THE REUNION

Roisin Meaney was born in Listowel, County Kerry. She has lived in the US, Canada, Africa and Europe but is now based in Limerick city. She is the author of numerous bestselling novels, including *Love in the Making*, *One Summer* and *Something in Common*, and has also written several children's books, two of which have been published so far. On the first Saturday of each month, she tells stories to toddlers and their teddies in her local library.

Her motto is 'Have laptop, will travel', and she regularly packs her bags and relocates somewhere new in search of writing inspiration. She is also a fan of the random acts of kindness movement: 'they make me feel as good as the person on the receiving end'.

www.roisinmeaney.com
@roisinmeaney
www.facebook.com/roisinmeaney

ALSO BY ROISIN MEANEY

I'll Be Home for Christmas
Two Fridays in April
After the Wedding
Something in Common
One Summer
The Things We Do For Love
Love in the Making
Half Seven on a Thursday
The People Next Door
The Last Week of May
Putting Out the Stars
The Daisy Picker

CHILDREN'S BOOKS
Don't Even Think About It
See If I Care

The Reunion

ROISIN MEANEY

HACHETTE
BOOKS
IRELAND

First published in Ireland in 2016 by HACHETTE BOOKS IRELAND
First published in paperback on 2017

1

Cataloguing in Publication Data is available from the British Library

ISBN 978 1 4447 9972 9

Typeset in Book Antiqua by Bookends Publishing Services.
Printed and bound in Great Britain by Clays Ltd, St Ives plc

Hachette Books Ireland policy is to use papers that are natural,
renewable and recyclable products and made from wood grown
in sustainable forests. The logging and manufacturing processes
are expected to conform to the environmental regulations
of the country of origin.

Hachette Books Ireland
8 Castlecourt Centre, Castleknock, Dublin 15, Ireland

A division of Hachette UK Ltd
Carmelite House, 50 Victoria Embankment, EC4Y 0DZ

www.hachettebooksireland.ie

In memory of Olivia and John

September 2015

LEAVING CERT CLASS OF 1995

The principal and staff of
St Finian's Secondary School
are delighted to invite you to a twenty-year
reunion

on Saturday October 10 @ 7.30pm
in The Abbey Lodge Hotel
for drinks and finger food

RSVP by September 26

Eleanor

'I NEED A TENNER.'

She turns from the sink and regards his glum face across the room. When did she last see him smile?

'A tenner,' he repeats. A hair's breadth more slowly, for the benefit of his retarded mother.

She doesn't miss it. 'What for?'

'A book. For school.'

'A book? I thought we got them all.'

A millisecond of silence, filled with his impatience. Overflowing with it. 'It's notes. For history.'

'Notes? Were they not on the list?'

He shoves back his chair abruptly. It screeches across the tiles, making her start. 'Forget it,' he says, and something else under his breath that she doesn't hear.

He's gone before she can respond, letting the door swing not quite closed after him. She hears him galloping up the stairs like he always does, taking three, four steps at a time in giant bounds, with the long legs he didn't inherit from either of his parents.

He'll wake Gordon, who never gets to bed before one.

Of course she'll give him the money. It might be for notes, like he says, and she doesn't want to get on the wrong side of his new school this early on. Or it might be for something else entirely, like the cigarettes he thinks she doesn't smell on him, or the alcohol he may well be sampling by now. She had her first swig of cider when she wasn't much older than fourteen: she can still remember the excitement, the tart, forbidden burn of it. She'd be surprised if he wasn't up to something similar by now.

Hopefully he's not into anything worse. She knows so little about him. Such a gulf there is between them.

She wipes her hands on her apron and tries to squeeze the dripping hot tap shut again. A washer, she knows that's all it needs, but she's afraid to chance doing it herself. Gordon keeps promising to get it sorted but she's still waiting. She'll ask Mike, two doors down, next time she sees him. Retired plumber, could do it with his eyes closed. Gordon won't even notice.

She takes her purse from her bag and finds two fivers. She folds them and places them carefully on the edge of the white plate that holds the remains of Jacob's breakfast: the smear of egg yolk, the curves of toast crust.

As she waits for him she picks at crumbs on the tablecloth, which is white like the crockery, and crisp with starch. She likes a nicely dressed table, a legacy from her days of working in Fennellys, and washing and ironing the cloths gives her something to do.

She dabs butter onto Jacob's crusts and eats them one by one, standing at the sink. She sips lukewarm coffee and watches the second hand of the wall clock float around silently. The radio presenter is indulging in painfully humourless banter with the AA Roadwatch girl. He plays decent music: if only she could tune out the blather in between.

The upstairs toilet flushes: the bathroom door is flung open immediately afterwards. No hands washed, she'll bet. She hears him crashing about in his room, yanking out drawers, slamming them shut. Ironic that someone so frugal with his words, so silent in her presence, can be so noisy in other ways.

Then again, he always has plenty to say to his father.

She brings his dishes to the sink, scrubs the egg residue from his plate. She enjoys washing up, likes the feel of the hot sudsy water, the shiny crockery that emerges from it. She rubs a finger across the wet plate just to hear it squeak. She pulls out the plug and watches the water swirl away.

'Come and get it,' she calls, when she hears him flying down the stairs. Damned if she's going to bring it out to him.

He reappears and stands on the threshold, rucksack slung across a shoulder, hip jutting out beneath. Looking but not looking at her. The fourteen-year-old mystery she and Gordon created.

'There's your money,' she says, and he crosses to the table and claims it.

'Thanks.' He shoves it into his trouser pocket.

'How's school?' she asks. 'How are you liking it?'

'Fine.'

He leaves the room. She listens to the click of the front door closing. 'Goodbye,' she says, to nobody at all. 'Have a lovely day.'

He'll leave this house for good as soon as he can, probably as abruptly as that. He'll never visit again unless he needs something from her. He and Gordon will still see one another but it'll be somewhere else, somewhere she's not.

Or he and Gordon might leave together. The thought slices into her like a blade. She elbows it away.

She dries the dishes and stores them in neat bundles in the press. She leans against the sink and finishes her coffee, cold by now, as a washed-out sunbeam lights up the dust motes in the air and Hozier sings about rhythm and blues, and Clarence paces on the outside sill, mewing crossly. Poor old Clarence, she forgot about him again.

The reunion invitation sits where she dropped it on the worktop. She scans the few lines for the second time. Can it really be twenty years? Who is principal of the school now? She has no idea. Sister Carmody died, didn't she? A good while back, she thinks. Dad it must have been who told her – he always kept an eye on the death columns, still does.

As a schoolgirl, Eleanor came to know Sister

Carmody's office well. Usually she was summoned after a teacher complained – homework not done, cheek given – but one time, towards the end of her Junior Cert year, it was because she'd been spotted coming out of a pub with Andrew and a few others. Some busybody with nothing better to do, ringing the school to report her.

Your parents would be so disappointed, Sister Carmody had said, like getting a bit sloshed at sixteen was the worst thing you could do. Poor woman didn't know the half of it.

St Finian's is co-ed now – she knows that much from Mum. Joined forces with the Christian Brothers down the road eight or nine years ago. Did away with the uniforms too: no more tartan tunics to be seen on the streets when she goes back home to visit. Probably no nuns left on the staff now either, or brothers. Vocations a thing of the past, people reluctant to ally themselves with a toxic institution.

Twenty years since Leaving Cert, though: hard to believe. She turned eighteen that year, three months after Caroline's nineteenth birthday in May. Chalk and cheese the two of them, Caroline the quiet sensible older one, her nose always stuck in a book. No wonder the nuns couldn't believe she and Eleanor were sisters.

But despite their differences – or maybe because of them – they never had a falling-out, or nothing serious, all through childhood and puberty and adolescence. They weren't close, not in the way you'd expect two sisters so near in age to be, particularly when they had no other siblings – but they weren't enemies either.

Ironic that it was Caroline, not Eleanor, who ended up in trouble when she was just seventeen. Packed off to England by Mum before she could disgrace them all. And Eleanor, to her surprise, found that she missed her elder sister.

Nothing was ever the same after that. Caroline was changed when she came home to them, no denying it. Still quiet, still the perfect student, but there was something different about her. Never really settled again, never really fitted in the way she used to, at home or in school. And the minute she could, she went back to England. Couldn't wait to get back.

She and Eleanor have kept in touch, of course. They talk on the phone roughly once a week. Granted, their conversations aren't exactly deep and meaningful; they're more like the chit-chat you'd put on someone beside you in the doctor's waiting room. But the main thing is they're keeping track of one another, not letting their lives drift apart.

Twenty years: Eleanor still can't get her head around it. All the plans she had growing up, her future mapped out at sixteen. Nothing turned out like she'd expected it to; nothing went the way she'd thought it would after she left school.

It started off OK though. When she married Gordon Fennelly she was just twenty, and mad about him. She was five foot four in her stockinged feet and weighed eight and a half stone, give or take a pound or two. Her stomach was flat and firm, her thighs lean, her curves where she wanted them.

Those days she lived in tight size eight jeans and skimpy T-shirts, or sweaters that moulded to her shape, clothes designed to show off her figure. Same weight no matter what she ate, no matter how little exercise she took. She was lucky, everyone said so.

And then came two pregnancies in rapid succession, and her weight went shooting off the Richter scale, of course it did. She was happy and in love and well able to cook, and she had a husband who was very good at feeding her, and who didn't give a damn what the scales said when she stepped up on them. But by the time her second child was born she weighed over twelve stone, and she decided, happy as she was, that enough was enough, and she set out to lose the extra blubber.

And she did, pretty much.

By the beginning of July 2002, ten months after giving birth to baby number two, she weighed just under nine stone. And if her stomach wasn't anything like as flat as it used to be, and her thighs had a bit more wobble to them than before, she didn't much care. She was a mother of two: she was entitled to a few wobbles.

And then, on the fifth of July that year, a few weeks before her twenty-fifth birthday, Eleanor Plunkett Fennelly's world collapsed around her, and she stopped caring about her weight or anything else – and all the fat came tumbling back, and more with it.

Imagine showing her face at the reunion, looking the way she does now. Imagine the glances of pity and disbelief, the turning heads when she'd appear, bringing her high blood pressure and cholesterol and increased risk of heart disease and stroke along with her. Imagine the stares she'd get, all decked out in a tent dress and nice shoes. She can still wear nice shoes, her feet the only part of her that hasn't gone completely to pot: she just can't stand in them for any length of time.

The principal and staff are delighted to invite you.

She opens the back door and Clarence hops down and sidles in, giving his guttural mew as he pours himself around her ankles, threading in and out as she attempts to cross the room. One of these days he's going to trip her up: she'll fall and break a hip, and he'll walk over her on the way to his food. But for some reason she's fond of him, the old scrounger. He doesn't pretend to give a tinker's curse about anyone but himself as he pads single-mindedly through his nine lives.

Clarence was never planned, he simply appeared. He invited himself into the kitchen one morning when Eleanor was in the garden hanging clothes on the line. When she came back there he was, sitting just inside the door washing his face, ignoring her until she found some cold meat in the fridge and set it on the floor beside him. That was six years ago, and he still turns up twice or three times each day.

Jacob used to watch out for him – he was the one who gave him the name – but around the time he entered his teens his interest in the cat trailed away, and now he pays him scant attention if their paths intersect. He'd like a dog, according to Gordon, but Eleanor can't face the prospect of another creature around the place. She can just about handle Clarence.

She shakes pellets into the cracked saucer that serves as his bowl. By the way he attacks them, diving in, shoving her hand out of the way with his big head, you'd swear he hadn't eaten in a week. A mouse-sized portion, the vet says, more than enough – but Clarence snuffles his way through twice that and looks for seconds. Having him around means Eleanor isn't the only fatty in the house: maybe that's why she likes him.

She sticks the invitation to the door of the fridge with a magnet that says *I love to cook with wine. Sometimes I even put it in the food.* A joke present from Caroline when Eleanor and Gordon opened Fennellys the year they got married, attached to the fridge door for the past seventeen years. When they'd been awarded the Michelin star in May 2002 Caroline had got them a crystal decanter from Avoca; another magnet would hardly have done Michelin justice.

Tenth of October the reunion is, less than six weeks away. Just for the hell of it she circles the date with a highlighter pen on the calendar that hangs by the door. Of course she's not going. No way is she going. She lets the September page drop back into place and the twelfth stares out at her, five days from now.

She'll get through it. She always does.

She turns her thoughts back to Jacob, beginning his second week in the school. Must be tough being the new boy in Junior Cert year, joining a group who'd already spent two years together. Boys that age not the most welcoming, maybe.

A few months before the summer, Gordon said they'd have to take him out of boarding school. *The fees are crippling. We need to economise.*

It was unexpected. She knew the restaurant was going through a lean time, but was it really necessary to move Jacob? He'd been boarding at a school fifty miles away for two years, coming home on the bus at weekends. He'd seemed happy enough there, and privately Eleanor found it easier without him around all the time – but now he was to be uprooted, just before his Junior Cert.

Still, what could she do, with Gordon saying they couldn't afford the fees? It might be for the best, she told herself, if they had to live together full time. It might help to fix what was broken between them.

So far it hasn't made a difference. He comes home in the afternoon, he makes a sandwich, he vanishes. Up to his room, or out with the few friends he's kept in touch with since primary school. He reappears for dinner at seven, which he eats with Eleanor in near-silence – impossible to have a conversation with him: whatever she tries gets her nowhere – and takes his leave of her again as soon as he can.

The new school is a bit of a trek. It's on the far side of Galway, because Gordon was dead set against the

Christian Brothers down the road – *You'd understand*, he told Eleanor, *if you'd gone there*. So each morning Jacob gets a bus, and each afternoon the bus brings him home again, and so far he hasn't complained.

Or not to her. When she asks, everything is fine. But Gordon hasn't mentioned anything either, so hopefully the move is working out.

The morning passes like it always does. Gordon puts in an appearance around ten. He makes coffee and toasts sourdough while Eleanor loads the washing machine in the utility room and takes the ashes from the sitting-room fireplace and empties the various wastepaper baskets and checks the fridge to see what they're out of.

He reads the paper as rapidly as he eats. He's gone by half ten, calling goodbye from the hall. She can't remember the last time he kissed her goodbye, or kissed her at all.

Around an hour later, as she plugs in the kettle for more coffee, her phone rings. She follows the sound and sees it sitting by the bread bin. She reads her husband's name on the screen.

'I need a clean shirt,' he says. 'My pen leaked on this one.'

'I'll drop it in,' she replies, lifting the bread bin lid to peer inside.

'No need, I'll send Keith. He'll be there in twenty minutes.'

He doesn't want her in the restaurant: she bats away the thought before it can take root. 'I got an invitation,' she says quickly, not giving him time to hang up. 'My school, a twenty-year reunion.' As she speaks she pulls a piece of crust from the remains of the sourdough.

'Right.' His absent tone means he's doing something else. Checking the lunch menu, or seeing what the bookings look like for this evening.

'I won't go,' she says. 'They'd laugh if they saw me now.'

'Whatever you think,' he says. 'Look, I'd better get moving.'

She hears the tiny click of his disconnect. She can't blame him. She pushed him away, pushed them both away, and now they're out of her reach. There's nothing left of what she and Gordon had, nothing except Jacob to hold them together, for however long he does.

She spreads butter on the crust and chews it silently as Paloma Faith sings on the radio. Eleanor saw her in some music video not so long ago, all blonde hair and red lipstick. Perfect dainty little figure.

She brushes crumbs from her hands. She unties her apron and drapes it over the back of a chair. As she heads upstairs to find a clean shirt and to put on a bit of lipstick for Keith, she thinks about giving her sister a ring.

Or she might wait until tomorrow.

Caroline

THE LAST TIME SHE WAS IN THE ABBEY
Lodge Hotel was in May 2000. She was a week past
twenty-four, wearing a fake tan and a green dress
she'd made herself. Sparkly clips in her hair, a
smudge of gold on her eyelids.

You're looking well, he'd said. Fortified, no
doubt, by a few Harvey Wallbangers, or whatever
concoction he'd gone for at the cocktail bar. Lying in
wait for her near the women's loo, his wife Sophie
safely out of earshot. Caroline could see her near the
buffet table in conversation with Eleanor, who had
yet to tell anyone that she was pregnant with Jacob,
and widowed Mrs Lee, second next door to the
Plunketts, whose only son Douglas, Dougie, would
be dead in sixteen months.

Tragic Mrs Lee, who'd boast to everyone she met
about Dougie and the fine job he'd landed himself
in New York, who'd show them the postcard he'd
sent of the monstrously tall silver towers where his
office was located. *The ninety-fourth floor,* she'd say,

pointing to the red oval he'd drawn around a row of tiny windows. *Imagine being up that high every day.* Pitiable Mrs Lee, who'd taught Caroline the piano, or tried to, years before. Eleanor, of course, had flatly refused any kind of music lessons.

So how are you? he'd asked, looking good still at fifty-four, in his white shirt and black suit and red dicky bow, his drink cradled in the manicured hand that seven years earlier had found its way inside her underwear. He'd pulled twenty pounds from his wallet fifteen minutes later with the same hand, thanking her for babysitting Nadine, telling her that Sophie would be in touch when they got back from France. Cool as a cucumber, as if he hadn't taken a detour when he was driving her back to her parents' house. As if he hadn't done what he'd done when he'd parked the car.

So how are you? he'd had the gall to ask, after turning his back on her when she'd gone to him six weeks later in tears, after his denials and his insinuations and his snarled threats. Throwing money at her, as if it could fix what he'd broken.

None of your business, she'd replied, whisking her dress out of the way as she steered around him, continuing on her way to the ladies' toilet while her mother tapped a fork against a glass so that everyone would shut up and listen to the speech she'd written for her husband to recite. Their silver wedding anniversary, twenty-five years of her telling him what to do. Twenty-five years of golf outings and tennis tournaments and two foreign holidays a year, and never, ever a hint of a scandal. A quarter of a century of happy family life, if you didn't count the time that poor Caroline had her breakdown and had to spend the best part of a year away from them.

Only of course that wasn't what had happened at all. What had happened was Jasper D'Arcy, and everything that had followed him. But things are better now, most of them. Truth be told, they're better than better now.

Most of them.

She drops the invitation onto the dressing table and sprays floral, talcum-powdery scent from Italy on her wrists and behind her ears. The aroma brings Matteo to mind, as it always does. *Put some here*, he would whisper, *and here*. Wicked man.

Today is Tuesday. In three days she'll see him. She smiles into the mirror as she sets down the perfume bottle. Four more days and she'll be spraying perfume in different places.

She scans the invitation again. *Finger food*, it says. That'll be cubes of rubbery cheese impaled between grapes on wooden sticks. That'll be wings of chickens, more bone than flesh. That'll be baby tomatoes with their insides replaced, and halves of hardboiled eggs cowering under yellowing mayonnaise.

Finger food. They couldn't even stump up for a proper dinner.

She won't go, of course. No question. She drops the invitation into the tin bucket that serves as her bin. She painted it red, stuck some flower transfers onto it. *You missed your calling*, Florence had said when she saw it. *You should have been a hippie.*

Her phone rings. Her sister's name on the screen evokes the same mix of guilt and impatience that it has done for years.

'Hi there,' she says, hearing the horrible jollity that her voice always assumes for Eleanor.

'Did you get an invite to the reunion?'

'I did, this morning.'

'Mine came yesterday. Are you going?'

'Probably not.' Definitely not. Absolutely not.

'Me neither. Wild horses wouldn't drag me.'

No surprises there. Eleanor doesn't do socialising any more, unless Gordon asks her along to some Fennellys thing – but as far as Caroline knows, that hasn't happened in quite a while. Eleanor doesn't do fun any more.

But Caroline must be kind, with Beth's fourteenth birthday coming up in four days. 'How are things?' she asks. 'How are you feeling, El?'

'I'm alright.' Pause. 'You know yourself.'

But Caroline doesn't know, because her child didn't fall into a swimming pool before he was one. As far as she knows her child is still alive, still out there somewhere. Twenty-one since March, a man now – and the hope still fervent in her that one day he'll come looking for her.

'Why don't you come for a visit?' she asks, like she has so often asked. 'You could stay for a night or two. I'm not going to Italy till Friday evening. We'd love to have you.' Hating herself briefly for the lie –

Florence would *not* love to have her – but it's a safe lie because Eleanor never takes up the invitation.

'Not just now, maybe another time. Thanks.'

Same answer as always, and neither of them ever pins down another time.

Caroline lets the silence drift, turning her head to look through the tiny square of bedroom window. Putty-grey sky again today, no Indian summer for them yet, no consolation for a dismal July and an only marginally better August. Thank God for Italy, with its mile-high blue skies and sun that shines when it's supposed to. September in Italy is magical. She thinks of Matteo again, and smiles again.

'How's Jacob?' she asks. 'How's the new school?'

Her sister's sigh rushes into her ear. 'Oh, he's alright – I think. He tells me nothing.'

'It's his age,' Caroline says, when both of them know his age has nothing to do with it.

'He asked for a tenner yesterday. For books, he says, but we paid his book list before the summer.'

'They must have forgotten one.'

'Mm.'

She feels sorry for Jacob, the child who didn't drown, whose mother pretty much abandoned him when Beth died. Poor Jacob, caught in the middle of that tragedy, too young to understand what had happened, but suffering the fallout ever since.

'Tell him his godmother says hello anyway. And how's Gordon?'

'Oh, he's … the same.' Her voice fading a little, as if she's turned her head to avoid the question.

Twenty when she married him, Gordon more than double that at forty-two. He's ageing well though, despite the sad, lost life he and Eleanor have had together. His face is nicely shabby, his melancholy smile endearing.

Hanging in there, he'd said, the last time Caroline asked how Fennellys was doing – but they'd lost their precious Michelin star last year, and Eleanor told her a month or so ago about another restaurant opening not too far from theirs. The recession finally being spoken about in the past tense, people daring to start new businesses again.

But Fennellys had weathered the bad times, had come through the recession when others were collapsing around it. Surely it will survive now; surely Gordon will pull it out of its slump. She remembers how hungry he was at the start, how driven to succeed he and Eleanor both were, working all hours to get the recognition Fennellys eventually achieved.

She remembers well the day they got married. Valentine's Day 1998, Eleanor looking radiant, happier than Caroline ever remembered. Twirling before her bedroom mirror in the ivory silk dress that had cost a bomb. *How do I look?* she'd asked, and Caroline told her beautiful, and it was true. Crazy about Gordon then, despite the age difference – you only had to look at her to know. Crazy about him still maybe, but the evidence, anytime Caroline meets them, is lacking.

He's only fifty-nine now, not old these days.

Funny how the gap between them seems to narrow as the years go on, as if Eleanor is catching up with him. If she'd only lose some of the weight, find a therapist, take some pride in her appearance —

She cuts off the thought: no point. *I suggested a counsellor*, Gordon had said, a few months after Beth's death. *She was having none of it.* Caroline has hinted at it too, more than once, but Eleanor brushes it aside. She can't, or won't, talk to someone.

'You're as busy as ever, I suppose.'

'I am. Off to London in a while: I have a meeting this afternoon.'

'Well for some.'

Again she's aware of the impatience her sister so often seems to invoke in her. *Pull yourself together: move on.* She glances at her watch. 'Better go, actually. We'll talk again soon.'

They'll talk on Saturday, the twelfth. Caroline will ring on Beth's birthday, like she always does. She'll be in Italy, but she won't forget to ring. And Eleanor will be morose, still wallowing in her grief after thirteen years. And Caroline will want to shake her and will hate herself for it.

There's nothing you can do, Florence said, *until she wants to help herself. Nothing except keep in touch, so she knows you're there if she comes looking.* But so far Eleanor hasn't come looking.

Caroline leaves the bedroom and goes in search of coffee, which is generally to be found on the ground floor around this time. Sure enough, as she makes her way down the steep, narrow stairs the aroma of newly ground beans floats up to meet her. For years she couldn't look at coffee: her taste for it didn't come back until she started going to Italy.

She opens the kitchen door.

'There you are. I heard you up early.' Florence misses nothing.

'I had things to sort for London.' Caroline takes a seat at the table, where delicate cups and saucers wait. Florence loves her pretty china, even if none of it matches. Every time she breaks a piece she replaces it with a charity shop one. As long as it says *fine bone china* on the bottom she's happy.

'How was yesterday?' she asks.

'Good.' Caroline had spent it in Cardiff, visiting shops with her samples, pausing at lunchtime to catch up with some college friends. Not home until after Florence's nine o'clock bedtime. 'I might have a new boutique. They're letting me know on Thursday.'

'That's all very well, but you're working too hard. I keep telling you, you need a holiday.'

'I'm getting one next week.'

'Italy? Italy is more work.'

'Not all the time.' She hasn't told Florence about Matteo. He's her secret, for a variety of reasons. 'And the weather will be better, so it'll feel like a holiday, even if I'm working.'

Florence pours boiled water onto the grounds. 'You must promise me you'll relax. Have a flirt with a waiter.'

Caroline laughs. 'I might just do that.' Matteo

is an electrician, not a waiter, and they passed the flirting stage quite a while ago. 'By the way, I got an invitation to my school reunion. Twenty years, can you believe it?'

'You must go,' Florence says immediately, bringing the cafetière to the table. 'When is it on?'

'October the tenth, but I—'

'I'm marking it on the calendar. Get me a biro.'

'Florence, I have no intention of going.'

'Don't be ridiculous. Why wouldn't you go?' She pulls open a drawer and rummages among the rubbish, and finds a red pen.

'I'm sorry I mentioned it,' Caroline says, watching as her cousin draws a circle around the date.

'Well, I'm not. You want some of that tea brack? I think there's a bit left.'

'No thanks.' Tea brack, even one as light and spicy as Florence's, never tempted her.

'Why would you not want to go? Give me one good reason.'

'Florence, I hated that year of school – you know I did. All my friends gone, and me having to join a class where the only one I really knew was Eleanor. I felt out of place there from the first day to the last. I was counting the days till I could come back here.'

'But that's exactly why you *should* go. Look at you, look how far you've come. You're a self-made successful businesswoman, and you look like a million dollars. You can hold your head up high and wear one of your beautiful creations, and let them see how well you turned out.'

Caroline watches the grounds swirling about in the cafetière. She breathes in the dark nutty scent of water turning itself into coffee. 'They wouldn't care, they'd hardly remember me. Anyway, my mind's made up – and Eleanor isn't going either.'

'Oh. Well, Eleanor.' Florence takes her seat, tucks her chair in. 'You spoke to her?'

'She rang, just now.'

Florence depresses the plunger and pours the coffee, her silence saying plenty. She and Eleanor met exactly once, thirteen years ago; they've spoken on the phone less than half a dozen times. Nothing has ever been said, but Caroline gets the impression that as far as Florence is concerned, that amount of interaction was quite enough.

'We never had school reunions.' Florence lets a single brown sugar lump fall with a plop into her cup. 'Nothing like that in my day. I wouldn't have minded – I'd have quite liked to see where everyone ended up, especially the no-hopers like myself.'

'Don't say that.'

'Why not? It's true. Nobody ever thought I'd make a go of anything – I'd say they were sure I'd get lost on my way to England.'

When she was almost nineteen, Florence Cassidy left Ireland on her own with no qualifications and took the boat across the Irish Sea, like so many others were doing at the time. It was 1953, and she didn't know a single soul in London. All she had to her name were the few pounds she'd managed to put by from the textile factory job she'd had since leaving school at fourteen. Her only skill was being able to operate a knitting machine.

What she found, she told Caroline, was a city that was still shaking off the horrors of a world war, with rationing still a way of life, not to end until the following year. What she found were people who were too busy pulling their lives back together to worry about anyone else, least of all an Irish immigrant. *I didn't let it stop me*, she said. *I made my way in spite of it.*

She located a hostel for girls that was run by Irish nuns, and she took what jobs she could find – leaflet distributor, church cleaner, cinema usherette, restaurant kitchen skivvy – hanging on to each one until the meagre wages or the deplorable conditions forced her to search for something better.

And then, coming home dispirited one chilly November evening from the restaurant, her hands red and raw from the scalding water in which they spent most of their time, she saw a notice in the window of the local greengrocer.

Experienced knitters needed, suit housewives, it said – and Florence, who wasn't a housewife, remembered the hours she'd spent hunched over her knitting machine each day in the textile factory, and recalled how she'd vowed to find a more uplifting way to spend her life. But so far that hadn't happened, and knitting was something she was good at. And whatever was being offered here might be altogether different from the soulless factory environment. Might pay better too.

She rang the number on the notice and spoke to a woman called Sybil, who didn't seem put out by Florence's Irish accent. *Let's meet*, she said, *and have a chat. Come to my place* – so later that week Florence rang the top doorbell on the wall of a tall narrow terraced house that lay just three streets north of the hostel. She was ushered up two flights of stairs and into the minuscule bedsit that Sybil rented on the top floor, and there she learnt that she would be expected to knit hats or scarves or socks, or all three, in return for no pay at all.

My brother is a missionary priest in Africa, Sybil told her, over a cup of Bovril. *The people he tries to help have nothing. His stories would break your heart. I want to sell knitted goods in the local market on Saturdays – a friend has a stall there – and send him whatever money I make, but I need a few more knitters to help me; I'm too slow on my own. I can supply the wool – I get end balls of dye lots for nothing from one of my aunts who runs a wool shop – but there wouldn't be any payment. That's why I said suit housewives. I thought they might do it to pass the time while their children were at school.*

Florence explained that she wasn't a housewife in search of a hobby. *I wash dishes in a restaurant*, she said. *I'm on my feet all day, and my boss is an ignorant man who pays me barely enough to survive on, and never offers me leftovers to take home. I was hoping to find something a bit better.*

But she'd taken to Sybil, plain and thirtyish and part-time social worker, whose narrow single bed had a tatty pink dressing gown in place of an eiderdown, whose floor beneath the window was piled high with dog-eared paperbacks, whose pale blue eyes were as innocent as a child's, whose guileless smile took over her face.

I'll knit for you in my spare time, Florence said, *and I'll ask the other girls in the hostel if they'll help.* She told Sybil about her experience in the textile factory. *I could hand knit, but a machine would be a lot quicker. Could your aunt find us a second-hand one, or would she know someone who'd loan us one, and I could teach you how to use it too?*

And a friendship was begun that lasted till Sybil's death in a plane crash almost twenty years later – on her way to Africa to visit her brother, a trip that had been long in the planning. After her death Florence packed up and moved out of London, taking with her the knitting machine she and Sybil had bought between them on the never-never, the savings she'd managed to scrape together over the years, and the few pounds left to her by Sybil.

She settled in a town eighty miles north of the capital and found herself a job in a garden centre, and a bedsit to rent above a chemist that was twice as big as, and half the price of, the tiny basement flat she and Sybil had ended up sharing in London. Ten months later she walked into the bank and came out with a modest mortgage on a small rundown cottage whose three-hundred-year-old walls were still rock solid.

In the meantime she'd discovered another market in which to sell the hats and scarves and socks she still churned out in her spare time, the proceeds of which she continued to send to Sybil's brother – and after his death, to the community of priests that survived him – until she'd finally given up the market stall a few years ago, when the standing and the weather became too much for her arthritic hips.

And when Caroline Plunkett was seventeen, Florence saved her life.

Caroline came to her, broken and despairing – and Florence, who was almost sixty by then, opened her door and took her in, and never once allowed Caroline to feel sorry for herself. *What happened happened*, she said. *You're not the first and you won't be the last. Deal with it* – and because she backed up her blunt words with endless patience and countless acts of kindness, Caroline learnt how to put the past behind her and move on, and over the course of the year they spent together she fell thoroughly in love with Florence.

At the end of the year she went home to Ireland and completed her final year of secondary school. She moved to Wales the following autumn to take up the college place she'd secured there, much to her mother's disapproval, and graduated four years later with a degree in fashion design.

Immediately afterwards she returned again to Ireland, staying only long enough to move out of the house she and Eleanor had grown up in. She stripped her bed and vacuumed her room and took her posters from the walls. She boxed up her books and packed two suitcases and put what was left over into a bag for the charity shop. And six years after their first encounter, Caroline flew back across the Irish Sea to be reunited with Florence.

And since then she's lived in the collection of tiny slant-ceilinged rooms that are tucked beneath the roof of her cousin's little cottage, and Florence potters about below her in the ground-floor rooms. The arrangement suits both of them perfectly.

Florence, whose precise relationship to Caroline has never been properly worked out – some class of a cousin, two or three times removed – will be eighty-one at the beginning of October. The number means precisely nothing to her. *You're as old as you decide to be*, she says. *I've been forty for the past forty years.*

For as long as Caroline has known her, Florence has danced to her own melody. Never married, frequently broke,unflinchingly honest. She's the bravest person Caroline has ever met.

'What are you doing with yourself today?'

'I'm going shopping.'

Florence's shopping takes the whole afternoon. She does the rounds of the town's charity shops, and tries on an impressive proportion of its offerings, and spends a maximum of ten pounds in total. Her wardrobe is never the same from one week to the next: for every sweater she brings home she donates one or two she bought the month before, or a handbag she's used twice, or trousers she's sick of.

'I'm doing steaks tonight,' Caroline says. 'Don't be late.' Every Tuesday Florence climbs the stairs for dinner; the rest of the week they dine separately, apart from Sunday when they go out for lunch – Caroline's treat – to the Hound and Hare a quarter of a mile away. Florence has a glass of beer beforehand and an Irish coffee afterwards, and never touches alcohol otherwise, apart from the mulled wine she takes each New Year's Eve.

And every morning that Caroline is at home, they drink excellent Italian coffee in Florence's kitchen.

They sit and talk as a watery September sun splashes onto the cracked terracotta tiles that Florence refuses to allow Caroline to replace. They talk about Angie in the library whose daughter was caught shoplifting in Boots in Oxford, and about Phil the postwoman who found a canvas shopping bag full of live kittens by the riverbank, and about Caroline's plan to introduce a new line of babywear to her range.

And as Caroline is getting to her feet, Florence urges her again to attend the school reunion, and Caroline assures her again that she has no intention of it.

'I'm going to keep on at you,' Florence warns, 'until you change your mind.'

'Good luck with that.' Once she fixes on a thing, Florence's tenacity is truly impressive – but Caroline can be every bit as stubborn.

'Nearly forgot,' Florence says, pulling an envelope from behind the stacked saucepans on the worktop. 'This came for you yesterday.'

Handwriting she doesn't recognise. Brighton

postmark, no return address. The only people she knows in Brighton are those who work in the boutique she sells into.

'See you later, have a good day.' She studies the envelope as she climbs the stairs. A new enquiry, maybe – she gets the occasional letter, although most people email or phone now.

In her room she takes the reunion invitation from the wastepaper basket and studies it for several seconds before tearing it into pieces that float back down like snowflakes. Despite what Florence says, she has nothing she wants to prove: let them reunite without her.

She slides a finger under the flap of the other envelope. She pulls out the single page and unfolds it, and begins to read.

Her hand flies to her mouth.

She sinks onto a chair.

Her eyes fill. The words swim together.

PART ONE

June 1993

Eleanor

SHE TAPPED ON THE DOOR.

'Come in.'

How well she knew that voice, how often it had invited her in. She turned the handle and entered the room.

'Ah, Eleanor.' It was sighed out by Sister Carmody, who wasn't seated behind her big wooden desk but standing with her back to one of the windows that began at the level of her shoulders and climbed upwards. 'Please close the door, and have a seat.'

She herself remained standing, arms disappearing behind her, hands presumably clasped above her substantial grey tweed backside. 'I've had a phone call,' she said, in the same mournful tone.

Pause. Eleanor waited, her eyes fixed on the black pen that extended on a tilt from its brass holder on the desk. She wondered who'd been on the phone, and what they'd caught her doing. She imagined grabbing the pen and driving it into Sister Carmody's pink-cardiganed chest.

'Would you care to hear what it was about, Eleanor?' The barest suggestion of impatience, just that. Sister Carmody never lost her temper at school. She must have a punching bag in her bedroom that got the brunt every night: Take *that*, Eleanor Plunkett, and *that*.

Eleanor shifted in her seat and made a noncommittal sound. What was needed here was some show of repentance, some evidence of shame. She ducked her head and looked at her shoes: that might do it.

'On Saturday night, Eleanor, you were seen coming out of a public house on Dominic Street, in the company of several males. It would appear ...' another pause '... that you were not completely sober.'

Not completely sober, no. She and Andrew had gone to McMurragh's with Tony, whose eighteenth birthday it was, and a few of the others. They'd sat at a corner table and she'd laced her glasses of orange juice with gin she'd swiped from the sitting-room cabinet. By eleven o'clock she was giddy and giggling, and trying to recite Hamlet's soliloquy. Yes, she'd definitely have looked a bit unsteady coming out, hanging on to Andrew as they made their way to Enzio's for chips. She wondered who'd squealed on her.

'I don't think I need to remind you, Eleanor, that your exams begin in three days.'

No, you need not. She was hardly likely to forget about the Junior Cert. Everyone getting summer holidays tomorrow, apart from the third and sixth years who were facing into two weeks of exams. But she'd get by, she always managed to get by. Let Caroline slog all she wanted for her A grades: Eleanor had no use or desire for them.

Her left shoe was marked on the toe, a grey smudge on the brown leather. It might come off with a swipe of a damp cloth. She hated when her shoes weren't clean.

'Your parents would be so disappointed, Eleanor.'

Here it came, the guilt trip. Her parents would almost certainly have heard her coming in last night – she'd practically fallen up the stairs – but as long as she was out with Andrew D'Arcy, whose father could buy and sell the Plunketts several times over, she got away with it.

'Now, I've decided not to involve them on this occasion, provided I have your solemn promise that it won't happen again.'

Eleanor looked up. 'I promise, Sister.'

I promise I won't get caught next time. I promise I'll wear a hoodie next time. She wondered if Andrew had given up waiting for her. She could murder a can of Coke.

Sister Carmody gave a final sigh and turned away to face the window. 'You may go, Eleanor.'

She lifted her rucksack and got to her feet and left the office, closing the door silently. No need to give the old bat anything else to moan about. She scooted down the deserted corridor and out the front door –

and there he was, sitting on the wall by the gate. He hopped down as she approached.

'Thought you'd be gone,' she said.

'What kept you?'

She handed him her rucksack. 'I was called into the office. Someone saw us coming out of McMurragh's on Saturday and phoned the school.'

'Who?'

'No idea. Come on, I need Coke.'

'What did she say? Is she going to tell your parents?'

'No, I got off with a warning. You're so lucky to be finished with all this.'

In September he was moving to Dublin to begin his teacher-training course: no question of him not getting enough points in the Leaving. He was a D'Arcy – naturally he was clever enough to get loads of points without killing himself. That family was charmed.

Being separated from him by sixty miles would take some getting used to though: they'd lived a few minutes apart all their lives, they'd seen one another several times a week. On the plus side, his moving to Dublin would mean more freedom for them.

Coming up to three years together, their first date a week after her thirteenth birthday. They'd gone to see *Back to the Future III*, her stomach knotted with anxiety at the thought of being on her own with Andrew D'Arcy. Half an hour in, he'd put his arm across the back of her seat: their first kiss – *her* first ever kiss – had happened a few minutes after that.

She'd taken no pleasure in it, too anxious in case she wasn't doing it right.

She'd had plenty of practice since then.

Lots of other stuff since then too, lots of fooling around. A few times they'd come close to going all the way – she was dying to do it, eager to see what all the fuss was about – but she wanted their first time to be right, not some rushed uncomfortable fumble somewhere, so she was holding out for Dublin, and whatever bed he ended up renting.

She had it all planned. She'd hop on the bus every second Saturday: nobody could object as long as she came home that night. The first bus got to Dublin at ten: they could spend the whole day in bed. The thought sent a delicious hot swoosh through her. She'd thought of everything, from the omelettes she'd make for their lunch – wearing only his shirt – to the bag of Bewley's coffee he was going to have ready for her to take home.

Of course they'd have to use protection: she had no intention of getting caught out. She knew, everyone did, about the dangerous days that she could simply avoid, as long as she kept an eye on her temperature – but that wouldn't work if they were limited to once a fortnight. Andrew would have to get condoms. He could sort that out.

His father probably had a stash. The old goat had to be doing it with half the women in town. Do it with *her* if she gave him half a chance, leering at her chest anytime she wore something that showed it off a bit. The only downside to marrying Andrew was getting Jasper for a father-in-law. Still, she'd think of the money they'd inherit one day, and put up with him.

Neither she nor Andrew had mentioned marriage yet, but it was there in their future, waiting for them. It was like a natural law that they'd end up together, that she'd change her name to Eleanor D'Arcy. She loved the sound of it, like a character straight out of Jane Austen.

She almost felt guilty sometimes that finding her soulmate had been so simple. She and Andrew had sort of gravitated together – around the time that she was beginning to have feelings for him, he'd asked if she'd like to go to the cinema. And just like that, they'd become a couple.

And one day they'd be man and wife.

She'd wear red, or maybe burgundy: white did nothing for her. Caroline would be her bridesmaid, of course – she could hardly pass her over in favour of one of her friends. She didn't imagine her sister would ever get married. Seventeen a month ago, and never out on a date, not a single one. Caroline wasn't interested in boys: she was too busy studying for her Leaving Cert, which was still a year away. She was good at everything in school, even art: little wonder their teachers found it hard to believe that she and Eleanor were sisters.

They didn't look remotely alike either. Eleanor was prettier, no one could deny that – eyes, hair, figure, everything was better – but if Caroline made an effort, wore some makeup, did something with her hair, ditched the boring long skirts and started wearing normal clothes, she mightn't be bad.

Eleanor could try fixing her up with one of Andrew's friends. Not Tony, he was daft – and Josh wouldn't be interested: he only had eyes for blondes. Maybe Patrick. He wasn't exactly an intellectual but opposites might attract, and at least he was as tall as her.

'What about Patrick and Caroline?' she asked.

Andrew kicked a pebble on the path, sent it bouncing ahead of them. 'What about them?'

'Would he go for her?'

He hitched her rucksack higher on his shoulder. 'Would he *go* for her?' He aimed at another pebble, missed it.

Was he being deliberately obtuse? 'I think we should get them together,' she said.

'Why?'

'She'll never get a boyfriend unless we help her out.'

He gave her a funny look. 'What makes you think she'll never get a boyfriend?'

'Oh, come on – look at her. She's older than me and she's never been on a date.'

'She will,' he said, 'when she's ready. There's nothing wrong with taking your time. Leave her alone.'

He sounded almost cross. She wondered what was eating him. They reached the shop and he went in without a word, and emerged with two cans of Coke. He handed her one and flicked open the other and drank without stopping until it was empty. He crushed it and flung it away, and she watched it clattering onto the road. Not like him to litter the place.

'I can't go out tonight,' he said. 'Dad and Sophie are going to some dinner. I have to stay with Nadine.'

Nadine's mother Sophie had been the D'Arcys' au pair before Jasper had decided, five years earlier, to ditch Andrew's mother in favour of a twenty-two-year-old Frenchwoman who happened to be pregnant with his child. Anyone else would have been ostracised by his social circle for bad behaviour. Because it was Jasper, everyone took a deep breath and got over it, and Sophie was invited to the dinner parties and art exhibition launches that Lorraine had attended in the past.

Being Jasper, he also got to hang on to the family home. Lorraine didn't do too badly though – she ended up in a gorgeous townhouse down by the river, where Andrew had spent half his time since the split. Tonight he was back with his father – and apparently too busy to see Eleanor.

'Why can't they get Caroline to babysit?'

He shrugged. 'You know they don't like asking her on a school night.'

'Well, why didn't you say you had plans? I was dying to see *Groundhog Day*.'

'Can't you go with Tina?'

'I don't want to go with Tina, I want to go with you.' She could slap him sometimes.

'Sorry.' He didn't look sorry.

She should be cross, but some instinct told her to hold her patience. 'I'll come over then – we can watch a video. What time are they going out?'

'Actually, I've a splitting headache,' he said. 'We might give it a miss.'

She studied him. 'Are you mad at me? Did I do something to annoy you?'

'Don't be daft.' He was already walking away. 'Come on, it's going to rain.'

The sky was grey, but she could see no sign of rain. He *was* mad at her, and he wasn't saying why.

He'd get over it. She drank Coke and followed him, taking her time.

Caroline

'THANK YOU, *CHÉRIE*.'

Sophie stepped forward to kiss her lightly on both cheeks – she was so *French* – bringing with her the same heady scent that wafted from the bottle on their bathroom shelf each time Caroline opened it. Opium by Yves St Laurent, a tiny illicit dab now also resting in the hollow between Caroline's breasts. It smelt of intrigue, of dark, delicious sin, and she couldn't resist stealing a drop every time she babysat.

Had Sophie been wearing it when Jasper first seduced her? It was, Caroline thought, the kind of exotic, intoxicating scent a full-blooded man would find irresistible; probably as potent and teasing to him as, say, the sight of a woman clad only in lacy black underclothes.

She imagined Jasper and Sophie swept into a clandestine embrace, enjoying snatched moments of passion in the utility room while Sophie was still the au pair and Lorraine the unsuspecting wife. Despite feeling some sympathy for Lorraine, the romance, the drama of Jasper's infidelity thrilled her.

The truth of it was, for as long as she could remember, the D'Arcys had held a fascination for Caroline. Everything about them enthralled her, from their house with its polished parquet-floored drawing room and beautifully appointed kitchen, all gleaming copper pots and jars of spices, its wide curving staircase and tastefully furnished bedrooms, its perfect lawns and impeccable shrubberies, to the stately silver Bentley with its personalised number plates – JAS 10 – that would shortly be ferrying her home.

'Ready?' Jasper asked, shirtsleeves rolled to the elbows on that balmy evening, reaching again for the car keys he'd tossed seconds earlier onto the marble worktop.

But of course it was the D'Arcys themselves, the sole inhabitants of their flawless world, who held the greatest attraction for Caroline. Sophie with her creamy skin, cat-green eyes and voluptuous curves; Jasper almost twenty years her senior, broad and muscular and craggily, charmingly attractive; Nadine, the child they'd produced together, elfin and adorable, equally fluent in French and English. Jasper was Papa, not Daddy.

And Andrew was lovely too, always friendly when they met. She was glad he was Eleanor's boyfriend – and it was surely inevitable, wasn't it, that in time the two families would be related by marriage? She hoped so.

Sophie walked with them to the front door. 'Nadine will miss you for ze summer,' she told Caroline. 'She will look forward to seeing you again when we come back.'

When Nadine was born four years earlier, thirteen-year-old Caroline – sensible, responsible Caroline – had become the babysitter of choice when Andrew wasn't around to do it. Now mother and daughter were flying to France the following day to spend the summer with Nadine's *grand-maman* in Provence. Jasper would flit over and back, too busy and important to be absent for long from his company – something to do with exports and imports.

His car smelt of leather and Sophie's perfume, and something else, a not unpleasant sharpish tang that she thought might be sweat. His sweat. She got into her seatbelt as he switched on the ignition, self-consciousness making her clumsy, causing her to fumble with the belt until she managed to click it into place.

He draped an arm across the back of her seat while he reversed from the driveway, leaning slightly in her direction to look through the rear windscreen. She smelt again the musky odour – peppery aftershave in there too – that he was giving off this evening. No, not unpleasant at all.

They were out on the road. Before moving off he pressed a button on the steering wheel. A second later she heard drumsticks tapping out a soft tattoo – ta-ta-ta *taa*, ta-ta-ta *taa*, tah, tah, ta-ta-ta taa, ta-ta-ta-

ta-ta-ta-ta-ta-ta-*taa* – and she recognised the opening sequence of *Boléro*. One of her favourites, so full of melodrama and passion.

'Ravel,' he said. 'Wait for it.'

She opened her mouth to say she knew it, and closed it again – might sound like she was showing off. She settled back in her seat to enjoy it. He didn't normally play music; this was a pleasant development.

She could easily walk home – it was less than a ten-minute stroll along well-lit streets – but Jasper always drove her, and she never objected to being brought to her front door in such luxury. Her parents' cars were perfectly presentable – her father's Volkswagen, her mother's Mazda – but they didn't compare to the soft leather seats, the walnut dashboard, the discreet hum of the Bentley's engine.

Before they reached the end of the road the drum was joined by a single flute beginning to snake through the melody. Jasper slowed at the junction, then turned left instead of right. Caroline looked at him in surprise: had he forgotten where she lived?

'Such a beautiful night,' he said, giving her a quick smile. 'I thought we might go the long way home for a change. That OK?'

What could she say but yes? This was a first: he always brought her straight home – but it *was* a lovely evening, calm and warm, and whatever route he took couldn't take much longer. Why not relax and enjoy it?

His words had left a waft of alcohol in the air. He

and Sophie had been out to dinner, something they did at least once a week. She hoped he hadn't drunk too much. He seemed sober, not that she was much of a judge.

The music flowed around them, the same dipping and swooping melody being repeated and repeated and repeated by a series of instruments. She picked out the clarinet, the bassoon, the oboe – and here came the trumpet, and here the saxophone, all of them underlined by the original drum tattoo. There was something hypnotic about it, the notes sliding and falling as they travelled again and again through the tune, the steady beat tapping out all the while beneath.

She watched the streetlights floating by as he drove. She was alone with the great Jasper D'Arcy, sitting where Sophie usually sat.

She stole a look at his profile, lit only by the muted dashboard lights, and the intermittent streetlight flashes. The slightly hooked nose, the jutting chin, the heavy eyebrows. He was so masculine, so … *definite*. Such a strong look, while not conventionally handsome, held a certain attraction – why deny it?

She guessed he was formidable in business. Not afraid of risks, ruthless, maybe a little intimidating in his dealings. Maybe even a little shady, a little … dangerous.

'So,' he said, glancing at her again, 'what have you planned for the summer?'

Planned? She had no plans, or none that would seem remotely interesting. 'Um, I'll do a bit of painting, and reading ...' She trailed off, hearing how dull it must sound to him, but he didn't seem disappointed.

'Ah, painting. Eleanor tells us you're a bit of an artist.' Another darting smile in her direction.

'Well ... I like it. I'm not sure how good I am.'

'She says you're not bad at all.'

Caroline made no response, unsure if he was mocking her. Why was she always so tongue-tied with him? It sounded like Eleanor had no such problem.

He probably considered Eleanor far more interesting.

'Listen to me,' he said, throwing her another smile, 'gabbing on. Sophie says I love the sound of my own voice.' His left hand, resting on the gear stick, moved to land for an instant on her thigh. 'Feel free to tell me to shut up.'

The touch, so unexpected, was shocking. She felt the heat of his hand through the thin cotton of her skirt. His fingers pressed briefly, prompting an alarming lurch in her groin – and then they were gone, his hand back on the gear stick, his eyes on the road ahead.

She shifted slightly in her seat, felt her skirt brushing against the fine hairs on her skin. It had been nothing, a friendly gesture, that was all. He'd probably done it without thinking.

His index finger tapped on the steering wheel, keeping time with the music that was gaining in intensity now, more instruments involved, the notes skipping and leaping and tumbling, the drums booming.

'Marvellous, isn't it?'

'Yes.'

They passed a parade of shops, all dark and shuttered apart from a pub on the corner. She saw a group of youths lounging outside, none of whom she recognised. They eyed the Bentley as it passed; she was aware of them looking in at her and Jasper. Father and daughter, they must look like.

They were pretty far from home. They were almost on the other side of town.

'I'd say you go in for the classical music, do you?'

'I do.'

It kept building, strings involved now, increasing in intensity, moving all the while towards its crescendo. Over and over went the melody, each repetition a little more forceful, a little more passionate.

'You're a woman of few words,' he said, slowing as they approached a roundabout. 'I have to say I find that refreshing.'

A woman – was that how he saw her? She'd turned seventeen last month. His tone was light: again she wondered if he was laughing at her, or just making conversation. He glanced once more in her direction: their eyes met for a millisecond. She turned away quickly, her face warm.

She shifted again. The dashboard clock read ten past eleven. How long were they going to keep driving? She wished he'd turn off the music; it was

... too much, too intense in the close confines of the car. She wished he'd turn for home.

'You're not afraid of me, are you, Caroline?' he asked then.

'... No.' But she didn't move, didn't dare look at him. For the first time she felt a stab of unease, she felt a change in the air between them. She should laugh it off. Eleanor would. Eleanor would know what to say, which remark to make that would sweep away the tension.

They turned a corner, leaving the main part of the town behind. No more shops now, just rows of houses separated by low fences. Calm down, she told herself. It's Jasper D'Arcy, he's friends with Mum and Dad.

'Because you know I would never hurt you, don't you?'

She nodded, still turned away, keeping her eyes fixed on the houses as they flashed by; doors, windows, gates, driveways all whipping past. Her pulse was thumping in her ears. The music, turn off the music. Her breath was coming fast, her forehead and palms damp. She sensed something was about to happen, but she didn't know what.

And then, without warning, he pulled in and brought the car to a halt. Her heart did a giant leap in her chest – it almost sprang out of her as she felt his hand on her thigh again, and this time it stayed put.

'Caroline,' he breathed, leaning towards her. She backed away, horrified. Through the window she saw railings that gleamed in the moonlight, and behind them trees, a row of trees, some park she didn't recognise. There was nobody about, nobody at all. If she screamed, no one would hear her.

'You want it,' he whispered, sharply enough to be heard above the music, 'don't you?' His hand hot, blazing on her thigh.

No, this couldn't be happening. No, it was completely wrong. No, she didn't want it.

'No,' she said, her throat tight, her breath coming in shuddering waves, trying to move away but there was nowhere to go, no way to escape from him. What was he *doing*? 'Please,' she said, beginning to cry, fumbling for the door handle and not finding it. 'Please stop, please, Mr D'Arcy—'

'Ssh,' he whispered, sliding her skirt up. 'I can make you feel good, Caroline, I know how.' Pushing the fabric past her knees till his warm fingers finally touched her bare leg, the sudden sensation of skin on skin causing an involuntary terrified gasp while she continued to scrabble uselessly at the door. 'I'll be gentle, Caroline, I won't hurt you.'

'Please,' she wept, 'I don't want this, please—'

'Ah,' he murmured, his face inches from hers, his alcohol breath warm, 'that's it, that's beautiful – dipping his head suddenly, his lips against her neck. 'Aaaah,' he said, 'I smell Sophie,' his head moving lower, finding the spot where she'd dabbed the perfume. 'Mmmm.' She felt the hot wet press of his tongue on her throat as his hand travelled further up her thigh, burrowing into her underwear, finding what he wanted.

'Please don't, please stop—' She shrank away from him, felt the stiff ridges of his gelled hair against her throat. 'Please take me home—'

'So soft,' he murmured. It was like he didn't hear her. She tasted the salt of the tears that rushed down her face as she squeezed her eyes closed, drowning in shame and fright as she continued her useless efforts to make him stop.

'Don't worry,' he whispered, suddenly yanking down her underwear, making her cry out in renewed terror – 'just relax, I know how to make you feel wonderful' – and she kept her eyes closed as he tilted back her seat and moved across to cover her body with his, to force her thighs apart as he fumbled with his clothes, and she kept her eyes closed as she cried out again with a sudden awful sharp pain, and she never once looked at him as he rammed into her again and again, each movement bringing fresh scalding agony as he panted and grunted, his mouth inches from hers, the smell of his sweat engulfing her, suffocating her as she wept and screamed and died of fright.

And in the immediate aftermath, as she lay limp and damp and panting and disbelieving beneath him, she realised that somewhere along the way, the music had stopped.

July 1993

Eleanor

SUMMER WASN'T GOING AT ALL AS planned.

For a start, the exams were every bit as horrible as she'd been expecting. Subject after subject had seen her sitting in the exam hall trying to conjure up scraps of knowledge, trying to put something, anything, down as everyone around her scribbled like mad. She'd done her best to waffle her way through essays, to remember dates, to figure out the answers to maddening geometry questions, but she suspected, particularly when it came to maths and history, that she'd be lucky to scrape passes.

Her own fault, of course. If she put her mind to it she didn't think she'd do too badly, but she'd never been into studying. She remembered Dad sitting beside her each afternoon as she ploughed through her primary school homework. She remembered him quizzing her on spellings, guiding her through maths problems, telling her that history was just the story of the past.

But why do I have to learn it? she'd demand. *It's all over now.*

Aren't you curious about your ancestors? Don't you want to find out what happened before you were born?

No and no. She had zero interest in any of the school subjects, apart from home economics, which she'd started in secondary. She liked the cookery part of it – at least you were using your hands and making something, not trying to memorise dates of things that had happened years ago. Cooking would come in handy when she left school: how would knowing when the Famine happened ever be of use?

Caroline, of course, would disagree. Caroline loved history. She could name all the kings of England back to whoever the first one was. She could list off every battle of both world wars, and she knew about Cromwell and Sarsfield and Brian Boru and the Wild Geese, all the stuff that sailed merrily over Eleanor's head. Caroline was planning to study history in college; Eleanor could think of nothing more boring or useless.

Caroline came top in almost every subject in her class: exams held no fear for her. She was the darling of all the teachers, and Sister Carmody's special pet. No doubt she'd be made head girl next year – she was the obvious choice.

But now the exams were over, and holidays had begun, and just when Eleanor should have been enjoying more time with Andrew, he wasn't there.

I told you, he said, *weeks ago* – but she was certain he'd said nothing. *It's only for ten days*, he said, as if ten days wasn't an eternity when you knew you were going to spend every minute of it imagining him hanging out with his buddies on the Costa del Sol, surrounded by blondes in bikinis with just one thing on their minds.

Swear you won't look at anyone else, Eleanor said. *Swear you won't even talk to another girl* – and he laughed and told her to cop herself on, which wasn't swearing anything.

So here she was, left twiddling her thumbs while he was getting up to whatever with Tony and Josh and Patrick and the rest of them. Ten of them altogether, each one trying to impress the others, she bet, seeing who could chat up the most females, who could get the prettiest ones to kiss them, and more. And they'd have drinking competitions, and do whatever they felt like after that.

'I'm sure nothing will happen,' she said to Tina. 'It's just with all those girls around ... but Andrew's not like that.' Was he?

'They're all like that,' Tina said gloomily. Evan O'Flaherty had dumped Tina a week before the Junior Cert; she was still stinging. 'You can't trust any of them.'

'No, I *do* trust Andrew.' But did she? Hadn't he been off with her lately? Wasn't he finding more excuses to spend less time with her? Going with Josh to a match that he'd have dragged her to in the past, even though football bored her stupid. Travelling to Dublin with his father to check out accommodation – well, she supposed that was genuine, although it would have been nice to be invited along. Telling her he should be spending more time at home with his father, now that Sophie and Nadine were in France – as if Jasper D'Arcy needed his son to babysit him.

And to make matters worse, the weather was awful. Dull and grey and chilly, rain nearly every day, Mum lighting the fire each evening just like in winter. It made things twice as bad to think about Andrew basking in the Spanish sunshine. He'd be perfectly tanned when he got home – he had only to look at the sun to get a colour, of *course* – and she'd be pasty and horrible.

And then there was Caroline, who clearly had a knot in her knickers over something. Snapping at Eleanor last week when Eleanor asked for the loan of a fiver till pocket money arrived; staring into space at mealtimes like a zombie; forgetting to collect Mum's dry cleaning on her way home from town yesterday. Caroline never forgot *anything*.

If Eleanor didn't know her better, she'd wonder if she was in love – but obviously that wasn't the case. No, far more likely that she'd had a falling out with the swots she hung around with – no sign of them at the house lately. They'd probably disagreed about which foreign film to go and see, or whose turn it was to have the others around for tea and cake and a chat about Napoleon.

Oh, who cared about Caroline? Her life was perfect, pretty much. She didn't have to worry about an absent boyfriend, and she *never* dreaded exam results. She was probably counting the days until she could go back to school. Maybe that was what was wrong with her: maybe she was fed up because she was on holidays.

Eleanor cast her sister aside and turned her attention to a more pressing problem: how to persuade Mum to buy her the dress she absolutely had to have for Andrew's graduation in September. It was pricey, even in the summer sale – but she'd tried it on, and twirled before the dressing room's mirror, and put a twenty pound deposit on it before she could think about it.

It was gorgeous. It was a shade between blue and purple, not a colour she'd ever gone for before, and the fitted bodice had a plunging neckline, and the skirt was full and swirly, and she felt like a goddess in it. Andrew would take one look at her, and he'd fall in love all over again.

That was all he needed, just a nudge back in the right direction. Just a reminder of why he'd gone for her in the first place. And the fact that the dress was for his graduation would make it a whole lot easier to persuade Mum to buy it.

Maybe she'd go to the shop this afternoon and try it on again: she could do with a lift. She'd ask Tina to go with her, but Tina didn't need having her nose shoved into Eleanor and Andrew's relationship. No, she'd go alone, and twirl in front of the mirror again, and cheer herself up.

Might even find a pair of shoes to go with it.

Caroline

SHE WAS LATE. SHE WAS NEVER LATE.

Like clockwork, every twenty-eight days. And now she was – how late? She counted again, knowing it was thirty-six, but still hoping for a mistake. Maybe she'd made a mistake.

But there was no mistake. She'd gone through one full cycle and was late for the second time. One week, two weeks, three weeks, four weeks, five weeks. Five weeks and a day.

It wasn't happening, it couldn't be happening. It *couldn't*.

It was stress, that was all it was. Sometimes it could delay things, couldn't it? In the run-up to the end-of-year exams she'd been studying too hard – she'd brought it on herself. Yesterday she'd woken up with a horrible nauseous feeling in her stomach. She'd rushed to the bathroom where she'd retched emptily, nothing to come up.

Stress, overwork. It wasn't anything else. It *wasn't*.

Over six weeks since— *No.* Stop.

She'd take it easy for the rest of the summer; she wouldn't open a textbook or anything school-related until September. She'd shake this off, her period would come back and everything would return to normal.

By day she could almost convince herself that this was true. She read nothing but novels, unable to remember a word of their plots as soon as she turned the final page. She tried to paint, and failed utterly. Nothing came out right. She went for long walks in an effort to tire herself out. She met her friends in town, she drank peppermint tea with them – *No coffee?* they asked, and she told them she was giving up caffeine for a while. For some reason, she'd gone right off coffee.

She went through her wardrobe and brought a bag of skirts to the Vincent de Paul shop. She painted her room a paler shade of cream and repositioned her posters of Leonard Cohen and Ernest Hemingway and Nelson Mandela, and sorted her books alphabetically according to titles, not authors. She kept busy, told herself that nothing was amiss.

But in the darkness of her room at night there were no distractions, no avoiding the nightmare scenario that became more and more likely as time passed, no stopping the sequence of events in the Bentley replaying itself over and over.

She cried terrified tears into her pillow as quietly as she could. How could it be possible, after one horrible encounter that had lasted less than five minutes? How could such a brief episode bring about such far-reaching consequences? If it was true – and she knew, didn't she, that it was true? – her entire future had been rendered uncertain.

What was to be done? Where was she to turn?

Not Eleanor, definitely not Eleanor. How could she possibly tell her what Andrew's father had done? Anyway, what could Eleanor do to help? Nothing, absolutely nothing.

Telling Dad was out – she'd die if she had to tell him that. And telling Mum was worse – she'd hit the roof. She'd probably march straight to Jasper and let him have it. That or call the guards, which didn't bear thinking about. All the questions she'd have to answer – maybe a court case: nightmare.

Her friends, Mary and Ciara and Ellen: maybe she could confide in them – or could she? They studied together in the library, or in one another's houses, they often met in town at the weekends, they went to the cinema and to the theatre – but when it came down to it they were companions rather than close friends. It was awful that there wasn't one single person she felt she could be completely open with now.

She hadn't laid eyes on Jasper since it happened. Lying awake that night, still shaken by what had taken place, the feel of him, the *smell* of him, still on her skin, she'd replayed the scene in its entirety, from the first quick press of his hand on her thigh to the matter-of-fact way he'd driven her home afterwards, as if nothing had happened. *Thanks,* he'd said, handing her the usual twenty-pound note, pretending not to notice as she scrambled back into her underwear, still trembling with fear and shame, still aching from his invasion. *Sophie will be in touch when they get back.*

Had he planned it all, or was it a spur-of-the-moment thing, decided as he'd approached the end of his road, and turned left instead of right? Or maybe it was before that. Maybe it was when he'd turned on the music that he never normally played. Had he been setting the scene with the music? Had that been part of it?

She should have been more forceful. She should have pushed him away, pulled her skirt down, insisted he drive her straight home. Hit out at him if she had to – but she *had* tried, she'd done her best to make him stop, for all the good her efforts had done. He was big and solid; he was far stronger than her.

She should have managed to open the door and run away from him then. At the very least she should have thrown his money back at him when he'd brought her home, instead of pocketing it meekly. Had she even *thanked* him for it? She thought maybe she had, still immeasurably shocked at what had taken place.

Thank God nobody was about when she'd let herself in. Mum and Dad out with some friends, Eleanor in her room playing Chris de Burgh. Caroline had crept shivering into bed, trying to blot out the entire episode. The following morning, after a couple of hours' sleep at the most, she wondered if she'd dreamt it, so fantastical it seemed in the light of day. But when she soaped in the shower, when she explored herself cautiously she was tender, and she knew it was no dream.

In the ensuing days and weeks she avoided his neighbourhood, not knowing what would happen if they came face to face again. She knew he'd act like nothing had occurred, like he'd done directly afterwards, but she was sure she wouldn't be able to.

Thankfully, Mum hadn't organised a dinner party since then. He and Sophie would surely have been invited: they were always on the guest list. He *had* been briefly mentioned one breakfast time – Mum had remarked that he must be missing Sophie and Nadine – and Caroline had had to duck her head to cover her sudden deep flush.

He was a friend of Mum and Dad's – that was what she couldn't understand. He was someone she'd trusted, the father of sweet little Nadine, the husband of Sophie, who always baked a batch of Caroline's favourite almond biscuits when she was coming to babysit. How could he have done what he did, how could he have possibly thought it was alright?

And now, finally, there was no more avoiding it. She'd have to go and see him, and ask for his help – and it would have to be today, before another frightened sleepless night went by. The idea of telling him, of giving voice to the horrifying words, was truly dreadful – but she had no other option.

It was three o'clock on a Thursday afternoon, and nobody was around. Dad was at work, Mum was playing tennis. She had no idea where Eleanor was. She'd go to his workplace, not to the house where she might encounter Andrew. She knew where Jasper worked; everyone in town knew where D'Arcy Enterprises was located.

The day was dry, but rain threatened. She pulled on a jacket and took Dad's golf umbrella from the hallstand: there was something comforting about its crooked handle. She set off, walking briskly. *Say what has to be said. Just say it out. He'll have to listen, he'll have to help.*

Jasper's company was located in an industrial estate on the outskirts of the town. It took her forty-five minutes to get there, her stomach cartwheeling all the way. While she was still some way off she could read the company name in giant red letters on the side of the brown brick building.

The Bentley was parked outside, in front of the low sign that read *Managing Director*. The sight of it stopped her in her tracks, brought the events of the night flooding back. The terror returned too: she could feel her skin crawling with it.

She couldn't go in. She couldn't face him.

She had to go in. She had to face him. She had no choice.

She took a steadying breath, and another. She forced herself to walk to the main door, feeling everything in her clamped tight. She entered and approached the reception desk, her footfalls obscenely loud in the overheated stillness.

The woman behind the desk looked up. Green eyes behind glasses with thin gold frames. A mouth the precise purple shade of her long oval fingernails. A tumble of brunette curls. A tailored shirt, white with navy pinstripes, top two buttons open.

A smile as painted on as the lipstick. 'Good afternoon.'

'Hello. I wonder –' Caroline broke off; the words wouldn't come. She began again. 'I'm looking for ... Jasper D'Arcy. Mr D'Arcy. I need to talk to him.'

'You have an appointment?' Ignoring the open diary on her desk. Knowing full well that an appointment didn't exist.

'No, I – But I must speak to him. It's urgent – it's an urgent – Tell him it's Caroline Plunkett. He'll see me.'

'I'm afraid Mr D'Arcy is tied up all afternoon. Maybe you could –'

Caroline shook her head. 'No, I can't come back. I *must* see him today, it's really terribly urgent. Could you please tell him I'm here? Just ring him and tell him, please. Caroline Plunkett.'

The woman pursed her purple lips. 'I'm sorry, but Mr D'Arcy really doesn't appreciate being interrupted when he's –'

'It's personal,' Caroline said, desperation giving her courage. 'I'm a neighbour, I babysit for his daughter. Look, I know he'd want to see me if he knew I was here.' Knowing nothing of the sort – she wasn't exactly bringing good news – but there was no way she was leaving, not after the effort it had taken to come here. 'Won't you please just ring him? Please?'

For a few seconds there was silence. Was she going to have to barge through the double doors that must lead to the interior of the building, search the place until she found him? What exactly could this dolly bird do to stop her?

Finally the phone's receiver was lifted. 'What was the name?' Cool. Pretend smile gone.

'Caroline Plunkett.'

A button was pressed. 'Sorry to disturb you, Mr D'Arcy, but there's a Caroline Plunkett in Reception who's–'

Pause. Caroline heard the tiny scrabble of his response.

'Yes, I've told her, but she's insisting on seeing you.' Managing to drench the words with disapproval. A second pause followed, more scrabbling.

'Thank you, Mr D'Arcy.' She hung up. 'He'll be with you when he's ready.' She reached for a nearby folder and opened it, and began flicking through its pages: she might as well have held up a *Do not disturb* sign.

Caroline took a seat on the beige couch that might or might not have been leather. No, of course it was leather. She folded her hands on her lap, ignoring the glossy magazines arranged in neat columns on the low coffee table. Her gaze swept over the modern artwork on the walls, the grouping of what looked like framed certificates behind the reception desk, the opaque glass of the doors through which he was bound to emerge.

The seconds, the minutes ticked around. He knew she was there. He must know why she'd come. She wondered how long she was going to be left waiting.

Not long, as it turned out. Within ten minutes the doors were pushed open and he appeared with another man. The sudden sight of him, although expected, made her heart hop. Dark-suited, clean-shaven, as well groomed as he always was. His eyes flicked over her, his face unchanging – no sign of recognition, not even a nod – as he swept past in murmured conversation with his companion. Was he leaving? She made to get up – but now he was shaking hands with his visitor, they were bidding one another farewell at the front door.

He turned back. 'Caroline,' he said smoothly. 'Come this way.' Not smiling, but not looking too put out either. He led her past the desk – 'No calls, Amanda' – and back through the double doors, where a lift stood waiting.

'We'll go to my office,' he said, entering ahead of her. 'We won't be interrupted.'

Still no indication as to how her presence was being received. She might be a business colleague, come to discuss a new contract with him. He was pulling down his shirt cuffs, straightening his tie, clearing his throat as the lift bore them upwards.

Standing next to her, looking straight ahead as she remained silent and fearful. She caught a waft of something unpleasant – had she stepped in dog dirt on the way? – that caused her uncertain stomach to turn gently.

The doors opened. He exited the lift; she followed him into his office. Pale carpet, outer wall of floor-to-ceiling plate glass. Massive desk in dark wood. Chairs, couch, plants, coat stand. Filing cabinets. Paintings, lots of paintings.

He closed the door and immediately crossed his arms, feet planted solidly. He issued no invitation for her to sit. He looked directly at her. She felt accusation, confrontation, even before he opened his mouth. 'So,' he said mildly, 'am I to guess what you've come about, or are you going to tell me?'

'You must know,' she said. She closed her hands into fists and squeezed tightly. 'I'm pregnant.'

In the silence that followed, she listened to the echo of her words in the quiet room: *I'm pregnant. I'm pregnant.* The first time she'd said it aloud. She watched his face change, his mouth tighten, his eyes narrow.

At length he spoke. 'And am I to assume,' he said, his voice changed too, something new and careful and dangerous in it now, 'that you're accusing me of having something to do with it?'

Icy. No feeling. She felt a fresh prickle of apprehension.

'Yes.' Her voice tiny, the word barely audible. 'You know you have.'

'Actually, dear, I know nothing of the sort,' he replied in the same chill tone. Staring at her, holding her gaze so she couldn't pull away. 'For all I know you might open your legs for any man who gives you a second look.'

She felt her eyes stinging, felt the colour deepening in her face. How could he say that? How could he be so cruel? She blinked hard, grabbed her cheek between her teeth. No crying, she couldn't cry.

'I didn't— Of course it's yours. I never— That was my first time, I would never—' She broke off, and he waited. He knew she was telling the truth, and still he tormented her. 'It's yours,' she repeated, her voice quavering horribly, tears a heartbeat away, despite her efforts to keep them at bay.

He drew in his breath, let it out unhurriedly. 'And do you think,' he enquired quietly, 'that anyone at all would believe you, if you told them?'

Real menace in his voice now, unmistakable. Quiet, but real. She felt her heart trying to leap out of her, her legs quivering. *Don't faint.* 'Why wouldn't they believe me?'

'Well,' he went on, 'look at you, dear. Why on earth would anyone think I'd be interested?'

Tears began to roll down her face then; she was powerless to stem them. She blinked them away, felt them reach her chin and drop off. He watched, his expression unchanged, as she cried silently, unable to speak. At length he sighed, uncrossed his arms and stepped forward. Instinctively she flinched, waiting for a blow – he was surely capable of it – but instead he walked around her.

She dashed more tears away and turned to watch as he moved behind his desk and slid open a drawer. What was happening, what was he doing? She imagined him pointing a gun at her, smiling as he pulled the trigger. She waited, rigid with fear as he rummaged in one drawer and then another, eventually producing a long white envelope.

He approached her once more: she felt another wave of terror. He thrust the envelope at her. 'One thousand pounds,' he said, 'provided you sort it out, and never mention it again, to me or to anyone. Understood?'

She looked from his face to the envelope, and back again. 'Sort it out?'

Again he held her gaze. 'This is not the time to be coy,' he said coldly. 'You know exactly what I mean. You get rid of it, you tell nobody. You go to England, plenty of places to get it done there. Tell your parents you want to see Buckingham Palace. You're a clever girl, you'll figure it out.'

He was giving her money for an abortion. She looked at the envelope again, but made no move to take it.

An abortion.

But what had she expected him to do when he heard the news? What choice did he have, if he wanted to keep his family and his reputation intact? This was *his* only option, wasn't it? She'd expected

him to wave a magic wand and make it all go away
– and that was precisely what he was doing.

But an abortion: the prospect horrified her. All
her life she'd had a fear of needles, a fear of being
anaesthetised. And she'd read about abortions going
wrong, about women dying from them.

'I can't,' she said. 'I can't—'

He shook the envelope angrily. 'Take it,' he
ordered. 'Don't be an idiot. *Take* it, and thank your
lucky stars I'm giving it to you. I'm doing this to
help you out, that's all.'

She found her voice. 'I don't want your money,'
she said. 'You can't make me do this. It's yours, it's
your baby—'

'Prove it,' he shot back.

'You know it's—'

'How do I know? You gave in to me easily
enough, didn't you?'

A flash of memory – his hand crawling up her
thigh, her attempts to make him stop, her desperate
pleas – caused the blood to rush suddenly to her
face.

'I asked you to stop!' she cried. 'This is all your
fault! My parents will believe me if I tell them. I can
prove it's yours – I can *demand* that you have a DNA
test!'

'Go ahead,' he said evenly. 'Tell Mummy and
Daddy what a bad man I am, tell them what I did.
Make me do a test – and what will it show? Only that
someone with my DNA was responsible. Someone
in my bloodline.'

Someone in his bloodline? Could that be right? His eyes remained locked on her face. Watching her. Waiting for her to get it – and then she got it.

Andrew. Andrew was in his bloodline. Andrew would be implicated if she insisted on a DNA test. People might be more inclined to suspect Jasper, given his history – but Andrew would be tainted. Andrew, who was completely innocent. Andrew, who was in love with Eleanor. She'd ruin their future together, it would all be over if this came out.

'Take it,' he repeated, shoving the envelope at her again. 'Do the sensible thing, there's a good girl.'

She took it. What else was she to do?

'But know this,' he said, stepping closer, forcing her to move back until she felt the door behind her. Trapping her, like he'd trapped her in his car. 'Remember this,' he said, his face inches from hers. 'You breathe one word of our conversation here, you tell anyone, anyone at all, about what you allege went on between us, or about this money, and you will suffer. I'll make quite sure of that.'

His breath smelt of coffee. A fleck of his spittle hit her lip as he spoke. His fingerprints were on the envelope, she thought wildly. He could be identified from them. And then what?

'Nobody will be able to prove it was me,' he said. 'I'll take you to court, I'll sue you for defamation of character. I'll ruin your family – they'll be lepers in this town when I've finished with them.'

Had she really admired him, looked up to him, this monster in an expensive suit who was spewing threats at her, who was menacingly, intimidatingly close to her, who had no qualms about risking his son's good name to protect his own? All she felt now was fear and revulsion.

'Do it,' he said tightly, watching her face. 'Tell them you fancy a few days in London. Tell them anything you want. But keep your mouth *shut*. Understand?'

She managed to nod. His eyes were like flint. Was this how he intimidated his business rivals? The envelope he'd given her was clenched in her fist, one thousand of his pounds inside it. She should throw it back at him.

His arm came up, and again she tensed – but he reached behind her for the door handle. Before pressing it down he paused, so close she could feel the heat of his body.

'You weren't bad, though,' he said. 'Nice and tight.' A smile that wasn't a smile on his face now: a smirk was what it was. He was laughing at her. He was laughing at what he'd done to her.

She was thoroughly sickened. She pushed him away and fled. She ignored the lift – no lift: he might follow her in – and found the stairwell and stumbled her way back to the ground floor. She shoved open the double doors and strode through the lobby, not looking once in the direction of the desk.

Walking away from the building, she imagined him watching her from his office window. The back of her neck prickled. Every inch of her felt dirty, contaminated by him. His envelope was still bunched in her clenched fingers: she had a sudden urge to throw it away, to fling it from her and let whoever found it take it. Or stuff it into a bin, push it down under all the other rubbish. He was buying her off, paying for her silence.

But she didn't throw it away. She wasn't that stupid.

'Anyone seen my golf umbrella?' Dad asked that evening – and as soon as he asked, she saw it propped by the beige couch in Jasper D'Arcy's lobby.

'Not me,' she said.

Eleanor

'YOU'RE GOING *WHERE*?'

'To France. Look—'

'I don't believe it – you're just back from Spain, and you're going away *again*?'

'I'm not just back, I've been back ten days.'

'You *know* what I mean!'

'El—'

He broke off. He wasn't looking at her. Why was he not looking at her? What was *wrong* with him lately?

'Look,' he said in a rush, 'I think we should take a break.'

'A break?' She frowned. 'What are you talking about? We *had* a break, when you were in Spain with your buddies.'

Still not looking at her. Seeming fascinated by her knee, or maybe by the park bench they were sitting on. 'No – I mean a break. From us.'

Her thoughts skidded to a halt. She stared at him.

He glanced up then. 'It's not you, El – honest, it's not.'

'Did you say a *break*?' This wasn't real. It wasn't happening. She felt her face going cold. 'You mean ... break *up*?' She could hardly get the words out. 'Are you ... breaking up with me?'

'It's not you,' he repeated, addressing her knee again. Hands thrust into his jacket pockets, looking as if he wished to be anywhere else in the world. His skin was golden after Spain: he was unbearably gorgeous. 'It's nobody's fault, nobody is to blame. It's just with me going away to college in September, and us being apart ... and, look, it doesn't have to be forever, it might not be forever. I just think it might be— Look, we've never gone out with anyone else – maybe we should just ... give ourselves a chance, you know?'

He was breaking up with her. Andrew D'Arcy was finishing with her. It was impossible. She was dreaming. It had to be a dream.

And then it came to her: he was joking. He was messing with her head, that was all it was. Relief flooded through her. He wasn't serious, he didn't mean it.

'I'm on to you, Andrew D'Arcy,' she said. 'I see what you're doing.'

He finally looked properly at her. 'What?'

'You're not going to France at all, are you? You made that up, because I got mad about Spain.'

'El—'

'And the rest of it. You're not serious, I know you're not. You're just having a laugh.'

'Listen—'

'Well, it's not funny. I nearly believed you.' She thumped his arm, hard. 'How could you think that was funny? It was horrible.' She thumped him again, anger taking over from the relief. Not funny, not in the least.

'Ow,' he said. 'That hurt.'

'Horrible,' she repeated, too loudly: a passing couple turned simultaneously. 'How could you *do* that?' she hissed.

He slid along the bench, out of her reach, rubbing at his arm.

'Well?' she demanded. 'It *is* a joke, isn't it?' Anxiety beginning to creep in again, to gnaw at her edges. 'You *are* joking, I know you are.'

'No, El,' he said. 'I'm not. I'm sorry, it's not a joke.'

Of course it was. She took another tack. 'You're doing this because you're mad at me,' she said. 'You're mad at me for some reason – it's why you went to Spain, I know it is. You're mad and you won't say why. That's so childish.'

'I'm not mad—'

'You are, I *know* you are. It's cruel not to tell me what's up.'

'Nothing's up, it's not a—'

'Just tell me what I did,' she said, sliding closer, forcing herself to sound calm, even though her anxiety was becoming real fear now. 'Come on, please tell me, because I haven't a clue. Stop being so mean. I can't fix it until you tell me.'

She reached towards him – but before she could touch him he sprang to his feet, as if she'd contaminate him.

'I'm sorry,' he said again. 'I'm sorry, El. I wish there was something I could say.'

She felt her throat tighten. She swallowed. Could this actually be happening? Could it?

'I'm really sorry,' he repeated.

She looked up at him, blinking hard to stop tears that threatened. 'Don't you ... love me any more, is that it?'

'It's not that simple—'

'Did you meet someone in Spain?'

'No – there's nobody else. Look, I just—'

'*No*,' she said, hating the wobble in her voice. She got to her feet. 'You can't do this, you can't just say it's over, it's not fair. You're just going through a phase, and that's OK. Go to France if it's what you want, but don't – don't talk about a break. We don't need a break, just a bit of time apart. We're *made* for each other, you know that.'

'El, I'm sorry—'

'Stop *saying* that!' She hit him again, a swipe this time to the side of his head with her open hand. 'I bought a *dress*,' she cried, tears finally spilling out, 'Mum bought it. It's for your graduation. It cost a *bomb*. Does that mean *nothing* to you?'

He began to back away. 'I have to go.'

He couldn't go: she had to stop him leaving.

'Please,' she said, grabbing his sleeve, 'I didn't mean it about the dress – the dress doesn't matter. But we love each other, you know we do. We're meant to be together, everyone says it. Please don't go.' Hearing the horrible pleading in her voice, but unable to control it. 'Please, don't. Don't leave me.'

'El, come on.' He tugged, but she wouldn't let go. 'Look,' he said then, 'I don't love you any more, OK?'

She stared at him, horrified. In the silence that followed she released her hold on him, allowed her arm to drop.

'I just don't. I don't know how it happened, but—'

'No!' She couldn't listen, couldn't hear. She lashed out again, hitting whatever part of him she could reach. She had to shut him up, had to stop him talking. 'No!' Shouting it, thumping his face, his neck, his chest, his stomach. He recoiled, backed away, hands raised to protect himself as she continued her attack. 'No!' she shouted again, raining blows on him, yelling obscenities now, words she'd never used before as the truth dawned, as he turned and ran away from her.

He ran away from her.

Andrew D'Arcy ran away from her.

She ran after him, her anger dissolving once more. 'Come back!' she cried. 'I'm sorry, I didn't mean it, please—' But he didn't stop, didn't come back. He easily outran her, disappearing from view before she'd gone any distance at all. She gave up then, weeping and breathless and stunned, her blurring gaze still fixed on the spot where the path turned, willing him to reappear even now, to come running back, laughing at how completely he'd managed to fool her.

She'd kill him. No, she wouldn't.

People threw her curious looks as they passed: she ignored them. What did they matter, what did anything matter now?

Eventually she staggered across the grass, still sobbing, and slumped beside a tree. She leant against the trunk, her back to the path. She hid her face with her hands, trying to take it in.

He was gone.

They were finished.

It was over.

There was no sense to be made of it. All the plans they'd had – no, all the plans *she*'d had, all *her* dreams. Not his, clearly never his. Her whole future rewritten, just like that. Had he never once meant it when he'd told her he loved her?

It might not be over though. He might change his mind – he might come back. He'd said it was just for a while, hadn't he? He just wanted some space, she'd been crowding him. He needed some time on his own, that was all. This was just temporary, this was a break. Lots of couples had breaks. Of course he still loved her.

At length she lowered her hands, turned to look again at the spot where he'd vanished. Maybe he was already returning, maybe he was regretting what he'd said – but all she saw was a scatter of strangers. A young woman on a bench – the same bench they'd sat on – pushing a buggy to and fro. An old man shuffling by, a raggy little dog on a lead trotting alongside. Two small tousle-haired girls in identical blue coats, each holding the hand of a man, each throwing glances at her as they skipped past.

She had just been dumped for the first time. She had an ex-boyfriend. Three years gone, just like that.

This prompted a fresh torrent of weeping. How was she supposed to go on without him? She *loved* him – did that count for nothing?

And wait till word got round, wait till everyone heard. She could say she was the one who'd put an end to it – but nobody would believe her. They'd know she was lying, they'd look at her with pity. She couldn't bear it.

A new and ghastly thought occurred: maybe he'd been lying when he said there was nobody else. Maybe he'd fallen for someone – maybe that was why he'd been distant over the past few weeks. He might be going to her right now to tell her he'd broken it off. It made her feel physically ill, picturing him with another girl. It made her heart contract, caused her to groan in actual pain. What if it was someone she knew? What if she met them together? She'd *die* if that happened, she was certain.

And even if there wasn't anyone else now there would be, just as soon as he started college. He'd be surrounded by girls – he'd be bound to fall for one of them. Oh, it was unbearable, all of it.

Time passed. Rain came and went again. Still she

sat hunched on the ground, arms wrapped around her knees, torturing herself with dire possibilities. Love, she decided wretchedly, was not for her. She'd never look at another boy, never give her heart away again. She'd end up old and alone – or maybe she'd live with Caroline, who would also be alone. The scenario was so bleak, so devoid of any possibility of happiness, that it prompted a wash of yet more tears.

Eventually she struggled to her feet, cold and stiff and damp. She walked home slowly, taking the long way around so she didn't have to pass his house. She was aware of the curious glances she was attracting. No doubt she looked a mess: she'd never been a pretty crier.

She decided not to tell anyone. He was going to France in two days, and he'd be there for the rest of the summer. Chances were he wouldn't be spreading the news around before he left. So she'd say nothing, act like they were still together.

Because he might come back to her, mightn't he? This might turn out to be exactly what he'd called it: a break. He was restless now, he wanted to make sure he wasn't missing out. She'd give him space, let him have his flings if that was what he wanted. In time he'd come back to her, she was sure. They had to end up together: anything else was simply unthinkable.

'Where have you been?' Mum asked, standing in the kitchen doorway. 'You missed dinner.'

'I'm not hungry.'

'Are you alright?'

'I'm fine.'

She'd go on a diet, lose half a stone. She'd be waif-like by the time he came back, he'd see how she'd pined for him. She hung her damp jacket on the hallstand and turned towards the stairs.

'What's wrong? Did something happen?'

'I had a row with Andrew,' she said. Perfectly true. 'He's going to France for the rest of the summer.'

'Oh no, that's awful. Over to Sophie and Nadine?'

'Yes.'

'You won't feel it, darling. The weeks will fly by.'

'I know. I'll just miss him.'

She trailed upstairs and found a Whitney Houston tape. She lay on her bed, lacking the energy to peel off jeans that clung unpleasantly. She imagined their reconciliation. She'd be gracious as he begged for her forgiveness. She'd forgive him too, she wouldn't make him feel guilty for what he'd put her through. And she'd never nag him again, ever.

She awoke hours later, starving. She peeled off her crumpled clothes and pulled on pyjamas, and crept downstairs to raid the fridge. She'd start on the weight loss plan tomorrow.

It wasn't over, she told herself, piling chicken onto granary bread. No way was it over.

Caroline

SHE TOLD HER EVERYTHING. SHE LEFT
nothing out. When she stopped talking there was
silence. She watched her mother's face, but it was
entirely without expression.

Eventually she spoke. 'Why didn't you say
something when it happened?' Her voice, like her
face, gave nothing away: impossible to know what
she was thinking. 'Why didn't you tell us?'

'I couldn't. I ... just couldn't. I hoped I'd never
have to.'

'You're quite sure you're pregnant.'

'Well, I haven't done a test, but—'

'And you haven't been to see Dr Connolly?'

'No.' Going to the doctor had never occurred to
her. 'But I've missed two periods, and ... I've been
sick – I've been throwing up.'

Her mother got up and walked to the window,
and stood with her back to Caroline. What was she
thinking? Why wasn't she more shocked, more
sympathetic? Why did Caroline feel as if she was

being interrogated, as if she'd done something wrong?

At length her mother turned to face her again. 'So,' she said, 'here's what will happen. I'll go now to the late pharmacy and get a pregnancy test.'

'OK.'

'You can take it first thing in the morning, and if it's positive – and it sounds like it will be – I'll contact my cousin Florence in England. She'll look after you.'

Caroline stared at her. 'What? England? No. Why?' But she knew why. 'No,' she repeated. 'I don't want that.' She felt the colour leaving her face. 'You can't, I won't–'

'You will.' Cutting crisply across Caroline's words, silencing her. 'You will, because we have no choice here. You *cannot* have Jasper D'Arcy's child. You must see that it's simply out of the question.'

'Why? We needn't tell anyone whose it is. We can say I was attacked by a stranger.'

'No!'

So forcefully, it made Caroline start.

A beat passed. The mantel clock sounded unnaturally loud. Her mother left her position by the window and came to sit next to her on the couch.

'Nobody is going to be told anything.' More measured, back in control. 'You are not having this child. It is simply not going to happen.'

'But *why*? I've done nothing wrong–'

'Caroline, you are seventeen years old. You can't

saddle yourself with a baby – you'd be throwing away your whole future. I won't let you.'

'I *wouldn't* be throwing away my future – I wouldn't want to *keep* it, I'd give it up for adoption. You think I'd want to keep his child?'

'Caroline, there is no question of you having a baby. There's only one solution here.'

'I can't do it,' she said. 'It's dangerous, I don't want to. You know I hate operations – remember when I had my tonsils out –'

Her mother waved an impatient hand. 'Tonsils – and you made such a fuss. Anyway, you were a child then, you're practically an adult now. And the procedure is perfectly straightforward – lots of women have it done. Look at that poor young girl last year, desperate to go to England.'

The X case, she meant, a fourteen-year-old girl raped and made pregnant by a neighbour. The courts involved when it had come to the attention of the authorities that she intended travelling for an abortion. People arguing about it on the radio every day. But in the end the poor girl had miscarried, and after that it faded out of the news.

'That was entirely different,' Caroline said. 'She was much younger.'

'Three years isn't that much. You're still a child, still our responsibility.'

'You can't force me –'

'For God's sake – listen to yourself! You want everyone to think we'd be happy for you to have some anonymous rapist's baby? Have some sense!'

'I can't face the thought—'

'Can you imagine the reaction if we let you have it? Can you imagine the wagging tongues? We'd be the talk of the town.'

'So what? Let people talk.' She shrank from it too, the pointing fingers, the nudges, the whispers – but it would be over in nine months, less than that now. In time, people would find something else to talk about. 'I haven't done anything wrong,' she repeated. 'Why are you making me feel like I have?'

'Nonsense: I'm doing—'

'I thought you'd help. That's why I told you.'

'Can't you see I *am* helping? I'm doing what must be done. I'll book your flights, and then I'll ring Florence and get her to—'

'Who's Florence? I've never heard of her.'

'I told you, she's a cousin. She's lived in England for years. She'll collect you at the airport. I'll arrange everything. If your friends ask, you can say you fancied a few nights in London – tell them there was an art exhibition you were interested in or something.'

Just like he'd said. How had he put it? *Tell your parents you want to see Buckingham Palace.*

'You will go to England,' her mother went on, 'tomorrow or the next day. It will be over before you know it, and you can put it all behind you.'

It was intolerable. She had no voice. She pressed icy hands to hot cheeks. 'I've a good mind to tell everyone!' she burst out. 'Why do I have to sneak away like a criminal when it was his fault? It's not *fair!*'

'And what about Eleanor?' her mother demanded. 'If you did that, if you named him, it would mean the end of her and Andrew. Do you really want that on your conscience?'

That had been *his* trump card, of course, his veiled reference to Andrew being implicated in a DNA test.

'Well, I won't then, I won't name him – but you can't make me go to England, you just *can't*. Please let me stay here, please don't send me away.'

'Caroline ...' her mother began, in a new voice. Studying her nails now, the perfect ovals that reminded Caroline of Jasper's pretty but unfriendly receptionist. 'I'm not sure,' she went on, raising her head to regard Caroline once more, 'that I entirely go along with your version of events, to be honest.'

'... *What?*'

'Can you truthfully tell me that you did nothing at all to encourage him?'

Caroline was aghast. '*Encourage* him? How can you—'

'I've seen the way you are in his company. I know you're infatuated with him, and I can understand it. He's an attractive and charming man. I wouldn't blame you if you were flattered.'

Flattered. Charming. Was she hearing right?

'And men can be weak, Caroline. They can give in easily to moments of temptation. If he felt that you were attracted—'

Caroline sprang to her feet, thoroughly repulsed.

'Mum, are you actually trying to say this was *my* fault? That I ... led him on?'

'Not exactly, or not deliberately. I'm just saying that he may have misread the situation. And if you stay here and have his child, it will eventually get out that it's his.'

'Not if we don't—'

'It will, Caroline. This town is too small for something like that to stay hidden. And can you imagine what that would do to his marriage, to his reputation, if he was only following his instincts, and imagining that it was what you wanted too?'

What *she* wanted: Caroline couldn't credit it. Her mother was worried about *Jasper*. She was trying to make out that Caroline had somehow tempted him, that she was as culpable as he was. The injustice of it took her breath away.

But you did admire him, a voice in her head reminded her. *You considered him attractive, you enjoyed being ferried home in his big car.* What if she'd been giving out signals without knowing it, making him think she *wanted* him to do what he'd done?

'Listen to me,' her mother said, reaching for hands that Caroline snatched away. 'However it happened it's done now, and our job is to make it go away. Blaming anyone will get us nowhere.'

'But you're blaming *me*!' Caroline cried, her outrage flooding back. 'You can't bear to think of him doing anything wrong, can you? He's perfect in your eyes, isn't he? It was all *my* fault, wasn't it?'

Her mother's face tightened. 'Now you're being ridiculous.'

'Am I? I don't think so.' She paused to catch her breath. A pulse pounded in her temple. She regarded her mother's pressed-together lips, her narrowed eyes. 'I think,' she said, the words coming out unbidden, 'you might be in love with him yourself.'

The slap took her completely by surprise. It didn't hurt – Mum's hand glanced off her cheek, no more – but the shock of it brought instant tears to her eyes. She blinked them away.

A beat passed. Another.

'I'm sorry,' her mother said. She didn't sound sorry. 'That was unforgivable.'

Was she referring to the slap, or to Caroline's suggestion that she was in love with Jasper D'Arcy? Caroline suddenly felt weary, out of words. What was the point, with her mother's mind clearly made up? She got to her feet and walked silently to the door.

'Caroline.'

She stopped.

'Not a word to anyone, not to Eleanor or your father. Promise me.'

She nodded dumbly.

'I'll tell them, after you've gone away. I'll say it was someone you didn't know, that you were attacked on your way home from the library.'

Caroline left the room without another word. She went upstairs – thankfully Dad and Eleanor weren't about – and sat on her bed, trying to take it in. Instead of having someone on her side, she was being sent away before she disgraced them all.

She would have been content not to name Jasper, only for Eleanor's sake. She would have gone along with the story that her rapist was a stranger. She'd expected sympathy and support – but she hadn't got it.

She should have confided in Dad, not Mum – but even as this thought was forming, she recognised the futility of it. Dad did what Mum wanted: he always had and he always would. He'd have believed Caroline's account, he'd have been furious at Jasper – but in the end Mum would have got her way, and events would have unfolded precisely as they were unfolding now.

She played out the following few days in her head. The test, of course, would be positive. When it was, Mum would go into action. She'd book return flights to London, she'd phone the cousin Caroline had never heard of, and whose name she'd already forgotten. She'd hunt down a clinic and make an appointment. When the time came she'd spin the other two a yarn and drive Caroline to the airport – and no doubt she'd go right in with her, to make sure Caroline didn't try to escape. How dramatic, how ridiculous it sounded.

But here was where events would take a different turn. Once she landed in England, Caroline was going to disappear. She'd give the cousin the slip in the airport – how hard would that be, when neither of them had ever laid eyes on one another? – and take a train to Scotland, or Wales, or wherever. Somewhere she couldn't be found.

She'd find a job, and some kind of accommodation: she'd have Jasper D'Arcy's money for a deposit, and the first month's rent. She'd change her name, tell people as little as she could, allow nobody to get close to her. She'd work for as long as she was able, and she'd have the baby when the time came.

And then she'd hand it over to whatever adoption agency she'd made arrangements with, and after that she'd come home, and face whatever music awaited her.

She packed a weekend bag – all she could take without arousing Mum's suspicions. She tucked Jasper's envelope into one of the shoes at the bottom of the bag.

In due course there was a tap on her bedroom door. 'I have the test,' her mother said. 'I'll call you around seven, before the others are up. Try to get some sleep.'

Some sleep: as if. For the remainder of the evening Caroline remained in her room, listening to the others coming in and going to bed. She lay awake the whole night, watching the display on her clock radio crawling towards morning.

And everything happened exactly as she'd known it would.

'Your return flight is a week from today,' Mum said as they made their way to the airport. 'Florence will meet you in London – I've given her a description, she'll have no trouble picking you out.

I've told her a stranger was responsible: there's no need for her to know the truth. You're booked into the clinic the day after tomorrow.'

Taking control like she always did.

'I know you hate me now,' she said at the desk that led into the departure area. 'I'm doing what's best for you. I hope some day you'll understand that. I'll be here to meet you when you come home.'

She handed Caroline a folded slip of paper. 'It's a sterling draft, made out to Florence. I've asked her to keep half and give the rest to you. Treat yourself to something nice when it's all over.'

Treat yourself to something nice: if she only knew. Caroline took it wordlessly. Maybe she could call herself Florence, wherever she ended up; maybe she could get some bank to believe her.

At the departure gates she turned away without a goodbye.

'I'm sorry I slapped you,' Mum said. Caroline kept walking.

She waited with the other passengers by the gate. She unfolded the bank draft and saw that it was for six hundred British pounds, and wondered again if she dared to try and cash it.

When the flight was called she boarded the plane. Her first flight alone, something she'd always looked forward to. Rome, she'd thought, for the art and the history – or maybe Paris, to sip coffee on the Champs-Elysées, wander through the Louvre, buy a book or two in Shakespeare and Company.

She would be dressed in clothes bought specially for the trip, and full of excitement as she packed her bag. Instead she was going against her will, desperate and frightened and sick.

She dreaded to think of Mum's reaction, once she discovered the change of plan. She imagined how angry she'd be, how she'd be forced to tell everyone – because there could be no other rational explanation, could there, for a seventeen-year-old female to vanish for the best part of a year? The family would have to suffer the nudges and whispers that Mum had been so anxious to avoid.

Pity about her. She'd brought it on herself by trying to force Caroline to do what she couldn't do. All of this was Mum's fault: the embarrassment and the shame were no less than she deserved.

She wondered what would happen about school. Would the nuns open their doors to her again, or would the fact that she'd had a baby, under whatever circumstances, be too much for them to live with? Caroline Plunkett, so full of promise, letting us all down like that.

There'd been a girl in school, Paula O'Connor, who'd had an abortion. She was in Junior Cert when it happened, a year ahead of Caroline. Everyone knew where she'd gone, and why – how had they all known? There'd been no talk of rape, or none that Caroline remembered – but that wasn't to say it hadn't happened.

The news of her pregnancy had done the rounds. It was whispered about in the school toilets, it spread as quickly as ashes in the wind. Within days it had made its way all over town.

Caroline remembered them all being deliciously shocked by the scandal, everyone waiting for Paula to come back, in awe of someone who'd actually had an abortion. In the end though, she didn't return to the school – word went around that she'd transferred to the comp. Had the nuns thrown her out, or had she been too ashamed to come back?

She thought of her friends moving into Leaving Cert year without her. She felt bad going away without a word to them – she could imagine how betrayed they'd feel – but the fewer who knew what she was planning the better, for now anyway. She might write to Mary once she was settled somewhere; she might explain everything and ask her to let the others know.

She thought of Jasper D'Arcy, who had caused such a seismic change in her life, her whole future altered because of him. She thought of his hand on her thigh in the darkness of his car, the weight of his body on hers as he took what he wanted with no thought for the consequences, betraying his second wife like he'd betrayed the first.

The plane's intercom beeped, interrupting her thoughts: their descent into London had commenced. Her stomach turned somersaults as they lost altitude. She used to enjoy flying when they'd gone on family holidays, but today she was enduring rather than enjoying it.

The airport was all crowds and heat and noise.

She showed her passport to an unsmiling official and walked past the carousel in the baggage hall: nothing to reclaim. She entered Arrivals and kept walking, looking straight ahead, catching nobody's eye. The exit doors were directly ahead, another dozen paces and —

'Caroline Plunkett.'

A woman stepped right in front of her, blocking her way. She saw a knitted hat in stripes of green and grey, pale red curls poking out. Blue-framed glasses sitting halfway down a large open-pored nose. Scarlet lipstick, worn off in spots. A foot or so shorter than Caroline.

'I'm your cousin Florence,' she said. 'You're the image of your mother; I'd have known you anywhere.' An Irish lilt to her words, with a pinch of England thrown in.

'I'm not going with you,' Caroline said, moving swiftly around her. This stocky little woman, who had to be well over fifty, couldn't make her. The plan would still work.

'Hang on —'

She didn't hang on. She kept going, pushing open the exit door, walking quickly into the English sunshine, casting around for a train station sign.

'*Wait!*' Rapped out sharply, causing several people to look in their direction.

Caroline whirled around. 'Leave me alone,' she hissed. 'I'm *not* having an abortion.' She strode off again, searching for information. Bus or train, she'd take whatever she found.

'Doesn't bother me whether you have one or not.'

Too loud, even with the surrounding noise, for Caroline to miss it. She halted for the second time and turned slowly, fearful of a trick.

The woman approached, hands thrust into the oversize pockets of a ridiculous patchwork coat. What did she need a coat for on a day like this?

'I told your mother I'd give you a place to stay, bed and board while you were here. I took the morning off to collect you.'

'She booked a clinic,' Caroline said. 'She must have told you.'

'She did – but that has nothing to do with me.'

'I'm not having an abortion. I'm going away where they won't find me. I'm having this baby, and you can't stop me.'

Florence raised her eyebrows. 'I wouldn't dream of stopping you, if that's what you want to do. And what then?'

'What do you mean?'

Florence sighed, taking a hand from her pocket to push up her glasses. 'What happens when you get to wherever you're heading? How are you going to live? How are you going to cope with a baby on your own?'

'I have money – and I'll get a job until … it comes, and then I'll give it up for adoption. I'll manage.'

Florence lifted her shoulders. 'Fair enough. You seem to have it all worked out. Where are you headed for?'

Caroline hesitated. 'I'd rather not say.'

Florence tipped her head to the side. 'You think I'll tell, is that it?'

Her bluntness was disconcerting. 'I … think it's best if you don't know.'

Another shrug. 'Off you go so, and good luck to you.'

'Thank you … and sorry you had to miss work.'

It wasn't her fault, she was only doing what Mum had asked. Caroline moved off, anxious now to be gone. Even though Florence wasn't protesting, she could still find a phone, couldn't she, as soon as Caroline was out of sight, and blab to her parents? There was no time to be lost. She spotted an airport official and approached him.

'A train to Scotland? You'll need to get to Victoria or King's Cross in London for that. Timetables and tickets back in the terminal.'

She thanked him and turned – and almost collided with Florence, standing right behind her.

'Scotland – that's your big plan? You're going to hide in *Scotland*? They'll find you in a day, child. You haven't a hope.'

Caroline glared at her. 'You have no right to interfere. This is *my* decision. It's got nothing to do with you.'

Florence took off her glasses and lifted the hem of her coat to polish them. 'Child, would you ever have a bit of sense? I'm quite happy for you to come and stay in my house for as long as you need to – and since I'm guessing you don't know another soul in the UK, I think you'd be wise to forget your cockeyed plan to scoot off to Scotland and take me up on my offer.'

Caroline stared down at her. 'Are you saying you'll let me live with you until I have the baby?'

Florence replaced her glasses. Her eyes were midway between blue and green. She held Caroline's gaze unblinkingly. 'Yes, child. That's exactly what I'm saying.'

There had to be a catch. It couldn't be this easy. 'What about my mother?'

Another lift of the shoulders. 'What about her?'

'She's going to object.'

Florence took Caroline's arm and began to steer her away from the building. 'You let me worry about your mother,' she said. 'There's only so much objecting she can do, and I've stood up to bigger bullies than Ronnie Plunkett in my day. Now let's go and find my jalopy, and we can be on our way.'

And for the first time in weeks, Caroline felt a tiny unclenching within her, a speck of hope taking root in the space that Florence's words were creating. It wasn't ideal, it was far from ideal – she was still exiled, still miles from family and friends at this horrendous time – but for now she had a place to stay, even if it was with someone she wasn't at all sure of.

For the time being, she had a roof over her head. It would do.

September 1993

Eleanor

EVERYTHING WAS HORRIBLE. NOTHING WAS turning out the way it was supposed to.

First there was the shock of Caroline, raped and pregnant. Sent by Mum to England for an abortion but still there weeks later, having refused to go ahead with it. Caroline, living now with a cousin called Florence, who seemed to have materialised out of nowhere. Caroline, defying Mum, going to have a baby at the age of seventeen. Unbelievable.

Mum was livid, just livid. She'd followed Caroline over, just as soon as she could arrange time off work. She'd returned home a day later, even angrier. Turned out she hadn't actually met Caroline, just this cousin person.

The woman is impossible: if I'd known she was going to turn traitor like this, I wouldn't have gone near her. I can phone, if you don't mind, once a week, but she's not going to let me talk to Caroline until it's too late for an abortion. Can you believe she's laying down the law like that?

Made a change, someone laying down the law to Mum. Raped, though: poor Caroline. On her way home from the library, in a part of town that Eleanor walked through regularly, which was very scary. She could trace Caroline's route exactly: down Larchfield Avenue, through the housing estate, past the parade of shops and the park and the hospital, across the bridge and along Stewarts Road. All very busy and public, hard to see where anyone would have had a chance to attack her in broad daylight without being seen.

Maybe Caroline had taken a detour through the park. Wouldn't have made the trip any shorter, just varied it. Eleanor hadn't set foot in the park since Andrew had broken it off. She used to like it, until he'd ruined it for her. But someone could have been lurking there that day – someone could have been waiting in a quiet part for a lone female to come along.

Yes, the park must have been where it had happened. Had he approached Caroline first, asked for the time maybe, or for change, or had he just pounced silently? She imagined Caroline with an armload of books, crying out when he'd grabbed her, the books flying in all directions. He must have dragged her behind a tree, a hand over her mouth. He must have wrestled her to the ground as he'd forced himself on her.

Hard to fathom how he'd got away with it though. The park wasn't all that big: it didn't really have places so isolated that something like that could happen – or did it? Clearly it must, if that was where it had taken place.

No question of letting the guards know, of course – not with Mum determined to keep it quiet. So what were the chances that he'd do it again to someone else? And in the meantime, Caroline was living with a stranger when she should have been at home being looked after by her family. It was wrong, it was all wrong.

Of course, nobody outside the family was ever going to know about the rape: Mum would make sure of that. *We'll tell people she's had a breakdown,* she said. *We'll say we've sent her to Switzerland to recuperate.* So now they were all sworn to secrecy. Mum and Dad had rowed about it – Eleanor had heard the raised voices, had heard enough to get the gist. Dad wanted Caroline to come home and have the baby here; Mum was having none of it. And guess who got the final say?

It seemed to Eleanor that the whole world was going bad. A few months back, a sweet-faced little toddler in England had been murdered by two ten-year-old boys; every night on the news there were reports of people being killed in the North; a bomb had exploded at the World Trade Center in New York. Horrible things were happening everywhere, wars and plane hijackings and ferry sinkings – and now this calamity, right on their own doorstep.

And if that wasn't bad enough, there was

Andrew. He'd finally reappeared towards the end of August: Eleanor had literally bumped into him on her way out of HMV.

Hey, he said. Deeply tanned, blond hair lifted to gold by the French sun. *How's things?*

Her heart jumped at the sight of him, her mouth curved into an unbidden smile. How long had it been since they'd held hands, kissed, done more than kissed, done as much as they'd dared? She couldn't bear to do the sums.

How was France? she asked.

Full of French people. How was your summer? Perfectly friendly, no sign of resentment after her physical attack. So far so good.

Oh, you know, just ... hanging around with the gang. God, pathetic. *Having fun.*

Her smile was getting stiff. There was a second of silence, two seconds. Say something, she begged silently. Tell me what I want to hear. Tell me you missed me.

But he said nothing, so to break the silence she pulled out Annie Lennox. *I got a CD player for my birthday; I'm building up a collection.*

Happy belated.

Thanks.

August the twentieth: he knew the date well. For her fifteenth last year he'd given her a heart-shaped gold locket on a chain, and she'd snipped off an inch of his hair and stored it inside. *Don't go. Don't leave me.*

So when are you off to college? Nice and casual, not probing.

Couple of weeks. Finally got sorted with a flat.

Oh, that's good. His bed. Wine, candles, music.

How's Caroline? he asked then. *I heard she was sick* – and she trotted out the lie they'd been telling everyone over the past few weeks, reciting the lines her mother had drilled into her. She'd said it so often it was beginning to feel like the truth.

Sorry to hear that, he said. *Give her my best when you're talking to her*, and she promised she would.

Well, he said, moving off, lifting a brown hand, *see you around. Be good.*

See you – and he was gone.

He was gone.

He hadn't missed her at all. After weeks apart, he didn't want her back.

And there and then, standing on the path outside HMV, forcing people to swerve around her, she'd had to face up to the fact that they'd never be a couple again. There and then, she'd stopped fooling herself.

She'd walked home, feeling horribly lonely. That afternoon she boxed up all her reminders of him – gifts, photos, Valentine cards, cinema tickets, scribbled notes – and consigned them to the attic, the hurt too raw yet to let them go out with the rubbish. When her room had been scoured of him she listened to Annie Lennox and Kate Bush and Whitney, and tortured herself with memories.

She told Mum that evening. She made it sound like a mutual decision, but she could see Mum wasn't fooled.

It might only be temporary, you never know.

It wasn't temporary. She did know.

And since then, he'd dropped off the radar again. She'd seen his father around a few times: he'd even stopped her in the street once to ask after Caroline – wondering, probably, how long they'd be left without their babysitter. Another time she bumped into Sophie, who gave her a pitying smile and called her *chérie* – but of Andrew there was no further sign.

And now it was the middle of September, and he was more than likely in Dublin, getting used to the place before college began. Moving on with his life, leaving her behind with his school uniform and all his other discarded things. Another girl christening his bed before long, more than one maybe. He might have a new one every weekend, making up for lost time.

Tears ambushed her regularly. It didn't take much: a snatch of a song, a film on TV that they'd seen together in the cinema. The echo of his voice in her head, the memory of his laugh. A chance waft, on the street or in a crowd, of the Calvin Klein scent she used to get for him.

One thing she was sure of: she'd never be interested in anyone else. Andrew had been it, her soulmate, her one and only – and now he was gone.

Her life yawned emptily ahead, years and years of loneliness to be endured.

Not that she couldn't get someone else if she wanted to. Not that there hadn't already been interest. *My brother fancies you*, Karen Doherty had said the week before. They were in the sports hall, waiting on the sidelines for their basketball team to be called into play.

Niall Doherty hung around with a few lads Eleanor knew slightly. He was nothing like as good-looking as Andrew. He was stockier, and acne had left mini craters in his face, and he used too much hair gel. Eleanor couldn't recall ever having had a proper conversation with him.

But he was funny. She'd overheard him more than once make a laconic remark that had everyone in stitches. And he had a car, a silver Corolla, and a job as a mechanic in the local garage.

He might be worth keeping in mind, if she ever felt remotely like seeing someone again.

But today she wasn't thinking about Niall Doherty. The Junior Cert results had come out – and if she hadn't exactly covered herself in glory, at least she'd passed all her subjects, no doubt against Mum and Dad's expectations, and the three of them were going out to dinner to celebrate.

Eating out with her parents wasn't Eleanor's idea of a celebration. If she'd still been with Andrew she'd have been going somewhere with him and the others; she'd have told her parents that she'd made plans. But tonight she had no plans, and no wish to go to the disco that more than half her classmates were attending, no intention of standing around with all the other pathetic unattached girls.

She put on her favourite Levi's and an oversized tartan flannel shirt that she usually wore in place of a dressing gown. Her father gave her outfit a disappointed look when he saw it: if he had his way she'd live in skirts like Caroline.

Mum, wearing one of her little black dresses, didn't limit herself to a look. 'Darling, you could make an effort. This dinner is in your honour, and we're going to Ricardo's' – so to keep the peace Eleanor changed into black jeans and a plain blue shirt, and ditched her Doc Martens for a pair of ballet flats. That would have to do them.

Ricardo's was pretty full. Family groups mostly by the look of them, doing exactly what Eleanor and her parents were doing. She took some comfort from the fact that she wasn't the only one reduced to spending Junior Cert night with her parents.

It was strange with just the three of them around the table though. For every family occasion up to this, every birthday, every anniversary, they'd been a group of four. She wondered what Caroline was doing right now, at eight o'clock on a Wednesday night. Seven weeks since Eleanor had laid eyes on her, six since they'd spoken.

A week or so after Mum's fruitless trip to England, Eleanor had searched for and found Florence's number in Mum's address book. She'd copied it onto a page and dialled it from a phone box the following day.

Yes? An unfamiliar female voice. A trace of impatience in the word, as if she'd been interrupted.

It's Eleanor, Caroline's sister.

Oh. Yes. Pause. *I suppose your mother put you up to this.*

No – she doesn't know I'm ringing.

Hmmm. So how is she?

Well … she's not happy.

Of course she's not happy. *Ronnie was never happy unless things were going her way. Has she accepted that Caroline is going to have this child?*

Um … we don't really talk about it.

Florence made a kind of grunting sound. Silence followed.

I just wanted, Eleanor said, *to have a word with Caroline.*

As long as you don't mention an abortion: I won't have it.

The remark annoyed Eleanor – none of her business what they talked about – but she couldn't be sure this sharp-voiced person wouldn't hang up on her. *I won't say anything about it.*

The receiver clattered down without another word. Poor Caroline, stuck with someone who sounded so unfriendly. Several seconds ticked by – her money would be gone – and then the phone was picked up again.

Eleanor?

Caroline, are you OK?

Yes, she answered, just that. Maybe Florence was lurking.

What's going on? Are you really having the baby? Mum's fit to kill you.

I'm not changing my mind.

The words quiet, and very definite. Caroline had always been the placid one, the pliable, obedient one. Where was this sudden rebelliousness coming from?

But have you thought it through? I mean –

I don't want an abortion. I'm not having an abortion. I don't care what Mum says: it's not going to happen.

So you're just going to stay there, with that woman?

Yes, I'm staying with Florence.

But what about school? Caroline lived for school – or she had, up to this.

A pause, for the first time. *It will just have to wait.*

Until when, though?

Till after.

The silence stretched as Eleanor tried to put a shape on her next question.

What are you – she began, but she was interrupted by a series of short beeps.

Caroline, I'm out of change, I'm in a phone box.

Silence.

Are you still there?

The line went dead.

She bought chewing gum with a pound in a nearby shop and dialled again, and again Florence answered with her single taut *Yes?*

It's Eleanor – can I have your address? She scribbled

it on the same page that had the phone number. *Don't tell Mum you gave it to me*, she said, before hanging up quickly. Since then she'd sent a letter each week to England, full of boring nonsense really, but it was all she could think of to do.

'Eleanor, have you chosen?'

She glanced up. The waiter stood by their table, pen poised. She'd been looking at the menu and seeing nothing. 'Pizza,' she said, 'pepperoni and mushroom.' Pizza was a safe bet at Ricardo's.

Caroline's name wasn't mentioned at home. Every Friday evening Mum rang Florence's house and conducted a stiff conversation with her that lasted less than a minute. In between the weekly phone calls Caroline simply wasn't discussed, at least not in Eleanor's presence. Was this how it was going to be until the baby was born? And what then? Would Caroline come home – and would she have the baby with her? Would she dare to do that?

Eleanor wished Dad would put his foot down sometimes. Look how Florence was standing up to Mum, refusing to let her talk to Caroline – why couldn't Dad be firm like that? But he was taking care not to rock the boat, as usual. Anything for peace, even if it meant turning his back on his elder daughter.

And what about Eleanor, caught in the middle? Did they think she didn't care about her sister? Of course she cared. Caroline needed their support, and all she was getting was a series of dull letters to which she couldn't even respond, because Mum would probably hit the roof and call Eleanor a traitor too.

She made no mention in her letters of her split with Andrew. She wasn't deliberately keeping it from Caroline, she just couldn't bring herself to write the words down. It wouldn't matter to Caroline anyway – she had enough on her mind.

'Look who's just come in.'

Eleanor turned to see – and her heart fell as she saw Andrew and his family entering the restaurant. Jasper paused on the threshold, sweeping the room with his eyes as if he was looking for someone. Making sure everyone saw *him*, more like. When his gaze fell in their direction he gave them a nod, and Mum smiled and waved back. Still friends with him, despite his son having broken her daughter's heart.

A waiter approached and they followed him to a table at the far side. Eleanor saw Andrew pull out his chair and sit. He was thirty feet away but he might as well have been on the moon. She felt a wrench, an urge to cross the room and throw herself at his feet and beg him to come back to her. Didn't she have enough love for the two of them?

'Eleanor, don't stare like that,' Mum ordered. 'People will notice.'

In that instant she despised her mother. 'I'm *not* staring – and you're the one who told me to look when they came in. Can I have some wine?' She'd have preferred gin, but she'd take what she could get. They allowed her half a glass from the bottle they'd ordered, and as she sipped it she fancied

Andrew's eyes on her, and knew they weren't.

'You could go over in a while,' Mum said, 'and say hello. Pity you didn't wear a nice dress.'

'I have no intention of going over.' She could imagine the glances she'd attract, the nudges, the whispers from those who knew their history. Poor Eleanor, can't let him go. She thought of the horrible, over-bright conversation she and Andrew would have about nothing at all.

As she chewed pizza she didn't want, she felt a sudden flare of resentment. He'd tossed her aside like a book he was finished with: why should she waste any more time pining for him? Tomorrow she'd give Karen Doherty her phone number and tell her she could pass it on to her brother. He'd be a distraction if nothing else.

She was sixteen. Andrew D'Arcy might have ruined her summer, but she was damned if he was going to ruin her life.

Caroline

SEVEN AND A HALF WEEKS AGO THEY'D MET.
Fifty-two nights they'd spent under the same roof.
Little by little, she was coming to terms with what
had happened. Little by little, she was learning how
to live with it.

Florence's cottage, one of half a dozen on a
narrow cul-de-sac that straggled away from the main
part of the town, was like something out of a Hans
Christian Andersen fairy tale. Its sharply sloping
roof was interrupted in the front by two small leaded
windows, one of which belonged to Caroline's
bedroom. Its thick walls were whitewashed; a bay
window, also leaded, sat to the left of a dark blue
front door that had a tarnished brass toad for a
knocker. A mat on the doorstep featured a faded
silhouette of a seated black cat.

Running in a curve from the cast-iron gate to the
door, an old crazy-paving path was bordered on both
sides by a slanting tumble of tall flowers in blues and
purples and reds, flowers whose names Caroline

didn't know but whose scent crept on warm evenings through her open bedroom window. The garden was surrounded by a waist-high wall, also whitewashed, inside which numerous leafy and flowering shrubs had been planted. The place was a mass of colour and scent, and alive on these long days with drowsily buzzing bees and flapping butterflies.

Inside there was a network of little dimly lit rooms filled with disparate items of furniture and curious knick-knacks – a dusty grandfather clock, far too big for the narrow hall in which it was positioned, half its roman numerals worn off and a chime that sounded at ten past the hour; a life-size papier-mâché Yorkshire terrier perching on a windowsill; a pair of painted wooden castanets dangling from a wall lamp; a blue china hare, minus one ear, on the floor beside the fireplace.

A knitting machine that resembled some medieval instrument of torture sat in the bay window, a jumble of baskets on the floor beside it that were overflowing with balls of wool in various shades, swathes of fabric and cushions with spilling-out stuffing.

The kitchen was practically devoid of gadgetry or any suggestion of modernity. There was an ancient gas cooker, a fridge incorporating a minuscule freezer, a twin-tub washing machine well past its prime. A trio of battered saucepans, a frying pan missing its handle and a whistling kettle were the only cookware, apart from the dented baking sheet and roasting dish that lived in the oven.

A cracked earthenware jar on the windowsill housed a hand whisk, a wooden spoon, a pair of scissors speckled with rust and a couple of knives. By the condition of them, the terracotta floor tiles might have been there since the house was built.

The whole thing shouldn't have worked, but it did. The mismatched armchairs were accommodating, the clock's out-of-sync chime deep and comforting. The dim lighting offered by the wall lamps softened evening shadows and hid the dust balls that lodged in every corner. The kettle was rarely off the boil, the sitting-room fire, even in the heart of summer, never fully out. Despite its thrown-together character, there was an indefinable charm about the place, a warmth and appeal that were missing from the larger and far more carefully furnished house where Caroline had grown up.

And the small square garden to the rear held its own attraction. A companion paved path to the one in front zigzagged its way down the shrub-bordered lawn to a gate at the end. Daisy-like flowers in rich violets and deep pinks poked from a bed outside the kitchen window, other flowers – blue, orange, white – spilt from hanging baskets on the fence. Something fragrant clambered over the back wall.

A bird table sat on a wooden post that was set into the centre of the lawn. Two nut feeders were suspended from the branches of a crab apple tree that nodded in from the neighbouring garden. There was a sagging clothesline, and a weathered wooden bench sat on the grass within comfortable sniffing distance of the fragrant climber.

The back garden also contained Pip the cat, a jet-black giant of an animal that Florence had brought home from the rescue centre eight years previously. Half an ear was missing, and a hip injury had given him a curious lolloping gait. He could be found most of the time curled under a shrub or sitting on the edge of the garden seat, regarding the various birds that hopped and flew about with a singular lack of interest. He ignored food offerings until they were left unattended, slept in the plastic crate that Florence had positioned between two shrubs, and disappeared regularly for days at a time.

On the rare occasions that he entered the house he stayed by the open back door, darting out if anyone came too near. He paid no attention to Caroline when she tried to coax him closer to her with morsels of meat. She persevered, sensing something, some vulnerability, that drew her to him.

He had a bad time of it, Florence told her. *Lots of abuse. No wonder he trusts no one now. Don't get too pally, he could give you a fine scratch* – but Caroline didn't think she had anything to fear from him. In time, he might learn that he had nothing to fear either.

All in all, considering the upheaval that had brought her there and the uncertain nature of what lay ahead, in spite of the sense of dread that ambushed her each morning on waking in her tiny bedroom, she had to acknowledge that after seven and a half weeks she was becoming attached to the place.

And Florence, who had been her saviour, who had fought Caroline's mother and won, was growing on her too. Little by little, Caroline was becoming accustomed to her. Was becoming fond of her.

Not that it had been easy at first. No, not at all.

A few things we need to get straight, Florence had said, as they sped north along the motorway from the airport in her small ramshackle grey van. *I have no problem with you staying in my house, but I won't be waiting hand and foot on you. I work Monday to Friday, and I'm gone Saturday mornings too, so you'll be fending for yourself until we find you something to do. And there's no point in feeling sorry for yourself either: that'll get you nowhere. You were unlucky, but what happened happened. You're not the first and you won't be the last, so deal with it.*

Deal with it. She'd been told that Caroline had been raped by a stranger, and here she was telling her to get over it. There was truth, of course, in what she said – no point in dwelling on it, nothing to be gained from self-pity – but couldn't she have softened her delivery? Did she feel no sympathy at all for Caroline's plight?

The small hope that Caroline had experienced in the airport began to ooze away. She caught her bottom lip to keep it from trembling, and looked out at fields of grazing cows – the motorway left behind by now – and she wondered bleakly if she'd made a terrible mistake. How were the two of them going to get along, living together for the next several months? She knew nothing about this woman, apart from the fact that they were related. Maybe she should have stuck to her original plan and gone off on her own.

Can you cook?

The question caught her off-guard. *I – I haven't had much practice.*

Not much practice? You're seventeen, aren't you?

Yes.

When I was your age I was well able to cook. How are you on gardening?

Er, I'm not –

Look at that – he shouldn't be on the road. Florence ground the gears and swerved out to overtake a slow-moving jeep that was pulling a trailer of piglets, the sudden shift in direction sending Caroline lurching against the door. Florence's driving was atrocious, all sharp braking and haphazard lane changes: since leaving the airport they'd been hooted at more than once.

I suppose you have a man to do that.

… What?

A sigh, glasses pushed up again. *The garden. Have you a man who comes in to do it?*

We don't really have a garden – I mean not a lawn, it's paved.

Paved? She sounded as scandalised as if Caroline had told her they danced naked on the paving stones whenever there was a full moon. *What – the whole thing, back and front?*

Yes. We got it done a few years ago. We have a barbecue out the back, and a pond with fish.

Florence scowled at the road. *A pond with fish*, she muttered. *Save us.* They approached a crossroads, and Florence took the right turn without warning, ignoring a horn that blared furiously behind them. Caroline grabbed the sides of her seat, thankful that she hadn't eaten on the plane.

Now, Florence said, whooshing too fast through a small village, *we'll tell people you're my cousin, which is quite true, and we'll say due to unforeseen circumstances you're spending some time with me, and leave it at that. No need to give them any more: it's none of their business.*

What about ... when I'm showing?

What about it?

Won't people wonder?

Let them wonder all they like. You can tell who you want, and the rest won't ask – the English are far too polite.

Tongues would surely wag though – people were people, whatever the nationality. But the prospect didn't seem to bother Florence in the least. So unlike Mum, who lived in terror of giving people the smallest excuse to gossip.

Caroline ventured another question. *Do you live alone?*

Florence braked sharply as they approached a bend. *I do, unless you count Pip. I hope you're alright with cats – not that he comes in much.*

They'd never had a pet of any kind at home.

Caroline thought it might be nice to have a cat about the place. *Where do you live?* she asked.

Florence named a town: Caroline had never heard of it. *It's not that big, about the size of Listowel, if you've ever been there.*

Caroline hadn't. *Have you lived there long?*

The best part of twenty years, since I left London. Suits me fine.

And where were you before London? And when did you come to live in England? And why did you leave Ireland? And how did I never hear a word about you until now? Nothing, she knew nothing – and yet here she was, her immediate future at least in this odd little woman's hands.

When they eventually arrived Florence parked crookedly on the road outside and whisked Caroline up the garden path, giving her scant time to take in anything of the exterior. She led her through the small ground-floor rooms, naming each one – kitchen, pantry, sitting room, dining room – but otherwise making no comment.

Caroline gazed around, trying to get a feel for the place that was to be her home for several months. She tried to define the peculiar smell: there was a cloggy element to it, like wet cement, and a sharp chemical note that reminded her of nail varnish remover.

What's that? she asked in the sitting room.

Knitting machine. I have a market stall with a friend. You can help when you've settled in.

She didn't elaborate. Caroline had never seen a

knitting machine, would hardly have known that such a contraption existed. She followed her cousin silently up the narrow stairs, the pattern on its carpet long since faded, the pile completely worn off in spots. It felt like a week since she'd set off from home in her mother's car, her head full of other plans.

Your bedroom, Florence announced, pushing open a door that scraped its way across the bare wooden floor. Like the rest of the house, the walls were papered rather than painted, and this room's wallpaper featured faded pink roses. There was a single bed with a folded blanket sitting on its bare mattress, a narrow wardrobe, a dressing table ringed with watermarks and a spotted-with-age mirror on the wall above it.

Bathroom across the way. Sheets in the linen cupboard on the landing. Lunch in ten minutes: it's a salad, nothing fancy. And she was gone, leaving Caroline to set her case on the floor and sink onto the bed and look through the tiny window at a segment of sky, and wonder again what on earth she'd let herself in for.

Lunch, as promised, was simple – lettuce, hard-boiled eggs, halved tomatoes, roughly cut slices of ham, brown soda bread – but after a morning of no food at all, Caroline was glad of it.

The bread is nice, she said.

Took two minutes to put it together.

You made it?

Of course I did. Any fool can make bread.

Everything she said had an edge to it. Everything sounded confrontational. Was it just her manner, or did she resent the impulse that had led her to invite Caroline to stay?

Maybe a compromise could be found that suited both of them.

You don't have to keep me, Caroline said. *I can find someplace else in town. I have money.* She might be glad of Florence's help later on; it might be best after all to have someone she knew nearby when the time came.

Florence frowned at her over her glasses. *What are you talking about? I said you could stay here, didn't I?*

Yes, but – it was only going to be for a week, and now it's going to be months, and you don't sound as if you're all that happy with it.

Florence gave a kind of a bark. *Lord above, child, that's just my way. You'll get used to it. Of course you're staying here – why would you be looking for anywhere else when I have the spare room?*

And that seemed to be that.

I have money for you, from Mum, Caroline said then, suddenly remembering the sterling draft.

Florence flapped the words away. *We'll sort money out another time. And once you've settled in we'll find you a little job to keep you busy. You'll need something to do or you'll be bored.*

A little job – something told Caroline she wouldn't have much of a say in whatever that might turn out to be. She'd just have to hope it was something she enjoyed, or at least didn't hate too much.

When they'd finished the meal Florence got to her feet. *Now, you can start the washing-up while I ring*

Ronnie and tell her about the change of plan. May as well get it over with.

At the mention of her mother, all of Caroline's earlier fears came rushing back. *No, you mustn't – they can't know where I am.*

Florence stared at her. *What? You want me to pretend you're not here? You want them to think you gave me the slip in the airport like you were planning to? Would I not have rung them there and then to say you'd never arrived?*

Well, maybe, but if Mum knows I'm here she'll come and get me – she'll force me to have an abortion. Couldn't you say you tried to ring from the airport and couldn't get through, or something?

Florence snorted. *You want me to lie? Lying isn't my style, child – when you know me better you'll realise that. And as for your mother forcing you to do anything, she'll have to get past me first. You leave her to me.*

She stomped out to the hall, and Caroline filled the sink and washed the dishes, and listened with increasing dread to the snatches that came through the half-open door – *Now, Ronnie, there's no need to be so dramatic … Yes, you asked me to take care of her, and this is – Well, I'm afraid I don't see it like that, and she seems to know her own mind … I'm sorry you feel that way, but I couldn't in conscience – No, I think it's best if she doesn't come to the phone.*

And so on.

At length Florence reappeared. *She'll probably ring back when she thinks of something else to threaten me with. Do not under any circumstances answer that phone.*

She sounded so matter-of-fact, so unafraid, that Caroline felt again the flicker of hope she'd experienced at the airport. *She'll have to get past me first.* Someone was finally on her side. Someone was standing up to Mum. The war had commenced, and Florence had just won the first battle.

It was far from resolved though. No cause for celebration yet.

The phone rang again that evening. They were tidying up after the tomato and cheese omelettes that Caroline had made for dinner – one of the few dishes she could manage, although working with Florence's battered frying pan had been a challenge. *I'll go*, Florence said immediately – and once more Caroline heard her stoutly refusing to allow Mum to talk to her.

She wondered how long it would be before Mum arrived – because she had no doubt that it would happen. And what then? Florence would have to give way when they came face to face. On the other hand, Mum could hardly physically force Caroline to go with her, could she?

Lying in bed later, she wondered if after all she should just go, disappear like she'd planned and hope for the best. She would, she decided, once Mum announced that she was coming. It wasn't fair to put Florence into the firing line like this, even if she seemed more than a match for Mum. No, it would be best all round if Caroline left.

The following day, with Florence gone to work, she made her way through the list of jobs she'd been given. She topped up the bird feeders, cleaned out the fridge, took the cracked plastic laundry basket to the clothesline, collected the pillowcases and blouses that hung there, and ironed them as best she could on the rickety kitchen table with an iron whose flex had electrical tape wound around at least half of it.

The rest of the time she wandered through the house, getting to know it. She ran her fingers along the carriage of the knitting machine, she pulled out drawers, she lifted the lids of various tins and boxes on the pantry shelves to peer inside. When lunchtime came she cut a couple of slices from the fresh loaf of brown soda bread whose aroma had been filling the kitchen when she'd got up, and topped them with some of the ham.

In the afternoon the sun appeared and she sat on the garden seat among Florence's shrubs and flowers, listening to the buzzing and chirruping around her. It was nice here, it was peaceful. She wondered how long it would be before she'd have to flee.

Maybe she wouldn't go too far. As long as Mum didn't find her, that was all that mattered. Maybe she could come back when Mum went home again.

She wished she had a sketchpad with her, and her set of pens, or some charcoal. She resolved to buy some the first chance she got. She sat on as the afternoon passed, ignoring the phone which rang faintly from the house, roughly once an hour.

In the evening she chopped carrots and onions as Florence browned chicken pieces, and then they threw everything into the roasting dish, and Florence splashed on the chicken stock she'd made with a carcass the day before, and tossed in bay leaves she'd pulled from a bush in the garden. After dinner the phone rang again, and Florence answered it, and dealt with Mum as Caroline clattered dishes with more enthusiasm than they warranted.

The following day Caroline again hung around the house and garden, not yet brave enough to venture further. Nobody dropped by; her only interruption was the post that slithered through the letterbox around eleven, and the telephone that continued to ring at regular intervals – each time more shrilly, it seemed to her.

That evening, under Florence's instructions, she coated whiting fillets in egg and flour. *I lost my faith years ago*, Florence said, laying them in the frying pan that sizzled with melted butter, *but I still do fish on Fridays: funny the things you hang on to. Stick a fork into those potatoes, see if they're done.*

As they were about to eat, the phone rang. Florence sighed and got to her feet. *Should have taken it off the hook. Eat away, won't be long.*

But Caroline couldn't eat. *Get on with it*, she said silently. *Come over if you're coming.*

She's coming, Florence reported, resuming her seat and picking up her cutlery. *She's flying in tomorrow – I told her to take a train to Oxford, I couldn't come and collect her with the market. She'll be here in time for lunch. Why aren't you eating?*

I can't. I can't let you keep fighting with her. I'll leave first thing tomorrow, and then you can tell her the truth, and say I'm gone, and you don't know where.

Florence stared. *What? Don't be ridiculous. You'll do no such thing.*

But it's not fair to you. This isn't your problem, it's mine.

Florence jabbed her fork at Caroline. *Now you listen to me – I'll be the judge of what's fair. There'll be no more nonsense about you leaving. I told you I'm well able for your mother.*

You may be, but I'm not. I can't face her.

Child, I have no intention of letting you face her. I said I'd deal with her, didn't I?

Florence, you don't know her. She'll insist on meeting me. She'll just barge into my room.

Bless us – she's not getting near this house. I'm meeting her in Oxford. I'm not bringing her within twenty miles of here.

But she could just come – she could get a taxi or something.

Florence snorted. *Child, you watch too much television. What do you think she's going to do – drag you by the hair out of here?*

Well, no, but –

But nothing. You leave her to me. Now can I please get on with my dinner before it's stone cold?

She seemed so sure of herself, so adamant that Mum wasn't going to show up at the house. Caroline would just have to hope fervently that she was right.

The following morning Florence left the house early, before Caroline was up. *Gone to the market,* the note on the kitchen table said, scribbled along the margin of a torn-out newspaper page. *Home around three. Ignore phone.* The last bit in capitals, and underlined three times.

The hours crawled by. Caroline swept floors and shook out rugs. She made tea and poured it untouched into the sink. She switched on the radio and switched it off again. She tried and failed to read the previous day's newspaper, and paced the newly swept floors as the minutes crawled around until Florence reappeared at ten past three.

Alone.

That's that, she said, shaking raindrops from her plastic hat, handing Caroline a bag of groceries. *I picked up a few things as long as I was out.*

She's gone?

She is – back to London. She's booked into a hotel for the night, flying home in the morning. Is the kettle on?

No. Mum vanquished, just like that. *Was she very angry?*

Florence walked ahead of her into the kitchen and held the kettle under the tap. *She was, for all the good it did her.*

But she's going to let me stay?

She is. I didn't give her a lot of choice. Now, we'll have a cuppa and then I'm going to show you how to make bread – it's high time you learnt.

Relief swept over Caroline. She imagined Mum, dressed to the nines no doubt, determined to have her way as usual – and Florence in her baggy trousers and man's sweater and badly drawn-on lipstick standing her ground and refusing to be intimidated.

No abortion then. The baby to be born after all. Her problems far from over, but the most immediate threat averted – and her living arrangements sorted until the baby came.

I don't know how to thank you.

For what? I did what had to be done, that's all. I don't agree with bullying – and I'm sorry, but your mother is the biggest bully I know. She's going to ring every Friday to check up on you, and I'm going to talk to her for the time being – I told her I'd let you on the phone when it was safe.

Safe?

Too late for her to persuade you to change your mind, I mean.

Caroline couldn't imagine dictating like that to Mum. *What did she say to that?*

Oh, she had plenty to say, Florence replied, *none of it good. I'm fairly sure I'll be cut out of the will. Get the milk, would you?*

When the promised call came the following Friday evening, Florence was quite a while in the hall. Caroline grew anxious, suspecting some new hitch. Maybe Mum was sending Dad over to try to reason with her. It would be harder to refuse him.

You won't believe it, Florence said on her return. *You've had a nervous breakdown – you were working too hard. They've sent you to a clinic in Switzerland.*

What are you talking about?

That's what your mother is telling everyone, and

that's what you'll have to say when you go home. I'd like to see the breakdown that would keep someone in a clinic for seven months. She gave a sudden bark of laughter. *You must be at death's door.*

Caroline couldn't see the joke. People were being told that she was in a clinic in Switzerland, recovering from some imaginary illness? Could Mum really be so afraid of being the subject of gossip that she was prepared to tie them all into a ridiculous lie that would have to be told for the rest of their lives?

Our doctor will know I wasn't sick.

Oh, you can be sure she's thought of that. She'll say they took you straight to a specialist, or went private, or something.

Yes, no doubt Mum had thought of everything. Caroline resolved not to worry about whatever awaited her on her return home: getting through the next few months was all she felt able to focus on.

Days turned into weeks, and she made no attempt to contact her friends. What was the point, if she had to lie to them? In time they'd hear what everyone else heard, and they'd feel sorry for Caroline, who must be too ill to make contact. They might enquire about writing to her, and her mother would think of another lie to put them off, because she didn't have cousins living conveniently in Switzerland who could pretend to be a health clinic.

The longer Caroline lived with Florence, the more accustomed she grew to her cousin's ways, the more she realised all that lay beneath the gruff exterior. Florence was unswerving in her course to protect Caroline, fielding the weekly phone calls that Caroline tried not to listen to.

She was also terribly bossy.

I've made an appointment for you to see my doctor on Thursday evening – you need regular visits. And I was thinking you could learn how to use the knitting machine – that'll fill your time till we find you a job. I'll give you a lesson tomorrow when I get home from work. And we need to get you more clothes – we can do that on Saturday, after the market.

And at times she could be unfailingly kind.

I got some ginger to make tea. It's great for sick stomachs. And I'll do soup with those chicken wings – you might feel like some in a while. Here, give me that hot-water bottle – it's due a refill. And when you're better I'll bring you down to the library and you can join up.

She rarely spoke of herself, of her life before she met Caroline, but little by little Caroline was filling gaps. *Do you go back to Ireland much?* she asked one evening.

Florence threw a block onto the fire, causing sparks to fly upwards. *Hardly ever.*

Don't you have family there – I mean close family? Brothers or sisters?

I have not. There were three of us, two girls and a boy. My sister went to America before I left school – she married a farmer in Delaware. We're not good at keeping in touch. The last time I saw her was at our brother's funeral, fourteen years ago – his car skidded on black ice and went into a wall.

Have you nieces and nephews?

I have. We have little enough contact. She looked into the fire, winding grey wool slowly into a ball. *Ireland had nothing for me,* she went on. *I didn't suit it. I was wrong for it.*

It seemed a strange thing to say, but Caroline wasn't brave enough to query it, and the topic was dropped.

The knitting machine was a revelation. She was surprised at how easy it was to operate, and how enjoyable a process she found it. She'd learnt to hand knit in school, years ago; as far as she could recall she'd produced a hairband, and one sock – had she ever made its partner? She remembered the annoyance of dropped stitches, the frustration of tangled wool, the near-impossibility of making her fingers do what was needed. She'd passed her plastic needles on to Eleanor with great relief when the class had begun some other craft.

But this was something entirely different. Knitting on a machine, once she'd mastered the basics, was infinitely more rewarding. Her first scarf, in plain navy, took just a few hours to complete. After that, she got Florence to teach her how to change colours so she could play with stripes.

Knitting indulged her creative side: within weeks she'd moved on to hats and wraps. All terribly basic – Florence didn't believe in patterns, and her range of colours was disheartening, but Caroline planned to hunt down new supplies, and some simple patterns too. She wanted to experiment with shapes and styles – she wanted to see what she could get the machine to do.

In the meantime she bought a toaster for the kitchen in perfect condition for four pounds in one of the charity shops, and a frying pan that actually possessed a handle, and a new set of wooden spoons that Florence said they didn't need at all, despite their only existing one having just half its bowl intact.

She met Gretta and Barney, owners of next door's crab apple tree, and Donald, who shared his market stall with Florence, and eighty-something retired clockmaker Frankie from three doors down, who still mended clocks and watches in the neighbourhood, and who regularly won the ten-pound jackpot at the Tuesday-night bingo in the community centre.

She met Joan, the local Avon lady who also delivered the free local newspaper once a week, along with any gossip she liked to call news. As Florence had predicted, nobody asked questions, nobody wondered aloud why Caroline wasn't going to school once September arrived.

The town where Florence lived was large enough for two churches, several pubs, a library and one police station, but small enough to walk from end to end in less than half an hour. Its weekly market was held on Saturday mornings in a little park behind the community centre, and comprised twenty-odd stalls, most of them shared, selling home-baked goods and artisan foods and patchwork items and second-hand books and antiques and bottles of homemade lemonade and seasonal vegetables and hand-carved wooden toys, and Florence's knitted hats and scarves and stuffed toys.

Some weeks I mightn't make much, she told Caroline, *especially in the summer, when nobody's looking for a scarf – but the toys sell anytime, and it's a nice social gathering.*

The toys were cute little monkeys and elephants, owls and fishes, made from fabric shapes that Florence cut and sewed by hand – again she used no patterns – and stuffed with the insides of old pillows and cushions donated to her by the town's charity shops, where she was well known. The proceeds of the stall, minus the pittance she kept back for new supplies, were sent faithfully to Africa every month, to the community of missionary priests she'd apparently been helping out for years.

Donald, her stall colleague of indeterminate age – fifties? sixties? – made exquisite patchwork quilts and cushion covers and bunting and table runners and placemats in beautifully coordinated florals and checks and stripes. His offerings, although expensive by market standards, never stayed unsold for long.

I studied fashion design at a London art college, back in the Dark Ages, he told Caroline, in his beautiful cultured accent, *and for years I worked as one of the plebs in a ridiculously exclusive men's bespoke tailoring business while I tried to be the next Vivienne Westwood, but my real talents were never appreciated, and in the end I upped sticks and discovered this delightful little backwater. I'd far rather be my own boss here every Saturday morning. The rest of the week I sell my body to whoever will have it.* An arching of an eyebrow. *What can I say? It pays the bills.*

Stop corrupting the child, you old queen, Florence said, without turning around. *She comes from a good Catholic family. Don't mind him, Caroline, it's all fantasy. He's loaded, he doesn't need to work another day in his life – and anyway, who'd have him?*

Donald rolled his eyes. *I don't know what I did to deserve this witch working alongside me, my dear. Although I must say she draws the crowds – they're all far too frightened to pass her by.*

They were clearly fond of one another. Each week Donald treated them to flapjacks or shortbread squares from a nearby stall, and Florence brought along a big flask of tea to accompany them.

So tell me your story, Donald said, the first time Caroline accompanied Florence to the market, a couple of weeks after Mum's failed crusade. *What has brought you winging your way across the Irish Sea to throw yourself on Great-aunt Florence's mercy? I'm hoping it was something truly scandalous. Tell Uncle Donald, it shall go no further.*

Tell him nothing, Florence said. *Let him make it up; it'll be far more interesting. And I'm not her great-aunt: I told you we're cousins.*

Whatever you say, dear. I'm guessing, he added to Caroline, *that Florence is the real skeleton in your family's cupboard. She definitely created a scandal, donkey's years ago, that caused her to be banished forever to England, but she refuses to tell me what it was. Would you happen to know, my dear?*

Caroline smiled. *I'm sorry to disappoint you, but I presume she came over here for work, like all the other Irish.* She glanced at Florence, who was eating shortbread and taking no notice. Caroline hadn't yet been told her story.

Oh, nonsense – it had to be some great trauma that brought her washing up on England's shore. Was it a fling with a parish priest, do you think, or perhaps a bishop?

She enjoyed helping out in the market, loved the interaction between the stallholders – cheesemonger Ernie, two stalls away, and the hilarious sisters, Brenda and Janet, who ran the farm co-op stall, and beekeeper Anton, locally known as 'the honey man', who'd come on holiday from France twenty years earlier and stayed put. She particularly loved Florence and Donald's banter, with one another and with their customers. It helped her forget her predicament for a few hours, until everyone began packing up and dismantling their trestle tables, until she and Florence returned their unsold items to the rear of the battered van, and went home for a late lunch.

But of course her problems hadn't gone away.

I estimate around mid-March, Florence's doctor had said, *which puts you at around thirteen weeks now. I'll arrange a scan at the clinic in the next few days.* The scan showed that so far all appeared well, that she was due on the seventeenth of March, St Patrick's Day, and that she was having one child. Caroline hadn't looked at the screen, and the nurse had made no comment.

And now she was over fourteen weeks gone, and the last time she'd spoken with her family was fifty-three days ago, apart from one brief unexpected phone call from Eleanor that had left her feeling even more lonely and confused than she already did. When the call hadn't been repeated she'd been half disappointed, half relieved.

But then a letter had come in Eleanor's looping handwriting, a week after the call, and it was followed a week later by another, and then another. The letters were short, no more than a couple of pages, and devoid of anything of real significance – their father's modest win on the scratch cards, a new family moving in at the end of the road, the weather turning cool – but they were a link to home, and she read and reread them, touched that Eleanor would bother.

No mention was made of Andrew, which she thought strange. Of course he'd be in college now; maybe Eleanor was finding it hard to be separated from him. They probably wouldn't get married until he graduated. She thought about her baby being a half-brother or -sister to Andrew: how strange and wrong that felt.

A month after her arrival in England she got a job, thanks to Joan-the-Avon-lady's brother-in-law's friend, who worked as a porter in the local hospital. Every weekday morning she sat on a wooden chair in the hospital kitchen and peeled dozens of potatoes and prepared a mountain of sundry vegetables and listened to the chef, whose name was Pearl, and who was forty and twice divorced and very large, telling her about her first mother-in-law who had tried to set fire to Pearl's car when she heard that Pearl was divorcing her son, and about the abusive drunken phone calls that she still occasionally got from her second ex-husband's sister.

Every Friday Caroline handed over three-quarters of her salary to Florence, who didn't want to take that much but for once gave in when Caroline insisted. Jasper's money went largely unspent: Florence refused to let her buy groceries, so her only real expenses were wool in all colours, which she bought regularly in the town's only wool shop, and a steady supply of sketchpads and charcoal.

Soon she'd be talking to her family again. Once abortion was no longer an option she would take the weekly phone call instead of Florence. She looked forward to making contact with Dad and Eleanor, but she wasn't at all sure she wanted to talk to Mum. She still felt deeply betrayed by her.

Most days she was well, if a little tired. Her figure, as far as she could see, remained unchanged. Occasionally she suffered from heartburn, and tenderness in her breasts, and her calves ached intermittently, but the nausea that had plagued her for several weeks had finally ebbed away.

Each afternoon she lay for an hour or two on her narrow bed – Florence encouraged a daily rest – and watched the diamond patterns from the leaded window that the sun threw onto the opposite wall, and listened to the soft chirps and buzzing from the garden below. She thought about the tiny being that was growing inside her, and she travelled in her mind along the months ahead, and the changes that lay in store, and she stopped at the part where her baby was born, and she became a mother.

She had no idea what came after that. She tried not to be afraid of it.

December 1993

Eleanor

'IT'S NOT YOU,' SHE SAID. 'IT'S ME.'

But of course it was him, with his damp hands and his gingery stubble and his too-high laugh. It was the mints he sucked wetly, and it was the way he coughed into fingers that were curled into a tube, and it was his white socks, and it was how he said her name, as if it only had two syllables.

Andrew had spoilt her. None of the boys she'd been out with since had lived up to him. None was half as good-looking, none made her heart beat faster or her insides turn to liquid like he had. But he was gone, and the others were still here, so she had to make do.

As she walked home alone she thought again about giving up on relationships for good, and living a single and celibate life. It might be lonely, but it would be easier than this endless searching and raising of hopes and inevitable disappointment, wouldn't it?

She crossed the street by the cinema, noting the

lone youth in a denim jacket standing outside, hands tucked into his armpits, away from the December chill. Waiting, no doubt, for his date to show up. Hoping to God she showed up. How pathetic the whole thing was.

As she turned onto their road her thoughts drifted to Caroline, as they often did these days. She tried to picture what her sister must look like by now. Six months gone into her pregnancy, or near enough: it must be obvious to everyone. Had she ballooned out like Mrs McCarthy down the road did on all her babies, legs like tree trunks, face swollen and puffy? Had her walk morphed into the laboured waddle that seemed the preserve of heavily expectant women?

She wondered what story they were spinning in England to explain Caroline's presence – or had they simply told the truth, that she'd been banished, sent away in disgrace by her Irish family?

Mum remained adamant that the secret would stay within the family. *We are not going down that road: the Plunketts are better than that. Once the child is adopted Caroline will come home, and we'll all be able to move on from this terrible business.*

At least now they were talking to her. Since mid-October, Caroline rather than Florence had been taking the weekly phone call. Conversation, when Eleanor was handed the receiver, was necessarily stilted, with Mum generally in earshot – but Caroline sounded content enough.

I've got a job, she'd told Eleanor in the very first

phone call. *Florence thought I should have something to do.*

Yes, Eleanor bet she did. Probably made her hand over her wages too.

In a hospital kitchen. She gave a small laugh. *I'm mostly peeling potatoes, but the people are nice.*

Peeling potatoes, after all her perfect school reports. After all her hours of study, all her straight As. How could she laugh? *Well, that's ... good.*

It's only part time, five mornings a week, and it doesn't pay very much, but it's fine. And I help out at a market too, on Saturday mornings. Florence has a stall with a man called Donald.

OK ... That sounded a bit more fun, but still. *Andrew and I have split up, by the way.* Might as well let her know: everyone else did. Surprising how shocked Caroline seemed at the news. Eleanor wouldn't have thought it would matter that much to her.

Maybe she had a crush on Jasper.

The baby was never mentioned, by any of them. All talk of the future was avoided too. Mum spent most of the first call letting Caroline know exactly how hurt and betrayed she felt. Since then, she asked stiffly about Caroline's health, and enquired whether she was sleeping, and if she needed money, before handing the phone over – exactly the sort of conversation they would be having, Eleanor thought, if Caroline really *was* in a Swiss clinic, recovering from a nervous breakdown – except that presumably Mum would sound a bit friendlier if that were the case.

Their father was kinder.

We miss you, he'd say. *The house is quiet with only the three of us.* As if Caroline had ever made it any noisier.

He also gave her the news, such as it was. Jenny Corbett had fallen off a stepladder and broken her hip. There were road works on the main street; traffic was even more chaotic than usual. The new people in number ten were building a conservatory. The Sullivans' poodle had gone missing in a suspected kidnapping. Tommy Dalton was getting married for the second time, to a widow with six children.

And now it was the Saturday before Christmas, and Eleanor had been on holidays since yesterday, and in the past few months an IRA bomb had exploded in a Belfast fish shop. A week later two gunmen had walked into a County Derry bar in the middle of a Hallowe'en party and begun firing. The night after that, River Phoenix had taken an overdose, and died outside a Hollywood nightclub, Michael Jackson had been accused of child abuse, and was under investigation. Few people, she guessed, would be sorry to see the end of 1993.

And she was tired of lying to Sister Carmody, who asked at least once a fortnight how poor Caroline was getting on, and tired of pretending to the rest of the world that she herself was fine, just fine.

She wasn't fine. She was lonely and fed up, and not looking forward to her first Christmas without Andrew. For the past three Christmases they'd met on Christmas morning – twice in his house, once in hers – to exchange presents. At the D'Arcys', Sophie had produced a platter of shortbread shaped like tiny stars and topped with powdery sugar, and buttery almond cookies the size of fat communion wafers, which they had washed down with small cups of deliciously rich hot chocolate.

On the one occasion that Andrew had come to the Plunkett house, the Christmas before last, Mum had spent the hour before his arrival trying far too hard to impress him with asparagus wrapped in prosciutto, and Camembert cubes fried in breadcrumbs, and something involving poached pears and filo pastry. Then she'd gone into raptures about the earrings he'd brought for Eleanor before quizzing him about the gift Sophie had got from Jasper. Beyond embarrassing.

But this year, Christmas would be very different. They were packing up, the three of them, and taking a plane to England. Eleanor had mixed feelings about the trip. In a way she was glad of the change of scene – it might be easier to be without him if she was in unfamiliar surroundings – but she was also apprehensive of what lay ahead.

Four nights in Brighton, Mum had announced at the end of November. *The twenty-third till St Stephen's Day. I've found us a little hotel just off the seafront. If anyone asks, we're having a quiet family Christmas with Caroline.*

A quiet family Christmas in Brighton with Caroline, who was supposed to be in Switzerland – but of course Mum had thought of that too.

We'll tell people she's making a good recovery, and we've moved her to a convalescent home in England.

There's a nice one not far from Brighton: we can say she's staying there for the next few months.

At first it had amazed Eleanor how everyone seemed to swallow Mum's absurd fantasy without question. But then it had hit her: of course everyone believed it, because it was Caroline they were talking about. If Eleanor had disappeared for the best part of a year, people would have shaken their heads and said they'd seen it coming, but Caroline was a whole other story – Caroline Plunkett, pregnant? Never! – so they were getting away with it.

The irony was that Eleanor hadn't yet done the deed with anyone. Why would she, when the only person she wanted to do it with was gone? It was horribly unfair.

Sometimes, when she was particularly fed up, she'd find herself feeling conflicted about Caroline. On the one hand there was guilt that she hadn't had an inkling of what her sister must have gone through, both from the rape itself and during the weeks that followed, when the suspicion that she might be pregnant was growing. Awful that Eleanor hadn't been there for her – weren't sisters supposed to look out for one another? Shouldn't she have sensed that something was badly wrong with Caroline?

On the other hand … something hiding behind her guilt, some malicious voice inside her head, would yank at the edge of her consciousness and insist on being heard. Wasn't it just a tiny bit … *humiliating*, it would ask, that Caroline had had sex before her? Wasn't it just a small bit … *deflating* that

her quiet, serious elder sister had been first to cross
that particular line?

She was aware of how hideously warped this
thinking was. It was despicable to turn Caroline's
terrible ordeal into the outcome of some freakish
competition. And yet, at times, the hard blunt truth
poked at her, taunted her: plainer, quieter Caroline
had had sex, and pretty, fun Eleanor hadn't.

Some sister she was.

Cousin Florence, of course, wouldn't be joining
them for their Brighton adventure. She hadn't been
invited: she was still the black sheep, the one who'd
led Caroline astray. Not, Eleanor was sure, that she'd
have been dying to spend Christmas with Mum –
imagine the scene when Mum had confronted her
in Oxford, demanding to see Caroline, and been
refused. No, Florence was doubtless far happier
left alone to open her can of soup and watch *It's a
Wonderful Life* in peace.

And when you thought about it, Caroline herself
mightn't be looking forward to meeting up with
them again. She hadn't exactly left them in a blaze
of glory.

One thing was for sure: Christmas 1993 would be
interesting.

When she got home Eleanor let herself in and
slipped upstairs, not in the mood to talk to anyone.
She lay on her bed and flicked through the December
issue of *Seventeen*. 'Makeup that Dazzles,' she read.
'Flirty Dresses for under a Tenner'. 'Hollywood's
Hip Kids: what they're wearing'. So trite it all
sounded – who cared what a bunch of spoilt rich

kids wore? Who needed a flirty dress when there was nobody worth flirting with?

Half an hour later there was a rap on her bedroom door.

'Eleanor? Are you there?'

She closed the magazine. 'Come in.'

Mum was all sequins and sparkle, off with Dad to the D'Arcys' Christmas cocktail party, the highlight of the town's social calendar. She stood before the dressing table and fussed with her hair, amber and sandalwood trailing into the room after her. 'Darling, are you not going out tonight?'

'I'm not bothered.'

'But you *should* be. You're young, and it's almost Christmas. Why aren't you meeting Ian?'

'I just finished with him.'

'Oh dear ...' Mum came to sit on the bed. 'Darling, I know it's difficult, after being so long with Andrew, but you'll find someone else eventually, I know you will.' She'd finally given up on him, months after Eleanor had. Must have been hard for her, her heart set on joining forces with the D'Arcys. 'I just don't like to think of you moping here all on your own.'

'I might invite Tina around.' Making it sound as if she'd just that minute thought it up. 'We could watch a video.'

'Well, that would be better than nothing,' Mum said doubtfully. Tina's father worked behind the counter of someone else's hardware shop: not exactly in Jasper D'Arcy's league. 'Sweetheart, you will pack something nice for Christmas Day, won't you? What about the lovely blue dress we got?'

The dress that had cost far too much. The dress that still hung in its plastic wrapper, not needed after all for Andrew's graduation. In fairness, Mum hadn't gone on about the expense of it.

'OK, I'll pack it.' She might as well give it an outing, get at least one wear out of it.

'And shoes – will your black ones do, or would we go shopping on Monday?'

'The black will do.' The last thing she needed was a day of traipsing around the shops with her mother.

'Right then, better get a move on. We'll probably be late, but we'll be like mice.' A tiny brush of her lips on Eleanor's cheek – not enough to do damage to her lipstick – and she was gone. Eleanor waited through the sounds of their departure – click of heels in the hall, her father's voice calling goodbye to her, clink of keys, soft sound of the front door closing.

She counted to a hundred before leaving the room. In the hall she dialled Tina's number.

'They're gone.'

'Five minutes.'

Tina was bringing around a bottle of Bacardi that her brother's friend, who looked eighteen, had bought for her in the off-licence.

Eleanor got out glasses and took Coke from the fridge. She filled bowls with crisps and nuts. In the sitting room she plugged in the electric fire and slotted *Wayne's World* into the video player.

You had to make your fun where you could.

Next year might be better.

Caroline

'I WISH YOU WERE COMING.' BUT SHE DIDN'T, not really. What she really wanted was not to have to go herself.

'Well, I'm very glad I'm staying here.' Florence looped yellow wool onto the needles of the knitting machine. 'Could you imagine me and your mother sitting around a dinner table? Only a matter of time before one of us picked up the carving knife.'

'I don't like the thought of you here on your own.'

Florence gave her bark of laughter. 'Child, you don't have to worry about me. I won't be on my own – I always go to Donald's on Christmas Day. He feeds half a dozen waifs and strays every year, and whatever else I say about him, that man can cook.'

Caroline could just imagine it. Beautifully presented turkey and ham in Donald's stylish apartment that overlooked the park where the Saturday market was held. It sounded wonderful. Christmas with people who didn't judge her for being pregnant: that was all she wanted.

Donald knew. Well, everyone had probably guessed at this stage, now that her skirts and blouses had stopped closing, now that she'd switched to looser dresses and pinafores that she picked up in the charity shops – but Donald was the first she'd admitted it to.

It had happened a few weeks earlier. They were managing the market stall without Florence, who had taken herself off to the dentist for a root-canal job. The November day was uncharacteristically mild, forcing Caroline to shed the silver-grey cashmere wrap that she'd run up for herself on the knitting machine a few days before, one of her few indulgences.

As soon as she took it off, she became acutely conscious that her condition must be pretty apparent to anyone who gave her more than a cursory glance: they need only notice the way her dress was pulled taut across the widest part of her midsection. And suddenly she felt almost deceitful in not coming out with it to Donald. *Let them think what they like*, Florence had declared – but not Donald. She couldn't leave him wondering: it didn't seem right.

She chose a moment when the stall was quiet, and then she told him. Not the full story, just that she was pregnant. *It's why I came to England. You probably guessed.*

I did wonder, he admitted. Caroline waited for his usual gentle teasing – he'd have a field day with this – but none came.

You shouldn't be standing. He draped his jacket over the wooden crate they used to sit on. *Not good*

*for the ankles, and we don't want you getting varicose
veins. Next week I'll bring a folding chair for you, and
peppermint tea. And you must come home with me for
lunch today, since it's just the two of us. I have some
exquisite smoked salmon. Are you taking iron?*

No judgement, no intrusive questions, no
pointing finger. And because of this, Caroline found
the whole story spilling out as they sat on Donald's
tiny balcony and ate salmon drenched in lemon
juice and scattered with capers on deliciously nutty
brown bread.

She told him about Jasper and the momentous
journey home in his car, and their subsequent
meeting in his office when she revealed her
pregnancy to him. She described her mother's
reaction to her confession, and how she'd been
packed off to England. She told him of her plan to
disappear, and Florence's offer instead to take her
in, and the abortion that hadn't happened after all. It
was such a relief to pour out the story finally.

My dear, he said, topping up her glass of
elderflower cordial, *you've certainly been through the
mill. Taken advantage of by a scoundrel, abandoned by
your family. Thank goodness for old Florence – whatever
her faults, and as we know they are legion, the woman has
a heart of the purest gold.*

Caroline smiled. *I'm not sure that Mum would agree
with you – she came over and had it out with Florence at
the start – but I certainly do. She frightened me a bit at
first, but I'm very fond of her now, and I'm so grateful to
her for taking me in.*

Indeed. So may I ask what happens next? What do you intend to do with your little arrival?

I'll ... have it adopted, and go home.

The pause, full of her uncertainty. The words halting in her throat, unwilling to come out. Have it adopted. Give it away to another woman, who would become its mother.

If Donald noticed the hesitation, he made no sign. *If that's what you've decided.*

It is. I'll go back home and finish school. I have one year to go.

In October she'd felt it move inside her for the first time, the little unexpected nudge causing her, in the act of reaching for a knife, to draw in her breath.

You alright? Florence, who missed nothing.

Yes – I think the baby just ...

Since then it had become a familiar sensation. It was more than a flutter, it was a shifting, a small resettling within her. Proof, not that she needed it, that it was alive, that it was growing. Her body was changing on a daily basis now, it seemed; her hips spreading, her ankles thickening, her breasts grown by two cup sizes. Her waist completely gone, everything merging into the bulbous growing mound that cradled her baby within it.

At her second scan a few days ago, the nurse had asked if she wanted to know the sex and she'd said no – and a minute later she'd changed her mind and said yes, and the nurse had told her it was a boy.

She was having a boy. A son.

It wasn't his fault that Jasper D'Arcy was his father. He was completely innocent.

I'm going to study history in college, she told Donald.

Very good: history is a worthy pursuit. Now, what would you say to some of Delia's irresistible macaroons? Delia was a market trader, producing home-baked confections each Saturday that were indeed hard to resist – but Caroline said no, she was anxious to get back to Florence, who would surely be home by now, so he wrapped three of them in parchment – *two for you, in your condition* – and saw her out.

At the door she stopped. *Donald, you won't … say it to anyone, will you? How I got pregnant, I mean.*

My lips are sealed, he promised – and although he ordinarily loved nothing more than a bit of gossip, some instinct told her that in this case she could believe him.

She leaned across and kissed his cheek. *Thank you,* she said. *For the lunch, and … for being kind.*

My dear, the pleasure was completely mine. Do give Florence my best, and tell her we simply wilted *without her today.*

Walking home, the cashmere shawl trailing from her hand, she replayed their conversation, and the mixed feelings it had evoked. She *did* want to go to college: it had always been the plan. Eleanor had no intention of going further than secondary school, couldn't wait for it to be over, but for Caroline, college was a natural progression. Get a degree, follow it with a master's, and in time a doctorate. The years of study that would involve didn't faze her: she was in her element with a textbook in front of her.

Or rather, she had been.

Now it was different. Now everything was on hold: naturally her priorities had shifted. She wasn't at school, she had a job, humble as it was, and a baby on the way. She was also discovering a love of knitting, and an impatience to learn more about the intricacies of creating garments from wool.

Maybe it was inevitable, with all that had changed, with all that was still changing, that she wouldn't feel the same as before about book-learning. She assumed the phenomenon was temporary: surely once she was back in Ireland, and back at school, her life would resume and she'd be the enthusiastic scholar she once was.

Wouldn't she?

Maybe she shouldn't desert her studies completely while she was here though. She'd been to the library in town, signed up and got a membership card. Their stock of non-fiction was limited, but they might be able to put in an order for some textbooks if she asked. On the other hand, she'd be picking up where she'd left off when she got home, so you could say she'd be missing nothing, just delaying it by a year. A bit of revision, a few weeks of rereading her old textbooks would be sure to bring it all back.

She and Eleanor would be in the same Leaving Cert class. She wasn't sure how she felt about that. In one way it would be good to have Eleanor in a class where she knew most of the others only by sight, but the biggest difference between them was probably academic: how would it be when they were at the same level, studying the same course, working on the same assignments? How would Eleanor feel about it, with Caroline's results inevitably better? Hopefully it wouldn't bother her; she wouldn't feel like she was being shown up.

Now that they were living in different countries, Caroline found that she missed her younger sister. She hadn't expected to, they'd lived such separate lives at home, but somehow it felt strange not to have her around. Eleanor had always been so vivacious, so definite a presence in the house.

Lately she'd changed, though. In their weekly phone conversations, short as they were, Caroline sensed a dimming of her sister's natural exuberance. No doubt this was down to her and Andrew being over, which had astounded Caroline when she'd heard. Finished, separated, after three years together.

No need after all to try to protect Eleanor's future happiness; no reason any more to keep well in with the D'Arcys, and protect Jasper. Not that it mattered now, she supposed. Who cared about Jasper? Certainly not her.

But she would have to talk about him again; she would have to reveal his identity to someone else. Now that Donald knew the true circumstances surrounding Caroline's pregnancy, it didn't seem fair to keep it from Florence, who still thought a stranger had been responsible.

The thought of telling her was unsettling. Florence

had offered her a refuge; she'd been her ally when Caroline desperately needed one. Over the past few months she'd become a friend. How was she going to take the fact that she'd been fed a lie for all this time?

No matter: however she took it, she had a right to know the truth. Caroline would tell her, as soon as she found the courage.

The weeks passed. November turned into December. As Florence had predicted, nobody asked pointed questions about what had become a patently obvious pregnancy, nobody looked curiously or judgementally at Caroline. On the contrary, Gretta next door gave her a little bottle of massage oil: *Rub it into your calves and feet when you feel tired, works wonders.* Constance from one of the charity shops crocheted a bed jacket for her. Donald made her a small cushion for her back.

And then, the Friday before she was to be reunited with her family for Christmas, she spoke to them on the phone as usual.

Looking forward to seeing you, Mum said. *It'll be nice to spend Christmas together* – and Caroline wanted to believe her, but her voice was entirely without warmth, like it had been since Caroline had gone against her. *We'll be at the bus station to meet you.* Caroline shrank at the thought of their encounter.

Mum passed the phone to Dad. Poor innocent Dad, unaware of what Jasper had done to his daughter.

We're off to the D'Arcys' cocktail party tomorrow

night, he said – and it was all Caroline could do not to tell him then, not to blurt it out. The thought of the friendship continuing, of his complete ignorance of the facts, bit deeply into her.

But that was all Mum really cared about, wasn't it? Drinking cocktails with Jasper D'Arcy and his like, attending the same dinner parties, the same summer barbecues as the society people in the town. That was all she cared about, despite everything.

She should have stood up to Mum. She should have refused point blank to go to England. Jasper should have been held responsible; she should have gone straight to a garda station the morning after it happened – the same night, even – and reported him, whatever the consequences. She hadn't been thinking right: she'd been shocked, and confused.

Oh, but it was too late for regrets, too late for accusations. Telling Dad now would only turn him against Mum, who'd kept the knowledge from him, and who'd forced Caroline to do the same. What was the point of creating more havoc? She was going to have the baby, give it up, and resume her life. End of story.

And if she hadn't come to England, she'd probably never have met Florence. Hard to imagine that: even though it had been only a few months it was becoming difficult to remember when Florence hadn't been part of her life, or to envisage a future that didn't include her cousin.

Now it was two days to Christmas, and tomorrow Caroline would be taking the bus to London en route for Brighton. She'd tell Florence tonight, she wouldn't put it off any longer. She waited until there was a pause in the to-ing and fro-ing of the knitting machine while Florence adjusted needles for a cable row.

'Florence, there's something you should – there's something I want to tell you.'

Florence turned, threads of yellow wool peppering her hair.

'I haven't been completely honest with you,' Caroline began – and out it all tumbled in a stuttery heap, words and sentences clambering over each other in their haste to be said as Florence listened without interruption, and occasionally blinked.

When Caroline finished speaking, the room had never seemed so quiet.

'So you knew him,' Florence said at length.

'I did.'

'He employed you as his babysitter.'

'Yes.'

'And when you told him you were expecting, he gave you money for an abortion.'

'He did.'

A long silence followed.

'I'm sorry,' Caroline said eventually. 'I should have told you everything from the start. Mum didn't want me saying it.'

'You've told me now,' Florence replied, 'and I'm glad about that. It's not good to keep things bottled up.' She nodded slowly several times. 'And your mother knows all of this.'

'Yes – but not Dad or Eleanor. They still think it was a stranger.'

'Your mother knew you were raped by a family friend, and she did nothing.'

The word, uttered so calmly, so matter-of-factly, was shocking. 'Well, it wasn't – I mean, she didn't think it was … rape, exactly.'

Florence's eyes narrowed. 'And what did she think it was, exactly?'

'Well, she thought I might have … given him the wrong impression.'

'Given him the wrong impression,' Florence repeated flatly. 'I've only known you a few months, and I'm quite certain you've never once given a man the wrong impression. You got into a car with a friend of your parents', a man you trusted, and he forced himself on you – he *raped* you – and instead of raising holy murder and having him arrested, your mother tried to make out that you led him on.'

Caroline said nothing. The grandfather clock in the hall bonged; ten past eight. It *was* rape. She *had* been raped. Why had she not once admitted that, even to herself?

'Holy mother of God,' Florence said slowly. 'That woman. Didn't want the scandal, I suppose.'

'No …'

The seconds ticked on. A log collapsed gently into the fire, causing a small shower of ashes to tip onto the hearth. Caroline bent to scoop them up with a little brass shovel.

'You could still do it if you wanted.'

She turned. 'Do what?'

'Go to the guards and tell them what he did. I'd be a character witness if you needed me.'

'No.' What was the point now, with everyone believing Caroline to be recuperating in Switzerland? Why rake it all up now, just to get back at him? Look at the lives that would be rocked: Sophie, Andrew, Nadine. Look how ridiculous Mum and the rest of them would appear, having fed everyone the fantasy for months. 'No,' she repeated. 'I'd rather leave it.'

'He'll know you didn't get rid of it, unless he's stupid. He won't swallow the fairy tale that Ronnie is spinning for everyone.'

'No.'

Let him wonder, she thought. Let him wait and wonder. When she arrived home with no baby he'd know that she must have put it up for adoption – and he was hardly likely to come looking for his money back. He'd probably do his level best to avoid her, which would suit her fine.

And he'd spend the whole of his life not knowing if he'd had a son or a daughter. There was some small satisfaction to be had from the thought.

'You might put the kettle on,' Florence said, turning back to the machine, and just like that, the subject was closed. As she spooned tea into the pot, Caroline felt the same sensation of a load being lifted as she had when she'd confided in Donald. No more secrets between them now. And Florence had believed her utterly, despite not knowing her for very long, despite never having set eyes on Jasper D'Arcy. She found great comfort in that.

The next morning Florence took time off work to drive her to the bus station. 'I can walk,' Caroline said – the station was only twenty minutes on foot – but Florence pretended not to hear. The day was damp and grey, the cold biting. Caroline wore the heather-coloured herringbone wool coat that Florence had found in one of her weekly trawls through the charity shops. It was slightly big on the shoulders, but roomy enough to accommodate her new shape. Around her neck she'd wrapped the cashmere shawl, its softness and warmth a blessing.

'Be back before you know it,' Florence said, rubbing condensation from the windscreen with her gloved hand. 'Three days, two nights. It'll fly by.'

Caroline doubted that, but she made no reply as they pulled away from the cottage. Outside the station Florence parked in a loading bay, something she did regularly. As far as Caroline knew, she never got a parking ticket. The traffic wardens must recognise the grey van, and decide to leave well enough alone.

They walked in. Caroline joined the queue at the ticket desk. 'Return to Brighton,' she said to the clerk when her turn came.

'Change in London,' he replied, barely glancing at her.

Out in the area at the rear, they scanned the parked buses. 'There's yours,' Florence said, pointing. 'Get on and find a seat before they're gone.'

They'd exchanged presents the night before, after Caroline's confession. Florence had given her a jar of hand cream and a pair of fur-lined boots. *They're not new*, she'd said of the boots, *but they'll keep you warm*. Caroline's gift to her was a sky blue cashmere wrap that she'd knitted one afternoon when Florence was out at work. Predictably, Florence had tut-tutted at the expense – *You have more money than sense* – but when Caroline had wrapped it around her neck she'd fallen silent.

'What are you waiting for?' she said now. 'You don't want to be standing all the way to London, do you?'

Caroline's feet tingled with the cold, even in the fur-lined boots that weren't new, but still she lingered, the thought of coming face to face with Mum more daunting by the minute. She couldn't imagine an hour in her presence, let alone a whole Christmas. 'I don't want to go.'

Florence took her arm. 'Child, I honestly can't blame you, but we've been through this. You'll have to meet her eventually – and if you don't get it over with now, how much harder will it be next year?' She steered Caroline towards the bus door. 'You'll be grand, wait till you see. Hold your head up high, don't be afraid of anyone. You stuck by your principles, and you should be proud of that. Now get up those steps and I'll see you in three days.'

With her free hand Caroline gave Florence's solid shoulder an awkward squeeze, the closest they'd got to an embrace. 'Happy Christmas,' she said, her voice wobbling. 'Thank you so much for everything you're doing for me.'

'Would you stop – aren't you company for me, and aren't you paying your way? Now get on, before you catch your death.'

Caroline planted her foot on the first step, still hating to go.

'Happy Christmas,' Florence added. 'Try and enjoy it. See you soon.'

'Need some help, love?' the driver asked, and Caroline shook her head and grabbed the rail and climbed higher. At the top she looked back and Florence had vanished. She ducked her head and saw her through the window, a stout little woman stumping back to her illegally parked van in a second-hand grey coat that was unravelling at the hem, and a brand new cashmere wrap.

Florence. Her saviour.

The bus was warm, and almost full. Caroline sat next to a headphones-wearing youth, who completely ignored her as they travelled south, the traffic increasing the closer they got to the Greater London area. She watched people in the cars that whizzed past them and wondered how many of them were driving home for Christmas, like in the Chris Rea song.

For the first time, Christmas held no appeal for her. In her bag were three scarves, one for each of the people she was going to meet. It felt like so much longer than five months since they'd been together, since she'd set off with her mother for the airport.

Now they were meeting again under very different circumstances.

Florence had sent no presents to the family. *Why would I? It would be hypocrisy of the highest order.* How wonderful to be like Florence, afraid of nobody, striding through life unencumbered by insecurities or apprehension. *Hold your head up high, don't be afraid of anyone.* Easier said than done.

Victoria Coach Station was thronged with harried parents, whining children, bawling infants. Everyone seemed to be in a rush. A breeze whistled its way around, lifting dropped food wrappers into the air, tugging at coats. Caroline pushed her way through the crowds and located the toilets. Afterwards she found the Brighton bus and took her place in the long queue as it inched towards the doors.

She needn't go. It wasn't too late to change her plans. She could walk out of the station and find a hotel and book in for the three nights. Florence would be mad when she went back, but it wouldn't last. On principle, Florence never stayed annoyed with anyone for long: *what good does that do, only make you bitter?*

The queue moved on. Caroline moved on with it. Of course she'd go. Florence was right, she'd only be postponing the inevitable if she didn't. And it would be good to see Dad again, and Eleanor.

Hold your head up high. Her legs ached, her back was stiff. Her fingers and toes smarted with cold. Her bag felt much heavier than it had starting out.

The woman ahead of her wore a mac that didn't look warm enough. Her black tights had a hole the size of a thumbprint behind one knee, and a ladder running upwards from it that vanished underneath her coat. Hair that had been bleached a lemony yellow emerged from a red knitted hat.

The cable pattern on the hat was the rope, one Florence often used. *Cables are easy, they're just knitting stitches out of their usual sequence. As long as you place the needles in the right positions you'll be fine.* She was a patient teacher, which Caroline hadn't been expecting. *Take your time*, she'd say, *and get it right. Better than rushing and having to rip it out again.*

By now Caroline was producing a wide variety of hats, for children and adults. She'd worked from patterns for just long enough to learn how to figure out the stitches for designs of her own: the process challenged and engaged her. The little elf hats she'd created in December, some red, some green, had been a big seller. *You're a natural*, Florence had told her. *Flying it.*

Already the women in the town's wool shop knew her by name; already she'd decided she needed to find a wider variety of wools than they supplied. In the library she studied books on knitting; she pored over yarn compositions and weights and characteristics as avidly as she'd once studied the battles and dates of the Crimean War, or learnt the names and various fates of Henry the Eighth's unfortunate wives.

She thought she might try her hand at a dress for herself. A long dress that flowed like water, one she could wear after she'd had the baby. She caught herself, as she peeled vegetables in the hospital kitchen, trying to figure out the line of it, the small flare that would happen at the hip.

Would it all stop, she wondered, when she went back to Ireland and resumed her old life? Would she forget about knitting? Would it simply become something that had made her time in England pass a little faster?

The woman in front of her turned. 'Got the time, love?'

Caroline checked her watch and told her twenty to one.

'Freezing, innit?'

'It is.'

The queue moved. They reached the bus door. The woman got on and Caroline followed. Most of the seats had been filled, but she found one next to an elderly man who had already fallen asleep, his head tilted towards the window, resting on a folded scarf.

The air was thick with the scent of damp coats and newsprint, and what smelt like someone's bag of vinegary chips that made her stomach rumble. She pulled off her gloves and unzipped her bag and found the little greaseproof-paper package that Florence had handed her just before they left the house. *Put that in your bag*, she'd told Caroline, *for when you get peckish*. Inside she found two slices of Florence's griddle bread, her favourite, spread thickly with butter and slices of ham.

Ridiculously, her eyes filled with tears. It was bread, she told herself, nothing to cry about. She blinked and began to eat as the bus pulled out of the bay and left the station.

Two hours at the most before she met them. No escape now.

Eleanor

SHE'D CHANGED.

Her hair was short, for the first time that Eleanor remembered. Still the same light brown colour, but cut now in a boyish, choppy style that made her look younger than seventeen, and her eyes appear larger.

Still no makeup that Eleanor could discern. Pale and a little crumpled. Dressed in an unfamiliar purplish coat that was at least two sizes too big, and tan ankle boots that didn't go with it, and a beautiful silvery grey scarf that draped itself in soft folds about her neck and shoulders.

Eleanor watched as she picked her way carefully down the steps of the bus, a black handbag hanging from a shoulder, a canvas holdall clutched to her chest. The three of them waited silently until she spotted them.

'Hello,' she said, lowering the holdall but keeping a grip on it, the ghost of a smile passing across her face, her eyes flicking over them but not, it seemed, meeting anyone else's.

Dad stepped forward and embraced her, murmuring something that Eleanor didn't catch above the noise of a departing bus. Mum leant in to brush her lips wordlessly against Caroline's cheek. Eleanor gave her sister a quick, somewhat self-conscious hug – they never hugged – registering as she did Caroline's new girth, the small hard press of it as they came together.

A moment of awful silence followed, the chatter of the people who swarmed past them only serving to emphasise the muteness of their little group. The three of them were ranged in a semi-circle around Caroline – taking her in, it felt like to Eleanor, reminding themselves of her, while Caroline stood and waited, her lips pressed together, her gaze having dropped to somewhere around their waists.

'Stephen,' their mother said finally, eyes still on Caroline, 'will you take her bag?' and he reached for it. Caroline immediately folded her empty arms: protecting herself from them, Eleanor thought – or maybe just keeping herself warm. Eleanor tried not to stare at the bulge beneath her folded arms as she searched for something to say, something to reassure or distract her sister.

'I like your scarf.'

Another fleeting smile. Definitely seemed ill at ease: must have been dreading this reunion. Couldn't be easy for her, coming face to face with Mum. Of course, the alternative was Christmas with Florence – not much of a choice, when you thought about it.

'So,' Mum said, 'how was your journey?'

'Alright … I had to change in London.' The soft timbre of her voice hadn't altered, or the way she tilted her head minutely when she spoke.

'Yes. Shame there was no direct coach. You weren't waiting too long?'

'No. Less than an hour. But the traffic was bad, coming out of London.'

They were going to start discussing the weather in a minute, like two polite strangers thrown together in a waiting room. But at least there were no angry words, no recriminations. Eleanor prayed they could get through the few days in peace, even if it meant constant small talk.

It began to rain again as they made their way out of the station – since early morning it had been showery – so Dad hailed a passing taxi. 'You go in front,' he said to Caroline, opening the door for her, and she lowered herself into the seat without comment. Her movements had become slower, more cautious. The trip back to the hotel took less than a minute, and was conducted in total silence.

Eleanor watched the back of her sister's head as the taxi sloshed through logs of water along by the prom. An inch of pale neck, exposed by the haircut, rose up from the grey scarf. What was going through her mind?

They hurried through the rain into the hotel. Mum turned to Caroline in the foyer. 'Eleanor will show you to your room: you can have a lie-down before dinner.'

Eleanor took the canvas bag from their father. It weighed little.

'And ... let's try to have a nice Christmas, alright?' Mum's voice was brittle, but at least she was making an effort.

Caroline let a beat pass. 'Yes.' Wondering, maybe, if it were possible.

They glided up in the lift, accompanied by a low-sized white-haired woman in a brown fur coat that looked like the real thing and smelt of grass.

'We're sharing a room,' Eleanor said. 'It's nice, looking out on the sea. We got here yesterday – our flight was delayed for two hours because of fog at Heathrow. We just made the last bus to Brighton. There were people swimming in the sea today, can you believe it? I saw them this morning after breakfast. Must be mad. The pier is lovely, lots of restaurants and touristy shops and things. You'll have to take a walk there, if it ever stops raining.'

She was prattling. She stopped.

'Can we make tea?' Caroline asked. 'In the room?'

'Yes.'

'Good.'

The lift doors opened at the first floor and the woman got out without a word or a look in their direction. 'Sorry about Andrew,' Caroline said as they waited to move off again. 'Are you OK?'

He was the last person she wanted to talk about. 'I'm fine. I'm over him. He's in college now.' The lift bore them upwards. The doors swept open. 'We're down at the end.'

In the room Eleanor dropped the bag and filled the kettle from the bathroom tap. Caroline pulled off her gloves and placed them on the dressing table. She unwound her scarf and unbuttoned her coat, and as it slid from her shoulders Eleanor saw the mound of her pregnancy rising clearly beneath the bottle green woollen dress. Her sister was *pregnant*: until now the full sense of it hadn't sunk in. Her sister was going to have a baby.

'Which is mine?'

She'd been caught staring. Her face grew hot.

'Which bed is mine?'

Eleanor indicated, and Caroline lowered herself onto the side of it with a sigh. She looked worn out.

Some instinct made Eleanor want to help her. 'Here, let me take off your boots.'

'Thanks.'

She knelt and pulled them off one by one. 'Your feet are cold,' she said. She rubbed them briskly in turn. 'You should have socks on over those tights; if you haven't brought any, I can lend you some.'

No response. She looked up.

'Sorry.' Caroline shook her head, her voice thick. 'It's just ...' She swiped tears away with her thumb. Her face had gone pink, her nose red at the tip. 'Sorry,' she repeated.

Eleanor got up, looked uncertainly at her. 'Are you OK? Do you need me to get something?'

'I'm fine, just tired, and I wasn't sure about ... all this.' She shook her head again, brushing at more tears with the back of her hand. 'You should go down, they'll be waiting for you.'

Her hands had a raw look to them. Her nails were bitten, every one of them. She never used to bite her nails.

'Let them wait,' Eleanor said. She got tissues from the bathroom. 'Get into bed,' she said, taking extra blankets from the wardrobe. The room was warm, but maybe you felt the cold more when you were pregnant. The kettle boiled and clicked off. 'Tea or coffee?'

'Tea. I can't drink coffee any more.'

She dropped a teabag into the small pot, trying to remember if Caroline took sugar. How could she not remember?

She tore the cellophane wrapping from some ginger biscuits and poured tea as Caroline wiped her eyes and blew her nose and attempted a smile. 'Don't take any notice,' she said. 'This happens all the time. It's my hormones. Florence says the worst thing I can do is feel sorry for myself, but I can't help it. I cry at nothing at all these days.'

Florence sounded like a monster. Eleanor looked out the window and saw sea and sky merged together in a grey-white mass. Rain tapped at the glass, coming down in a steady flow now. From three floors below came the muted sound of traffic whooshing over the wet road.

'I wish there was something I could do,' Eleanor said. 'It must be awful, having to live with that woman – on top of everything else.'

'Florence?' Caroline's blotchy face took on a new softness. 'No,' she said, 'you've got it all wrong. Florence has been so kind to me. I don't know how I would have managed without her.'

Florence, who sounded so fierce on the phone? Florence, who'd taken on Mum and won? Florence, who forced Caroline to get a job peeling potatoes, who refused to let her feel sorry for herself?

'She brought me to her doctor, and she makes sure I'm eating right, and I'm learning how to cook, and bake bread – and she's got this knitting machine, she taught me how to use it, and we knit hats and stuff and sell them in the market. And you should see her garden – she works in a garden centre, she knows *everything* about plants and flowers.'

She stopped. 'The look on your face,' she said. 'It's like you don't believe me.'

'Of course I believe you. It's just ... I'm surprised. She wouldn't allow you to talk to us on the phone for ages.'

'It wasn't like that, she wasn't forbidding me. It was just that she wanted to be sure Mum wouldn't talk me into having an abortion. She said I should wait until it was too late. She was right.'

'But she didn't sound all that nice, the time I talked to her.'

'Until you get to know her she can seem a bit scary, but it's just the way she is. It took me a while to get used to her, but now that I have ... honestly, she's lovely.'

Eleanor still had her doubts. Anyone might seem lovely if you had nobody else.

'Thanks for your letters, by the way. I was glad to get them.'

'I thought there was no need to keep writing when we started talking on the phone, but if you still want me to ...'

'No, it's fine.'

For a while neither of them spoke. The light was beginning to fade; soon they'd need to switch on a lamp. Eleanor watched a gull wheel soundlessly in the leaden sky, and thought Mum and Dad would probably be wondering what was keeping her.

There was so much she wanted to ask, so much she didn't know about what her sister was going through.

'Caroline,' she began, her eyes still on the bird, 'are you OK? I mean, are you happy?'

Caroline made a soft sound that could have been a sigh, or something else. 'Happy?'

Eleanor turned. 'No, I don't mean happy – I mean, are you ... alright?' She didn't know what exactly she was asking. They'd never talked like this.

'Well, I hate that it happened,' Caroline said quietly. 'I'm angry that it happened to me – but I'm getting through it. Thanks to Florence, I'll survive.'

Was that a dig at her family? Hard to tell. Eleanor came to sit on the side of her bed. 'I wish I could help.'

'Thanks ... but I don't think there's anything you can do.'

'Would you come home with us if you could, I mean right now, if Mum agreed?'

Her sister was silent for so long, Eleanor thought she wasn't going to answer. Then: 'No,' she said. 'No, I wouldn't. Anyway, Mum wouldn't want that.'

'Are you scared though? Of having it, I mean.' As soon as the question was out, she heard how stupid it sounded. Of course she must be scared.

'I'm not exactly scared,' Caroline replied slowly. 'Not of that bit, not really. I mean ... that'll be awful, but it'll only last for a while, and then it'll be over.'

'Are you ... going to have it adopted then, or what?'

A beat passed, two. Then: 'Yes, of course I am.' Flat, final. She reached up to pull pillows out from behind her: they thumped softly onto the floor. 'I'm going to try to sleep now,' she said, lying down, turning away. 'Would you close the curtains please?'

Eleanor had the feeling she was being shut out. She crossed to the window and drew the curtains and made her way in the dim light to the door. 'We'll be in the drawing room,' she said. 'It's nice. It's to the left of the reception desk. And they're having a special dinner at eight this evening. I'll come and call you if you're not up before then.'

No response. She left the room and closed the door softly. She took the stairs to the ground floor, encountering nobody. She scanned the drawing room with its dark red wallpaper, floor-to-ceiling shelves of books and two fireplaces. Her gaze travelled around the little groups until she found her father sitting alone by one of the fires.

He lowered his newspaper at her approach. 'How's Caroline?'

'She's having a nap. Where's Mum?'

'She's gone for a facial. She said you could follow her if you want one.' Eleanor shook her head. She took the armchair beside his and let her gaze roam around the room. Nobody looked under sixty.

'I feel like I've failed her.'

Eleanor turned, astonished. He wasn't looking at her, his gaze was on the fire. Had he meant to say that aloud? She was embarrassed, unsure whether to respond.

The silence between them stretched. He *had* failed Caroline, of course. He'd let Mum have her way instead of insisting that Caroline come home, and now he was going along with the breakdown story, like Eleanor was. You could say they'd both failed her. *Thanks to Florence, I'll survive.*

He looked up then, attempted a bleak smile. 'Sorry, love, don't mind me. Talking to myself.'

'She likes living with Florence,' she told him. 'That's what she said anyway. It sounds like they're getting on OK together.'

He nodded, cleared his throat. 'Right,' he said. 'Well, that's something. Thank you.' He folded the newspaper and placed it on the coffee table. He got to his feet. 'I think I'll take a walk. I could do with some fresh air.'

'It's still raining. It looks heavy.'

'I'll bring an umbrella – there's bound to be one I can borrow. I won't be long.'

She watched him walk out, and it came to her that she pitied him. The thought wasn't one she wanted to dwell on. She picked up his newspaper and flicked through it without interest.

It was Christmas Eve. She had to keep reminding herself of that. Despite the decorations, and the carols that were piped into every public area pretty much all the time, and the giant tree in the lobby, it had never felt less like Christmas.

Caroline

SHE SURVIVED.

She ate dinner on Christmas Eve, smoked salmon followed by beef Wellington followed by berry crumble followed by fancy little chocolates. Talk consisted mainly of Eleanor's running commentary on their fellow guests: an attempt, Caroline suspected, to avoid the silence that might otherwise dominate. Afterwards Dad suggested a short walk on the pebble beach – *might stretch your legs after that bus trip* – and Caroline agreed, glad of an excuse to escape. The rain had finally stopped, but there was a breeze that whipped in from the sea and made her pull her wrap more tightly around her.

He told her about a break-in at Jasper D'Arcy's company – she was glad of the darkness that hid her face – and about the golf club being closed for renovations, and the nurses picketing the hospital for better conditions. She told him about the people she'd met through Florence, and her fellow workers in the hospital kitchen, and the Saturday market.

She's good to you? he asked. *She treats you well?*
She does. She's very good.

I'm sorry, he said then. *I didn't know what happened.*
I got home from work and you'd already gone to London.

Raped by a stranger, he would have been told. Such a shock he must have got.

I wish I could have done more for you, love.

It's OK, she said. *I'm not unhappy. Honestly, I'm not. And I'll be home in a few months.*

He opened his wallet and gave her two hundred pounds. *Treat yourself to something nice when you get back,* he said, and she took it to make him feel better.

They walked as far as the pier, which was very long and strung with lights, and familiar to her from images on television and in books. It looked magical in the darkness. *Victorian,* Dad said. *Lots of bars and restaurants and shops, and a fairground at the end. We had a look around this morning.*

Eleanor told me.

On their return to the hotel they found the others listening to a group that was singing carols in the drawing room, and Caroline thought how strange, how different a Christmas the four of them were having.

She went upstairs before Eleanor, and slept almost as soon as she climbed into bed, lulled by the wash of the sea. In the middle of the night she woke and padded out to the bathroom. Afterwards she lay in the dark, listening to Eleanor's steady breathing in the next bed.

There was something comforting about it. They hadn't shared a room in years.

After breakfast – fruit, cereal, croissants – the four of them exchanged presents. *How lovely*, her mother said when she opened Caroline's scarf. *Beautiful colour, thank you*. But she didn't try it on, like Eleanor and her father did theirs. From her parents Caroline got a watch – *What does anyone need a second watch for?* she heard Florence ask in her head – and from Eleanor a book of Nelson Mandela's speeches and a jar of bath salts.

Having a bath wasn't an option in Florence's house: the tub was cast iron and enormous, and Florence said the hot-water tank only heated enough water at a time to cover the bottom of it, so they both used the shower hose she'd attached to the taps. The bath salts could be passed on to Gretta or Delia, or donated to charity.

They went out to eleven o'clock Mass. After yesterday's rain everyplace was sodden, but a milky sun shone low in the sky and made the sea dance with lights, and lit the fronts of the Regency houses. The choir was made up of young boys dressed in white robes: the sound of their perfectly pure voices was almost too beautiful to bear. As Caroline brushed away the never-far tears she was conscious of her mother's eyes on her.

They walked home through the Lanes, an area of interconnecting narrow cobblestone alleys in which antiques and jewellery shops nestled between expensive-looking boutiques, impossibly quaint tea rooms and sweet shops. Not one of them was open, of course, much to Eleanor's disappointment.

After a light lunch – dinner was at five – she and Eleanor bundled up and walked along the prom while their parents watched a film on television. *I've been out with a few other boys*, Eleanor told her. *I'm not really interested in any of them, though*. Her hands tucked into her coat pockets, Caroline's new scarf around her neck.

Are you seeing anyone now?

No. Boys are overrated, she said, kicking up clods of pebbles as they walked. *I can't see me ever getting married*.

But of course she'd get married. She was Eleanor.

The long beach was dotted with couples. A man skimmed stones, a little boy by his side. Caroline thought about how Mum hadn't worn her new scarf to Mass. It shouldn't have bothered her. It wouldn't have bothered Florence: she'd have tossed her head and said, *Let her – what do you care?* But she did care.

Back at the hotel she slept until Eleanor appeared. *Dinner in ten minutes*, she said, and changed into a striking lavender blue dress that Caroline hadn't seen before.

That's lovely.

I got it for Andrew's graduation, Eleanor replied. *Never got worn till now. Cost a bomb, so I thought I'd better wear it to keep Mum happy.*

She didn't sound upset. She must be over him, like she'd said. Caroline got into the grey wool dress she'd bought second hand a fortnight before, already a bit tight around the middle. *I feel totally dowdy compared to you*, she said.

Don't worry – I'm sure nobody expects you to be glamorous. As soon as she'd said it, Eleanor flushed deep red. *Because of the baby, I mean.*

I know what you mean. But she hadn't really meant it like that. Caroline didn't mind. Eleanor was prettier; that was all there was to it.

Downstairs they ate turkey and ham and cranberry sauce and the rest of it. They pulled crackers and wore paper hats, and applauded along with the other hotel guests when the giant plum pudding was wheeled into the dining room and set alight.

And afterwards, for the first time since they'd met in the bus station, Caroline found herself alone with her mother. Had she given a private signal to the others? Had they arranged beforehand to disappear after the meal? Whether planned or unplanned, it happened – their father said something about catching a news bulletin, Eleanor said she needed the loo – and there the two of them suddenly were, left sitting alone at the table as people gathered their things and began to drift in the direction of the hotel bar.

Your hair, Mum said, pleating the yellow paper hat she'd taken off before the pudding. *When did you cut it?*

Last month.

I like it. It suits you.

Thank you.

Are you feeling alright? Not sick?

I'm fine.

I was sick all the way through with Eleanor. Not you, though. With you I just went off oranges, of all things.

Pause. The hat had become a narrow strip that she began to fold in on itself. Her nails were perfect crimson ovals, redone each week in the beauty salon where she worked.

I know, she said, *that I'm not exactly your favourite person right now.*

Caroline's heart sank: not this. Where was Eleanor? Why hadn't she come back?

You don't believe that I had your interests at heart, but I did. If you'd stayed at home everyone would have pitied you, and I wasn't having that. The hat a tiny fat yellow square now that she dropped onto her saucer. She placed her hands on the tablecloth, rings flashing.

I wish you'd done what I wanted, Caroline. This would all be over now, and you'd be home. But you chose to do it this way, and I have to respect that.

She had to respect it when she'd been given no other choice, when Florence had given her no other choice. A waiter passed by their table just then, carrying a tray of empty glasses. *We'll be happy to have you home*, her mother said when he was out of earshot. *You know that, when it's all over.*

Caroline forced herself to look directly at her. *You mean when my baby is born, and given away.*

Yes.

The baby that nobody must know about.

A sigh. *Caroline, we've been through this. I'm looking out for —*

I know what you're looking out for. Keeping her voice low and controlled. No tears threatening, not now. Now she was perfectly calm. *You're still friends with him, even when there's no need any more, now that Eleanor and Andrew have split up.*

Caroline, it's not as easy as just breaking off the friendship. Your father would wonder why, for one thing.

Maybe he should know why.

Her mother's eyes bored into hers. *He is* not *to be told – there's nothing to be gained by that. Think of the damage you would do, telling him at this late stage.*

She had a point. Silence fell.

Caroline, I need you to promise –

Don't worry, she said. *I'll play along.*

I'll ruin your family, Jasper had said. *They'll be lepers in this town when I've finished with them.* No, there was nothing Dad could do if she told him.

More silence. They were the last two in the dining room apart from the waiting staff, who moved among the tables stacking plates and gathering glasses. Caroline caught snatches of a piano plinking somewhere, a burst of laughter, the shrill clatter of falling cutlery.

I assume the school will have a place for me when I get home.

Yes, I've sorted all that with Sister Carmody. Her mother leant slightly forward then. *Caroline, it might be for the best if you stayed in England until August.*

August?

It will take a while for you to get your figure back. Her gaze slid from Caroline's face to the table top, which was littered with the remains of their plum pudding, smeared glasses, crumpled napkins, discarded paper hats. *It would be a shame if we gave the game away at this stage, don't you think? I'm sure you understand.* Raising her eyes to meet Caroline's again. *You do understand, don't you? It's not that we don't want you, it isn't that at all.*

It wasn't like Caroline had been counting the days till she could go home, far from it. On the contrary, she'd been planning to stay with Florence until the last possible moment. It shouldn't have hurt, the knowledge that she wasn't wanted back home till then. It shouldn't have hurt.

She pushed her chair back from the table. *I'm tired. I'm going to bed.* She would have liked to stay and listen to the classical Yuletide concert they'd been promised, but bed seemed like the best idea just then.

Caroline, I hope you —

Goodnight, she said, and left the room, aware of the gaze that followed her all the way, forgetting about the pink paper hat she was still wearing until she caught sight of it in the lift mirror, and pulled it off.

She didn't see her mother again. *She has a headache*, Dad reported at the breakfast table. *She's going to have a lie-in.* By eleven o'clock, when it was time to head to the bus station, there was still no sign of her. *I'll see if she's up*, Dad said – but Caroline told him not to disturb her. It was easier that way, easier to leave without another encounter.

The three of them walked to the station. The day was bright and still and bitterly cold. *Look after yourself*, Dad said as he hugged her. *We'll be thinking of you*.

Another hug from Eleanor, who had insisted on giving her a pair of socks that morning to wear over her tights on the return journey. *Talk soon*, she whispered. *Best of luck.*

Caroline waved to them as the bus pulled out. When they had disappeared from view she sat back and closed her eyes. Next time they met she'd have borne a child. She'd be a mother, even if she wouldn't have the evidence to prove it.

The further she travelled from Brighton, the more she could feel herself unclenching, letting go of the tension of the past three days. In the seat directly in front of her was a woman with a baby. At one stage she propped it against her shoulder, and it regarded Caroline with a solemn, unblinking gaze.

A boy, she thought, going by the navy fur-lined hat that covered his ears, and the miniature powder blue padded jacket. So bright his eyes were, the whites so milky and clear. How soft his cheek must feel. She imagined holding him in her arms, the small warm heft of him. He belched loudly, his placid expression not altering a whit, and she couldn't help smiling at his complete unselfconsciousness.

The journey, which included a freezing, two-hour stopover in Victoria, seemed endless. When she reached her destination, she stepped off the bus and saw Florence, all wrapped up in her patchwork coat and her scarf and her plastic hat, and she felt like she'd come home.

How was Christmas?

Grand – although he gave us a goose this year, bit bony. Don't tell him I said that. Lovely pudding though; he got it from Delia. I'm going to buy one of her leftovers – she'll be selling them half price on the stall. Are you frozen? It's been like this since you left. You survived anyway.

I did.

Told you you would. Ronnie behaved herself?

Most of the time. I'm not allowed home till the end of August – she's afraid I might still look pregnant up to then.

Pity about you, and you living in luxury with me. Don't let it bother you one iota, put it down to her ignorance. Brighton is nice, isn't it? Lovely pier.

Yes, she was home.

Now it was approaching midnight on New Year's Eve, and a group of them were sitting around the fire that Florence had lit that morning: Donald in a beautiful dark grey suit and bottle-green bow tie, Gretta and Barney from next door, clockmaker Frankie, three houses away on the other side, and Florence's friend Constance, the charity shop volunteer who'd given Caroline a crocheted bed jacket. All of them assembled at Florence's as they did every year to see the old one out and to usher in the new.

Caroline drank camomile tea. The others cradled glasses of the mulled wine that had been filling the kitchen with scents of cinnamon and orange and cloves since teatime. Delia's cranberry and dark chocolate cookies, presented via Donald, were doing the rounds, along with fingers of Florence's Christmas cake. Frankie had brought two jars of Anton the Frenchman's honey, Gretta and Barney a box of Florence's favourite rum and raisin fudge.

Constance's contribution was the lucky dip, which Caroline gathered was an annual staple: a bag of wrapped offerings that she'd put together from the bric-à-brac section of the charity shop. They all pulled something out, and opened their various spoils.

Barney expressed delight at a rust-spotted tin of snuff, promptly opening it and taking a pinch, much to Gretta's disapproval; Donald insisted on wearing his faux-pearl clip-on earrings immediately, declaring that he'd never felt fully dressed until that very minute.

Florence got a pair of brass candlesticks, which Caroline suspected would be back on the charity shop shelves before long; Frankie valiantly attempted to attach a couple of mismatched cufflinks to the ends of his pullover sleeves. Gretta donated her trio of highlighter pens to Frankie for his bingo cards; Caroline pulled out a small battered watering can.

The evening was rich with laughter, everyone in good spirits. Donald entertained them with anecdotes of well-known theatrical people whom he swore had been customers, if not friends, in his tailoring years in London. Constance recounted various past mishaps in the charity shop: a priceless first edition of a book inadvertently donated; a man accidentally – or maybe not – buying back the jacket his wife had handed in a few days earlier; a 1,000-piece jigsaw returned, and a refund demanded because a single piece turned out to be missing – a day before the customer in question reappeared, shamefaced, with the piece in question.

Caroline found herself comparing the evening, so full of merriment, to the three days she'd spent in Brighton. Three days brimming with unspoken criticism and regret, three days soaked in guilt and apprehension.

Sssh! Florence lifted a hand and everyone stopped chattering and listened to the radio host – no television in the house – counting down to midnight. A general round of kissing and hugging and well-wishing ensued, along with an almost tuneful chorus of 'Auld Lang Syne', and shortly afterwards people began to pack up, and the gathering was over.

Lying in bed later, drifting towards sleep, Caroline wondered what 1994 held in store. However it went, it promised to be momentous. This time next year Florence would be hosting her New Year's Eve party without her. Caroline would be halfway through her Leaving Cert year and her baby, nine months old or so, would be lying in someone else's cot, in an unknown family's house.

Since she'd got back from Brighton, babies were all she saw. They were everywhere she looked, in buggies and in their mothers' arms and in their fathers' slings. Cherub faces, heartbreakingly beautiful. Clear liquid eyes, tiny button noses, plump little rose-pink lips. Curves of dimpled cheeks that begged to be stroked, fingernails no bigger than lentils, folds at their wrists that made her want to weep in adoration.

She and Florence were travelling to London in a week or so. They were meeting someone from the adoption agency that Florence had found in the phone book. Caroline was going to fill in whatever forms were required, she was going to sign along the dotted line and give permission for her baby to be taken from her.

The baby who moved constantly inside her these days. There he was now, pushing against the wall of her womb with his minuscule limbs. A part of her, whether she had chosen him or not. Fully dependent on her to survive.

Her boy, her son.

She tried to quell the feeling of desolation. It was for the best, she told herself. It was the way it had to be. She turned her face to the wall and surrendered to sleep.

March 1994

Eleanor

'HOW'S THE PATIENT? ANY NEWS FROM England?'

God, would she never stop asking? 'Getting stronger every day, Sister.'

'Ah, that's marvellous. The sea air must be doing her the world of good. She'll be back to us in September so.'

'She will.'

'We'll have to keep an eye on her, make sure she doesn't work too hard.'

'Yes, Sister.'

'And I believe, Eleanor, you're making a real mark for yourself in the home economics department. Miss Rowley was only saying to me lately that you're really applying yourself there.'

'I like it, Sister.'

'Good girl, I'm so pleased to hear that. You'll make us proud of you yet. Well, say hello to your parents.' And off she went, happy in her state of blissful ignorance about the baby her prize pupil was going to give birth to any day now.

'She was asking about Caroline again,' she told Mum that evening.

'That's good,' Mum said, turning salmon steaks on the grill.

'I hate lying all the time.'

'I know, darling, but it's not for much longer. Once Caroline's been home a while people will forget she was ever away. By the way, I told you we'd been invited to the Fennellys' housewarming on Saturday, didn't I?'

'Yes.'

The Fennellys had moved into number ten last October – two parents, three kids. Within days of their arrival, snippets of information began to filter about the neighbourhood. He was in finance; his company had promoted and transferred him from Galway. She was planning to open a chiropody practice in the town. Shortly after their arrival she joined the tennis club. Mum played with her a few times.

Before they moved in there had been a succession of skips and trucks and workmen coming and going to the house – they might as well have demolished it and started again. Now, after months of finishing touches – painting, landscaping, a conservatory – they were ready to show it off, and everyone on the road had been invited.

Eleanor had no interest in the housewarming. She'd already met Conor Fennelly.

Hello, she'd said, encountering him on the street a few weeks after they'd moved in. *I'm Eleanor*

Plunkett, I live in number two – because you had to be friendly, didn't you? Particularly when someone looked interesting, and he did, with his lanky frame and caramel hair, his pale, flawless skin and general air of unkemptness, even in a school uniform. She bet he was a Nirvana fan.

Conor is hoping to go to art college after school, Mum had reported a few days earlier. *Apparently he's very artistic. You should get to know him.*

Artistic could go either way – he might be limp and moody, or fiery and unpredictable. Eleanor needed to find out, so she'd introduced herself next time they met.

He'd looked down at her thoughtfully. He was as tall as Caroline, taller. *I know who you are*, he'd replied, in a softer voice than she'd been expecting.

A beat passed. Was that it? She'd begun to move away, not knowing what else to say, his continuing scrutiny making her feel awkward.

See you around, Eleanor Plunkett. And off he went.

Gratifying that he was aware of her – but a bit full of himself. Assuming she knew his name, or not concerned if she didn't. Limp and moody, she decided. 'See you around' indeed. Not if she saw him first.

But after that he was everywhere. Hunched over a book in the library, looking pensively at a bag of lentils in the supermarket, waiting to cross the street as she passed by in a bus, coming out of the dry cleaner's with a plastic-covered something. And anytime they came face to face he'd say, *Hi there,*

Eleanor Plunkett. Mocking her, it felt like. Making fun of her because she'd had the manners to introduce herself.

Once again she vowed to stay away from boys. There had been nobody at all since she'd finished with Ian, just before Christmas. She'd had offers but she'd turned them down, unable to summon the interest. It had happened the wrong way around, she thought. She'd met her prince at the beginning, and now it was the turn of all the frogs. Fate had been unkind to her, fooling her into believing she'd been one of the lucky ones.

Then again, she was luckier than Caroline.

I'm feeling fine, she'd told Eleanor last week on the phone – but it was the middle of March and her baby was due anytime now, and every time the phone rang, Eleanor imagined it was to tell them that it had arrived. *Florence will let you know*, Caroline said, and Eleanor hoped that she or Dad answered that particular call.

She was going to give birth miles from home, with only a distant cousin to keep her company. Or maybe Florence wasn't even planning to be present at the birth: Caroline might only have anonymous hospital staff around her. She would have to go through all that pain and trauma with no baby to show for it at the end.

And how did she feel about that? *Are you going to have it adopted, or what?* Eleanor had asked her in Brighton, and Caroline had said yes, and then turned away. Was she having second thoughts? Could she really want to keep a baby who'd been conceived under such terrifying circumstances, whose father was a rapist? Or was she simply reluctant to dwell on the whole business of the birth and its aftermath?

Eleanor couldn't begin to imagine what it must be like, knowing you were carrying the child of a violent stranger. How could Caroline bear it? She had no choice, of course – she'd turned down the option of aborting it until it was too late. Maybe she was regretting that now: awful if she was. Eleanor wished again that she could be of some help – but what was to be done now except await the inevitable, and hope things worked out for Caroline?

Saturday came, and with it, the Fennellys' housewarming party. Eleanor went along mainly to keep Mum happy, but also because she was curious to see what they'd done to Tom Gallagher's old house.

She tried on six jeans-and-shirt combinations, and in the end settled on the fourth. She pinned up her hair and let it down again. She plaited it and undid it. She dabbed on the spicy perfume Sophie D'Arcy had given her the Christmas before last, the one she kept in the darkness of her wardrobe and eked out drop by drop.

The house was packed, neighbours milling from renovated kitchen to extended living room to brand new conservatory. Conor's mother, whose name was Jenny, poured drinks and pointed them in the direction of the caterers, who were dishing out hot food.

There was no sign of him. Eleanor told herself she was delighted. She ate a chicken kebab and wandered through the knots of people, looking for an unattended glass of wine she could swipe. She saw her parents talking to Jasper and Sophie D'Arcy, who'd been invited even though they didn't live on the road: typical.

Eleanor Plunkett.

She turned. He wore a black T-shirt and blue jeans. His hair was more tousled than usual. He held a paper cup.

I wish you wouldn't keep calling me that, she said. She hoped there weren't flecks of chicken on her face.

He looked at her in surprise. *Isn't that your name?*

Impossible to know if he was making fun of her. *It's the way you say it. Like you're mocking me.*

He seemed to consider this. *So what way would you like me to say it?*

He was ridiculous. *Just one name is enough.*

Plunkett, then.

She smiled. She couldn't help it.

Would you pose for me sometime? he asked, raising the cup to his lips, watching her over the rim of it as he drank.

It was totally unexpected. *Pose* for him?

You know, he said, *sit without moving while I paint you.*

I know what it means, she said stiffly. She should walk away. Why wasn't she walking away?

Hey, he said, smiling now, *calm down, I'm joking.*

But I really would like to paint you. I'm putting a portfolio together, and you'd make a good subject.

His smile, she had to admit, was lazy and warm and lovely, his voice mellow and soft as a cat's purr. But she was still unsure.

I wouldn't ask you to take off your clothes, he went on, *if that's what you're worried about. Not unless you want to.*

Smartass. *My parents are behind you*, she told him.

He didn't look around. *Glad they could make it. Anyway, you have nothing to fear.*

Except fear itself, she said. His eyes were midway between brown and yellow, with a splash of green.

Exactly. So will you do it?

She wanted to. Despite his mocking tone – was it mocking? – she was intrigued. *What would it involve?*

You turning up here, tomorrow afternoon if you're free. Wearing something bright.

OK, she said. An artist's model. She'd wear her red shirt and her favourite jeans.

Three o'clock they settled on, before he was dragged away by his twin sisters, who looked about ten. She wondered if he'd found a girlfriend in town yet.

The following morning the news arrived that they'd been waiting for. When Eleanor went down for breakfast she met her father in the hall, his face tight with concern.

'Florence rang, just a few minutes ago,' he said. 'Your sister has gone into labour.'

Caroline

'YOU WON'T LEAVE ME? PLEASE DON'T LEAVE me.'

'I haven't a notion of it.'

The pain came again, a hot, sharp knife. She gritted her teeth and tried not to squeeze Florence's hand too tightly.

'Squeeze it all you want,' Florence ordered. 'I can take it.'

'I'm scared,' she said, when she could talk again. 'Florence, I'm so scared.'

'Don't be. Women do this every day. It's the most natural thing in the world.'

'I can't. It's too hard, it hurts too much. I can't do it.'

'Child, you're hardly in a position to back out of it now. You'll be fine, you'll get through it, you're strong enough – and I'll be here. I'm not going anywhere.'

Time passed. She had no idea how much time passed. She was aware of nothing now but the scalding pain: she was inside the white-hot pain, she was living in it, she was immersed in it. It made her bellow and curse, it made her shout at Florence and the nurses. It made her bawl, tears and snot running from her as fast as the sweat that soaked the sheet beneath her.

Breathe, the nurses told her, *like this*. Panting at her. *Don't push yet*, they said, as she grunted like an animal and screamed some more and tried to breathe like they showed her, and hung on to Florence's hand like it was the only thing keeping her alive.

More time passed. Someone was stroking her arm, someone was telling her she was doing great, she was nearly there now, telling her to hang on, and it was Florence, her friend, her rock. *I love you*, Caroline said, or tried to say, even in the middle of her agony, but more pain came, pain on pain on pain, a fresh and unbearable lance of it – and *Now, push now*, someone said, some man said, and with the last of her strength she pushed, and she roared and pushed, and she moaned and screamed and pushed and pushed with every ounce of her strength – and at last, at last, at last she pushed her baby out of her.

'Thanks be to God that's over,' Florence said. 'I don't know about you, but I could murder a cup of tea.

'You did great, child,' she said. 'You didn't give up, you kept going – and you were a topper on the breathing. I was very proud of you.

'Mind you,' she said, 'your language was

appalling at times, but considering the state you were in, I suppose we can overlook it.

'I'm going to be black and blue after you,' she said, flexing her hand, 'but I did tell you to squeeze, so I have nobody to blame but myself. You're stronger than you look, I'll grant you that.

'When you get home,' she said, 'we must paint that room of yours: it could do with being freshened up. You can be thinking about the colour you'd like – you'll be the one looking at it till August.

'Drink your tea,' she said, 'and eat that toast before it goes cold. It'll do you good. Go on.'

She talked and talked, ignoring the river of tears that flooded from Caroline as the nurses held out her baby and coaxed her to look at him, to hold him, just for a little while, didn't she want to take a photo as a memento? She talked on as Caroline turned away from him and told them no, she couldn't, she couldn't, because if she did she'd never let him go. She kept talking as they finally gave up and took him away, as they took her precious son away from Caroline.

Couldn't she see that the last thing Caroline wanted was to lose him, that it was smashing her heart into tiny pieces to let him go? Didn't she understand that for Caroline this was worse, far worse, than the other pain?

But of course she saw. Of course she knew. Even though she'd never had her own child she understood it all, every bit of it. She talked because there was nothing else she could do. Even in the midst of her grief and her anguish, a part of Caroline realised that.

'You'll be home in a few days,' Florence said. 'You won't feel it,' as Caroline wept and wept and let her tea go cold, as the nurses replaced her sodden sheet with a fresh one and sponged the sweat from her body and helped her into a clean nightdress and wheeled her back to the ward for the remainder of the night, and pulled the curtains around her so the other new mothers could cuddle their babies unseen.

'I'll phone your parents first thing in the morning,' Florence said, finding Caroline's hand again and patting it. 'They'll be happy to hear that all went well.' She pulled tissues from the box that someone had placed on the locker and passed them to Caroline. 'Dry your eyes now, child,' she said. 'It's for the best, it is. Try and sleep, you'll feel better after a sleep. Things will seem brighter, you'll see. I'll be in to you tomorrow,' she said, pulling her plastic hat from her pocket. 'I'll be in as soon as they let me, and we'll get you home.'

'Stay,' Caroline begged, through the tears that refused to stop. 'Don't go, stay for another while. Keep talking.' So Florence shoved the hat back into her pocket and resumed her seat by the bed, and pestered the nurse on duty until she brought more tea and toast, and practically force-fed it to Caroline when it arrived.

'Did I ever tell you,' she said then, 'about my friend Sybil?' Reaching again for Caroline's hand, running her thumb absently over Caroline's knuckles as she spoke. 'I don't think I did. I met Sybil a long time ago, about a year after I came to live in London. We're going back forty years now. I was nineteen or twenty at the time. She put up a notice in a shop window looking for knitters, and I chanced to read it on my way home from work one evening. I had a job washing dishes in a restaurant, but I wasn't happy. My boss was an unchristian man who treated me like dirt because I was Irish, so I decided to ring the number on the notice, in the hopes that I'd get a better job out of it, and Sybil was one of the few people who didn't remark on my accent when she heard it ...'

And Caroline hung on to the sound of her voice, and let the story of Sybil wash around the grief and the loneliness and the devastation that was inside her.

And Florence was still talking when she toppled, finally, into exhausted oblivion.

August 1994

Eleanor

'I'VE GOT PINS AND NEEDLES.'

'Two minutes.'

She sat where she always sat, on the cream couch in the conservatory. The day was fine; the sun made stripes across her jeans. The place was full of the cloggy smell of the oil paints that covered the fold-up table, and the sharp tang of white spirit. She felt a trickle of sweat running down her back.

'Will you stay to dinner, Eleanor?' his mother called from the kitchen. 'We're having lamb.'

'Careful,' Conor said, dabbing colours into one another on a dinner plate, 'or she'll adopt you. She wanted a family of daughters; I was a big disappointment to her. Thank God the twins came along.'

'Don't mind him, Eleanor – he loves to tease. Take no notice.'

He was funny, once you learnt not to take him seriously. His sisters, Avril and Justine, were endearing chatterboxes.

'He painted us, lots of times,' they told Eleanor. 'We can show you if you want. He does weird paintings.'

His work surprised her: she'd never seen anything like it. He filled his canvases with wild darts and streaks of colour that somehow coalesced into semblances of his sitters – not mirror images by any means but recognisable all the same, almost as if he'd captured their essence rather than their features. They were so vibrant and alive, you almost waited for them to speak. He'd painted his entire family, and other people Eleanor didn't know.

Other girls. She was jealous of them, even though they were all fully clothed.

After about two weeks her portrait was done. *When is your birthday?* he asked, and when she told him August, still months away, he told her he'd give it to her as a gift as soon as it was dry – *on condition that I can do some more sketches for my art college portfolio. And I'll have to borrow it back if anyone calls me for interview.*

She loved that someone had painted her. Caroline had sketched her lots of times, with charcoal or pen and ink, but this was altogether different. Caroline's drawings were good – at least, they looked quite like Eleanor – but compared to Conor's they were boring. She thought he'd made her more striking than she was – eyes darker, mouth fuller – but if that was how he saw her, she wasn't complaining.

We must get it framed, Mum said when she saw it, so Eleanor chose a simple one of pale wood. She hung the finished work in her room, and traced the tiny black CF he'd inscribed in the bottom right corner.

Eleanor Fennelly. Eleanor Plunkett Fennelly.

She liked sitting for him, liked how it felt to have his eyes on her. She sneaked looks at him as he worked, watched him frown when he mixed colours, saw him catch his bottom lip as he dabbed and daubed with brushes and palette knives, and sometimes with his fingers. Once he got a smudge of blue on his cheek: she wanted to wipe it away with her thumb.

She imagined undressing for him, lying naked while he painted her. Feeling his eyes on her body. If he suggested it she'd say yes, but he didn't. Instead he asked if she'd like to go to the opening of an art exhibition in town.

My teacher gave me an invite, he thought I'd like it. The artist is a German expressionist.

Sure, she said, trying to sound casual. Trying not to look as if the invitation delighted her. She'd never been to an art exhibition in her life – Caroline was the one for all that – and she had no idea what 'expressionist' meant, but she didn't care.

I'll call around and collect you.

Her mother was thrilled. *Darling, I'm so happy for you. Jenny says it's high time he got himself a girlfriend.*

She loved the thought that he might never have had a girlfriend. *Mum, it's not a date. We're only going to an exhibition. We're just friends.*

But she hoped it was a date, hoped that she'd be his

first love, like she'd been Andrew's first. Although he made no attempt to hold her hand throughout the evening, and didn't put an arm around her as they walked home, or try to kiss her when he said goodnight at her gate, she knew it was only a matter of time.

She wanted him to be the first to take her to bed. That was only a matter of time, too, she was convinced. It would be better than her imaginings with Andrew; for one thing, she was a year older – and Conor would be sensitive, she was sure, and gentle. She couldn't wait.

The weeks passed. They went other places together, they met up for coffee after school, and sometimes they went for a burger at weekends. She sat for him, lots of times; he called her his muse. They had fun together. He made her laugh.

But he could be serious too. *I have an uncle*, he'd told her, just the other day. *Gordon, Dad's brother. He's head chef in a hotel in Galway. If you mean it about wanting to cook for a living I could talk to him. He'd have contacts. He might be able to point you in the right direction.*

She'd been to Galway a few times. She liked it.

We could visit the hotel sometime, you could meet him.

That'd be good. A day trip to Galway, just the two of them.

She found herself thinking about him when he wasn't around – she'd remember something he'd said when she was in the middle of making a batch of scones or a quiche, and she'd have to smile.

He's just eight houses away, she'd think at odd moments. He was filling the gaping hole that Andrew had left. It had taken a year, but now it was finally happening again.

She saw Andrew from time to time, when he was home from college. He looked as good as he always had – better, maybe, with his hair a little longer now. The sight of him caused no more than the mild pleasure she'd feel on meeting, say, a relative she was moderately fond of.

He and Eleanor had kissed on their first date; there had been no waiting around, no will-he-won't-he angst with Andrew D'Arcy.

For her seventeenth birthday Conor gave her a CD by The Divine Comedy, a group she knew little about. *It's a concept album*, he told her, *Baroque pop*. She had no idea what any of that meant. The CD was a weird mix of classical and modern: she couldn't decide if she loved or hated it but she treasured it, and the *Happy Birthday, pretty girl* message he'd scrawled on the back, along with a big X.

How's it going? Tina would ask, and Eleanor would say great – but was it great? For over four months they'd been what everyone else regarded as a couple, and still the most she'd got from him in terms of physical affection was a hug at the end of an evening that could legitimately have come from her grandmother, and that left her wanting so much more.

Despite his easygoing manner, his general air of confidence, she decided it must be shyness that was holding him back. He'd had no practice: he might be terrified of messing up. The thought of this vulnerability made him even more appealing. Eleanor had never had to make the first move in the past, but it looked like it was up to her now. Should be easy: a nudge was all he'd need.

Tonight they were going to a classical concert. *Mozart*, he'd said, as if that was a good thing. She didn't tell him she'd rather Madonna, or Jon Bon Jovi, or pretty much anyone else. Didn't matter, as long as they were going together.

The doorbell rang just after seven, as they were finishing dinner. 'Bring him in,' Mum said. 'He can have coffee.'

'Can't,' Eleanor replied, grabbing her bag. 'We're meeting a few others.' She couldn't subject him to Mum's small talk, her not-so-subtle nosing into his family's goings-on, not tonight.

The sight of him on the doorstep brought a rush of happiness. 'Plunkett,' he said – since the night of the housewarming that was what he'd called her, and occasionally El, 'you look splendid, as usual.'

He was always complimenting her. A nudge would definitely do it. They walked down the driveway and turned left towards town. 'Did I tell you Caroline is coming home, day after tomorrow?'

'Several times. Might have to paint her. Does she look like you?'

'Not a bit – nobody would take us for sisters. She likes to paint too, but her stuff isn't anything like yours, it's more ... ordinary.'

A boy, Caroline had had. Eleanor had a nephew. One she'd never meet, but still. Aunt Eleanor, she decided, had a nice ring to it. Shame she couldn't tell anyone.

Caroline had changed, after the baby. *How are you?* Eleanor enquired, just like Mum and Dad had asked before her. It was three days after the birth: Caroline was back in Florence's house, had only been kept in hospital for a day and a night.

I'm alright.

She didn't sound alright, she sounded ... wrong. Was it just the after-effects of what she'd been through, or was it more than that? Was she missing the baby, was that it? Or – a new thought occurred – had she changed her mind and kept him, and was the note in her voice one of wariness? Eleanor couldn't ask, not with Mum in earshot, but she could ring back later, when her parents were out.

Florence answered.

It's Eleanor.

She's resting.

It's OK. I just wanted to know ... if she gave the baby up for adoption.

What? Sharply, an octave higher. *Of course she did! Why would you think otherwise? Did your mother put you up to this?*

No – she doesn't know I'm ringing. I just thought Caroline sounded ... a bit different.

There was a kind of a snort at the other end of the line. *A bit different? She's just had a baby – of* course *she's different!*

I only meant –

That girl has been through a lot, and she's still getting over it – the last thing she needs is someone asking silly questions. Is that clear?

Eleanor prickled with annoyance. Awful woman: how could Caroline like her?

Your sister is very fragile right now, and I won't have her upset.

I wasn't trying to upset her, Eleanor said, as crossly as she dared. *I just wanted to make sure she was OK, that was all.*

She'll be fine. Now, was there anything else? I have things to do.

In the weeks that followed, the baby wasn't mentioned. Caroline's voice, when Eleanor spoke to her each Friday, sounded hollow, as if someone had sucked the insides out of her. Or ... defeated, yes, that was it. She was defeated by what had happened.

And in just two days she was coming home. Eleanor wondered how she felt about it: something else they hadn't talked about. Over the past year, an awful lot of stuff had been left unsaid.

The concert proved every bit as boring as she'd anticipated: what did anyone see in classical music? It was as pointless as opera, or ballet. She passed the time imagining their first kiss, which would be happening shortly. She'd suggest they walk home by the embankment, tell him she wanted to sit and watch the sunset. The rest should be easy.

'What did you think?' he asked as they filed out.

'It was fine,' she said, unwilling to admit her complete lack of interest.

He wasn't fooled. He pushed the hair out of his eyes. 'Plunkett, you're a lost cause. I'll have to give you a cultural injection.'

'Ha ha.' They snaked with the rest of the audience towards the door.

'Bet your sister would have enjoyed it. Bet she's into classical.'

'Why would you think that?'

'Because you said she's the opposite of you.'

'You're right, actually. She'd have loved this.'

'She can come with us next time then,' he said.

Eleanor felt everything stiffen in her.

She can come with us? He wanted *Caroline* to come out with them? Was it a *threesome* he was after – or was this his clumsy way of telling her he wasn't interested?

She waited until they were out on the street. Once they were free of the crowds she marched away, hands buried deep in her pockets, face hot with anger.

'Plunkett – hold up. Where's the fire?'

She kept going until she got to the corner. She stopped and wheeled to face him.

'What's going on?' she demanded. The embankment could go to hell – she needed answers.

He looked baffled. 'In what sense?'

'What are we doing? What are you doing with me?'

'What am I *doing* with you?'

'Where are we going?' Her voice climbed higher with every word: she could hear exactly how shrill she sounded. 'You *know* what I mean – stop pretending you don't. Are we together or aren't we? And if we are, why don't you – why don't we *ever* –'

She broke off. She couldn't. She couldn't form the words.

He stood looking thoughtfully down at her.

'Why?' she repeated. 'Why don't we? Don't you fancy me, is that it?'

He sighed. He reached for her hand, caught it.

'Listen,' he said, 'El, we need to talk.'

'We *are* talking.'

'Not here.' He led her down the next street, and she went with him because it was easier than demanding answers to humiliating questions. Twilight was underway, the sky streaked with bronze and grey, the colour leaching from the hanging baskets that were displayed outside several shop fronts.

They were holding hands for the first time: how ironic. She'd handled it all wrong; she'd sounded needy, not desirable. Even if he'd fancied her up to this, she'd killed it tonight. She felt dejected, miserable.

'Where are we going?'

'Hang on.'

They came to a bus stop with a wooden seat, and nobody at all sitting on it.

'This'll do,' he said. They sat. He didn't let her hand go. He held on to it, he looked at it for a few seconds before lifting his head. 'El,' he said, 'I really like you, I do. You're fun to be with, and I look forward to seeing you.'

But. There was a but coming. She waited for it.

He paused. He chewed his lip. His hand was warm, his fingers long and slender and beautiful. Artist's fingers.

'El,' he said. 'I'm sorry. I'm really sorry. I should have seen this coming. I was being selfish, and a bit cowardly, I suppose, and I apologise for that. It's just that ... well, I haven't really told anyone yet. My parents have no idea. I think I'm still getting my head around it myself.'

He halted again.

My parents have no idea. I'm still getting my head around it.

And then, suddenly, she knew.

'Turns out,' he said, 'that I'm gay.'

Of course he was.

'I'm sorry,' he said again. 'I thought you might have guessed. I'm really sorry.'

She felt her cheeks flushing. Mortified didn't come close. She pulled her hand away from his, and he let it go.

'I'm sorry, El. I really didn't mean to lead you on.'

'No.' She found her voice. It had become tiny. She turned away, watched the cars passing. They sat side by side in silence for several seconds. 'You should have said.'

'I know. I know that now.'

She had no idea what to do. She couldn't think

what to say. Eventually she got to her feet. 'I'm
going home. I'd like to be by myself.'

'OK. I'll call around in a few days.'

She didn't answer. All the way home she puzzled
it out. Now that she knew, she couldn't understand
how she hadn't guessed. In the months she'd known
him, in all the time they'd spent together, it had
never once crossed her mind.

But now that she knew, it was so obvious.

Fool. She was a fool.

The only good thing, she thought, the only thing
she could take comfort from was that he wouldn't
tell anyone how she'd made an idiot of herself.
He wouldn't do it because it would blow his own
cover – but even if everyone knew he was gay, he
still wouldn't expose her humiliation. He wouldn't
because he was decent and kind.

He was exactly, she realised, the sort of friend
you'd want, if you were looking for a friend, rather
than a boyfriend.

And he was trusting her to be discreet too. He
hadn't told his parents yet; he hadn't told anyone.
She could tell the world if she wanted, she could
expose him – but of course she wouldn't because,
for all her faults, she was a decent person too.

She'd let some time go by. If anyone asked, she'd
tell them that it hadn't really worked out, but they
were still friends. A mutual decision, she'd say, no
hearts broken. And hopefully, by the time people
learnt the truth about him, they'd have forgotten

that he and Eleanor were ever a couple – in everyone else's eyes at least.

He said he'd come around in a few days. Hopefully she'd be able to meet him without wanting the ground to swallow her. They *should* be friends – they were pretty good at it.

She got home. She went inside, pressing cool hands to cheeks that still burnt.

Caroline

IT DIDN'T TAKE HER LONG TO PACK. SHE folded her new clothes carefully in tissue paper and placed two sketch pads on top, filled with pen-and-ink drawings of the friends she'd made here, and some of Pip the cat, who had finally learnt to trust her enough to sit next to her on the garden seat, and to endure the lightest stroke of his black fur.

She tucked a photo of herself and Florence, taken the previous Saturday by Gretta, between the layers of her clothes. She slipped Donald's farewell gift, a folder of handmade notecards and envelopes, into the front pocket of the case. *You must keep in touch*, he said. *You have no excuse now. I shall expect regular updates, full of Irish scandal.*

She pinned Gretta and Barney's present, a tiny porcelain brooch of a bird in flight, white with pale blue wing tips, to her jacket lapel.

The new wrought-iron garden seat had been delivered the previous day. She'd agonised over what to get for Florence, what she could possibly give her to say thank you. In the end, she decided that nothing would be enough, and settled on the seat as the best she could do.

What do I want that for? Florence had demanded when she'd seen it. *Haven't I got one already?* But it looked good sitting outside her kitchen window, next to the flowerbed that got all the afternoon sun, and she'd be glad of it when the existing wooden seat collapsed, as it had been threatening to do since Caroline had moved in.

Over a year she'd been living here: hard to believe. She perched on the side of her single bed and thought back to the day she'd arrived, full of apprehension, feeling utterly alone. She'd sat in this very spot and wondered how she was going to endure spending months under the same roof as a woman she'd only just met, and who sounded so gruff and unfriendly. Now she wondered how on earth she'd survive without her.

So much had happened to her here. She'd learnt how to use a knitting machine, and become quite accomplished on it. Her silk alpaca scarves – cheaper than cashmere, not as warm but just as soft – had been a strong seller at the market over the winter, and her other bits and pieces, hats, bags, purses, pencil cases, headbands, had sold consistently the rest of the time.

In the last few weeks she'd ventured a little further and run up simple vest tops in a fine cotton yarn, pastel pinks and greens and blues, and they'd proven popular too. Florence would often praise her efforts – *You've bumped up our profits no end* – and Donald, she knew, appreciated the increased traffic to the stall her offerings had brought about.

And last week she'd chanced making a tunic-style top for herself in a beautiful deep violet shade, and while it wasn't perfect – not quite long enough, not quite flared enough – for a first effort she was pleased.

She'd learnt to cook while she was living here. She was able to put a meal together with some confidence now, and bake a quite palatable loaf of brown bread, and she knew which cuts of beef and lamb needed longer, slower cooking. In the garden she could tell a delphinium from a larkspur. She knew when to prune what shrubs, and how to deadhead and take cuttings, and divide crocosmia corms. She'd learnt to recognise starlings and chaffinches and swallows and more, and she could distinguish between their various songs.

She'd got to know so many people here. All the neighbours on the road, Donald and Delia and the other market traders, and several of the townspeople who shopped there; the kitchen staff at the hospital, many of whom she still bumped into around town. She'd made the acquaintance of Constance and other volunteers in the charity shops, the women in the wool shop, the Pakistani couple who ran the small supermarket at the end of the next road.

She'd changed in appearance here. On Constance's advice she'd cut her hair – and at the beginning of June, when the baby weight was pretty much gone and she was still in the baggy dresses of her pregnancy, too disheartened to make any changes, she'd been taken in hand by Florence.

We need to get you some new clothes, she'd announced one day. *You look a holy show in those things. We're going to see Judith.*

Judith was the well-dressed manager of the town's largest charity shop. *I have an outfit that I think would be perfect for you*, she told Caroline. *It came in the other day, and it just might be your size.*

To keep them quiet, Caroline tried it on. The navy top was long and slim and gently flared at the end; the form-fitting navy skirt fell to an inch or two below the knee. A scarlet line no wider than the stroke of a pen ran around the skirt just above the hem; a trio of similar lines draped themselves over the top's left shoulder.

Caroline had never worn anything like it. Before she'd got pregnant, all her clothes had been designed to hide her figure, which she'd always considered to be too boyish, too uninteresting – particularly when she compared herself to curvier Eleanor.

But now things had changed. When the baby weight went, it left behind a little more roundness on top, a little more width in the hips. She felt more feminine – and this twosome, made from a fine wool that flowed like liquid when she moved, revealed her new curves without flaunting them. The label wasn't one she recognised, but she guessed the outfit had cost a fair bit first time round.

We'll take it, Florence had said when Caroline

emerged from the dressing room. *And we'll have to find you shoes, or boots or something, to go with it*. Over the following few weeks Caroline picked up another top and skirt and two dresses, all in the same flowing style – she liked it, it suited her – and not all second hand. She also bought black suede boots and two pairs of brand new shoes.

She'd turned eighteen here, on the eighth of May. She'd told no one. The day after her birthday a small package arrived for her: the address was in Eleanor's handwriting. Inside were a scented candle and a silver photo frame, and two fifty-pound notes folded into a card. Mum had written in the card along with the other two: *Hope you have a good day. Looking forward to having you home again.*

Why were they sending you a parcel? Florence wanted to know. When Caroline told her, she arranged a dinner party with the New Year's Eve gang, and they all brought gifts and wished Caroline a happy birthday in the new gentler voices they'd taken to using with her since the baby.

She turned her head to look out the window. Florence was standing at the gate talking to a passer-by: she talked to anyone who'd listen. In a few minutes she'd come inside and she'd call up the stairs to Caroline, and they'd get into the car and drive to the airport.

On the twentieth of March, three days later than promised, Caroline had become a mother here.

It was for the best, Florence had said, over and over since then. *What kind of life could you have given him, cut off from your family, never able to bring him home? He'll be with people who really want him, people who can provide all the things he'll need. He'll be happy, and you should be happy knowing that you've given him that.*

And Caroline listened and nodded and tried to believe it, but she didn't believe it because it wasn't true. It wasn't for the best: how could it be? How could it be for the best when she was his mother? How could it have been the right thing to do when she felt so emptied-out, so destroyed without him?

She should have kept him. She'd have figured out how to live the new kind of life she would have had with him. She'd have loved him enough to make up for a hundred families. They'd have got by, they'd have had one another, and they'd have had Florence, who would have been better than any grandmother.

But she hadn't kept him: she'd given him away. She'd failed him, she'd denied him his mother, and she had to live with that. She hadn't even given him a name, against the advice of the adoption agency. *Naming him will be good for you,* they'd said, but she wouldn't listen, couldn't bear the idea that a name would be all he'd get from her. But they'd been right, she could see that now. If she'd named him she'd have something to call him now when she thought about him.

Her most bitter regret was that she hadn't listened to the nurses in the delivery room, hadn't allowed herself to look at him, hadn't let them take his photo. How could she have been so stupid, how could she have denied herself the sight of his face, and a reminder of it?

And now she was trying to learn how to be without him, and how to live with the pain of having lost him, and it was the hardest thing she'd ever had to do. In time, in a million lifetimes, she might manage it. She might smile one day, and actually mean it.

And at some stage she might learn how to stop hating her mother.

She turned away from the window. She picked up her coat and put it on. She'd take it one day at a time. Today she was flying back to Ireland. In less than a week she'd begin her final year of secondary school. She'd study hard and get a good Leaving Cert.

And next summer she'd come back to England, to whatever college would take her in. She wasn't sure what she wanted to do after school, but she had several months to think about it. She'd refuse to apply to Irish colleges: she'd tell her parents it was England or nothing. They'd agree, they'd have to. And after she qualified, she was going to find a job here.

Her old life in Ireland was over: she had no interest in reclaiming it. Wanting to be a historian was part of that old life, part of what she used to want. That had all changed; everything was different now. Her future was in England. Florence was here, and so was her son. The two people she cared most about were here. She might never get to meet him again, but she'd feel closer to him.

She hadn't told anyone what she was planning, not even Florence. She was afraid to give voice to it, afraid she might jinx it if she said it aloud, so she was keeping it safe inside her until she could make it happen.

She heard the front door opening. 'Caroline? It's time we were moving.'

'Coming.'

She gave a last look around the room. It was pale green now, painted to match Donald's patchwork spread in blues and greens that had been covering her bed when she'd come home from the hospital. *Take that spread with you*, Florence had said. *It's yours, he gave it to you* – but it belonged here, so Caroline had left it.

The dressing table, the spotted mirror, the floorboards shiny with age. The cream bedside rug she'd picked up for half nothing. The cheap chipboard wardrobe Florence had paid fifteen pounds for, as good as new apart from a smear of red paint on the door that Caroline had covered with a postcard of Stonehenge.

The tears she'd shed in this room. The river she'd cried into that pillow.

Come on, time to move. She picked up her case and went downstairs.

The wind tugged at the car as they sped along the motorway. 'You'll be blown across the Irish Sea,' Florence remarked. 'Probably be home in half the time.'

'Mm.'

Her flight was at four, due into Dublin an hour later. The three of them were coming to meet the prodigal daughter. *We'll get dinner on the way home. We'll stop somewhere nice,* her father had said on the phone. *Wherever you fancy.*

'Don't let what happened ruin your life,' Florence said at the airport. 'Don't let it make you bitter. What happened happened.'

'That's what you said when I came to you. I thought it was a bit cruel of you at the time, but I know what you mean.'

'I said it because it's true. It's all in the past now, and you handled it as best you could. It's how you deal with what comes after it that matters.'

'I know. I know that.' She did know. It didn't help.

'It'll make you stronger, child. Things like this, things that take so much out of us, always do. You survived, and you'll be all the stronger for it.'

'Yes.'

'He might look you up some day, and he might not. It's up to him. You've left the letter, you've done all you could.'

The letter. A collection of pathetic stilted sentences that didn't come close to telling him how she felt. Written while she was still pregnant, to be passed on to his adoptive parents, a copy to be held at the agency.

I'm not in a position to keep you, although I very much want to. Please try to understand how hard it is for me to give you up, and try not to feel badly towards me. I want you to have the best life you can; that is my only reason for having you adopted. I would be very happy to meet you some day, if it's something you think you might like.

Written and rewritten, the words blurring on the page as she wept. She put her name at the end, along with Florence's contact details. Writing to a man who didn't yet exist.

'I won't say try to forget him,' Florence said, 'because that's not going to happen. But try not to let him get in the way of your life. Try not to let him take over. Make a space for him, and keep him in that space.'

Make a space for him. She might, if she had any idea how.

'And don't let this put you off men. They're not all bad, you know.'

Caroline managed a smile. 'You're a fine one to talk.'

Florence tossed her head. 'It wasn't for me, that life. I wasn't cut out for it. But a happy marriage can be a worthwhile thing: I've seen plenty examples of it. And you'll make someone a good wife, now that I've taught you how to cook.'

She made it sound so easy: learn to cook, find a husband. Tuck your broken heart away in a corner and live happily ever after.

'The place will be quiet without you,' Florence

said. 'You can always come back, you know that. There will always be a room for you in my house.'

Caroline bent and put her arms around her, and clung to her. 'I just might take you up on that,' she whispered.

Eventually Florence nudged her away. 'There,' she said, 'safe trip, off you go. Drop me a line soon, let me know how you're doing. Or give me a ring. Whatever suits.'

At the boarding gate she sat silently among the other waiting passengers. A little girl, two or three years old she thought, stared fixedly at her from her mother's knee, and Caroline returned her steady gaze until the child got bored and turned away.

'Were you on holiday?' the woman next to her on the plane asked, and Caroline said yes, just a few days.

'London is great, isn't it?'

'Yes, it's great.'

'I like your sweater. Did you buy it there?'

'Actually I designed it myself.'

'Did you really? It's beautiful.'

'Thank you.' She looked through the window as they left land behind and began to cross the Irish Sea. Leaving him behind. Just for a year, she promised silently. I'll be back.

She thought about being back at home, running the risk of meeting Jasper D'Arcy every time she ventured out. *Hold your head up high, give as good as you get.* She was stronger now: he'd knocked the innocence out of her. She'd look him in the eye if they met: she wouldn't show him fear.

Dublin was wetter than England, and just as windy. She pulled her coat around her as she walked across the tarmac to the terminal building.

'Welcome home, darling,' her mother said. 'It's so good to see you.'

'Welcome, love,' her father said. 'Home at last. Here, let me carry that.'

'Hi,' Eleanor said. 'You look good. I like that sweater – the colour really suits you.'

'We're going to stop for dinner on the way home,' her mother said. 'There's a lovely new hotel outside Kildare, I've heard great things about it. Or if there's anywhere you'd prefer ...'

'Do you want anything before we leave the airport?' her father asked. 'Are you thirsty? Will I get you some water?'

Falling over themselves to be nice to her, now that she was home. Now that she'd avoided bringing disgrace on the Plunkett family. But she was here, and she would remain here for the next several months, so they might as well get along.

'Dinner sounds good,' she said.

As they walked out to the car, the rain stopped.

PART TWO

PART TWO

September 2015

Eleanor

DEAR MR AND MRS FENNELLY,
I would appreciate a meeting with you at your
earliest convenience: there is an issue that
involves Jacob that we need to discuss. Please
call my secretary to make an appointment.

It's typed on headed cream manila paper and signed
by Philip Murray, the school principal. Lord, what's
this? Today is Friday, just two weeks into Jacob's
first term at the school: what could he have done
to warrant his parents being summoned to the
principal's office already?

There is an issue that involves Jacob – what does that
mean? Has he got caught up in something wrong?
She recalls the ten euro he looked for a few days ago,
and wonders again if he was telling the truth when
he said it was for history notes.

She needs to handle this: Gordon's too
preoccupied with Fennellys' struggles. She stows
the letter in her pocket until he's gone to work, and
then she phones the number.

'St Kevin's School, good morning.' A warm tone that stops it being too official.

Eleanor gives her name, says she'd like to make an appointment with Mr Murray.

The voice leaves her briefly, and returns. 'How's Monday for you, Mrs Fennelly, three fifteen?'

Monday is fine for Mrs Fennelly. She hangs up and makes a note in her phone. She'll say nothing to Gordon until afterwards, but she'll show Jacob the letter when he gets home and ask him what it's about. She won't sound confrontational, just concerned.

She empties the washing machine and hangs clothes on the line outside, even though a fine drizzle has begun to fall. She feeds Clarence and mops the kitchen floor as she listens to a man on the radio talking about the preparations for the 1916 commemorations next year. Road to the Rising, he's calling it. She wonders why the centenary of a failed rebellion is being celebrated.

She makes a fresh pot of coffee and gets biscuits from the press. She snaps a ginger nut in half and thinks about the past.

October the twenty-eighth, 2000, one of the best days of her life. Better, even, than the day she married Gordon. *A boy*, they'd said, placing him in her arms. *A healthy son*. She and Gordon had opted not to know the gender beforehand, preferring the surprise.

She remembers looking down at him, marvelling at the wonder of the brand new person she and

Gordon had made, the sight of him, the warm heft of his tiny perfect body banishing all the pain that had gone into his arrival. She remembers thinking, *I'm somebody's mother*, remembers knowing that nothing would ever be the same. His eyes were closed, hidden from her by papery eyelids. *Open them*, she whispered – and he did. Looked right at her, claimed her for his own.

She took to motherhood instantly. She loved him, she loved him to bits, unconditionally. She doted on him those first few weeks. Gordon complained, half joking: *You have a new man, I'm not wanted any more.* Jacob kept her up at night; he wailed for her when she was nearly sick with exhaustion, when her eyelids were glued together with sleep. He took over her life completely, and she didn't care a whit.

She was a mother; she had a son. He was her precious child; nobody had ever had a baby so beautiful. She flaunted him: she wore him in a little sling when she went out so everyone could admire him. She brought him into Fennellys, showed him off to the staff. She took a million photos of him.

Breastfeeding felt sacred to her, a communion between him and her that nobody else could share. She adored the fact that she was still nourishing him from her own body, loved the pull on her nipple from his eager little mouth.

She remembers thinking about her sister in those first few weeks, and the son she'd surrendered right after his birth. She couldn't imagine having to give up Jacob. How had Caroline borne it? Her anguish must have been immeasurable.

Or maybe not: maybe the fact that he'd been the product of a rape had changed the way Caroline felt about him. Maybe his departure had come as a relief. *That's that over with,* she might have thought.

But she remembered the emptiness in Caroline's voice when they'd spoken after his birth, the dispirited way she'd spoken. He was still her son, he was the innocent child who'd grown in her womb, regardless of the circumstances of his conception. Giving him away must surely have hurt.

Nobody had talked to her about it when she'd come home from England. Eleanor hadn't asked how she felt, hadn't once tried to get through to her sister. To tell the truth she'd been afraid of what might come out, what the enquiry might dislodge. Granted, Caroline didn't encourage confidences, she never had – but they should have tried, they shouldn't have ignored it the way they did.

By the time Jacob came along, Caroline had been back in England for over five years, having surprised them all with her announcement, in the spring of her Leaving Cert year, that she no longer wanted to become a historian, that she'd applied instead to several art colleges, all of them in the UK. That she intended to study fashion design, to make a career of it.

Eleanor couldn't believe it. Caroline, who'd never looked at a fashion magazine growing up, who'd never seemed to care what she wore. Mum kicked up, of course, but Caroline had stood her ground in her quiet way, and in the end they'd had to let her go. She ended up in an art college in Wales, and four years later she graduated with an honours degree – naturally – and got a job straight away at some clothing place in Oxford, just half an hour from the town where Florence lived.

She seemed to have put the past behind her. She moved right back in with Florence, which Eleanor thought was a bad idea – the memories that house must have for her! – but any time she came back to Ireland after that she seemed happy. Well, fairly happy.

Of course, Mum had another tantrum when she heard what Caroline was planning.

Live with Florence? You can't possibly impose on the woman like that. It was one thing staying with her when we had nobody else to call on – but moving in with her now just isn't on. You should be with young people, not stuck with someone old enough to be your grandmother.

But again Caroline refused to be told. *I can mix with young people all day at work. I'd like to live with Florence.*

Well, I daresay you might – you two seem to have become great friends – but Florence might well prefer to have her house to herself. Why don't you rent, and go to stay for the occasional weekend?

Actually, it was Florence's idea that I move in. And that was that. Mum had had to lump it, and from then on they hardly saw Caroline. She flew home each Christmas for a few days – still does – and in between she appeared for any occasion that demanded it, and that was pretty much it.

She came home for Eleanor's wedding, of course. She wore a beautiful bridesmaid's dress that she'd made herself, its rich ochre shade picking up the copper highlights she'd started getting in her hair. She arrived again for Jacob's christening, two years later: Eleanor had agonised about asking her to be godmother – would it be insensitive, in view of her history? – but in the end she'd gone ahead, thinking her sister might be more hurt if she were overlooked in favour of one of Eleanor's friends.

And Caroline is good to Jacob, always has been. Never forgets his birthday, presents at Christmas and Easter. She came to stay after Beth died, took two weeks off work and stayed in the spare room while Eleanor lay in the dark and wished for death. It was Caroline who suggested the crèche for Jacob, Caroline who went with Gordon to check it out.

She's been back a few times since then: she came for Jacob's communion, and again for his confirmation. Just short trips, a night or two in Ireland at the most – but it's good to see her, and catch up.

Maybe if they lived closer to one another, things might have been different. Maybe they'd have a better feel for one another's lives as adults than they'd had in their youth. Maybe Caroline could have helped Eleanor to find her way back to Jacob, when she finally felt able to cope with him again – or is that just wishful thinking?

She looks for another biscuit, and discovers

she's finished the packet. She bins the wrapper and washes up, and passes the day in the usual fashion until Jacob gets home from school.

He glances at the letter, hands it back. 'I don't know what that's about.'

'You must have some idea, love.' She can hear how careful she's being, how tentative she sounds. 'There must be some reason.'

'Well, I don't know what it is.' He walks past her into the kitchen and begins to make his usual sandwich.

'I'm going to see Mr Murray on Monday. I've made an appointment.'

'OK.' He seems unconcerned. Maybe all new parents are summoned like this as a matter of course. Maybe they need information about him that Gordon forgot to give when he was enrolling him.

There's an issue that involves Jacob.

No; this is more than a matter of course.

Caroline

AT LONG LAST, HE CAME TO FIND HER. AFTER twenty-one years of waiting and praying and wishing and hoping, his letter arrived on Monday the seventh of September 2015.

Dear Caroline
My name is Noah O'Reilly. I'm your son. I read your letter and I'd like to meet you. I live in Brighton, and would be happy if you wanted to give me a call. Or write and let me have your number, and I'll call you.
Regards,
Noah

Below there was a mobile phone number and an address. Her son's phone number, her son's address: she couldn't read them without crying. The page – blue pen, small, neat writing – became blotted with her tears, the number and the words smudged and illegible, but it didn't matter because she'd already copied the information into her phone, and she'd written it in her address book as well, in case something happened to her phone.

Noah O'Reilly, she wrote. His name. They'd named her son Noah – and with O'Reilly for a last name, they must have Irish connections.

He lives in Brighton, a hundred or so miles away. He grew up a couple of hours from her. She's been to Brighton often: for several years she's been stocking a boutique there with her clothing and accessories. She never leaves the town without a walk along the prom, and out to the end of the pier. She might have walked past him.

She thinks of her first visit to Brighton, the Christmas she was pregnant with him. The charade it was, the four of them pretending to have a good time when all they were doing was keeping up appearances.

He didn't enclose a photograph. She has no idea what he looks like, if he's tall or short, slender or big-boned. She doesn't know if he takes after her or his father.

She knows nothing about him; his likes, his fears, his hopes, his strengths. She thinks of the twenty-one years that have passed since she gave birth to him, the ache for him that time hasn't dimmed. She thinks of all the birthdays he celebrated without her, all the landmarks – first tooth, first step, first word – that she missed. He went through school without her, went through his childhood and his teens without her.

When his letter arrived she resolved to write back to him. She'd send him her number, let him be the one to make the call. The thought of phoning, of dialling and listening to his ringtone and waiting for him to answer, waiting to hear his voice for the first time, was much too frightening. And he didn't have her number, so he wouldn't know who was calling. She'd take him by surprise if she rang.

But it wouldn't really be a surprise, would it? He knew there was a chance she'd call, he'd be prepared for it. If an unfamiliar number came up he'd know it might be hers. And if she wrote she'd be sentencing herself to days, maybe longer, of waiting for him to ring. Days of uncertainty, and worry that he might have changed his mind, and jumping every time her phone rang, and disappointment every time it wasn't him.

Ring him, Florence said. *What are you waiting for? Haven't you waited long enough? Go on, get it over with.*

Easy for her to say, with her courage. Easy for her, with no son of her own, and no idea what this meant to Caroline.

No, that wasn't fair: Florence of all people knew exactly what this meant. Florence had been there when he'd been taken away, when Caroline's world had turned dark. Florence, as ever, was only trying to help.

So the day after receiving his letter Caroline went upstairs and closed her bedroom door and picked up her phone and selected *Noah* and pressed the call button. All in a rush, before she could change her mind, before she could chicken out. She listened to his phone ringing, eyes closed, heart clenched.

Hello?

It was him.

It was him.

It was him.

She opened her mouth and nothing came out.

Hello?

She felt sick. She tried to speak again, and again she failed.

Caroline? Is that you? An English accent. Of course an English accent.

Yes, she managed, her voice cracking even on that tiny single syllable.

Hi, he said. *It's me. It's Noah.* Warmth in the voice. A smile in the words.

She couldn't speak for the tears that spilt down her face. Her son was on the phone. Her son, on the phone. Speaking to her. She drew in a ragged, noisy breath.

It's OK, he said. *It's OK. I'm glad you rang. I'd like to meet you.*

Me too, she whispered, swiping at her face.

I presume you're still at the same address.

Yes.

I'll come to you, shall I? I'll drive – I can borrow Dad's car.

Dad's: the word jumped out at her. *Yes*, she said. *Yes, come.*

How about Saturday? Would the afternoon be good for you?

Saturday, three days away. Saturday the twelfth, a day after she was supposed to be flying to Italy for a week.

Italy could wait. *Saturday, yes. Anytime in the afternoon.*

Shall I come to the house?

She thought fast. He couldn't come here, not with Florence around. Somewhere quiet, somewhere unobserved, in case she went to pieces like she was doing now. She cast about, came up with nothing. There was no place she could think of in town that wouldn't have people about on Saturday afternoon.

But Florence, if asked, would make herself scarce – and if the day was fine they could sit out the back, with only Big Ears, the rescue cat that had replaced Pip, to witness her making a fool of herself.

Yes, she said. *Come to the house.*

OK. If I get lost I'll call you. I'll aim to be with you around three.

Alright. Saturday. Three days. She wouldn't sleep a wink between this and then.

There was a small pause. Was he still there?

Is it OK if I call you Caroline? he asked.

His voice, saying her name. *Yes*, she said. She had forfeited the right to Mother, or Mum, or anything similar.

Right – see you Saturday then.

Yes.

Looking forward to it.

Yes. Me too. Goodbye.

After hanging up she cried some more before drying her eyes and finding Florence.

I'll go to visit Constance, Florence said. *Haven't seen her in a fortnight.*

Constance would be ninety-six on the eighteenth of October, and had been living for the past three years in a nursing home on the edge of town. When Caroline visited her, once every six weeks or so, Constance called her Dolly – *I think that was her sister's name,* Florence said – and asked how Jeremiah and the children were. But she seemed content, and the place was warm and clean, and the staff pleasant.

That evening Caroline changed her Italian flight, pushed it back to Monday. *Something has come up,* she emailed Matteo. *I'm sorry. I'll see you after the weekend. I'll be there on Monday.*

Carolina, I am sad, he emailed back. *I count the days till Monday. I see you at the airport. Ti amo.*

He didn't know about Noah. She had never been able to tell him that she had a son who was only nine years younger than him.

She got in touch with the businessman in Italy she'd been due to meet on Monday – they were to discuss introducing her stock into his boutiques in Malta – and asked him to reschedule her appointment to later in the week. *A family matter,* she told him, and he didn't question it.

And now it's Friday evening, and time has been crawling since Wednesday, and she won't sleep a wink for the fluttering in her stomach.

She'll see him tomorrow. She can't wait.

Eleanor

ON THE TWELFTH OF SEPTEMBER 2002, on what should have been Beth Fennelly's first birthday but was instead two months after her death, her father took the day off work. He left her mother in bed while he dressed and fed Jacob, their surviving child who wasn't yet two years old, and brought him to his crèche. Eleanor lay unmoving, listening to her phone ringing every few minutes on the bedside table until Gordon eventually reappeared with a breakfast tray on which sat a plate of buttered toast, a large teapot, and a red rose in an eggcup.

Eat, he said, pouring tea into a cup – and she ate toast she didn't want as he answered the phone that had begun to ring again, and told her mother that Eleanor was in the shower.

He waited while she got dressed, and then he brought her out to the car. He took the coast road to Spiddal and parked by the sea. He walked along the beach with her, his arm tucked into hers. He told her he loved her, that he would always love her. He said they'd get through this together, that they had to for Jacob's sake. Eleanor kept her eyes on the horizon and saw the dark humps that were the Aran Islands, and said nothing in return.

Afterwards he brought her to a pub and got her a brandy that went straight to her head. She went to the ladies' toilet and leant her forehead against the wall, trying to quell the dizziness until the brandy reappeared, and was flushed down the toilet.

The following year, on what should have been Beth's second birthday, Gordon dropped Jacob to his crèche and carried on to the restaurant. *I'll stay home*, he'd said, but Eleanor had told him no. By then she'd succeeded in alienating him. By then they had little to say to one another beyond what was strictly necessary. They didn't fight, they just didn't connect any more. Didn't touch, didn't sleep together, didn't share thoughts or feelings.

She got up after he and Jacob had left. She took the white photo album from its home in her wardrobe and brought it downstairs. In the kitchen she drank tea and ate nothing while she drifted back into the past, when Beth was alive and they were happy. She gazed at images of Beth's smiling face, her sturdy little body, the wisps of white-blonde hair, just like Eleanor had had at that age. She fancied she heard the soft babble of her daughter's voice, smelt the soft powdery smell of her. She would be wearing a new birthday dress today. She would be just old enough at two to know that something special was happening.

No Clarence to feed back then, no interruption from the silenced phone in her bag, nothing to disturb her as she travelled slowly through the ten months of Beth's life.

When she got to the end of the album she closed it quietly. And then, without thinking about it, she assembled flour and sugar and butter and eggs, and baked a cake. She took her time with it, creaming the butter and sugar, adding the beaten eggs bit by bit with the sieved flour, stirring and folding carefully until everything was mixed.

When the finished cake had cooled she iced it in white, and piped *Happy Birthday Beth* on the top in wobbly pink.

Then, before the writing had set, she lifted the lid of the kitchen bin and dumped in the entire cake.

Not premeditated, not any of it.

An hour later Jacob was dropped home by Lavina, the neighbour who collected him every day from the crèche along with her own child. *Cake*, he said, as soon as he walked into the kitchen, even though Eleanor had opened all the windows. She shushed him and cooked dinner while he played with his toys. Afterwards she bathed him as usual and put him to bed.

Later that evening Gordon came home from the restaurant and found the cake while he was emptying the bin.

I think, he said, *you should consider counselling. I really think you could do with talking to someone.*

It wasn't the first time he'd suggested it. *No counselling*, she said, and he didn't pursue it.

The following year she made another cake. Jacob was three going on four, and attending the playschool Gordon had found for him. When the cake was finished Eleanor packed it up and deposited it in the litter bin at the end of the road. Again Jacob looked for the cake he could smell when he got home, and again she told him there was no cake.

Gordon didn't comment when he came home later that evening. If he also noted the lingering scent of baking in the kitchen, he gave no sign.

She makes a cake every year, and every cake goes into the public bin. Gordon and Jacob know about them – how can they not? – but they pretend they don't. She imagines Gordon took Jacob aside at some point. *It's just something your mother does*, he would have said, or words to that effect. *Better to ignore it, better to say nothing*. So no remark is ever made about the fact that Eleanor bakes a birthday cake every year for her dead daughter.

They don't know she bins it. Maybe they think she eats it in its entirety.

And now it's the twelfth of September again, and Gordon has left for work, and Jacob has made himself scarce too. *I'm going to Brian's*, he told her after breakfast. *I'll be home for dinner*.

Gordon won't be home till much later than dinner, as usual. He'll be thinking of Beth today too: she saw it in his face at breakfast. He'll have called to the cemetery on his way to the restaurant; he'll have left the bunch of bright pink daisies he always leaves there. She sees them every year when she goes later with her own bouquet.

Jacob never accompanies either of them to the cemetery, not since he kicked up at the age of eight, saying he didn't want Gordon to take him any more. She knows there's not much point in insisting, but it saddens Eleanor.

She crosses to the fridge and takes out a bottle of white wine. Not yet noon – but it's not as if she makes a habit of it. She uncorks it and pours herself a glass. The wine is cold and sharp, the same pale yellow Pinot Grigio that Fennellys offers as its house white. She never likes it until she's got halfway down the glass. She's not a big drinker these days – she probably drank more in her teenage years than she has in all the ones that followed – but she always has a glass on Beth's birthday. She replaces the bottle and assembles her ingredients and makes the cake. When it's in the oven she wipes down the table and gets the photo album.

Beth wasn't planned. They'd wait a year, maybe two, before having a second child; that was the plan. Eleanor would go back to work when Jacob was six months old – but he was just half that when she realised she was pregnant again. Once she'd got over the shock – no birth control infallible – she decided to embrace it. Tiring as it was, she loved being a mother; and could two babies really be all that much harder than one?

Let's have lots, she said to Gordon as they

celebrated the news with lasagne and banoffi pie. *Let's have six altogether, three of each.* She wanted a big, messy, noisy, happy family. She'd give up work to be a stay-at-home mum and wouldn't go back until the last baby was ready for school.

She secretly hoped for a girl this time. Beth she'd call her, after her favourite character in her favourite girls' book – and at two o'clock in the afternoon on the eleventh of September 2001, as news of a terrorist act in New York was beginning to filter through to Ireland, Eleanor had her first contraction.

For the rest of the day and into the small hours of September twelfth, while people were watching in horror as news bulletins showed and reshowed footage of a tiny dark smudge that was a plane full of people making a graceful arc through a perfect blue sky in order to aim itself at a tall silver tower full of other people, Eleanor was otherwise engaged.

She opens the album and looks at her daughter's newborn face, all pink and wizened and bewildered. Born just after four o'clock in the morning, emerging into the delivery room around the time that rescue workers were pulling the second last survivor from the rubble of the Twin Towers. Wrapped in the white blanket Caroline had knitted for her in softest alpaca wool, with its border of tiny yellow daisies. Lying in the arms of her mother, who was sweaty and worn out, and completely content. A boy, and now a girl. The start of their perfect family.

And there is Jacob in his father's arms, a month away from one year old, regarding his baby sister with deep distrust. Wearing an awful navy outfit – polyester top, stretchy bell-bottomed trousers – that someone, she can't remember who, had given him for Christmas, and that she'd forgotten to recycle. Easily known Gordon had dressed him that morning.

But nobody was looking at Jacob that day: they were all focused on the new arrival, who was going to be called Beth Maria Fennelly. Maria after Gordon's mother, because he wanted it.

Eleanor sips wine and turns the page – and there is her daughter asleep in her cot, their first night home from the hospital, as Mum and Dad and all their neighbours were praying that Mrs Lee's son Douglas would be found alive in the carnage. Beth slept through the night from three weeks old, a dream baby compared to Jacob. A small pink rabbit lies by her cheek, a gift from someone – who? Gordon's sister Lynn, she thinks. Lost a few weeks afterwards in a shopping centre, replaced with a pink pig they christened Porky, who was to become Beth's constant companion. Porky, who travelled to France with them less than a year later. Porky, who was found floating –

She cuts off the thought and turns the page. There they are on Beth's christening day a month later, while poor Mrs Lee was still saying novenas, still clutching onto hope that had become frail as a spider's web. There the four of them are, grouped in the porch of the church. There is Beth, magnificent in the Plunkett christening robe that her brother and mother and aunt and grandmother had worn before her. Beth, blue-eyed and pink-cheeked and smiling out from Eleanor's arms, unaware as yet of the trickle of cool water onto her head that is shortly to prompt outraged bawling.

There is Gordon in the charcoal grey pinstripe suit that Eleanor used to love on him. White shirt, a sky blue tie that had been a gift from her. She'd bought all his ties back then. She'd give him one along with his proper present every birthday and Christmas. Now her presents to him, and to Jacob, are gift vouchers or book tokens. Nothing she has to think about, nothing that couldn't equally be given to anyone at all.

She often wonders why he doesn't leave her. God knows she's given him reason enough. He'll be sixty at the end of this month: that's young enough to start again with someone else.

She doesn't want him to leave. The thought of it causes a pain in her that's almost physical. The idea of him with anyone else isn't something she can dwell on – but she can't understand why he stays.

She turns the page and sees a larger group from the same christening day, this time standing outside Fennellys, where they went to eat after the church. Mum stands on the far left of the photo, flatly refusing to be called Granny, wearing a sea-green dress and matching coat, and the kind of fixed smile that makes it plain she'd rather be elsewhere.

Mum never quite managed to hide the fact that Gordon, for all his ambition and success, had been somewhat of a disappointment to her as a son-in-law, bent as she'd been on Eleanor marrying into the D'Arcy family. Poor Mum, her hopes dashed with Andrew's departure.

Funny the way things turn out. Who would have predicted that Eleanor would end up marrying Conor Fennelly's uncle, head chef in the Galway hotel where she'd got her first job after graduating from catering college? Who would have foreseen Conor's success in the art world, his paintings selling regularly for six figures now in the galleries of London and Paris and Milan?

And who would have predicted that Andrew D'Arcy wouldn't yet be married, would be living in Spain now, wifeless and childless and forty since May? Not teaching any more, gave it up after just a few years to study horticulture, of all things. Last Eleanor heard he was planting trees with a group of environmentalists in Granada – much, she bets, to his businessman father's disgust.

Dad is in the christening snap, of course, looking handsome in the navy suit Mum picked out for him. He's holding Beth, and regarding her fondly – intent, no doubt, on spoiling her as much as he'd spoilt his own daughters. Always the soft one, the parent Eleanor and Caroline turned to with a problem, the one they knew would listen without criticism – even if, a lot of the time, Mum would ultimately be called upon to put things right.

Standing beside Dad is Caroline, home from England for the christening. Twenty-five and looking better than she'd ever looked at home. A wrap in swirling greens and blues draped across her shoulders, one of the pieces from her range of knitwear that was beginning to be talked about in England. *Caroline Knits* the name she traded under, her labels designed by up-and-coming artist Conor Fennelly, who was related by marriage to her sister.

Gordon, to the extreme right of the picture, has Jacob in his arms again. Eleanor studies her husband's face. A fortnight away from forty-six then, hair just beginning to recede. At the height of his game at work, the Celtic Tiger alive and kicking in 2001, and Fennellys benefiting from its bounty along with the best of them, crammed with people in business suits and cocktail dresses every night of the week.

Gordon's parents, of course, are absent from the photo, both of them claimed by cancer. His mother died in her fifties, several years before Eleanor and Gordon met; his father went the year before Beth was born, lasting just long enough to meet his brand new grandson.

In his seventies when they were introduced, William Fennelly had always felt more like a grandfather to Eleanor than a father-in-law. Lovely man, though. Always called her Eleanora. *Like Billie Holiday*, he told her. *Real name Eleanora Fagan*. Liked his jazz, William did.

Eleanor is missing from the christening group snap too – she'd been the one who'd taken it, preferring by then to stay on the other side of the camera when she could. She remembers handing

Beth to Dad: *No, I don't mind. I'm sick of being in photos!*

She makes her way slowly through the album, through the ten months of life that Beth had been given. They'd had it all that year, big house, two cars, plenty of money. Times were good, even if Eleanor was sleep-deprived more often than not, and wishing she saw more of her workaholic husband.

The final photo is of Eleanor and the two children on a pretty sun-filled patio that is bordered on one side by a neat row of lavender bushes, on the other by a shoulder-high stone wall over which bright pink bougainvillaea tumbles. Behind them is a pair of white-framed French windows, open just enough to reveal a glimpse of the pale blue tiled floor of the living room.

Eleanor sits in a cast-iron garden chair, Beth on her lap. Jacob stands alongside, leaning into his mother, chubby arms resting on her thigh. Beth wears a little peach sundress and matching bonnet; Jacob is in blue shorts and yellow T-shirt. Eleanor's hair is damp from a recent swim. She's wrapped in a purple sarong, and her smile is bright. All three are barefoot, the tiles beneath them warmed by the sun.

The snap was taken by Gordon, who was standing beside the swimming pool, the feature that had made Eleanor decide to book the villa. Their own private pool – why not? Didn't they deserve a bit of luxury, with Fennellys doing so well? And it was in France, where Gordon's career as a chef had begun: he'd worked his way up to head chef at a restaurant in Cannes, stayed there for almost ten years before returning to Ireland. Surely he'd love the chance to revisit the place.

Or maybe not. He wasn't exactly overjoyed when Eleanor told him she'd booked them into the villa. *You should have checked with me. You know how busy I am.*

But she didn't let it faze her: she knew how to get around him. *Darling, you're a successful restaurateur, you're always busy – but isn't that all the more reason for a break? We hardly ever get away. Your staff sees far more of you than we do. Come on, you know you want to – and it's just for ten days.*

They'd missed out on a honeymoon, too busy getting Fennellys off the ground. Their only holiday, if you could call it that, had been more than two years earlier, a snatched long weekend in Madrid where Eleanor suspects Jacob was conceived. Now, with their second child just a few months away from her first birthday, wasn't it time for another break? Hadn't they waited long enough?

Imagine the food, she said. *Imagine the wine, and the midnight swims in our own pool when the kids are in bed. You can resurrect your French, show me up. I got a D in the Leaving, and I haven't spoken a word of it since.*

In the end, it hadn't taken too much coaxing to win him over. By the time they were on their way to the airport, she'd swear he was looking forward to it as much as she was.

And the villa, when they pulled up outside it in their rental car, was perfect: situated on the outskirts of a charming little market town, clean and simply furnished and full of sunlight, ceiling fans and muslin curtains and cool floor tiles on which pretty pastel rugs were scattered. The bedroom at the top of a narrow staircase had a balcony that overlooked the pool and the little grove of orange trees that lay beyond it; the adjoining bathroom had a bidet, and a small claw-footed bath.

There were sprigs of lavender in an enamel jug on the kitchen table when they arrived – picked, no doubt, from the bushes that flanked the front door – along with a bottle of red wine, a jar of honeycomb and a basket of eggs. The following day they had a visit from Monsieur Clément, the neighbouring farmer and owner of the villa. He brought warm *pain au chocolat* from the small bakery down the road, and showed them the well at the rear of his farmhouse where they could draw spring water, and told them of a nearby vineyard where visitors were welcomed.

The photo had been taken on their third day. Earlier that morning Eleanor had counted four new little freckles on the bridge of Jacob's nose as she'd dabbed sun cream on his face. Day three, everyone blooming in the warmth. Even Gordon was beginning to slow down, lulled by the tranquillity of the place. The night before, he and Eleanor had sat with glasses of wine on the balcony in the heady evening air while their children slept in the room within, and Eleanor had thought, *It doesn't get any better*.

And less than twenty-four hours later, on the fifth of July, Beth Maria Fennelly drowned. Beth was taken from them in the middle of a perfect July afternoon. She'd woken from her nap on a little yellow blanket in the living room and crawled – how fast she could crawl! – out onto the patio and over to the swimming pool and tumbled in, while Eleanor was upstairs and Gordon had turned his back to take a phone call.

In less than a minute Beth's tiny lungs had filled with chlorinated water as her mother applied a plaster to the finger she'd cut on a page of her magazine, and her brother, not yet two, rolled a toy truck across the kitchen tiles, and her father listened to the manager of Fennellys telling him of a visit they'd had from a well-known restaurant critic, and the glowing report that had followed it.

Beth was no more. Beth had left the world ten months after she'd entered it. Beth's tiny body was shipped home in a white coffin and laid in the ground in a new grave, because Gordon's first wife was in the grave he already had, and Eleanor wasn't giving Beth to her.

People came to the funeral. People hugged her and shook her limp hand and told her they were so terribly sorry, and she sleepwalked through it all, and she kept waiting to wake up. Andrew D'Arcy came, and Jasper and Sophie came, and her old friend Tina. Caroline came from England with Florence, who was just a small, wide, pale-haired woman in a man's coat that smelt of tobacco.

My heart goes out to you, Florence said. *Nobody should have to bear this* – but Eleanor had to bear it. She had to bear the unbearable.

Angela Moloney, who lives around the corner, was born the same week as Beth: Eleanor had become acquainted with Angela's mother Ruth at their antenatal classes. Angela, fair-haired, smiling Angela, Irish-dancer Angela, image-of-her-mother Angela, fourteen-years-old-today Angela, is Eleanor's painful reminder of all she was denied.

The curious thing, the peculiar thing, the inexplicable thing, is that the day they lost Beth is not as tough as today: Eleanor simply blots out its significance when it comes around. She refuses to acknowledge the day Beth was taken from them, only the one when she came to them.

On the fifth of July each year she attacks the house. All day long she beats the living daylights out of rugs, and gets down on her knees to wipe dust from skirting boards. She squeegees the windows she can reach, and polishes mirrors until they gleam, and scrubs every inch of the kitchen and bathroom floors till the sweat runs off her. She vacuums carpets and washes fingerprints from doors and knobs. She scours toilets, she cleans out the fridge with bicarbonate of soda. She pummels the day until it's gone.

The cake is done: she waits for it to cool. She closes the album and returns it to its place in the wardrobe. She has another half-glass of wine. And when the cake is iced, when it has been inscribed with the birthday greeting, it goes the way of all the other cakes.

And it's not until much later, after she's been to the cemetery with her flowers, after Jacob has returned and their usual near-silent dinner has been eaten, after Eleanor has had a bath and washed her hair, after she's watched the news on television and read her book for an hour, it's not until almost midnight, when she's on the point of falling asleep, that it hits her.

Caroline never phoned. For the first time, she'd forgotten to ring on Beth's birthday.

Caroline

FLORENCE, AS PROMISED, IS TAKING HER leave in the brown hatchback, the replacement for the ancient grey van that eventually went beyond all attempts to revive it.

'You'll be fine,' she says. 'Just be yourself, and tell the truth, that's all you have to do – and if he's mean to you, he'll have me to answer to.'

He won't be mean: Caroline knows that from the phone call. After Florence drives off she paces the floor in the sitting room. She's lit a fire although the day doesn't really warrant it – warm and drizzly, so the garden is out – and she's assembled tea things on a tray in the kitchen. Does he drink tea?

She's said nothing to Eleanor, or her parents. She'll tell them: he won't be kept a secret from them. But not yet, not until she meets him herself.

She's made him a scarf: it was all she could think of, not knowing his size for anything else. She has no idea if the turquoise colour she chose will suit his skin tone.

At half past two she thinks, *He's on his way. He's somewhere between Brighton and here. He's driving to meet his birth mother for the first time.* Everything is fluttering inside her at the thought of seeing his face, hearing his voice properly. Will they shake hands? Will they hug? She is sick with apprehension. What if they have nothing in common? What if things are stilted between them? What if she bores him?

At three o'clock she hears the little blue cuckoo do his best from inside his house on the kitchen wall. The clock was a housewarming gift from clockmaker neighbour Frankie when Florence took possession of the cottage, well over forty years ago. It still keeps pretty near perfect time, but the mechanism that propelled the bird out each hour has died, and his song, still valiantly attempted, is little more these days than a series of little clicks.

At ten past three a maroon car drives slowly past the house. A minute later it reappears, having turned at the end of the cul-de-sac. It pulls up and a man gets out. Caroline watches from behind Florence's net curtains, heart pounding beneath hands she's pressed to her chest.

On the tall side. Blond hair, cut short. Features too far away yet to make out. Black leather jacket, grey jeans, a satchel of some kind hanging from a shoulder. He closes the car door and stands looking at the house as he pockets the keys: she takes a step back. He puts a hand on the small gate and pushes it open. He walks up the path: is he limping ever so slightly?

The doorbell rings. Even though she's expecting it, it makes her jump. She walks on shaky legs into the hall. He's here. They are about to have their first face-to-face conversation.

She opens the door.

'Hello,' he says. 'I'm Noah.'

His smile is tentative. He has Andrew D'Arcy's dark eyes. He's exactly her height.

'Hello,' she whispers.

He opens his arms then. 'Oh—' she says, and walks into them. She cries. Of course she cries. He cries too; she feels it in the quiver of his breathing. She clings to him in the narrow hallway. Her son is here. He's here. At last he's here.

Eventually they draw apart, and she leads him into the overheated sitting room, scrubbing at her eyes with a tissue, struggling to regain her composure. He'll think she can do nothing but cry.

She tells him as much as she's able. He sits in Florence's chair and doesn't interrupt.

'I was young and very innocent. I was in awe of your father, who was handsome, and a successful businessman. He was a lot older than me, and he was married. I used to babysit for him and his second wife. He was a friend of the family.'

She is as honest as she can be, but she softens parts, for his sake. She makes no mention of rape, lets him believe the act was consensual.

'He wasn't helpful when I told him I was pregnant. He … didn't want to have anything to do with you.' She leaves out the money that was handed over, the envelope of cash she was given to make her baby go away.

'My mother ... was embarrassed to tell people what had happened, so I came to England. I stayed here until you were born, and they told everyone at home that I was sick, and I was gone away for treatment. It was ... easier for everyone that way.'

She doesn't add that Mum wanted the abortion, too, that he wouldn't exist if his grandmother had had her way.

She tells him about Eleanor. 'She lives in Galway. They own a restaurant, and they have a son, Jacob, your cousin. He's nearly fifteen.'

As she speaks she keeps her eyes on him; she feasts on him; she wants to inhale everything she can about him.

Nose large, mouth on the generous side, teeth good. A suggestion of red in the light hair. Skin dotted with freckles, and pale like hers. She bets he takes forever to get a tan, like she does. She rejoices in their similarities. Dark lashes fringe the eyes, which are easily his best feature. His face, she decides, has character. It's a face that would stay with you, even after a short encounter. Or maybe she thinks this because she's his mother.

His mother. It's still sinking in.

She fancies she sees a touch of her father about him, around the mouth and chin. There's definitely a look of the Plunketts there, even if the D'Arcys gave him the eyes.

She finishes her account and falls silent, and

listens through the half-open door to the ponderous tock of the grandfather clock with its out-of-kilter chime that still sits in Florence's hall.

'I wanted to keep you,' she says, pressing fingernails into her palms to keep from crying all over him again. 'I wanted that more than anything, but I let them take you. I regretted it as soon as it was done. I've regretted it ever since. I hope you believe me.'

He smiles. His smile is big and warm and beautiful. 'I do believe you,' he says. 'It must have been very hard for you. You were young, you were trying to do what was best for me. I understand that, honestly.'

Every word is balm poured onto her old wounds.

He was adopted, he tells her, by a couple in their thirties. 'Dad's a bus driver, Mum works in a crèche. I have two sisters and a brother, all adopted. I was lucky. I had a great upbringing. We weren't that well off, but we were happy, and we had all we needed. Dad gets deals on the buses, so we took lots of day trips.'

She feels a stab of jealousy towards the strangers who gave him such a great upbringing. She's aware of how horribly mean-spirited this is – they looked after him, they were good to him: they deserve her thanks, not her resentment – but she mourns the years she missed out on, the birthdays and the Christmases, the sports days and the family outings, the disappointments and the celebrations. His head is filled with memories in which she played no part at all.

No, she mustn't think like that. She must look to the future now. They must make their own memories.

He's at college, he says, in his third year. 'I want to be a teacher: my subjects are history, maths and computer studies.'

History, her old love. Another bit of her coming out in him.

He has a girlfriend, he tells her, a new and delightful bashfulness entering his voice. 'Aideen, her parents are Irish. She's studying politics. She's very musical – she plays the piano in the college orchestra.'

They talk and they talk and they talk. The tea she made at some stage grows cold as little by little he makes himself known to her.

He doesn't have a sweet tooth. He enjoys all types of sport. He broke a leg aged five, cracked a couple of ribs in rugby training a few weeks ago: the small lean to the right she noticed as he walked up the path.

He isn't much of a cook, but he can make bread. His favourite cuisine is Indian; he dislikes all types of seafood. He's been to France, Italy and Portugal on holiday. He passed his driving test at seventeen. He's allergic to cats, loves dogs. He speaks fairly good French and very bad Spanish.

He's brought photographs, lots of them. She sees him as a baby in his adoptive mother's arms, as a toddler, as a little uniformed schoolboy. She sees him building sandcastles, and wailing on Santa's knee, and crowded onto a couch with his siblings. She sees him with an arm around his girlfriend, who's wearing a long pink dress: 'We were at her brother's wedding.'

He gives her a gift, a stack of what look like tea mallows in a cellophane box tied with a red ribbon on which 'Choccywoccydoodah' is stamped in gold lettering. 'They're called plumpies,' he tells her. 'My sisters thought you might like them. They're from a chocolate shop that's a Brighton institution.'

She tells him of the boutique on Brighton's Middle Street that stocks her wraps. 'I know it,' he says. 'My sisters often go there. The chocolate shop is at the far end of that street.'

He's also brought a letter from the woman who's been his mother for twenty-one years.

My dear Caroline
I want you to know that Noah has been a precious addition to our lives, and we felt blessed to have had him growing up in our house. He was a lovely boy who never gave us a minute of trouble, and he's grown into a wonderful man. I'm delighted that he chose to meet you, and I sincerely hope it all works out for both of you.
Best regards
Sheila

They're still talking at six o'clock. No sign yet of Florence, who surely guessed that lots of time would be needed.

'Is my father still alive?' he asks, as he eventually gets up to leave.

'Yes.' Her heart sinks. She was hoping he wouldn't ask, which was stupid. Of course he was going to ask.

'I know you said he didn't want to have anything to do with me, but could I ... get in touch with him anyway? Would that be OK?'

She's been dreading it. 'Let me contact him,' she says. 'Let me see if he'll agree to meet you. I'll go to Ireland. I'd rather do it in person.'

She quails at the thought of confronting Jasper, despite her resolution to stand up to him. Their paths have crossed briefly over the years – at her parents' silver wedding anniversary party, at a neighbours' Christmas drinks do some years later, in the street occasionally in her home town – but they've never exchanged more than a few words. A proper one-to-one encounter is a dreadful prospect, but for Noah's sake it will have to be done.

'I'll go as soon as I can,' she promises, 'but it mightn't be for a while. I'm going to Italy on business next week, and I have a lot on after that until the end of the month.'

She'll wait till she goes home to give her parents the news: it will keep till then. She wonders if her mother will agree to meet him, or if she'll disown her first-born grandson, the one she never wanted.

Before he leaves she presents him with the scarf. He thanks her and hugs her goodbye. 'I'm so glad we did this,' he says.

Tears threaten again. 'Me too.'

'I'll phone you tomorrow. We'll keep in touch, get to know one another. And I'll see you again soon. I want you to meet Aideen. Wait till she hears you're a fashion designer.'

She stands at the gate and waves as he drives away. *This is what happiness feels like*, she thinks, as his car moves off. *This is what pure happiness feels like.* All the good moments in her life – being accepted for a fashion design course at a Cardiff college, graduating with honours and moving back in with Florence, getting her first job at a clothing factory in Oxford, starting out on her own and making a success of it, meeting and falling for Matteo – all the good times were nothing compared to this. She's filled with joy; it spills out of her.

Matteo comes close though, Matteo who doesn't know Noah exists. In two days she'll see him: the thought delights her as it always does, but mixed now with the delight is uncertainty. She should have told him about Noah at the start, allowed him to walk away then if he chose: five years later, it has become something she kept from him.

But is it really necessary to tell either of them about the other? She and Matteo belong in Italy, and Noah is here in England. There's no reason why the two ever have to meet, is there? She'll just keep them separate, like she's always kept Matteo separate from her life over here.

She closes the gate. She'll bake a cake in

celebration of Noah: she'll bake a caraway-seed cake, the first one Florence taught her.

She returns to the house, her step light – and it's not until the following morning that she remembers Beth's birthday of the day before, and the phone call she forgot to make.

Eleanor

'I WAS SURPRISED,' SHE SAYS, TAKING THE
chair he indicates, 'to get a letter from you so early
on in the term. Nothing wrong, I hope?'

'Not as such,' he replies, in the soothing voice she
guesses he saves for just these occasions. She nods,
although she has no idea what 'as such' means.
Something is either wrong or it isn't.

The last time she sat in a principal's office was
over twenty years ago, in response to one of Sister
Carmody's regular summonses. This is different,
though: despite her being the innocent party, she
feels somehow more intimidated. She's unsure how
she should be around this prematurely balding man
– he's younger than her, she suspects – whose office
smells of eucalyptus, and who rests his hands on a
cardboard file that has her son's name on it.

This is her first time in the school, her first
encounter with its principal. He might not have been
impressed that she left the enrolment to Gordon,

that she didn't want to check out the school her son would be attending. He might think she isn't much of a mother.

'Would you care for tea or coffee, Mrs, uh, Fennelly?'

She says no, stifling her impatience. Why doesn't he just get on with it, let her know why he's called her in? The chair is too tight: she's wedged into it. Mentally she's uncomfortable too, tightly coiled against whatever the principal is about to tell her. She wishes she'd worn something looser: the navy skirt seemed the most suitable of what was in her wardrobe, but the waistband is digging into her. Why didn't she just leave this to Gordon?

There's a tap on the door. 'Come in,' he calls, and a young woman enters. Dark, compact, black trouser suit, cream shirt. Arm outstretched as she approaches, looking for Eleanor's hand.

'I asked Miss Collopy to attend,' the principal says. 'She is to be Jacob's form teacher this year. The other teachers report any concerns to her.'

Form teacher? She looks about nineteen. She crushes Eleanor's hand. 'Glad to meet you, Mrs Fennelly.' She slips into the neighbouring chair, fits in easily. 'We thought, Mr Murray and I, that we'd catch this early, nip it in the bud.'

How long before one of them gets to the point? The possibilities – drink, smoking, drugs – jab at Eleanor. Let it not be drugs: the others they could deal with. Maybe he's being bullied, the new boy made a target. That happens, doesn't it?

The principal begins speaking again. Have they rehearsed this? 'Three of Jacob's teachers contacted Miss Collopy with their concerns, so she checked with the others.'

He glances at the form teacher, gives her a tiny nod. *Your turn.* Eleanor's palms prickle: here it comes.

'It would appear, Mrs Fennelly,' the teacher says, 'that Jacob has not handed up any homework assignments so far, for any of his subjects.'

She stops. Eleanor waits, but nothing more comes. She looks at the principal. That's it? He hasn't done his homework?

The silence stretches. She's clearly expected to say something. She searches for the right response. 'Well, er, that's … not good. Would he have had … much homework in the first couple of weeks?' No, wrong. Not the point. 'I – his father and I will certainly have a word with him about that. We'll make sure it doesn't happen again.'

For God's sake – a bit of homework not handed in? His first fortnight in the school? They're right, she supposes, to catch it early – but would a phone call not have done? For all they know, she could have had to get time off from work.

'It's early days, of course,' the principal says in the same smooth tones. 'He's new to the school, he's just settling in – and I'm sure he'll be fine. But we thought it best to call you in at this stage, considering his Junior Cert is ahead of him this year.'

'I had a word with him on Friday.' The form

teacher again, whose name Eleanor has managed to forget. Cotter? Connolly? 'We had a good chat, he really opened up to me – and of course, we have every sympathy.'

That's unexpected. 'Sympathy?'

'He told us what happened, Mrs Fennelly. The swimming pool accident. Very sad.'

'He *told* you?'

Eleanor is astounded. He talked about Beth to her? He spoke to a near stranger about Beth? He hasn't mentioned his sister in years. None of them has.

Jacob looked for her, of course, after it happened. He asked where she was, often. He wasn't yet two: what did you tell a child that young? *She's gone to be an angel*, Gordon said, which surely made no sense at all to him, but it was the best they could do.

'It must have been terrible,' the form teacher goes on, 'to lose his mother so suddenly.'

Eleanor blinks. 'Pardon?'

For the first time, the woman's composure slips. A faint flush seeps into her face. 'I hope I'm not speaking out of turn, Mrs Fennelly – I know it can't be easy for you either.'

She picked it up wrong from him, that's what must have happened. He didn't make it clear that Beth was his sister, not his mother.

'Marrying a man with a teenage son, I mean. Jacob is at a tricky age, isn't he? It's understandable if there's a little ... tension at first. And maybe this is Jacob's way of showing it.'

What?

'Of course we'll make what allowances we can, under the circumstances, but we thought you and Mr Fennelly would want to know all the same.'

She talks on, but Eleanor has stopped listening.

There was no misunderstanding. He didn't tell them about Beth.

He told them his mother drowned in a swimming pool.

They think Eleanor is his stepmother – a recently acquired one, by the sound of it.

She doesn't correct them: how would that make him look? She sits and nods as they drone on about the school policy and pressure of exams and student care and parental involvement. Eventually she's allowed to lever herself from the chair.

'You could wait for him,' the principal says. 'He'll be finished in ten minutes.'

She can't. 'I can't,' she says. 'I have an appointment.'

She doesn't care if they believe her. She catches the look they exchange. *Poor Jacob*, the look says, *saddled with a new stepmother who won't wait ten minutes for him.*

'Miss Collopy will see you to the lobby,' he says – but Eleanor says no, no need, she can find her own way. She practically runs down the corridor in her haste to escape before the classroom doors open and the students begin to stream out.

She drives home, her thoughts whirling. He

disowned her. He told them she's not his mother. Why on earth would he do that? She has to talk to him – she can't possibly let this go.

When she's almost home she decides to go instead to Fennellys. She'll tell Gordon, see what he thinks. She turns the car around and drives across the bridge in thickening traffic. As she nears the restaurant she changes her mind again – Gordon will be getting ready for the evening: he won't have time to talk to her. She points the car towards home once more.

She parks in the driveway, looks towards the house. Is he home yet? Ten to four: he might be.

She stands in the hall and listens. No sound, no sense that he's there. She opens the kitchen door: the room is empty. She climbs the stairs and knocks on his door: no response. She returns to the kitchen and sits at the table. A minute later she gets up and paces the floor. She goes out to the hall, opens the front door, closes it again. She wanders around the kitchen until she hears his key in the lock, and then she flies back into the hall.

The door opens. His eyebrows lift a little at the sight of her, but he makes no comment.

'Jacob, I need to talk to you,' she says, keeping her voice calm and low. 'We need to have a chat.'

He drops his bag with a thud, shrugs off his jacket. 'What about?' His face bland, giving nothing away.

'Will you come into the kitchen?'

He drapes his jacket on the banister and follows her silently. *Please let this come out right*, she thinks. *Let this not fall apart.*

She sits – but he makes for the fridge. 'Jacob, can you wait to do that?'

'I'm hungry.' He takes out cheese and mayonnaise, gets bread from the bin, lifts the lid of the butter dish.

She tamps down irritation. 'Jacob, you know I was at the school today.'

He makes no response. He spreads butter, cuts cheese.

'Mrs Collopy told me—'

'Miss.'

She stops.

'It's Miss,' he repeats, his back to her. 'Miss Collopy.'

She takes a breath in, lets it out. 'Jacob,' she says, 'look, I know—' She breaks off. This is impossible.

He turns then, the knife still in his hand. For the first time in a long time, he looks right at her. The intensity of his stare unnerves her. Maybe, she thinks, she should be doing this with Gordon. Maybe it was a mistake to confront him on her own.

Too late for that now. 'Please,' she says, 'sit down, love. I can't talk to you like this.'

A beat passes. She waits, tensed. He drops the knife with a clatter and takes the chair across from hers. He leans back, folds his arms.

'Look,' she says, 'this isn't about you not doing homework, although I am concerned about that—'

'Are you?' Quietly, eyes still locked with hers.

He's looking at her, but it feels rather as if he's looking *through* her.

'Jacob, of *course* I am. If you're having problems—'

'I should bring them to you?' No emotion that she can discern.

'Yes, of course you should.' But even to her, the words don't ring true. When did he last confide in her? When did he ever look for her help? Why would he do it now?

Ask him. Ask him the question that's tormenting you.

She takes another breath, and plunges in. 'Jacob, why did you tell that woman – why did you lie to her about me? I don't understand why you'd say a thing like that.'

He shrugs. His gaze shifts an inch to the right, and comes back. 'I didn't think it would bother you,' he says.

She regards him in bewilderment. 'You didn't think it would *bother* me? How can you say that? How can you think that?'

'Because you don't feel like my mother,' he says, more forcefully. 'You've *never* felt like my mother, ever.'

She's horrified. 'Jacob, don't say—'

'You wished it was me, didn't you?' Louder, the colour darkening suddenly in his face. 'You were sorry it wasn't me, weren't you?'

She flinches. The words feel like a slap. 'What? No, of *course* not! How can you—'

'I used to wish it was me too. I used to dream about dying – I knew you wanted me out of the way.

I would have done it too, only I hadn't the guts.' Glaring at her, daring her to deny the charges.

She begins to cry. 'Jacob, don't *say* that, please don't say—'

'Why not?' he shoots back. 'It's the truth. It's how I feel, how I've *always* felt.'

'How could you *ever* think I wanted that?'

'Because you were never here, not really. You were here, but you weren't with me. You were with *her*.' The words flung out, hitting her, hurting her. 'You were *always* with her. You may as well not be my mother.'

She looks at him through tears. His face is blurred, but there's no mistaking his anger, his unhappiness. He's right. He's completely right. She turned her back on him when it happened, unable to see beyond her grief, unable to function in the face of her unconscionable heartbreak. She left Jacob to Caroline, and then to Gordon, and then to a crèche, and then a playschool. She left him to whoever would have him, still floundering around in her sorrow.

She missed his second birthday, three months after Beth's death. *I'm not doing a party*, she said to Gordon. *You can't possibly expect me to do that.*

You won't have to – I've asked Sarah to organise it. Sarah was a pastry chef at the restaurant. *You won't have to do anything, just be there.*

But even that was beyond her. She couldn't face the people who were coming, her parents and Caroline and Gordon's sister. She couldn't pretend to be happy, even for a single afternoon. An hour before Sarah was due to arrive, while Jacob was still at the crèche – Gordon was to bring him home – Eleanor slipped from the house and drove away. She spent the afternoon in a cinema, her gaze fixed on the screen but her mind empty, her phone vibrating regularly in her pocket.

It wasn't fair to Jacob, was all Gordon said when she returned – house emptied of guests, paper plates stacked on the draining board, wrapping paper folded on the couch, Jacob playing with his new Bob the Builder digger – but it was enough for her to move her things into the spare room. That night she lay in the dark in the unfamiliar bed and yearned for her dead daughter. She was twenty-five and her life was over. She'd lost one child and had lost the knack of loving the other.

She abandoned him when Beth died – she attended, silent and unsmiling, to his needs when he was brought back in the afternoons from the crèche, she put him to bed without a story – and by the time she felt able to take him back, he was gone too far for her to reach. For thirteen years they've been mother and son in name only, connecting on the surface but nowhere else.

She wants to embrace him, to pull him from the chair and lay her head on his shoulder and beg for his forgiveness – but she stays put, imagining his recoil.

'I'm sorry,' she says eventually, wiping a sleeve across her face. 'I messed up, I know I did. Losing a child was so hard ... I just went to pieces. I was too sad to cope with you for a while – but I never once wished it had been you. Never, ever.'

He says nothing. His eyes still glitter with what looks like rage.

'You must never think that,' she insists. 'I know I don't show it, but you mean the world to me, Jacob. I couldn't bear it if anything happened to you – you *must* believe me.'

'How can I? You still make her a birthday cake every year. You did it on Saturday. When did you ever make one for me? Mine comes from Fennellys. From Dad.'

It's true. She has no defence, there's nothing she can say – but she tries anyway. 'Things changed after Beth. Nothing was the same. The first year, Dad arranged your party through the restaurant, and ... it just became a habit for them to do the cake. It wasn't something I did deliberately.'

She stops, hearing it for the half-baked explanation that it is.

'I'm sorry,' she says again. Useless word, not half enough for him.

He gets to his feet. He looks down at her, and she waits for him to speak. She half rises, aching again to hold him – but he turns and leaves the room. She listens to him going upstairs; stomping up, not bounding like he usually does. His angry words resonate in her head.

I used to dream about dying. I would have done it, only

I hadn't the guts. What if he'd had the guts? What if he'd done it? It's unthinkable. She might have lost both her children.

He's right. She may as well not be his mother. She's failed utterly. How could she have turned her back on him, even in her terrible grief? How could she have allowed it to happen?

His half-made sandwich sits on the worktop like a reproach. She reaches for her phone. Who can she call? Who can she talk to? Not Gordon: twenty past six, he'll be up to his eyes. Not Caroline: she's in Italy. There's no friend she can call on – after Beth her friends became people to avoid, with their tentative pitying smiles, their useless suggestions of a walk, a bath, a massage. She shut herself away from them all, and one by one they gave up trying to get through.

She can't call her parents. Dad wouldn't know what to say; Mum would try to take over, like she always does, and end up making everything worse. A few months after Beth's death, when Eleanor had begun piling on the weight again, Mum arrived with cartons of plain yogurt and boxes of crispbread. *I know you're hurting*, she said, *but letting yourself go won't help.*

She went through the kitchen, throwing out Eleanor's stashes of peanuts and biscuits and chocolate, dumping the ready meals that were piled high in the freezer, and the tubs of ice-cream that were stacked behind them. *You're a qualified chef*, she said. *Start cooking healthy meals again for you and Jacob. And go back to work: moping around the house is doing you no good.*

The minute she was gone Eleanor salvaged what she could from the bin, poured the yogurts down the sink and fed the crispbread to next door's dog, who'd eat anything. That night she and Jacob ate fish fingers and instant mash for dinner, and afterwards she opened a family pack of Mikado and gave him two, and worked her way through the rest when she'd put him to bed.

No, she'd say nothing to Mum.

You should think about talking to someone, her doctor said a few weeks after Beth, when she sat hunched in his office, waiting for him to scribble on his pad again, to repeat her prescription for the Valium that rubbed the edges off her pain. *Pills are not a long-term solution*, he told her. *They won't help you to heal. I can recommend a counsellor –* but she couldn't bear the idea of discussing Beth with a stranger, couldn't bear someone digging about inside her, yanking out her secrets and resentments and regrets in an effort to help her 'get over' Beth and 'move on' – the very phrases made her shudder. She didn't want to move on: moving on meant leaving Beth behind, and no way was she doing that. She was never doing that.

Gordon said it too, after Jacob's missed birthday, after she'd moved out of his bed. *You need help*, he said. *We both do –* but still she resisted, afraid of what opening up, what talking about Beth might do to her, so for several weeks he went alone to a grief counsellor, where presumably he was told how to handle a wife who refused to look for help, a wife who had locked herself away and lost the key.

She lays her phone aside. What now? Where does she go from here? What does she do with her fractured going-nowhere life, her falling-apart family?

She has no idea.

Caroline

THEY MET IN JULY 2001, WHEN SHE WAS twenty-five and he was just fifteen. She was at a trade-only wool fair in Florence: she'd persuaded her boss at the knitwear factory in Oxford to let her go. She'd been dying to check out Pitti Filati since she'd heard about it from her work colleagues: an annual three-day knitting-yarn extravaganza, showcasing the best producers and suppliers in the industry. Already beginning to think about starting her own range of designer knitwear, Caroline was hungry to investigate, to seek out possible wool sources for the future.

The fair was like the biggest wool shop in the world, thousands of square metres of warehousing devoted exclusively to the knitwear fashion industry. She spent the three days prowling among the stalls of yarn collections, running a hand over the hanging rails of worked-up samples, leafing through innumerable folders of colour swatches. She noted brand names and photographed the samples; she collected business cards from the various dealers and tried to look like she knew what she was doing.

Around her, international buyers and designers were networking; everyone seemed acquainted with everyone else. Abandoned by her Dutch colleague Roos, who was busy doing her own networking, Caroline listened to snatches of the many languages being spoken around her. She watched the handshakes and embraces, and did her best to take it all in.

Can I 'elp you?

She turned. He stood behind a nearby stall. Olive-skinned, straight light brown hair that touched his shoulders, black T-shirt and dark green jeans. An air of easy confidence about him, for all his youth.

You want some 'elp? he repeated.

She must seem very much the amateur. *It's my first time, I'm just … looking around. Taking everything in.*

You are English?

Irish – but I work in England. Her gaze wandered over the array of wools set out before him. *These are beautiful. Are they yours?* He was surely too young to be in the business.

He shook his head. *I 'elp my mamma and 'er friends. They make the wools together. They are group, in Italian it is* cooperativa.

A co-operative.

Sì.

All women?

Sì. His glance flicked over her dress. *You are designer?*

She smiled: the novelty of her title hadn't yet waned. *I am. I work for a company now, but I want to design for myself.*

A women's co-operative sounded interesting: she took the small cream card he offered. Della Donna Lana Cooperativa, she read, and beneath it Nina Piccolo, and contact details.

Nina is my mamma, the boy said, indicating a low-sized blonde woman in conversation with a nearby stallholder. *We live in Napoli, to the south. Is near Amalfi coast.*

She knew exactly where Napoli was. *You have a brochure?*

He produced a small leaflet, far humbler than some of the glossy ones she'd already collected. *The wool they 'ave is not a lot, but is good quality and not so expensive.*

Thank you. She tucked it away with the rest, and bade him goodbye. They hadn't even exchanged names. Once he was out of sight she forgot about him – but towards the end of that year, when she was starting to approach boutiques with samples of her work, she emailed the address on the cream card and got a reply from Nina that included an invitation to visit the co-operative in Naples.

In the spring, when she'd secured a few sale or return deals, she took up the offer – and that was the start of a love affair with Italy, and the beginning of a business relationship and a friendship with the co-operative women that was to endure to the present day.

She and Matteo were to take a little longer to get together.

She adored everything about Italy. The honesty of its food, the warmth of its people, the musicality of its language, the landscape that rivalled Ireland's best, the history that oozed from every building, every fountain and statue. The drama and passion of Italian opera invariably reduced her to tears.

Later that year she took a deep breath and handed in her notice at the factory. She officially launched her own business, working out of Florence's house. She began to attract orders from shops and from individuals. She travelled to Italy for a few days in the autumn to renew her acquaintance with the co-op members, and to place new orders. She stayed in the same small hotel that Nina had arranged for her first visit, not far from the family home she shared with her husband Giacomo and son Matteo.

Caroline stayed three nights, and dined in a different co-operative house each night. At Nina's she ate fettuccine tossed in a pungent Gorgonzola sauce; at Patrizia's it was a crispy-based pizza topped with creamy *burrata* cheese and scattered with cherry tomatoes, basil, and rocket; Ava served up peppery bean soup accompanied by a focaccia loaf whose alternate dimples held olives and cubes of pancetta.

The trips to Naples became a regular occurrence, a few days every three months or so. Each time

Caroline stayed at the same hotel; each time her friends at the co-operative took it in turns to feed her. Sometimes Matteo was there when she ate at Nina and Giacomo's, other times he was absent. She enjoyed his company when he joined them – he was amusing, and his English was better than his parents' – but she wasn't bothered if he was missing. For the first few years he was Nina's son, no more.

And then, when she was in her early thirties, and he was approaching his mid-twenties, things began slowly to change.

Eyes somewhere between green and blue, teeth pleasingly white against his olive skin. The easy grace of a dancer about him, in the hand gestures that accompanied his speech, in his relaxed pose, whether sitting or standing, in the way he moved his head. Hair the colour of honey, several shades lighter in the summer.

She became aware of something tripping inside her when their eyes met. His lazy grin made her feel happy. She caught herself thinking about him when he wasn't there, making a special effort to look good when she was due at Nina's for dinner. Hoping he'd be there, disappointed when he wasn't.

She had a crush. It was ridiculous. He probably had a girlfriend. He probably had several. He was far too young for her. She was much too old for him. He looked on her as his mother's friend. She had borne a son who was just nine years his junior. They lived in different countries.

And yet there he was, floating around in her head every time she let her guard down. Shame that the first man to seriously catch her attention was Matteo Piccolo, attractive and charming and utterly out of the question.

She tried to displace him, tried to find someone more realistic to concentrate on. She arranged to meet her old colleagues from the knitwear factory in the evenings; they went to pubs and she fell into conversation with others. She was invited to lunch, or to dinner, and she accepted the invitations.

Naturally, Florence was delighted. *You see? Just a matter of time. You were a late starter, that's all.*

But none of the men worked out, none lasted beyond a couple of dates. Caroline turned them off, she knew she did, with the lack of interest she couldn't hide. And every time she said goodbye or goodnight to one of them, inventing excuses to avoid another meeting – too busy with work, getting over a broken relationship – Matteo would reappear in her head, mouth turned up in that irresistible grin. *See?* he'd say. *I'm still here.* There was no getting rid of him.

She found herself increasing her trips to Naples, booking flights every six or seven weeks. She told herself she needed to check out new colours, to touch base with the women, to improve her fledgling Italian. She knew it was pathetic, hankering after someone so much younger, but she told herself there was no harm in it. She had a crush: so what? The anticipation of seeing him added spice to the trips. It made her heart patter a little faster each time he materialised.

He always seemed pleased to see her. He called her Carolina, like the rest of them, and kissed her on both cheeks when they met or parted. He asked her how business was, and spoke in Italian with her, and smiled, not unkindly, at her efforts to respond.

Sometimes he showed up at his parents' house with a girl in tow – not always the same one – helmets under both their arms for the motorbike he drove. When he didn't appear, Caroline imagined him out with one of the girls, eating or drinking or dancing, and tried not to feel crushed.

And then it was September 2010, and Nina and Giacomo were throwing a twenty-fifth party for their only son, and Caroline was invited.

You must come, Nina said in an email. *It will be very good night, lots of delicious Italian foods, and dancing too. We will be very happy that you come.*

She was busy. Her designs had found favour with several boutiques throughout England. In addition, she was getting a steady number of private commissions that kept her occupied in between producing stock for the shops. There were developments at home too: they'd reconfigured Florence's house – now Caroline lived upstairs, with a kitchenette and an electronic knitting machine occupying the room that used to be Florence's.

But she was tempted by the invitation – and it was time she revisited Naples: she needed to prepare for the spring season. Yes, she replied, she'd be delighted to come – and what would Nina suggest she bring as a birthday gift?

One of your beautiful scarves, of course, Nina replied, so Caroline chose an alpaca, lambswool and silk blend in a chocolate brown shade to complement his olive skin. The day before the party she flew to Naples with a mauve and cream dress and a new haircut, already regretting her choice of colour for the scarf. It was too dark, he'd prefer something brighter. He'd never wear it.

He wore it. He unfolded the tissue paper she'd put around it, he lifted it out and pressed it to his face. He put it on and threw one end of it over his left shoulder.

Grazie, *Carolina,* he said, kissing her on both cheeks, his lips warm and soft on her skin. *It is beautiful.* He caught one of her hands and raised it to his lips to kiss it too. *Thank you.* He held her gaze until she looked away, flustered.

The party was held in their small back garden, which was rich with the scent of the jasmine that climbed up and over the entire end wall of the property. People milled about, helping themselves to the various dishes that were laid out on trestle tables. A trio of musician friends of Matteo grouped themselves outside the kitchen window with guitar and keyboard and violin, and played catchy jazzy tunes that a few were dancing to.

Caroline kept a furtive eye on Matteo as she stood on the edge of a group that included Nina and Patrizia, only half listening to their rapid Italian. She watched him wandering among his guests, chatting and laughing with girls who were younger and prettier than she was. He didn't seem to be with any of them in particular. Despite the warm evening, her scarf still hung about his neck.

And then, without warning, when she looked away to respond to a remark of Nina's, he materialised at her side. *Carolina, we will dance.* A statement, not a question. Holding out a hand, his mother and her friends watching so she had no choice but to allow him to take her into his arms as his friends played some soft tune she didn't recognise.

He smelt of almonds. He was a fraction taller than her. She relished the sensation of being so close to him, loved the warmth of his palm against her back. She wondered if everyone was looking at them, thinking how kind of Matteo to take pity on the older woman. The wine she'd drunk made her reckless: let them think what they liked.

What's the music? she asked, wanting to remember what they danced to.

Is Mancini. You like?

I do.

Then you must put your head here – indicating his shoulder. *I will not eat you, I have already enough food.*

She laughed and moved closer. She closed her eyes and swayed with him. This might be all she ever had; this might be the only time in her life she danced with him. She felt the heat of his skin through his shirt, felt the thud of his heart against her chest.

The music stopped. They drew apart. He smiled. Grazie, he said, lifting her hand once again to press his lips to it. Grazie, *Carolina.*

She returned to the others. The night wore on; he didn't ask for another dance. At two in the morning Patrizia and her husband offered to drop her at her hotel on their way home. Matteo kissed the three of them goodbye and thanked them for coming, and for their gifts.

She was one of three. She wasn't special at all to him.

Lying in bed, head spinning gently, she fantasised about undressing him. She imagined laying her body along the length of his, everything touching from shoulders to feet. She thought about how soft and warm and smooth his skin would be, how safe she would feel in his arms, how being with him would banish the memory of her long-ago encounter with Jasper. She fell asleep trying to recall his almond smell.

The next morning she awoke feeling sad. She packed her bag. Her flight was at one, her taxi to the airport booked for ten. She'd refused Nina's offer of a lift, thinking her friend would have enough to do after the party. Patrizia or her husband would have collected her if she'd asked, but taking a taxi didn't bother her. It wasn't far to the airport, just a handful of miles.

She ordered breakfast in her room, too downcast to face the dining room with its couples and families. She ate the soft sweet bread without tasting it;

she took no pleasure from the milky coffee or the freshly squeezed orange juice.

She was thirty-four, with a thriving business and an empty heart. She would stop visiting Naples so often: there was really no need. The co-op could just as easily send her samples of their new products. Anyway, she didn't have the time any more to flit over and back like she'd been doing.

Just as well, she decided, that Matteo had no interest in her. Imagine if they had a fling, and if Nina objected to her son being involved with an older woman, which she well might do. It could jeopardise their business relationship: it could mean the end of Caroline's dealings with the co-op. No, she would put Matteo out of her head for once and for all; she'd throw herself into her work at home and forget him.

At ten to ten she brought her bag downstairs. She crossed the lobby to the reception desk and checked out. She turned for the door – and almost collided with him.

Two motorcycle helmets dangled from a hand. Her brown scarf was again around his neck, even though the temperature gauge behind the desk read twenty-eight degrees.

Buongiorno, *Carolina*, he said.

Why are you here? she asked. There'd been an accident, something was wrong.

He gestured towards the helmets. *I will take you to the airport.*

What? No, you don't have to do that – I have a taxi ordered.

He regarded her for a few seconds in silence, an expression she couldn't read on his face. *One minute*, he said then. She watched him approach the desk, speak to the receptionist.

This wasn't his idea. His mother had probably insisted. Still, she was glad he was here. It might be the last time they would meet.

He turned. *Taxi is cancelled. No problem*.

He had cancelled her taxi, just like that. She had to smile.

Now you come with me, yes?

Yes … thank you.

In Italian, he ordered.

Sì. Grazie.

Buona.

He handed her a helmet and scooped up her bag, and they left the hotel. His motorbike stood at the kerb: he clipped the bag to its carrier.

Hold on to me, he instructed when she'd clambered on, forced to hitch her dress high to swing her leg over the seat: definitely not a dress for a motorbike.

She wrapped her arms around his waist and rested against him. He drove carefully through the traffic as she held on tight, trying simply to enjoy the sensation, like she'd done the night before while they were dancing.

The time flew. Far too soon they reached the airport. He pulled up and she released her hold on him and dismounted as modestly as she could.

You can leave me here, she told him, as he unhooked her bag, shyness overcoming her. *You don't have to come in.* She lunged towards him, bumping her cheek clumsily against his. Grazie, *Matteo.* Arrivederci. Turning away, not wanting to prolong this final leave-taking.

Carolina.

She stopped.

Look at me.

She turned.

You do not like me? he demanded.

She glanced around. Anyone could hear him. *What?*

You go, so fast. You say grazie, *Matteo, you say* arrivederci, *and then you go.*

Again he made her smile. He was adorable, looking at her now like a wounded pup. *I just didn't … want to delay you.*

He stepped closer. *Carolina,* he said quietly, *all the time I think about this beautiful quiet Irish girl. I like you very much, and I think you like me. I 'ope you like me.*

She couldn't believe it.

All around them people were getting into cars, getting out of cars, opening and banging doors, calling goodbye, embracing, rolling luggage past them into the building. She was dimly aware of it, but she saw only his face, heard only his words.

He liked her.

He *liked* her.

Do you? he asked, his blue-green eyes fixed on hers. *Do you like me, Carolina? You must tell me. I must know.*

She didn't know what to say. *I'm older*, she blurted out. *I'm a lot older than you.*

He dismissed the words with a flick of his wrist. *Carolina, that is not important. What is important is if you like me, if we likes one anothers. Do you?*

Yes, she said, so quietly that even she didn't hear it. *I do*, she said.

He smiled, his eyebrows shooting up. He beamed. *You do?*

Yes. Yes! Suddenly not caring who heard her.

He caught her up easily, whirled her around. She screamed delightedly, causing heads to turn. He lowered her to the ground and took her face in his hands – and for the first time in her life, at the age of thirty-four, Caroline Plunkett was kissed properly, right there outside the departures building, in full view of so many.

It wasn't his first kiss – he knew exactly what he was doing. The wonder of it made her head spin, made her cling to him in case she disgraced herself by fainting.

When you come back? he demanded, when he eventually released her. *When? Next month? You must come soon, Carolina, yes?*

And that was how it began. On the plane home she resolved to ignore the age gap, or try to. Jasper D'Arcy and Sophie – no, maybe that wasn't a great example. What about Eleanor, then? She'd fallen in love with a man nearly twice her age. The tragedy they'd endured, were still enduring, didn't alter the fact that once upon a time they'd loved one another. Love crossed age gaps, often.

Love? Was this love? She had nothing to measure it by. All she knew was that the thought of Matteo, the sight of him, the sound of him, everything about him made her happy, and the thought that she could make him happy too was wondrous.

It might not last. With her in England and him in Italy, with all those miles between them, she had to accept that it might not last. All the more reason to enjoy it for however long they did survive. Maybe it was best to think of it as a holiday romance, not to be taken too seriously. Yes, a holiday romance, something that happened only in Italy, something that nobody at home need know about.

And her son would not come into it: there was no need for Matteo to know about her son.

And as for jeopardising her business dealings with the co-op – well, she would just have to hope that it didn't, that Nina and Giacomo would be OK about her being involved with Matteo – if, indeed, they ever found out. He might be anxious to keep it from them, fearing their disapproval.

She was involved with Matteo – the thought brought a rush of heat to her face. In a relationship with Matteo. In love, maybe, with Matteo.

Twenty-six days later she flew back to Naples. She and Matteo had emailed daily; his were in broken English, hers in a mix of English and bad Italian. He ended his with *Ciao, bellissima Carolina*. Beautiful Caroline. He actually thought her beautiful.

She booked her usual hotel, trepidation beginning to curl itself around her edges. What was she doing, flying to Italy to meet a man she hardly knew?

Stop, she told herself. *You're having an adventure: enjoy it.*

She bought new lingerie. At the cash register she couldn't meet the shop assistant's eye.

He was waiting at the airport. She was caught up and swung around again, she was properly kissed once more before she had a chance to fully take him in.

We go, he announced, when they finally drew apart, *to 'ave dinner with my parents.*

She was dumbstruck. She hadn't told Nina she was coming. *Do they know*, she asked, *about us?*

He grinned. *Of course – I tell them. They are 'appy. Why not?*

He made it sound so simple. They *were* happy, or they appeared to be. Nina met them at the door and hugged Caroline with her usual warmth, Giacomo served monkfish and grilled vegetables, and poured wine into her glass. They enquired about her business, asked about the weather in England, told her of a festival that had just ended in Naples. She could find no evidence at all of resentment.

And now I take you back, Matteo declared, after the *caffè amaretto* – and Caroline thanked her hosts, her mortification making her hardly able to look them in the eye, and waved goodbye from the back of their son's motorbike, and felt her heart thumping loudly in her throat all the way to her hotel.

And then she was seduced, competently and thoroughly and with great tenderness, by a twenty-five-year-old Italian electrician, who had just become her lover.

Five years they've been together. Five years of snatched weekends in Naples, and occasional longer trips that included one memorable June week in Tuscany, and a rather forgettable September visit to Venice, where it rained pretty much non-stop, and Matteo, whose twenty-eighth birthday they were celebrating, had a cold and was miserable. But on the whole they're very happy.

He's never been to England, or Ireland. Neither of them has ever suggested it. If Florence has her suspicions, she says nothing.

Ti amo, he has said, many times, and *Ti amo*, Caroline has replied. I love you, beautiful in any language. She means it every time. She loves him; there is no doubt now.

And tonight, not five minutes ago, he asked if she would marry him, and she didn't say yes.

Her head spins, thinking of all the things she's kept from him. He knows of her parents' existence, knows she has one sister, and that she lives with a cousin in England, but she's never shared Eleanor's tragedy with him, never told him of her fractured relationship with her mother, never mentioned the son she bore. So much she hasn't told him.

He'll be thirty next week. In May she'll be forty.

His family, including all four grandparents, is

here in Italy. His friends are here – everyone he knows, apart from her, is here.

Her life is in England. Her clients are there; her contacts are there. Florence and Noah are there. She can't leave England, not with Noah part of her life there now.

She's never told him about Noah. That's the kicker, isn't it?

He's in the kitchen of the tiny apartment he's been renting for the past four years: she hears the pop as he pulls the cork from a bottle of Prosecco. The apartment is on the fifth floor, in a not terribly auspicious area of Naples, and the lift in the building is usually out of order, but they moved the bed so it faces the uncurtained window, and at night they can count the stars, and when they wake they can see the sea over the red rooftops, and they smell bread and vanilla and chocolate from the bakery four floors below.

He returns and hands her a glass. '*Salute*,' he says, tossing his back, refilling before she's even taken a sip. He's disappointed, and trying not to show it.

She didn't say no. She didn't say no because she can't tell him no to his face, she can't do that to him. *I need some time*, was what she said. *Give me some time*.

When she goes home she'll wait a week or two, and then she'll send him an email. She'll use the kindest words she knows and type them onto a screen, and they will reach him silently. It will be more cowardly, but hopefully less cruel, than saying the words aloud.

She can't marry him. It's out of the question. She loves him, he's the first man she's loved – but there are too many things in their way, too much mismatching.

The sadness bears down on her. The thought of never seeing him again is awful, but that's what will happen, because how can they go back to what they were once she turns him down? He won't want it: his pride won't allow him to get past it.

They drink Prosecco, the silence heavy between them.

Eleanor

'I CAN'T SEE ANY OTHER WAY,' HE SAYS.

He looks worn out. Beneath his eyes the skin is darkly hollowed. She wonders how long it's been since he slept through the night: his sleeping patterns have been an unknown quantity to her for thirteen years.

He's still handsome, though. You'd still drown in his eyes, if you had a mind to.

'Why didn't you tell me things were so bad?' she asks. 'I knew we were in trouble, but I had no idea it had come to this. Why did you keep it to yourself?' But she knows the answer before he gives it.

'I didn't think you'd be interested.'

And there it is, the ugly truth. There's no malice in his remark, she knows that. He's simply stating a fact, like Jacob did a week earlier.

She's mortally ashamed. She's overcome with shame. When he lost the Michelin star last year she sympathised, of course she did, but it didn't resonate with her as it must have done with him, so far removed from the restaurant she'd become. So far removed from him, and from everything that was important to him.

And now his business is collapsing around him, his dream is in ruins, the situation so dire that he's forced to tell even his wife, whom he didn't think would be interested.

'How bad is it really?'

'As bad as it can be.'

'Debts?'

He shrugs. 'Not debts as such ... just not enough coming in to keep us afloat.'

This she can believe. He was always scrupulous about paying his creditors, always popular with suppliers for that reason.

'But close the restaurant? Has it honestly come to that?'

Another shrug. 'Yes, without a big cash injection – and I don't see anyone offering.'

It was all he wanted when he met her. She remembers him telling her, the very first night they went out to dinner, or maybe the second. *I'm going to open my own place*, he said. *Next year, all going well*. He told her he'd been putting every spare penny aside for over a decade to afford it. And now, after struggling through Ireland's worst recession, after achieving the heights he did, he's about to lose it all.

'But you own the building. Can't you remortgage?'

He gives her a peculiar look. 'I did, last year. I have to sell it to pay back the bank.'

Did he tell her he'd remortgaged? He must have: his face says he did. Her shame deepens.

'When will you close?'

'End of the month.'

End of the month: eleven days away. The day after the sixtieth birthday that they weren't planning on celebrating. *Oh, you must have a party,* Mum said – she'd wanted a party for his fiftieth too. *No party,* Eleanor had said, then and now. No party for her own thirtieth either. Poor Mum, denied her chances to shine.

'What about the staff?' she asks.

'I've told them. I had to give them time to look around for something else.'

The staff knew before she did. Keith may even have known when he came by a couple of weeks ago to pick up a clean shirt for Gordon, after the ink in his pen had leaked. In the beginning Eleanor had worked with Keith, along with Charlie and Jennifer, the other waiting staff, and Frank the wine waiter, and Dolores the commis chef. Married to one another, Frank and Dolores. Both of them about to lose their jobs now.

She knows them all, and she knows Sarah who joined later, the pastry chef who came to the house for Jacob's second birthday, who organised his party because his mother was unable to cope. She knows Joe, the kitchen jack-of-all-trades, who joined Fennellys straight from school, his wage helping to pay for his disabled brother's home help.

She remembers the early days of the restaurant,

the first few months when they were getting it off the ground, trying to make a splash. She remembers the hectic, exhausting eighteen-hour days she and Gordon used to put in regularly, planning the menus, creating the dishes, helping to clear up. Doing their own marketing too, no spare cash to pay anyone else.

She remembers the bookings coming in, the plates being ferried from the kitchen, the frayed tempers when orders were piling up, the customers who were delightful and the ones who weren't.

She recalls the disasters – the pan fires, the spills, the break-ins, the case of food poisoning that almost closed them, the diners who made a run for it before their bill was paid. She recalls the triumphs, the accolades, the glowing reviews, the excitement of the Michelin star, the Hollywood celebrities, the famous writers and politicians who dropped in. The many Champagne corks that were popped in Fennellys.

She remembers the proposals too – rings hidden in desserts, bashful men dropping to one knee – and the parties they hosted: birthdays and staff nights out, retirements and golden wedding anniversaries.

'I'm sorry,' she tells him. 'I really am. I wish I could say something, do something. Is there anything I can do to help?'

He shakes his head. Too little, too late.

She regards his hands. They rest on the table, as familiar to her as her own. She remembers how he would run the back of a hand lightly down her cheek, how he would trace a path slowly along her jawline and on down to find the hollow of her throat, raising goose pimples as he went. She recalls how he would place his palms on either side of her head, so he could search her face before he kissed her.

She wants to take his hands in hers now, offer what comfort she can – but her courage fails her as it did with Jacob. How would any kind of physical contact be received, after so long with none?

He pushes back his chair, holds the edge of the table as he gets to his feet. 'I need to sleep,' he says, and leaves the room without bidding her goodnight. She's tired too: normally she'd be in bed hours before this. She'd stayed up to talk to him about Jacob, but before she had a chance he told her *his* news.

She switches off lights and locks up and climbs the stairs. She takes off her clothes and gets into bed. She closes her eyes and waits for sleep, but it refuses to come. Instead, she finds her mind straying back to the time when she and Gordon met.

It wasn't exactly love at first sight.

You won't be getting preferential treatment, he said, *just because you're friendly with my nephew. You'll work as hard as anyone else here or you won't last.*

I'm not looking for preferential treatment, she replied. Typical head chef, thought he was God Almighty. She'd got the job on her own merit; it had nothing to do with knowing Conor. He knew that as well as she did.

He didn't attract her in the least. Too short, five eight at the most. His black hair was peppered with grey, and cut too close to his head. Too lean of face, too beaky of nose, altogether too wiry. His eyes, dark as treacle, were the best part of him. You could melt into them, if they were in someone else's face.

He called her Plunkett, like his nephew did – but there was a world of difference in the way he rapped it out across the kitchen.

He's full of himself, she reported to Conor, the first time she went home from Galway. *He bosses everyone around. And I wish you hadn't told him you knew me: I think he feels obliged to pick on me in case I get notions above my station. Last week he pulled me up because my julienned carrots weren't all exactly the same size. I felt like shoving his face into them.*

Conor grinned. *Maybe he fancies you.*

Don't be daft.

Time passed. She endured his bossiness, learnt when to stay out of his way. On the whole she enjoyed the work. He was an inspired chef, you couldn't deny it – and a good teacher when he felt like it.

And then, a few months into the job, she was shopping in Galway. More mooching than shopping, three days before pay day and not much in her purse. She passed a bar and glanced in the window – and there he was, sitting at the counter nursing a glass of something. Nobody with him, no other drink next to his, nobody's jacket on the empty stool beside him.

She took in his slumped posture, watched him raise his drink to take a sip. There was a defeated air about him, something pitiful in the way he cradled the glass in both hands and looked into it.

His wife had died some years back – she knew this from Conor. He looked to be in his late thirties or thereabouts. She must have been young when she died.

He lifted his head then and she hurried off, not wanting to be spotted. Next day she found herself briefly alone with him in the kitchen, while he prepped fish for lunch and she chopped potatoes into chips.

I saw you yesterday, she remarked, for want of something to say. *In Malone's. I passed by the window.*

He was filleting a mackerel and made no response.

Do you live in the town? No cause not to be civil with him, even if he didn't encourage it.

He glanced up, knife still embedded in the fish. *Salthill.*

On the seafront?

... No.

She gave up then. It was their longest conversation, which was a bit sad when you thought about it.

His nails were neatly clipped. He was constantly washing his hands, and demanding that they did too. She caught him whistling 'Strangers in the Night' once when he thought nobody was around.

He wasn't that short; he was a good five inches taller than her. And better too lean than overweight, like a lot of other chefs. And she supposed his short hair was practical in the kitchen – she had to tie hers up every day.

Eighteen months after Eleanor joined the hotel staff, one of the waitresses got married. The reception took place on the premises, and Eleanor was invited. She brought Conor along as her guest, trying not to count the months (over forty) since she'd had a steady boyfriend. She'd had dates, plenty of first dates, and even a few second ones, but she'd met nobody she wanted to go out with more than twice – or if she did, they didn't.

Gordon was on duty in the kitchen. She caught sight of him once when the door swung open, head bent over a hotplate.

He works too hard, she said, half to herself.

Who? Conor, scraping the last of his crème brûlée from its bowl.

Your uncle. He takes about one day off a month.

He's always been like that.

Do you remember his wife?

No: I was four or five when she died.

How long were they married?

Not long – about three years.

Any kids?

No. He eyed her half-eaten dessert. *Are you going to finish that?*

She pushed her pavlova towards him. *Did he ever meet anyone else?*

Not to my knowledge. You're mighty curious about Uncle G.

I feel sorry for him, she said, and she did.

She imagined him living alone, going home to an empty house every night. He'd be less focused on his work if there was someone waiting for him.

She wondered if he had photos of his dead wife

about the place. She remembered how lost she'd been after Andrew finished with her, how she'd vowed not to lose her heart like that again. Maybe he was the same, determined never to risk more heartbreak. Conor was twenty, which meant he'd been alone for about sixteen years.

She turned to look at the bride and groom at the top table, watched him lean towards her and whisper something in her ear that made her push him away, smiling. She wondered if she'd ever have a wedding day of her own, if any man was destined to be her husband. She wasn't yet twenty, not for another two months. She knew she had plenty of time – but it would be good to meet him at least. It would be something to know he existed.

A fortnight later, Gordon Fennelly asked her out.

I'd like to take you to dinner, was what he said.

Eleanor was flabbergasted. He'd never given a hint he was interested in her: on the contrary, his singling her out for criticism hadn't abated. It was all she could do sometimes not to fling a saucepan at him, preferably a cast-iron one.

She couldn't go out with him. He was her boss. He was twice her age, or close to it. She didn't even like him.

That would be lovely, she said.

He took her to a seafood restaurant. She wore the orange dress she'd bought for the wedding, and the turquoise appliquéd wrap Caroline had made for her. Waiting for him to pick her up from the staff house she shared with three chambermaids, Eleanor was nervous almost to the point of vomiting.

What had possessed her to say yes? They'd have nothing to talk about: the evening would be filled with horrible silences. She wouldn't be able to eat a thing.

She put on the little heart-shaped locket from Andrew that she still had – and took it off again. She dabbed spicy perfume behind her ears, and then scrubbed it off in case he didn't like it.

She told the chambermaids. No point in hiding it, they'd see him when he arrived. He didn't seem bothered about people knowing: it had been his idea to pick her up.

You're going out with Gordon? She heard the envy in their voices, and her anxiety increased.

In the two hours that they sat across a table from one another, during which she managed to eat most of a plate of grilled whiting with an almond and basil pesto, and more than half a slice of the lemon tart that followed it, she finally admitted to herself that he'd grown on her, so slowly and gradually that she hadn't noticed. Every time their eyes met, her insides gave a queer little flip.

Thankfully, they found enough to talk about. He told her of his childhood in Meath, and the catering college he'd gone to after school, and the French Michelin-starred restaurant that had employed him for a decade, leading him in the process through the various grades of chef, from a *poissonier*, responsible only for the preparation of the fish dishes, to their *chef de cuisine*.

His wife wasn't mentioned. She wondered if they'd met in France.

I'm going to open my own place, he said. *Next year, all going well.*

He didn't smile a lot – this she knew already. When he did she felt rewarded, as if it was something she'd earned. She told him about her father, who worked in computers, and her mother who had a part-time receptionist job in a friend's beauty salon, and her sister who'd just finished her second year of fashion design at an art college in Wales. *She got the best Leaving Cert result of anyone in the school – I mean, ever. My parents weren't too pleased when she chose fashion design. They thought she should do something more with her results, but she seems to be enjoying it.*

Halfway through her second glass of an excellent white Bordeaux – chosen by him at her request – she felt bold enough to ask, half in jest, why he picked on her so much in the kitchen.

He didn't immediately reply. He regarded her in silence. She grew increasingly self-conscious under his unsmiling scrutiny.

Finally, he spoke. *Why do you think?* he asked quietly.

She had no idea what he meant, no idea what to say. All she knew was that her question had somehow changed things between them. Her earlier nervousness rushed back. *I don't know*, she admitted finally, when it became clear that he expected an answer.

He raised a hand: their waiter materialised. *I'll take the bill*, Gordon told him.

Eleanor's heart sank. She'd asked the wrong question. She'd blown it. She excused herself and made her way across the room to the door that led to the toilets. In the ladies' she freshened her lipstick and blotted her damp palms with toilet paper, and practised looking cheerful in the mirror.

They drove in silence back to her accommodation. The car smelt of the pine air freshener that dangled from the mirror. It was his loss, she told herself. He'd taken offence where none was meant: pity about him. Little wonder he was on his own.

She wouldn't put up with his tetchiness any more: she'd hand in her notice and find another job. Even if he refused to give her a reference – and there was every chance he would – she'd get one from Eoin, the general manager. Eoin liked her. Eoin wasn't contrary, or super-sensitive.

He pulled up outside the house. To her relief the place was in darkness: the others must be out, or already in bed. No questions to answer about the date, not tonight anyway. She'd be ready for them in the morning, say she'd decided the age gap was too wide.

Thank you for dinner, she said, reaching for the door handle.

I pick on you, as you call it, because I like you. That's the screwed-up way I operate.

Her hand stilled on the handle. She considered his words. He liked her. He was screwed up, but he liked her.

I can't figure you out, she replied.

Give it time.

She turned to look at him. It was too dark to see his expression clearly.

You want to risk this again? he asked.

Yes, she said – aware of the happiness that was creeping up through the soles of her feet, filling all the spaces in her. He wanted to see her again, and it was a revelation to her how much she wanted that too.

Would we say this day next week?

She had to wait a whole week. *Fine.*

A beat passed. He put a hand on her arm. *Can I kiss you?*

She'd ached for it all evening. *Yes.*

He leant across and brushed her lips with his. *Goodnight, Eleanor.*

Goodnight.

It was the first time he'd called her Eleanor. She got out and closed the car door. She let herself into the house, not looking back. She stood in the hall, listening to his car as it moved off. She closed her eyes and recalled his kiss, the whispery touch of it, and she felt the same electrifying current pass through her.

Gordon Fennelly, of all the men in the world. Who would have thought he'd be the one she'd been waiting for?

Six months later, a week before Christmas, he asked if she would marry him, and on the fourteenth of February 1998 she became Eleanor Plunkett Fennelly. She was in love – properly in love this time, not like the puppy love she'd felt for Andrew D'Arcy. A new life beckoned with Gordon, and she couldn't wait for it to start.

And look at them now. Look at the state of them now. A child died, her baby died, and she never got over it. Never allowed herself to get over it, pushed away all efforts to help her.

She turns her pillow, lays her cheek on the cool cotton. Is it too late now? Has too much damage been done to them? How can she possibly make amends, where can she start? All night she lies awake, searching for answers.

The following morning, she makes a phone call.

Caroline

'HE'S WONDERFUL,' SHE SAYS. 'HE'S BEEN here twice, and he's met Florence, and next time he's bringing his girlfriend: he says she's dying to meet me! I was so nervous before we came face to face. I thought he might resent my having given him up – but he doesn't, not in the least. He totally understands. He's clever and funny, and I think he's really good-looking, but I might be biased – oh, and he's in college, and history is one of his subjects! Remember when I wanted to be a historian? We've got so much catching up to do, we never run out of conversation. We talk on the phone nearly every day.'

She stops. 'Sorry – I'm going on a bit. But you'll have to meet him, I'd love you to meet him.'

'I should like that very much,' Donald replies. 'Perhaps you can bring him for tea.'

Donald had written to her when she went home to Ireland after having Noah. His letters were full of flowing fountain-pen sentences in perfect copperplate writing:

*It hasn't been the same since your departure;
I find myself missing your gentle company. I
do hope you're happy, after the year you went
through. Please don't leave it too long before
coming back to see us. We shall sit on my balcony
and eat shrimps, and put the world to rights – and
if Florence promises to behave, we shall allow her
to join us.*

He'd been fully behind her when she told him of her
wish to study fashion design instead of history.

*You must do what your soul tells you – and you
certainly have a fine creative flair. If I can be of
any use, I will. I still have friends in London, you
know, from my time in the tailoring business.*

He was good as his word. In her second year of
college he'd found her a six-month placement with
a London-based knitwear company, and he'd given
her the keys of the apartment in Russell Square
that he'd hung onto since his days of living in the
capital. *It's what estate agents would refer to as bijou,
just two little rooms with bath, but in a good location. I
use it rarely, and I've lent it to friends on occasion, but
otherwise it lies vacant. I always feel a tad guilty that it
is so unused, so you should be doing me a favour if you
gave it an airing.*

When she protested that she couldn't stay without
payment, he told her that his father had been a
merchant banker, and a shrewd investor – *and as his*

sole heir, I inherited rather a lot. I also made my own tidy sum from my days in London, and I am consequently in the rather embarrassing position of having far more funds than I shall ever need. I should be delighted to loan you my little place – and when you become a famous designer you may feel free to provide a steady supply of expensive scarves.

She'd adored London. Her art college course in Wales was marvellous – challenging and exciting, exhausting and rewarding in roughly equal measure – but in London she happily forgot it. At weekends she rambled on foot through the city, taking in its galleries and museums, its immaculately laid out parks, complete with lakes and boats, its department stores and boutiques full of designer collections.

In London her love of history was reignited. How could it not be, when the city was drenched in it? There was the Tower of London where doomed Anne Boleyn had spent her last night on earth more than four hundred years earlier; there were the same cobbled alleys through which Shakespeare and Thackeray had walked; there were the very Houses of Parliament that Guy Fawkes had tried to blow up on the fifth of a long-ago November.

The Charles Dickens Museum, a five-minute walk from Donald's apartment, was the actual house where Dickens had lived for a time, where *Oliver Twist* and *Nicholas Nickleby* were written: how could you hear that, and not be enthralled?

The various markets of London, with their cheerful, noisy stallholders and seemingly endless array of wares, charmed her too, so different from the peaceful, civilised little affair where Florence and Donald sold their respective offerings each Saturday. She unearthed all sorts of treasures to bring back to college – beautiful old buttons, lengths of lace, necklaces of colourful beads – as she rummaged through the bric-à-brac. She bought second-hand sweaters and painstakingly took them apart so she could use their wool to create something completely different.

In the Victoria and Albert Museum she studied knitting patterns from the 1940s, distributed free to British women who contributed to the war effort by knitting for soldiers on the front lines. In the Westminster Reference Library she read about the history of knitting in Britain and Ireland, and the diverse, distinctive styles that had developed over the years in different regions.

The many theatres of London were places of wonder to her. The only seats she could afford were high up in the gods, but she didn't care. *Les Misérables* and *Blood Brothers* and *Miss Saigon* broke her heart; *The Phantom of the Opera* transfixed her. Of all of them, *The Mousetrap*, running continuously on a London stage for forty-five years, was the only one that disappointed. Terribly dated, and with a lacklustre cast.

She brought a pot of Fortnum & Mason marmalade to Donald whenever she travelled north, and a brown paper bag of homemade toffee to Florence from a quaint little sweet shop in Lambeth that was run by two elderly brothers. *Rot your teeth*, Florence said, the first time Caroline produced it, before proceeding to make her way through the bag without further complaint.

Through the years that followed, through the remainder of her college course, her time with the knitwear company in Oxford, her tentative initial steps as an independent designer, Donald remained her friend. He still lives alone in his apartment that overlooks the park, still dresses in his beautifully tailored suits, but at eighty-six he is increasingly frail and fragile. He walks about carefully with a stick and tires easily, and he has Esther from the Philippines calling by each day to make his dinner.

'There's something else,' Caroline says. Needing to tell someone, and Donald is like the grave with secrets. 'There's a man in Italy,' she begins, and the story of Matteo emerges. 'What should I do?' she asks. 'There are so many obstacles to us getting married. And he has no idea that Noah exists.'

'You love this man?'

'Yes.'

'You're quite sure?'

'Yes.'

'And do you think,' he enquires, 'that he would have any less regard for you because another man once forced himself on you?'

'Well ... But it's not as simple as that. It's the age difference too, and the fact that he lives in Italy. And it's not so much that Noah exists, or how he came about, as the fact that I didn't tell him.'

'It seems to me,' Donald says slowly, 'that you are finding a lot of excuses. It seems that you are busy putting obstacles in your path.'

'What? No – I *do* want to marry him—'

'But you're afraid,' he says gently. 'Aren't you? You're afraid of the difference in your ages, which you tell me doesn't bother him—'

'Not now, but what about ten years' time, or twenty?'

Donald smiles. 'And you would jeopardise your chance of happiness, you would throw away this opportunity you're being given, because of what *might* happen in ten or twenty years? My dear, we could all be dead and buried next month, never mind next year, or in ten years' time.'

It was true. What he said was perfectly true.

'My dear, this is your decision to make. I can't help you. I can only tell you how the situation looks to me – and it would appear that a man you love has asked you to be his wife, and you haven't accepted him because you're afraid he might have second thoughts in 2025, or perhaps 2035.'

She laughs. 'When you put it like that …'

'I put it like that because that's how it is. You are worrying about something that may never happen, which is usually the way with worrying.'

Can it really be that simple? Is she making this harder than it needs to be? Carolina Piccolo – she loves the musical sound of it. Signora Piccolo, wife of Matteo Piccolo.

A week since his proposal, a week of no emails,

like he promised. *I will wait your answer*, he said. She's been missing him since she got home, missing his daily broken-English messages.

She'll write to him. She'll send him a proper letter, even though it'll take longer to reach him. She'll tell him everything, and she'll tell him yes, if he still wants her.

'I hear you're off to Ireland,' Donald says.

'Yes, the day after Florence's birthday.'

On Thursday, which is the first of October, Florence will be eighty-one. Unknown to her, Caroline has invited her friends to afternoon tea at the house. The following morning she will fly to Ireland, to tell his grandparents and his father about Noah making contact.

She kisses Donald goodbye and sees herself out. On the way home she rehearses sentences in her head.

Eleanor

SHE'S BEEN BUSY. THE DAY AFTER GORDON told her about Fennellys she phoned her doctor's surgery and made an appointment. *A check-up*, she told his secretary. She tried to remember the last time she'd been to see him, and couldn't.

The following day she arrived at the surgery. *Eleanor*, he said, coming around his desk to shake her hand, *I'm very glad you've come in.*

I need to get better, she said. *I need your help.* Because she couldn't attempt to repair the damage she'd caused to her relationships with Gordon and Jacob, could she, unless she fixed herself first?

They talked. He put her on the scales, and didn't remark on the result it showed. He gave her a diet sheet.

These are just guidelines, he said. *You're a chef. You'll have all sorts of recipes for low-fat dishes.*

I used to be a chef, she said.

He smiled. He'd often eaten at Fennellys. *Like riding a bike. I'm sure it'll come back.*

He gave her a business card. 'Cathy Prendergast', she read. 'Psychotherapist'. *She's good*, he said. *I think you should give her a call.*

He told her to drink water. *Lots, with lemon and cucumber in it. Fill a big jug every morning, make it a habit.*

He told her to walk. *Go as far as you can, as fast as you can, as often as you can. Don't let the weather stop you. Get yourself some waterproof gear, and a pair of good shoes.*

He told her not to weigh herself. *Come back and see me in a week – make an appointment with Dorothy on the way out. Let's take it week by week.*

When she left his surgery she drove into Galway and bought a size eighteen skirt in TK Maxx whose zip didn't quite make it to the top, and a pair of walking shoes in a sports store – ignoring the glances that passed from one young, slim staff member to another – and afterwards she did a supermarket shop for food from the diet sheet that would help the skirt to close fully.

Later that day, after a lunch whose putting together made her cry – the first salad she'd made for Gordon, with quinoa and beetroot and rocket and cherry tomatoes and crumbled feta cheese – and three glasses of lemon and cucumber water, she dialled the number on the card the doctor had given her.

I need to talk to someone, she said, in a voice that had started without warning to shake.

Come and see me, Cathy replied, in a voice that was

warm and steady and not at all shaky, *and we can decide if we're a good fit. I have a free slot on Monday morning, eleven o'clock – would that suit?*

Monday, five days from now. The day before Gordon's birthday. *That's fine*, she said. That evening she cooked wholewheat noodles and baby vegetables with garlic and ginger and chilli.

What's this? Jacob asked, and she told him.

You like it?

It's OK. But he took seconds.

Their conversation hadn't been brought up again. He acted like it had never happened, but the things he'd said had lodged in her head.

You've never felt like my mother, ever.

You wished it was me, didn't you? You were sorry it wasn't me, weren't you?

I used to wish it was me too.

Lodged in her head. Crucifying her every time she picked over them.

I won't be making cakes any more, she told him now. *For Beth, I mean.*

OK. That was all he said, but at least he knew.

After dinner she put on her new shoes and walked to the park, half a mile away. It was slow going: halfway there she had to stop and lean against a wall. When she got home she had blisters on both heels. She put on her slippers and drank three glasses of water. She found a photo of her and Gordon that had been taken shortly after they'd begun to go out, and she stuck it to the mirror in her bedroom to remind her of how she'd once looked, and how she could look again. She bathed her feet in salty water and went to bed.

Next day she breakfasted on porridge with goji berries and two glasses of water. Jacob glanced at the porridge – usually she ate twice the amount, and made toast as well – but he didn't comment. After Gordon had left for the restaurant she stuck plasters on her blisters and pushed her feet into the new shoes and limped to the park again. She sat on a bench for twenty minutes, watching a robin hop its way along the grass. When she got home she drank two more glasses of water and peeled off her sweaty clothes and stood under the shower.

That afternoon – lunch was ribbons of courgette tossed in a lemon mint dressing – she walked slowly to a hair salon she'd often passed but whose door she'd never opened. She booked an appointment for the following afternoon, and went home by the seafront so she could sit on another bench and watch the waves roll in, and smell the salt. *I'll get there*, she told herself, *however long it takes*.

She went home and drank more water as she stir-fried beef and garlic and bamboo shoots and vegetables in light soy sauce for dinner, with wholegrain rice instead of white. *It's nice*, Jacob said.

She'd never cooked for him, not properly. She'd eventually abandoned the ready meals she'd fallen back on after Beth, but the dishes she'd produced in their stead weren't much of an improvement. She'd taken the quickest option, preparing dinners that needed no imagination, dinners that were edible, and moderately healthy, but not in the least exciting.

She used to love working with food, playing around with ideas for dishes, inventing new flavour combinations. Pitting herself against Gordon sometimes, seeing which of them could come up with the most original pancake filling, or the tastiest dinner party main course that used fewer than five ingredients.

And then she'd given up on it, like she'd given up on everything. The following day she walked back to the hair salon where she was introduced to Neil. He had a nose ring and several tattoos, and his violet hair was gelled into stiff points. He looked younger than Jacob.

I don't know what I want, she told him. *Just keep some of the length, and give me something that you think will suit me* – and then she read her magazine and drank sparkling water with slices of lime while shanks of her hair dropped to the floor around her feet.

She liked the end result. *You've taken years off me*, she told him. She gave him a fiver tip and made another appointment for six weeks' time. *You should think about letting me put a few red lowlights into it*, he said, *really perk it up*, and she promised she would. That evening she drank water as she cooked a chickpea and red lentil curry, and Jacob asked for more, and didn't comment on her hair.

Gordon did though. *I like it*, he said the next morning. *It suits you*.

She hugged the comment to herself as she walked to the shopping centre and bought a pack of blister plasters and a shockingly expensive cleanser and moisturiser set, and a book called *Yoga for Beginners*. Mum swore by yoga; she'd been going to classes for years.

The day was warm. She opened the back door and sat on the step as she ate her lunch of lean minced beef cooked with garlic and chilli and wrapped, with shredded carrot and spring onion, in an iceberg lettuce leaf.

As she ate, her gaze roamed the garden. They had almost half an acre, bordered with overgrown shrubs and straggly climbers and long-ago flowerbeds that the weeds had long since claimed. Everything in the garden had been in situ when Gordon had bought the house, five years before Eleanor had moved in. All he did was cut the grass in the summer, and the only time Eleanor came out was to hang clothes on the line, or take them in again.

It hadn't always been like that though. She remembered when she was first married, she and Dad had spent a couple of afternoons weeding out the flowerbeds, and she'd scattered flower seeds, lots of them, onto the freshly-turned earth – but she had so little free time with Fennellys it was impossible to keep new weeds at bay, and by the time the flowers were beginning to poke up through them Jacob was well on the way, and the garden was forgotten.

She fed the last of her lunch to Clarence, who

gobbled the meat and ignored everything else. She found a rusting pair of hedge clippers in the cobwebby shed and did the best she could with the hydrangea outside the kitchen window. By the end of it the organic bin was full and her arms ached, not altogether unpleasantly – and the bush, she thought, was improved.

That evening she baked sea bass with couscous and Oriental vegetables, and Jacob told her, without being prompted, that he'd been selected to try out for the school rugby team.

That's wonderful, she said. *Well done.* She was thrilled. It was the first time he'd volunteered information. *Fingers crossed.*

I might not get in.

Still, being asked to try out is brilliant.

He had ice-cream to follow the sea bass; she had watermelon chunks.

Later, in the privacy of her room, wearing only her underwear, she struggled through the first few pages of her yoga book – bend from the waist without toppling over, and breathe too? It took supreme effort not to hate the willowy tutor in full makeup and leotard, who looked like she'd been born in the lotus position.

The following day everything ached. She hobbled downstairs and squeezed oranges, and cooked French toast and bacon for Gordon and Jacob.

What's the occasion? Gordon asked.

It's Sunday, she said. *I just thought we should make it special.* She drank three glasses of water and ate a small bowl of porridge with goji berries as she listened to Jacob telling his father about the rugby try-outs.

That afternoon she walked to a garden centre that was almost a mile away – by now, after at least two daily walks, her pace had quickened a little, and the blisters were all but gone. She bought secateurs and a trowel and new clippers, and a pair of lime green gardening gloves.

When she got home there was no sign of the other two. She spent the hour or so before dinner working on the shrubs, clipping off anything that looked like it should go. She had no idea if she was doing more harm than good – was this even the right time of the year to prune? – but she enjoyed being out in the fresh air, inhaling the clean scent of the earth, hearing the small snip of the secateurs mingling with the birdsong she'd never paid much heed to before.

That night she repeated her yoga exercises through gritted teeth, and rewarded herself with a long hot bubble bath.

The next morning she drove into Galway and found Cathy the psychotherapist. Cathy was in her sixties, with bobbed white hair and green-rimmed glasses and a warm handshake. She brought Eleanor into a room that didn't look in the least like an office, with its pink walls and chintz armchairs, its piano and little spindly-legged tables. Had she deliberately made it more homely to ease the troubled minds of those who came to her?

Sit anywhere you like, she said, *and tell me why you've come.*

So Eleanor sat by the window and watched a small ginger cat pottering about the garden and told Cathy, haltingly, about losing Beth, and what it had done to her, and Cathy listened.

I won't be able to fix what's broken, she said then, very gently. *I can't change the past, nobody can do that, but I can help you to cope with it, to live better with the broken stuff. How does that sound?*

It sounded worth a try. They arranged to meet again. Driving home, Eleanor stopped at the shopping centre and bought a pale blue tie with tiny tangerine spots, and paper to wrap it in, and a birthday card that said, *To my husband*. No mention of age: he might not like her to draw attention to it.

It was the first tie she'd got for him in years.

That evening she phoned home and told her parents about Fennellys closing its doors for good in two days.

Why didn't you tell us it was in trouble? Mum demanded. *We had no idea.*

We didn't want to worry you, Eleanor replied.

We'll come to see you as soon —

No, she said quickly. The last thing Gordon would want was his mother-in-law swooping in, full of triumphant pity. He'd never been quite good enough for Mum. *Leave it for now*, she said. *You can come later, when we've dealt with it.*

Anything we can do to help? Dad asked.

There is one thing, she said, and told him.

When she hung up she typed an email to her old friend Conor Fennelly. She and Conor hadn't met in a while. They'd lost touch after Beth – or rather, Eleanor had dropped him, like she'd dropped everyone else. He hadn't given up on her though – he emailed her every so often, giving her all his news, and once in a blue moon she replied.

He'd done well for himself. Almost immediately after leaving his prestigious London art college his work had begun having an impact. Based in Paris these days, living with his musician boyfriend, his paintings were snapped up by collectors for huge sums.

The last time they'd met was at his father's funeral, four or five years ago. Gordon's only brother Todd, dead after his third heart attack.

How are you, Plunkett? Conor asked, after the burial and before the dinner, when Gordon was talking to Todd's widow Jenny, and it was just t he two of them. *How are things?* As if he didn't know, as if he hadn't heard from Gordon how things were.

Oh, you know, she said, *I get up, and I put in the time until I go to bed again.* The truth slipping out after two glasses of wine.

He didn't tell her to get some help, or to pull herself together. *Come to Paris,* he said. *Get yourself on a plane and come over, even just for one night. I'll wine and dine you: I'm not short of a bob these days.*

She promised to think about it but of course she didn't. Go to Paris, when she hardly went as far as town? She hoped he wouldn't hold it against her now, when she needed him.

> I'm thinking of selling your painting. Remember the one you gave me for my birthday, a million years ago when we were young? You may or may not have heard that Fennellys is closing – I'm not sure if Gordon has told you, or your mother. It's just not viable any more, and Gordon has no choice, although he's very upset about it. So I was trying to think how I could help, and I remembered the painting. I thought it might be worth something, since you're doing so well. Maybe not enough for Gordon and me to get a new start, but a bank might give us a loan if we put it up as collateral or something. Would you mind very much?

And now it's the following morning, and Gordon is sixty, and so far there's been no response from Conor. Eleanor wraps the blue tie and signs the card and gets dressed. She's going to make pancakes for him and Jacob – but a note on the kitchen table tells her that he's already left for the restaurant. *Lots to do* is all he says by way of explanation. She puts his present aside and begins to set the table for herself and Jacob, pushing down her disappointment.

After breakfast she spends an hour in the garden until it's time for her doctor's appointment. She drives to the surgery, wishing she'd waited until afterwards to have her porridge. What if she's lost no weight at all?

She's down seven pounds. Half a stone lighter in one week. *Well done*, he says. *A great start. What about Cathy?*

I called her, I've been to see her. I think she'll help.

Marvellous, good for you. Come back to me next week, and keep doing what you're doing.

She's euphoric driving home. She's begun, and it's working. Things are going to get better: she can feel it. On impulse she takes the turn for the shopping centre. She'll visit Fennellys, she'll deliver Gordon's present – and she'll get something for the staff too, to thank them for their service.

She buys the largest box of chocolates she can see in the supermarket, and a thank-you card. On the way back to the car she catches sight of her reflection in a shop window and is disheartened by how enormous she still looks. *Stop*, she tells herself. *Seven pounds gone, more to go*. Lots more to go – but she'll get there.

At home she takes everything from her wardrobe and lays it on the bed. Most of her clothes don't fit, and she can't bear the ones that do. She looks at the skirt she bought the week before. She coaxes it past her hips and just about gets the zip to close. She can hardly breathe in it, but it's closed.

She teams it with a navy blouse that does its best to hide the bulge above the waistband, and slips her feet into navy court shoes that she can't walk very far in: no matter. She makes up her face and tidies her hair and leaves the house, her stomach rumbling from lack of lunch.

Moving in the skirt is challenging: she can almost hear the fabric protesting. As soon as she gets home she'll take it off, and wait another while before wearing it again.

She finds a parking space across the street from Fennellys. Through the front plate-glass window she can see people sitting at tables. Everything looks as it should, no sign of the imminent closure. But that's the way it goes, isn't it? Businesses collapse without warning, there one day, gone the next.

August 2013 she was here last, when the restaurant was celebrating fifteen years in business. She remembers feeling frumpy in black chiffon that had seemed a good idea in the shop but that she realised, as the night wore on, made her look like someone's recently widowed grandmother. She remembers eating too many canapés as she tried to make small talk with the skinny, glamorous women who had come with their business-suited husbands to congratulate Gordon, who was saddled with a fat wife.

But that's all behind her now. Those days are over. She reaches into the rear seat for the box of chocolates – and as she does, she hears a sharp tearing sound, and feels a great release.

She sinks back down hastily, feeling behind her with frantic fingers to assess the damage – and discovers that the entire back seam of her skirt has come apart from top to bottom. No way can she go near the restaurant: she can't even get out of the car.

Her euphoria vanishes, and is replaced by despair.

She's useless, worse than useless. She's pathetic, trying to change her life with glasses of water and a bit of wobbly yoga and some gardening. As if that's going to work. As if she's ever going to be the slim, vibrant, happy person she once was.

And as for saving her marriage and reclaiming Jacob, as for repairing her family, she hasn't a hope. What man in his right mind would want her, as pathetic as she is? What son would want to have anything to do with such a messed-up failure of a mother? They must be ashamed when people see them together; Gordon must wish he'd never laid eyes on her. He must be counting the days until Jacob moves out, and he can leave too.

She starts the car and pulls away from the restaurant. She drives home, blinking tears away. When she parks in the driveway she gets out carefully, holding her skirt together as best she can, keeping an eye out for neighbours.

As she slams her door she catches sight of the chocolates, sitting on the back seat. She'd forgotten them. She opens the rear door and slips into the seat, and takes the chocolates onto her lap.

She hasn't had chocolate in the last week. She's never gone a week without it in her life.

She turns the box over and sees pictures of what's inside: praline and hazelnut crunch, coffee creme and caramel swirl ... She imagines the tastes, and her empty stomach rumbles and her mouth waters.

She peels off the cellophane.

October 2015

Caroline

IT IS THE MIDDLE OF THE MORNING ON Thursday the first of October, and Florence Cassidy's eighty-first birthday. In the little kitchenette of her upstairs quarters, Florence's cousin hums as she spreads white icing on the cake she baked the previous evening.

Her letter to Matteo took three days to finish, but last night she copied out the final version on a fresh sheet of notepaper, and today she's going to post it. After Florence's party she'll walk to the letterbox in town and send it off, and wait for his response.

She smooths the top of the cake and sets it aside to dry. No doubt Florence knows well that she's up to something: at eighty-one, her cousin is as mentally sharp as ever. In fairly good physical shape too, apart from the hips that complain loudly in wet weather. Her market days are long behind her: in addition to the rain not agreeing with her hips, she doesn't have the strength in her wrists any more to move the fairly substantial carriage of the knitting machine to and fro. Without something to sell, there's not much point in having a market stall.

The machine still sits in the bay window. *Sentimental*, Florence said, when Caroline suggested donating it to a charity shop. *I couldn't part with it.* These days she does a bit of hand knitting, tea cosies and scarves and baby hats to give as gifts, but her fingers have begun, in the last few weeks, to stiffen up.

I should move to the sun, she said, not so long ago. *Myself and Donald could buy a little house in the Bahamas.*

Donald is dropping by this afternoon in a taxi ordered by Caroline, and Gretta and Barney are coming too. Tea and cake in the sitting room: anything more fancy than that and Florence would kill her. For her eightieth last year Caroline had just about got away with the same group at a lunch in the local hotel. *No fuss*, Florence had warned, in advance of the occasion, and a small lunch party was all Caroline had dared to arrange.

When the icing has set on the cake she takes a packet of candles from the press. Five she'll use, for the five who will celebrate this afternoon. As she pushes in the last one she hears a sound she can't identify, a kind of muffled thud.

She raises her head and listens: nothing more. She returns the leftover candles to the press. Half eleven, just in time for coffee. She makes her way downstairs and taps on the kitchen door before pushing it open.

Florence lies face down on the old tiles, looking as if someone had flung her there. Her head is turned to the left. One leg is bent at the knee, the other extended. Her right arm is pinned beneath her, the left is thrown out to the side, palm facing upwards.

She was the thud. Florence was the thud.

No.

No.

No.

Caroline's heart lurches. 'Florence!' She drops to the floor beside the unmoving form. 'Get up, Florence, come on, please—' What does she do? What does she *do*? She feels lightheaded with panic.

Pulse, find a pulse. She lays trembling fingers on the wrist of the out-flung arm – still warm, still warm – and searches frantically, and feels no beat. 'Florence, Florence, can you hear me? You're OK, you're fine, come on—' the words jumping out in little frightened gasps. She tries the side of Florence's neck, moves up, moves down, again finds nothing. Nothing.

Her eyes fill with tears. 'No, Florence, please, don't do this. Don't do this to me—' No sign or sound of breath issues from the half-open mouth – 'You're OK, you just had a fall, try to get up, you'll be fine' – a terrifying blankness in the eyes she knows so well. 'Florence, it's OK, it's OK, just lie still, don't try to move, I'm phoning the doctor. Hold on, hold on, Florence.'

It takes an eternity to find his number. She pulls things from drawers, knocks things from shelves, bumps into chairs as she darts about the room, her fear threatening at any moment to engulf her, to take the legs from under her, to reduce her to a helpless mess. Finally she pulls the falling-apart address book from the drawer beneath the cutlery that has a bit of everything in it.

She flips through pages that are full of Florence's big messy writing until she sees 'Dr Wharton', under X because the W section is full of names, half of them crossed out. She flies up the stairs for her phone, forgetting in her fright about the landline that sits on the hall table. 'Florence,' she says when she finally gets through to his secretary, 'she's collapsed, Florence Cassidy,' stumbling back down the stairs, the words jumping in frightened bunches from a mouth that has stopped working properly. 'Please hurry.'

'Hold on.'

She holds on for an aeon, weeping as she drops to a crouch again on the kitchen floor beside the still unmoving Florence, as she squeezes the limp hand. 'You'll be fine, just a turn, right as rain, I promise.'

'I've called 999,' the receptionist says. 'An ambulance is on the way. Is she breathing? Is there a pulse?'

'No, I can't find, I can't—'

'Can you do CPR?'

Her mind is blank. She can't remember what CPR means.

'Chest compressions – do you know how to do them?'

She can't, she can't think. 'Tell me,' she begs. 'Tell me what to do.'

'Can you fetch a neighbour?'

Neighbour. Gretta. Barney.

She races out, whacking a hand painfully against a gatepost. She hammers on their door until Barney's surprised face appears. 'Florence,' she says, she gasps, her breath gone, 'please, you must come—' and they come. The two of them rush back with her to Florence.

They turn her over, gently, so gently. Gretta pushes on her chest, Barney blows breath into her mouth while Caroline, useless, useless Caroline, weeps and weeps and squeezes her frozen hands together and runs a million times to the gate to see if the ambulance is coming.

And when it finally arrives, it takes the paramedics who rush from it no time at all to confirm what she already knows, what the three of them already know: on the morning of her eighty-first birthday, kindly, generous, honest Florence Cassidy has died, suddenly and without warning.

Florence is dead.

Florence is gone.

Florence has left them, with her birthday cake uneaten and her presents unopened. With nobody ready to let her go.

Caroline loses track of time. Florence is taken somewhere in an ambulance so they can find out why she died. The sitting room fills with people. Donald is there, crying quietly into an enormous handkerchief – when did he arrive? – and other faces from the market, Delia, and the honey man, and the farm co-op sisters, and Herbert with the fish stall who sold Florence two of his leftover salmon cutlets at half price every Saturday.

There's Angie the librarian's daughter who works in the butcher's, and Joan who used to ring the doorbell every week with her Avon case, even though Florence never bought a single thing from her. There's Pearl from the hospital kitchen with Lionel, her third husband. All day they continue to spill into the house, people from the charity shops and the wool shop and the garden centre. People who knew Florence, who loved her like Caroline loved her.

Loved: the past tense is an obscenity.

They speak in whispers, they make tea for Caroline, they cut her a slice from a Dundee cake that somebody brought. Eventually they leave, and she is alone.

Come next door, Gretta had said before she left. *Spend the night with us, I'll make up the bed in the spare room* – but Caroline said no, she wanted to stay, yes, she'd be alright, yes, she'd see them in the morning.

She sits in the empty room. The house is far too quiet. Someone lit the fire: she watches the flames as they leap. There is a pink mark on the back of her hand that's sore when she presses on it; she has no idea where it came from.

She wishes for Matteo. She wants to lay her

head on his chest, feel the solid warmth of him, the comfort of his arms enfolding her.

Time moves on: she's heedless of it. The grandfather clock chimes more than once as she sits there, too stunned by her sorrow to move. Every so often she hears the distant doomed efforts of the cuckoo to emerge from his blue house on the kitchen wall. The fire flickers and fades and goes out.

Her exhausted mind begins to play tricks. Florence is clattering about in the kitchen, getting dinner ready. Florence is standing by the window, saying *Holy mother of sweet divine, would you look at that?* Florence is in the garden, taking a cutting from her forsythia for someone she fell into conversation with in a charity shop, or at the market. Florence is busy at the knitting machine, shoving the carriage to and fro, pausing every so often to swipe threads off her face.

Eventually the cold forces Caroline from her chair. She finds a wrap and puts it about her shoulders. She wanders into the bedroom they created for Florence, in what used to be the dining room that nobody dined in.

She sits on the side of Florence's bed and lifts the pillow, wanting to hold it close – and something beneath it is revealed.

A photograph, black and white, faded to shades of brown. She picks it up and studies it.

She doesn't recognise the woman, who looks to be somewhere in her thirties. Nondescript features, nothing remarkable, face turned slightly away from the camera. Her belted dress – shirt-collared, button-through, wide-skirted – and primly waved hair suggests the 1950s. A white handbag hangs from an arm. There is an air of timidity, of vulnerability, about her smile.

Caroline turns it over. She reads, in Florence's distinctive hand, *Sybil, the love of my life. London 1960.*

Sybil: the name snags on her memory. Sybil. She closes her eyes and hears Florence's voice saying, *Did I ever tell you about my friend Sybil?*

And then she remembers. The night Noah was born, and she was trying not to break apart, Florence had told her the story of Sybil, the woman she'd befriended when she'd first come to London. Sybil whose brother was a missionary in Africa, Sybil who knitted and sold hats and scarves to make money for him. Sybil who was killed in a plane crash on her way to see him.

Never once in all the years that followed was Sybil's name mentioned between Caroline and Florence again, but the story had stuck in Caroline's head – maybe because of the traumatic circumstances of her hearing it – and she could recall every detail.

Did I ever tell you about my friend Sybil?

Sybil, who was the love of her life.

Another memory returns, another remark of Florence's: *Ireland didn't suit me,* she said. *I was wrong for it.*

It had struck Caroline as odd at the time, but now she thinks she understands. Florence left Ireland, a country that recognised only love between a woman and a man. She was wrong for Ireland, a country that regarded anything else as a sin.

Did Donald know? Had Florence confided in him, or had he sensed a kindred spirit in her? Was that what had brought them together, what had created such a solid friendship between them?

She rises to her feet. What does any of it matter now? She slips the photo into her pocket: tomorrow or the next day she'll find an opportunity to tuck it in next to Florence, where it belongs.

She stands on the threshold of the room, unwilling to leave, and thinks of all there is to be done. She must ring Ireland in the morning, give her parents and Eleanor the news, get them to spread the word among the cousins. She must go to the nursing home and let Constance know: that can't be left to anyone else, even if the sense of it doesn't penetrate the fog in the poor woman's brain.

She must organise the funeral. She has no idea how to go about it, but Gretta and Barney will help, and Donald too. She must get through the next few days somehow, without Florence, without Matteo.

And when this is over, and there is nothing more she can do for Florence, she must book a new flight to Ireland, and face what still has to be faced there.

She must tell Noah. She must let him know that Florence died. *He's a dote*, she'd said, after meeting him. *He deserves you as his mam.*

Florence, her greatest ally.

She switches off the light and leaves the room. She wanders into the kitchen, unwilling, despite her sadness and weariness, to move on from this day, the last day of Florence's life.

But the day has already passed: she sees from the clock that it's well after midnight. From now on, this date will be the anniversary of Florence's death as well as her birth, a new poignancy added to the first of October.

Her eye falls on the wall calendar that hangs by the fridge, and she sees that Florence had already turned the page to the new month. There's a red ring around the tenth, Saturday week: what was that? The tenth of October rings no bell with her.

She makes cocoa – she and Florence used to drink it sometimes at bedtime – but its sweet dark scent brings fresh tears, and she pours it down the sink. Time for bed, time to take her leave of this wretched day.

As she plods upstairs, so devastated, so bone weary she can hardly lift her feet, she hears a blackbird burst into song.

Eleanor

AND AFTER FLORENCE HAS BEEN BURIED, after they've wiped the graveyard from their shoes and driven back into town, after they've eaten the sandwiches and cakes that caterers brought to Florence's poky little house, after everyone has thanked Caroline and shaken her hand, and told Eleanor it was nice to meet her, after all of that is over, Eleanor remains with her sister in the emptied-out sitting room that still smells of tea and perfume.

You don't have to come, Caroline had said on the phone, *you didn't know her* – but Eleanor said why wouldn't she come, wasn't Florence family? Of course she was coming.

She wasn't going because Florence was family. She was going because Florence had flown to Ireland for Beth's funeral. Florence had gripped Eleanor's arms and looked straight into Eleanor's eyes and said, *My heart goes out to you. Nobody should have to bear this.* And in the midst of her devastation, Eleanor could see that she'd meant it.

But even if Florence hadn't shown up, hadn't said what she'd said, Eleanor would have made this trip anyway. Florence had been like a mother to Caroline; she needed someone from home around her now, and Mum and Dad weren't travelling because they'd been invited to Nadine D'Arcy's wedding on the same day, and no way was Mum missing out on that.

And here she and Caroline sit, in ancient lumpy mismatched armchairs, on either side of the fire that someone had been lighting when they'd got back from the graveyard.

'So,' Eleanor says. 'Noah.'

Caroline manages a small smile. 'You liked him?'

'You know I did.'

Last evening she'd been told about him. *There's something you have to know*, Caroline had said when she'd picked her up at Oxford station – and as they'd driven to Florence's house she'd told Eleanor about Noah having made contact. *You'll meet him tomorrow*, she said. *He's coming to the funeral. I told him there was no need, he only met her once – but he wants to come.*

Eleanor can't get over him, her twenty-one-year-old nephew. *Should I call you Aunt Eleanor?* he asked, and she assured him she wouldn't answer to it if he did – *Makes me sound like a hundred*. He's perfectly lovely, and has gorgeous dark eyes. He and Caroline seem so comfortable together, as if they've known one another all their lives. She's seen the smiles they exchange, and the way Caroline looks at him when she thinks nobody sees.

'When are you going to tell Mum and Dad?' Eleanor asks.

Caroline leans forward to add another log to the fire, making it blaze briefly. 'Saturday,' she says. 'I'm going home, I need to do it face to face.'

Saturday is five days away. 'What do you think Mum will say?'

'I have no idea.'

Silence falls. Outside the window a bird chirps. Eleanor thinks it sounds cross: a mother maybe, telling her babies to go to sleep.

'I'm sorry about Fennellys,' Caroline says. 'Gordon must be upset.'

'He is.'

'What'll he do now?'

'He'll look for a job. He's already started sending out his CV.' She wonders if Caroline is thinking, *Sixty*, like the recipients of the CVs must surely be.

Another beat passes. Eleanor opens her mouth, closes it again.

Opens it again. 'Caroline.'

'Yes?'

'It must have been so hard for you – giving up Noah, I mean.'

Caroline turns from the fire and looks at her.

'I hope you don't mind my saying it.' It's easier somehow, in this quiet twilit room, to bring up things that have never been spoken of.

'No, I don't mind.' She pauses. 'It was the hardest thing I ever had to do.'

'I didn't realise, until I had Jacob. We never talked about it when you came home.'

'No ...'

'We didn't have a clue, did we?'

Caroline shakes her head slowly. 'You weren't to know. Nobody could know, unless they'd been through it.'

'All you had was Florence.'

'She was all I needed. She was great. I nearly broke every bone in her hand from squeezing it so tightly.'

'It was so unfair though, Mum sending you away like that, not letting you home when you refused to have the abortion. Treating you like a criminal when you'd done nothing wrong, when you'd been raped by some stranger. I know Dad really wanted you to come back, he and Mum had awful rows about it.'

Caroline turns to gaze again into the fire. The silence stretches between them. A car crawls by on the road outside: its headlights travel along the wall. 'It wasn't a stranger.'

So softly, Eleanor barely hears it. 'What's that?'

'It was Jasper D'Arcy.'

'*What?*' She can't have heard right.

Caroline turns to look directly at her. 'Jasper D'Arcy raped me,' she says clearly. 'Noah is Jasper D'Arcy's son.'

'What? *Jasper* did it?' Eleanor looks at her in disbelief. 'No – he couldn't have.' But of all people, he could.

'He did.'

'How – I mean, where? When?'

'He was driving me home from babysitting.'

'*Jesus* … but why didn't you *say*? Why didn't you tell someone?'

'I did tell someone,' Caroline says calmly. 'I told Mum.'

'What – *Mum* knew?'

'Yes.'

Eleanor tries to take it in. Mum knew, and she'd said nothing. Mum had remained friends with the man who'd raped her daughter. Today Mum and Dad were at Nadine's wedding.

'Does Dad know?' She couldn't bear the thought that he'd gone along with it, that he'd turned a blind eye too.

'No, he doesn't know. Only Mum.'

'And Jasper? Does he know about Noah?'

'Oh, yes.' Caroline passes a hand across her face. 'I went to him, when I knew I was pregnant. He was awful. He gave me money for an abortion. He threatened me, said I'd be sorry if I told anyone.'

'God …' So much she'd kept to herself, so much she'd bottled up. Eleanor tries to work it out. 'So when you disappeared for a year, he knew it wasn't a breakdown.'

'Of course he did.'

Eleanor had met him in the street more than once while Caroline was in England. She remembered him asking her how Caroline was: bastard.

She regards her sister. The pale, drawn face, the

shadows beneath her eyes. Exhausted, like Gordon. 'Are you going to tell him now?'

'I have to. Noah wants to make contact with him.'

Eleanor can only imagine how the news will be received: the son he wanted killed, the son whose extinction he'd paid for, would like to meet him. 'I'll go with you,' she says, 'if you want me to. Moral support.'

Caroline gives a small smile. 'I appreciate the offer, but I can handle him. He has no power over me any more.'

'Why are you telling me all this now?' Eleanor asks.

Caroline sighs. 'Because I'm tired of keeping secrets, tired of pretending. Florence never pretended. She was never afraid of the truth. I told her about Jasper.'

'Did you?'

'Yes.'

'... You'll miss her.'

'I will.'

Silence falls between them again. Eleanor traces back in her mind to the year it happened. She'd just finished Junior Cert, so it was 1993. The summer she and Andrew split up.

Andrew. Noah is Andrew's half-brother.

Jasper might have been Eleanor's father-in-law, if things had gone according to her plan – and Caroline had borne his child. It was so messed up.

And Mum knew. Right from the start she'd

known. Eleanor can't get her head around that particular bit of it. How could she not have wanted to scratch Jasper's eyes out for what he'd done to Caroline? How can Caroline bear even to talk to her when they meet now?

'They're at Nadine's wedding today.'

'I know. Dad told me on the phone. He was sorry to miss the funeral.'

In the hall the grandfather clock begins to bong, although the mantel clock reads ten past eleven.

'The clock is wrong,' Eleanor says. 'One of them is. And that cuckoo is on his last legs.'

'The cuckoo is very old – and the grandfather clock tells the right time. It just bongs at ten past. It's always been like that, ever since I came here.'

Eleanor imagines her arrival, more than twenty years earlier. Pregnant and frightened, completely at Florence's mercy. What a time she must have had here that first year, even with Florence's support. And yet, as soon as she could, she moved right back here. For nearly half her life she's lived in this odd little house, so much less imposing than the one they grew up in. Cosy enough with the fire, but terribly dated. Still, it's where she wants to be.

'I really like your hair,' Caroline says. 'It's well cut.'

Eleanor tells her about Neil, the man-child with his nose-ring and tattoos and violet hair. 'He wants me to get red lights in it.'

'They'd be nice.'

'I've lost half a stone,' Eleanor says then. It comes

leaping out of nowhere. 'You can't see it, but I have. I went to my doctor. He's helping me.'

'Good for you.'

'And I'm seeing someone,' she says. 'A woman, Cathy. A counsellor.'

'Oh, I'm so glad.'

She won't mention the chocolates, the half-dozen she ate before making herself stop, before the prospect of getting on the doctor's scales again brought her to her senses. She gave the rest of them to a neighbouring house with five children. *Too tempting*, she told the mother.

'I'm trying to put things right,' she says. 'The hair is part of it.'

'I felt we failed you too,' Caroline says, 'after Beth. None of us knew what to do.'

'I know. I don't think there was anything you could have done really.'

Another silence. Eleanor looks about the darkening room, at all the bits and pieces that don't go together. She thinks of the woman who lived there, the woman whose heart went out to her when Beth died.

She thinks of Gordon who just might still love her, despite everything. She thinks of Jacob, who got picked last week for the rugby team, who told her about it when he came home from school, who thanked her for the tenner she gave him as a reward.

She imagines being happy again, really happy.

'There's another thing,' Caroline says, her voice

jumping into Eleanor's thoughts, scattering them. 'I'm going to the reunion on Saturday night.'

'What reunion?'

'Our school. Twenty years.'

Eleanor had completely forgotten it. 'I thought you said you weren't.'

'I wasn't planning to. I threw away the invitation when it came, but I said it at the time to Florence and she thought I should go. And now –' She breaks off, and Eleanor waits. 'And now she's gone, and I ... went into the kitchen, the night she died, and I saw the date circled on her calendar, and I couldn't think why. The tenth of October meant nothing ... but then after I went to bed I remembered it was the reunion, and I remembered Florence drawing a circle around it, and saying I should go. So I'm going, because she wanted me to.'

And Eleanor thinks about walking into the reunion and seeing the girls who used to be her friends, Tina and Carmel and Jo and Trish and the rest. She's changed, but they'll have changed too. They're going to be older, and some will be fatter, like her, and some will be carrying broken hearts around with them, like her.

She lost a daughter. It happened, and some of them will have heard, and maybe some of them won't. She can tell them, if they ask about children.

And she can buy another damn skirt, and get the right size this time.

'I'll go with you,' she says.

The Reunion

The Reunion

Caroline

CARO MATTEO

At last I am writing to you. I'm sorry it's taken me longer than I wanted, and I'm sure longer than you wanted, but I truly didn't know how to answer your question. I couldn't find the right words to use. Now I think I have found them, and I am sending them in a letter because they seemed too important for an email.

There is something I must tell you, something I should have told you a long time ago. When I was seventeen I gave birth to a child, a son. The father was an older man whom I did not love. He was a friend of the family, but he raped me one night. When I told my mother I was pregnant she wanted me to have an abortion, so she sent me to England, but I refused to go ahead with it, and insisted on having the child. I remained in England until the baby was born. My mother didn't want me returning to Ireland, so I lived with my cousin Florence, who looked after me. It was a very frightening and lonely time for me, but Florence was very kind.

My son was adopted in England and I was heartbroken, but I thought it was for the best. Even though he was the result of a rape I loved him, and I hated having to part from him. I gave Florence's address to the adoption agency, and wrote a letter to him saying that I would be happy if he ever wanted to get in touch – and a few weeks ago, shortly before my last visit to Italy, he wrote to me, and I met him. He was the reason I changed my flight, and arrived a few days later.

He lives in Brighton, which is in the south of England. I am very happy that he found me, I always hoped he would. He is a wonderful young man, and we took to one another straight away. We have met a few times since then, and we speak on the phone almost every day.

I'm sorry I never told you about him. I should have been honest with you, but I was afraid. I thought it might turn you against me. I felt having a son who is only nine years younger than you would make me seem older, and would make our age difference seem even greater than it is. I know you don't think the difference in our ages is important, but it was always in my mind. I think I was always waiting for you to tell me you'd met someone younger, and wanted to leave me. I can see now I was wrong not to have more faith in you, more faith in us. I talked with an old friend a few days ago and he made me see how foolish I was being.

Ti amo, caro Matteo. I love you. You have made me very happy, happier than I was in years. My answer to your question is yes, I would love to be your wife. I would love to grow even older with you! There are a lot of things we would have to decide, with your life there and mine here – but I think we could find a way, if we both want to. I will understand if you change your mind after reading this, and I will always remember you fondly. Your Carolina xxx

PS Since I wrote this letter, a very sad thing has happened. Florence died suddenly on Thursday. It was a big shock, as I loved her very much.

She posted it five days ago: he'll surely have got it by now. She put her address at the top. Maybe he's responding with a letter of his own, maybe that's why no email has come from him, like she thought it might. No email, no phone call or text. No response at all.

Whatever the outcome, she's glad she sent it, glad there are no more secrets between them now. Glad she said yes to his proposal, even if her letter changes his mind.

She bitterly regrets never telling Florence about him. She should have told her: why didn't she? Florence would have been happy for her, would have delighted in the thought that Caroline had found someone to love, someone to love her back. And she wouldn't have given tuppence for Caroline's reservations.

Have some sense, child, she'd have said. *Come clean to him about Noah. If he loves you it won't matter a damn to him if you have half a dozen sons. And for goodness sake forget about being a bit older – ages are just numbers: what do they matter if you're happy together?*

What she wouldn't give to hear that voice again.

She locks the back door and walks through the rooms, checking that windows are closed. In the hall she picks up her weekend bag and lets herself out. She stands by the gate and regards Florence's house.

She left it to you, the solicitor said. *She left everything to you, bar a few small bequests to friends.*

She may have left it to Caroline, but it'll always be Florence's house.

She drives down the motorway to the airport and leaves her car in the short-term car park. Just one night she'll be away; long enough.

She's given Jasper some notice. It seemed only fair.

I'll be home on Saturday and I need to meet you.
I'll be in St Joseph's church at four o'clock.

She figured a church was as safe a venue as any. She posted it three days ago to his work address. She signed it 'Caroline' and added her phone number. She didn't want to give the number, but she thought he deserved a chance to change the arrangement if it didn't suit him.

She's heard nothing. He'll have guessed what it's about. He'll either ignore the note or he'll turn up. She will hold her nerve and say her piece. She will not be intimidated by him.

And now she sits on the plane that has just taken off, and she wonders how he'll be with her, and she tells herself again not to let him frighten her. What can he do in a church, in broad daylight?

'Going on holidays, or going home?'

She turns to the woman next to her, who is about her mother's age.

'Neither. My home is in England now. I'm going to my school reunion.'

'How nice. You can catch up with all your old friends.'

'And I'm going to tell my parents about their grandson,' she adds.

'Lovely. Haven't they met him yet then?' A flick of her eyes to Caroline's abdomen, which is too flat to have contained a baby recently.

'Not yet, but soon, hopefully.'

Her companion decides not to delve further. 'I've been admiring your dress, very pretty.'

In Dublin airport she says goodbye to the woman, who has taken her business card and promised to be in touch. She collects the rental car she ordered from England and drives down the motorway to her parents' house, and finds a chicken and ham salad waiting for her. No sign yet of Eleanor.

And after lunch, during which Caroline listened to her mother's minute-by-minute account of Nadine D'Arcy's wedding, she says, 'There's something I have to tell you both,' because they think she's just come home for the reunion.

And then she tells them.

'I know you never wanted him,' she says, looking directly at her mother, 'but he was born, and you're his grandparents. And he's wonderful, and I'm so happy he got in touch, and I would very much like to bring him home to meet you.'

She wants it because he does. She wants to give him everything.

Her mother takes her napkin from her lap and dabs the edges of her mouth. She folds the napkin and lays it on her plate. 'Caroline, you cannot be serious,' she says calmly. 'You must know it's out of the question. You can't bring him here: you'll make us out to be liars.'

Caroline isn't surprised. It's what she expected. After all these years, nothing has changed. 'You *are* a liar,' she says. 'You turned us all into liars.'

'Only because you forced me to do it.'

She can't. She can't fight any more. She gets to her feet, the skin around her eyes hot and tight. 'You do realise,' she says, 'that if you refuse to acknowledge him, I will never set foot in this house again?'

'Caroline, that's unfair. You know why it had to be—'

'I don't care,' she says. 'I don't care what warped reasoning you want to use. All I know is you turned your back on me when I needed you, just to avoid a scandal, and you know that's true, even if you won't admit it. I'm leaving now. I'm booking into the Abbey Lodge Hotel for the night.'

'Caroline—' Dad says, but she keeps going. In the hall she lifts the weekend bag that hadn't gone further. She opens the front door and he follows her out.

'I want to meet him,' he says.

She turns back wearily. 'You won't be allowed. Mum won't allow it.'

'I want to meet him,' he repeats. 'I'll come to England.'

He'll come to England. It'll cost him dear. 'Are you sure?'

'Of course I'm sure.'

He looks sure. He looks like he means it. She hopes to God Mum doesn't try to persuade him against it.

'I'll give you a ring,' she says, 'next week, when you're at work.' He'll be sixty-five in December. He has three months of work left.

'I wish it didn't have to be this way,' he says, and she sees his eyes glittering with tears.

'Me too,' she replies. She gives him a quick hug and walks away. She wonders if he loves Mum, or if he stays because he's afraid to leave. She hopes it's love that keeps him there.

When she reaches the hotel her phone buzzes with a text from Eleanor. *Should be with you around six, presume you're landed.*

She rings her and fills her in. 'I'm at the hotel now. Come up to my room when you arrive.'

'Sorry you had to go through that.'

'I expected it.'

'Want me to talk to her?'

'I don't think there's much point, to be honest.' Although Eleanor was always better at handling Mum. They were always more in tune.

'I'll tell her I met Noah. I'll say he's lovely.'

For all the good it will do. 'Do, if you want.'

'Caroline,' Eleanor says quickly, 'it was good to talk to you, the night of Florence's funeral.'

'Yes. It was good.'

'I'm glad you told me – about Jasper, I mean. I'm glad we can talk like that now.'

'Me too.'

'When are you meeting him?'

'At four. I told him St Joseph's church.'

'Good idea. I'll be thinking of you.'

'Thanks … How have things been with you?'

'Better. Getting better.'

'Glad to hear it. See you soon.'

At ten to four she leaves the hotel and walks the relatively short distance to the church. The day is chilly, the wind sharp: she pulls her jacket more tightly around her. She passes the shopping centre where she used to meet her friends for coffee, Ciara and Ellen and Mary.

Last time she met Mary and Ellen was shortly after she'd started in art college. Mary was studying economics, Ellen had a year done of her teacher training course. They told her Ciara was living in an Israeli kibbutz, her law degree aspirations tossed aside. *Her parents are livid,* Ellen reported. *Can't say I blame them. I mean, a kibbutz is a bit of a comedown from a career in law, isn't it?*

Not if it's what she wants, Caroline replied.

There was a small baffled silence.

How's Wales? Mary asked, and Caroline told her it was wonderful, and pretended not to see the sidelong glances they exchanged as she described the course. Poor Caroline, the glances said, with all her academic promise, ending up as a glorified knitter. Poor thing, must have been the breakdown. No doubt they thought her as much of a lost cause as Ciara in her kibbutz.

She hasn't met either of them since. The coffee shop is a newsagent's now, or it was the last time she saw it.

Someone told her, about a year ago – was it Eleanor? – that Ciara is now living in New Zealand, with a doctor and their two little boys. She hopes their lives are full of happiness.

I will never set foot in this house again – had she really said that? It hadn't been planned. It hadn't occurred to her until the words came out. Never to go home again, never to see her old room again. Never to lay eyes on Mum again – or not at home anyway. Will it really come to that?

She reaches the church and walks through the open doors. It's empty apart from a figure, a woman she thinks, who kneels in the front pew. She turns left and takes a seat at the back, out of the cold and where she can watch the door. It is three minutes to four.

At a minute past four he walks in, wearing a dark overcoat and a hat. She stands, her skin tingling, her hand tight on the back of the next pew. She waits until he sees her.

He approaches. She doesn't resume her seat. They face one another: he gives a tiny nod. Years since their last encounter. He's in his late sixties now, but still in control of his business. He seems slightly shorter than before. He looks her in the eye – but she feels no enmity this time. If anything, he looks wary.

Could he possibly be *afraid*? Could he imagine he's going to be exposed, after all these years? The thought gives her sudden courage.

'Your son wants to meet you,' she says, her voice just loud enough for him to hear. 'He lives in England. I gave him up for adoption when he was born. He made contact with me a few weeks ago, and we've met. I told him you're married. I didn't tell him you raped me. I didn't want him thinking he began like that.'

He blinks. A muscle in his face twitches.

'My mother knows the truth. For a long time, she was the only one who knew. I thought she'd help me, but I was wrong.'

Still not a word from him.

'I told Eleanor,' she goes on, 'a few days ago. I don't imagine she'll bother spreading it around, but I can't promise anything.'

He makes a small sound in his throat, a small clearance, and she waits – but nothing else comes.

'My father thinks a stranger raped me. I won't tell him it was you – for his sake, not for yours.' She opens the bag that hangs from her shoulder and takes out an envelope. 'There's a photo of your son in here, and his name and address. I'm leaving it up to you. You won't hear from me again.'

She hands over the envelope: he takes it silently. She remembers another envelope passing between them, going in the opposite direction. She turns to leave.

'Caroline,' he says.

She stops, doesn't look back at him.

'I'm sorry.'

She moves off. She walks through the porch and out of the church. She thinks, *It's finished. It's over.* She feels a sense of elation. *Good for you*, Florence says in her head. *I'm proud of you, child.*

All that's left now is the reunion.

As she walks back to the hotel her phone rings. She sees Gretta's name on the screen. *Barney*, she thinks. *Something's happened to Barney.*

'Gretta – what's wrong?'

'Nothing,' Gretta says, 'but there's someone here who's *insisting* on talking to you.'

'Who?' she asks – who on earth could be ringing her from Gretta's phone?

'I'll let him tell you.'

Him?

'Is me.' He sounds irritated. 'Is Matteo. Your

neighbour give me her phone because mine is no battery.'

'*Matteo?*' She's dumbfounded. Matteo in England: she scrabbles to make sense of it. 'How did you – did you get my letter?'

'Of course I get letter,' he says indignantly. 'Is why I come to England. I come for surprise. I fly to 'Eathrow airport, I take train to Oxford, I take bus to your town, I find your 'ouse – and you are gone away. Your neighbour tell me you are in Ireland, Carolina.'

'Yes, I – what did you think?' she asks.

'What I think? About what?'

'About … my son. About Noah.'

'Carolina – you think your son is problem for me? Your son is no problem for me. Your son is problem only if he think I am not good enough for his mamma, because I am only electrician, and his mamma is big important fashion designer.'

She bursts out laughing: the relief is incredible. 'Matteo, of *course* he doesn't think that.' Better not mention that Noah isn't yet aware of his existence. 'You're not angry that I didn't tell you about him?'

'*Sì*, I am very angry. You think I am so *superficiale* that I run away because you have a son?'

'Sorry –'

'Carolina, if you have more childrens, you must tell me now. You must tell me immediately how many childrens you have.'

'No more, Matteo, I promise. Just Noah.'

'I am also angry that you are in Ireland. When

you are my wife, you must tell me when you go to Ireland.'

When you are my wife. It's a sonata.

'When you come back, Carolina? When?'

'Tomorrow,' she says, beaming at an approaching pedestrian, who gives a startled half-smile in return. '*Domani,*' she says. 'Wait for me. Let me talk to Gretta, she'll give you a key – and probably your dinner too. Don't go away, *caro*. Wait for me.'

Eleanor

I'M SORRY, SHE SAID. I'M SO SORRY. I CAN'T begin to tell you how sorry and ashamed I am. I blamed you. I held you responsible and I pushed you away. I treated you horribly.

I needed help, she said, *but I was afraid to look for it. I was afraid to let myself talk about what had happened, because I didn't know what it would do to me. I let losing Beth take over. I couldn't see beyond it. I didn't care about anything or anyone else.*

He was preparing dinner. He wasn't looking at her, he was putting a pan of water on to boil. But he was listening.

But I'm trying now, she said. *I've been to Dr Byrne and he's monitoring my progress – he's going to weigh me every week. I'm eating healthier, and exercising, and walking.*

It wasn't easy. Every day she had to give herself another pep talk, force herself to keep on track. She'd gained two pounds after England, her own fault for relaxing the rules a bit in Florence's house.

But she wasn't giving up. Since coming home she'd gone back to low-fat meals, upped her water intake, increased her walks and exercising.

And I'm getting into the gardening, I'm really liking it.

Every day she spent an hour or more out the back, pulling weeds from what used to be flowerbeds, hacking at briars, digging out the shrubs that had gone beyond rescuing. When everything was ready she was going to plant new shrubs, ones with colourful leaves, and fill the flowerbeds with bulbs. Tulips she wanted, those lovely dark purple ones, and white and yellow crocuses, and pink hyacinths. And snowdrops, lots and lots of snowdrops. Dozens of snowdrops.

And I'm seeing a woman, she said. *Her name is Cathy. She's a psychotherapist. I got her name from the doctor. I've had two sessions with her already. I like her: I think she's going to help.*

That bit wasn't easy either; it was far from easy. It was full of anger and pain and regret and shame. But the bad stuff was loosening and unravelling, she could feel it. *You're doing great*, Cathy told her. *You're doing exactly what you need to.* It helped a bit to hear that.

I never stopped loving you, she said. *Never. I hope you can believe that. I love you now as much as the day I married you.*

He shook salt into the water, took carrots from the vegetable drawer of the fridge. Didn't react at all to what she'd said. But he was still listening.

And there's something else, she said. *Something I want to run by you.*

Here was the tricky part, the part she'd been trying out in her head. The part she wasn't at all sure of.

You know the painting, she said, *the one Conor did of me, years ago, when we were teenagers. I showed it to you – it was hanging in my room at home. I'd forgotten all about it – I mean, I hardly saw it anytime I went home, I was so used to it. But I remembered it after you told me about Fennellys having to close. I got Dad to send it to me. It's upstairs now. I thought it might be worth something, now that Conor's such a big shot. I mean, I knew it was one of his early works, and maybe nobody would be interested – but I thought it might be worth finding out.*

I thought, she said, *if we could get decent money for it, or if a bank would accept it as security against a loan, it might help to set us up again, to start something new. Something smaller, something the two of us could manage together, without the expense of staff. A little bistro, maybe, something like that.*

She paused for breath, watching as he chopped carrots on the diagonal at lightning speed. She'd always loved to watch him at work, the confident way he handled ingredients, knowing exactly how he could make them come together. He swept the chopped carrots aside, split a garlic bulb into cloves, cracked them open one by one with the side of his knife.

So I got in contact with Conor. I asked if he'd be OK

with me selling it, and he came back and said no way was I to sell.

Ring me, was what he'd said first, in the email he'd sent back to her. *Ring me the second you get this. I haven't got a number for you, and we need to talk.*

Her first thought was that he was mad at her. He was deeply offended at the thought of her selling his gift. She rang him, bracing herself for his anger. He answered on the first ring.

Is that you, Plunkett?

Yes. I won't sell if you –

Damn right you won't, he said. *Have you never heard of sentimental value? I had no idea Fennellys was closing – my uncle is as bad as you for keeping in touch.*

Well, it is, and we need –

Listen to me, he ordered. *I have money, Plunkett. I have obscene amounts of it, and I need to invest it in something, and I would much rather put it behind you and Gordon than buy some anonymous shares in some stranger's business. Let's talk. When can we talk, the three of us?*

She watched as Gordon lit the gas under the wok, splashed in the rapeseed oil he favoured over olive.

So it turns out, she said, *that Conor's looking for something to invest in, and he wants to meet us.*

He peeled an onion and cut it crossways in half and sliced it thinly, his chopping hand a blur. He flung the lot into the hot oil, making it sizzle.

What do you think?

He shook the wok, scattered in the garlic. *You've been busy,* he said.

Well, I wanted to help.

I can see that. He gave the wok another shake: the onions leapt. He tumbled wholewheat pasta into the simmering water.

So what do you say? she asked again.

He turned. *Conor wants to give us money.*

Not give, invest. He's looking for something to invest in, he says his accountant is at him ... It would be a business arrangement, that's it. Let him not dismiss it out of hand. Let him at least consider it.

He threw the carrots into the wok. He chopped herbs.

Gordon, I'm trying to help, she said. *I want to help, I want to ... start making amends. Please let me.*

He shook the wok. He stirred the pasta.

Will you meet Conor, see what he has to say?

He turned again. *Yes*, he said. *I will.*

Just that, nothing more. But he didn't say no.

He didn't say no. She tells herself this as she drives across the country now to her parents' house. He didn't say he couldn't see them working together again. He didn't say he hated the idea of the bistro. He said none of that. He said he'd talk to Conor.

It's a start. It's enough for now. It has to be enough for now.

'I like your dress,' Mum says when she arrives. 'It suits you. Orange was always good on you.'

She'd found it in a tiny little shop, after trawling the boutiques of Galway. It has a crossover top, and gathers and folds across the front that do their best with her bulk, and sleeves that come to the elbow. It's a size eighteen, like the ill-fated skirt that ripped on its first outing, but now eighteen feels comfortable.

'Where's Dad?'

'Gone to get milk. He won't be long.'

'Caroline told me,' she says then. Might as well dive in. 'I know who Noah's father is.'

Mum's face doesn't exactly change, but everything in it seems to freeze. 'Eleanor—'

'I can't believe it,' Eleanor says. 'You knew, you knew all along, and you said nothing.'

'This is—'

'You actually stayed friends with him. You went to his parties, you invited him to yours.'

'Eleanor—'

'You were at Nadine's wedding just the other day. You missed Florence's *funeral* for it.'

'This is not your concern,' Mum says loudly, her voice harsh as sandpaper.

'Not my concern? How can it not be my concern? Caroline is my *sister*.'

'I did what I thought was best.'

'Did you, though? Was it best for Caroline? Whose best were you thinking of?'

'I don't have to—'

'It was certainly best for Jasper. Keep his name out of it, keep his nose clean. And it was best for you. No scandal in the Plunkett family, nobody whispering about us.'

'Eleanor,' Mum said angrily, 'I was thinking about you, if you must know. You were still with Andrew, we all thought—'

'You thought we'd get married. You'd have been happy letting me marry into that family, having a rapist as a father-in-law. Nice one, Mum. Nice parenting.'

'Watch your tongue, Eleanor.'

'You just couldn't see beyond his wealth, and his status, could you? God forbid any of us did anything to upset the great Jasper D'Arcy.'

'That's *enough*!'

'It's not half enough. I've met Noah, he's lovely – and you're refusing to meet him, as if he's done something wrong.'

'How *can* I meet him, after what we told everyone? How can Caroline ask us to let him come here? It's out of the question.'

'Mum, it's been years – do you honestly think anyone will care? And so what if they do? What does Dad say?'

A further tightening of the mouth. 'He's planning to go to England. "Good luck to you," I said. "Just don't expect me to go with you."'

Eleanor looks at her sadly. She's impossible. She's dug a hole for herself and now she can't get out of it. She reminds her of herself, stuck in the past, no way of escape. 'Mum, you've already alienated Caroline. If you insist on keeping Noah hidden, you're in danger of losing both daughters. Do you really want that?'

The front door opens: a key is withdrawn from the lock. She hears the soft whispery sound of her father taking off his coat and hanging it.

'Hi, love,' he says, crossing the kitchen to kiss her cheek. 'You look nice.'

'Thanks, Dad. Actually, I was just leaving – don't want to be late for the reunion.'

'You can't stay for a chat?'

'No time, sorry. We can talk tomorrow. I needn't rush back.'

For a second she feels like telling him; she feels like blurting it out to him. She darts a look at Mum, and sees fear in her face. No, she won't say it. She won't wipe the smile off his face. Better that he doesn't know, better that he never knows who fathered his first grandson.

'I might be late home,' she tells him. 'Don't wait up.'

She gets to the hotel just after seven. *St Finian's Reunion*, she reads on a notice by the door, *Gerard Suite*. She searches the lobby for familiar faces and finds none. She asks for Caroline Plunkett's room number. 'I'm her sister,' she says. 'She's expecting me.'

She walks past the lift and takes the stairs to the third floor. She emerges, breathless, from the stairwell to find Caroline waiting at the door of room 302.

'Well,' Caroline says, 'you look good.'

'You look better,' Eleanor replies, and she does. An elegant jade green dress that falls to her knee, soft black boots, a thick silver chain around her neck. And there's something else, something ... *charged* about her. A light flush in her cheeks that isn't usually there – but the centrally heated room might be to blame for that.

'Come in,' she says. 'Have a seat. I've got something to tell you.'

The room isn't bad, the first time Eleanor has seen one of them. A bit anaemic – cream walls, beige carpet, white linen on the double bed – but easy on the eye. A painting of the town's main bridge above the bed, a good-sized television set high on the opposite wall. Two bucket armchairs by the window, a wardrobe, a dressing table.

Eleanor lowers herself cautiously into one of the armchairs – but it's more generously proportioned than the one in the headmaster's office. From this height a fair bit of the town is visible. In the distance she can see the big red lettering on the side of Jasper D'Arcy's building: impossible to miss it. Look at me, look how successful I am.

'How did it go with Jasper?' she asks.

'Easier than I'd imagined. He said nothing at all, except sorry at the end.'

Eleanor snorts. 'Sorry my foot.'

'I told him you know, by the way. I sort of insinuated that you might spread the word, just to scare him – but you won't, will you?'

'Because of Dad,' Eleanor says, her eyes still on the giant red letters.

'Yes, because of Dad.'

'I'll say nothing – but I'll give him the filthiest look imaginable if I ever meet him again.'

She hears the bubble of Caroline's laughter behind

her. She can laugh about it now, now that Noah has come back to her. 'I saw nobody I recognised downstairs,' Eleanor says. 'I wonder if many will turn up.'

Another sound behind her, a sudden loud pop, makes her jump. She turns to see Caroline pouring what looks awfully like Champagne into two glasses. 'Is that what I think it is?'

'Certainly is. I got it in the off-licence at the corner.'

Eleanor hasn't tasted Champagne since the night of Fennellys' fifteenth anniversary celebrations. It's Moët: must have cost her a bomb. It's loaded with calories. She can walk them off tomorrow. 'What about the reunion?' she asks.

Caroline hands her a glass. 'We'll get there,' she says. 'We have lots to talk about first.'

She sits. She smiles at Eleanor; a real smile, full of joy. 'Let me tell you about Matteo,' she says.

Five months later:

March 2016

Caroline

I WANT TWO WEDDINGS, SHE SAID. *ONE IN Ireland and one in Italy.*

Two wedding impossible, he said. *Two wedding crazy. Nobody have two wedding.*

Two, she said. *Or due, if you'd prefer it in Italian –* and today, on a raw afternoon in mid-March, they are getting married for the first time in Ireland, in the seaside town of Salthill. They'll do it all again six weeks later in Naples, so his extended family and friends can be there.

And if she feels like it, they might well have another in England sometime, just for all the gang there. She has a feeling she's going to take to weddings.

They'll live in Italy, in Matteo's apartment, until they find a house they love. Caroline will travel back and forth to England as she needs to, using Florence's house as a base – or Donald's London apartment, to which she's always had access. She'll see plenty of Noah, who is delighted at the prospect of having a mother based in Italy. *It's one of my favourite places*, he told her.

So simple, after all her worrying. Everything falling into place.

For her first wedding she wears a pale green dress in a linen silk mix – her something new – and to keep out the cold she has the sky blue cashmere shawl she knitted for Florence at Christmas in 1993. It's her something old and her something blue.

Her something borrowed is a necklace of pearls that she'd never have chosen, but that she wears happily. They were presented to her the night before by her soon-to-be mother-in-law on her arrival in Ireland. *They are in Piccolo family a long time*, Nina told her. *All Piccolo womans wears for wedding*.

All Piccolo womans. Today she is becoming a Piccolo woman. She'll keep Caroline Plunkett for business, but everywhere else she'll be Carolina Piccolo.

And if the child she is carrying turns out to be a girl, she'll wear the pearls on *her* wedding day.

Caroline will be forty when she gives birth to her second child. It's no age these days. When she told Matteo two months earlier, when she was sure, he caught her up and whirled her around, like he'd done at Naples airport the day they'd admitted their feelings to one another. *I will be papa!* he shouted, much to the delight of passers-by. *I will be Papa Piccolo!*

'It's time,' her father says. 'They're waiting.'

He's come to Salthill on his own today. Caroline hasn't seen her mother since the day of the reunion. Mum has never met Noah or Matteo, never accompanied Dad on his trips to England, and now she's missing out on her daughter's wedding, because the grandson she can't bring herself to acknowledge will be there.

Caroline will send her photographs of today, and of her new baby when it arrives. Her mother will know of her happiness, even if she refuses to share it.

I told her I knew about Jasper, Eleanor said. *I told her she'd lose me too if she insisted on pretending that Noah doesn't exist* – but Caroline didn't want that.

Don't fall out with her on my account, she said. *I can't meet her if she won't acknowledge my son, but you can. Don't cut her off too, don't do that to her.*

Love has made her generous, love has made her want the best for everyone. And maybe one day, Mum will come round.

'Hang on,' Eleanor says, fussing with the ribbon on Caroline's bouquet, 'nearly done.'

Eleanor is her matron of honour. She wears a dress in a terracotta shade that picks up the dark red lights in her hair. *Size fourteen*, she told Caroline. *I'm getting there.*

She *is* getting there. Caroline hears it in her voice each time they chat on the phone, sees it in her face when they Skype one another. There's a new purpose to her, a new resolve to her that is pushing away her demons. Her sister is finally emerging from the lost place she was in; after all this time she's finding peace of mind again.

I think it's going to be alright, she said, the night of the reunion. *I have a feeling things are going to be alright.*

I can't believe, she said, *you never told me about Matteo. I'm so happy you found someone.* And she genuinely did sound happy.

And by the time they finally ran out of talk and Champagne they left room 302 and made their way downstairs, a bit tiddly, and found the room where the reunion was to take place.

And discovered they were too late.

It was over. They'd missed it.

The last ones have just left, a staff member told them, piling plates on top of one another. *They're only gone five minutes.*

They might make the thirty-year reunion – but Caroline wouldn't lay a bet on it.

Dad drives them from Eleanor and Gordon's house to the church, where the tiny wedding party awaits them at the side altar. They turn as she approaches on her father's arm, as the organist strikes up his version of the Mancini tune she and Matteo danced to in his parents' back garden at his twenty-fifth birthday party.

There is Noah, smiling and handsome in dark grey, and his girlfriend Aideen, whose parents come from Westport in Mayo, a couple of hours further up the Atlantic coast.

Jasper wrote to Noah, a month after Caroline

had passed on his address. He wished him well and enclosed a substantial cheque, and said it was best if there was no more contact between them. Noah signed the cheque over to Caroline, who spent the lot on prize bonds in both their names. *If we win small,* she said, *we'll buy more bonds. If we win big we'll buy a boat, and sail it from England to Italy every summer.*

Across the aisle from Noah and Aideen are Nina and Giacomo, her new Italian parents, trying to look as if they're not on the point of solidifying from the cold, bless them. They didn't have to be here, they could have waited till May, and the second wedding in Naples, but Caroline wanted them so they came.

She'll get them Irish coffees at the first opportunity, or hot ports.

There are Gretta and Barney, who have flown in from England for the occasion. Sadly, the journey was beyond Donald. *I'll be with you in spirit,* he told her, which makes two of them, because no way is Florence Cassidy missing out on this day.

There is Caroline's nephew Jacob, his hair cut especially for the occasion. Standing, as befits his station, next to the groom.

Matteo knows nobody here, Caroline had said. *I was wondering if you'd oblige your godmother.* They didn't really need a best man, neither of them was bothered – and Noah would certainly have stood in if they were – but she thought it might be good for Jacob. *You won't have to make a speech, promise.* So there he stands, looking, it has to be said, pretty damn handsome.

She thinks he's happier these days too. She hopes so.

And beside Jacob stands her man, the father of her next child. Here he is shaking Dad's hand, taking her by the arm, touching her cheek with his lips, whispering, '*Bella*,' for her ears only.

Here is the start of the rest of her life.

Eleanor

YOU COULDN'T MAKE IT UP. WELL, YOU could, but nobody would believe you.

They met Conor, who told Gordon what he'd already said to Eleanor. *I've accumulated a pot of money. My accountant has been nagging me to invest some of it, and I would love to keep it in the family.*

I'm not sure that I'm comfortable, Gordon replied, *taking money from my nephew.*

Uncle Gordon, Conor replied, *get over yourself. It's not charity: I'll be expecting a good return on my investment – and VIP treatment every time I grace the premises with my presence. Now say yes or I'll cut you off without a farthing.*

And eventually Gordon was persuaded to accept. He and Eleanor drew up a business plan and sent it to Conor's accountant, and at the start of January, after two months of hunting, they found the premises they were looking for, just off the seafront in Salthill.

And ten days ago, on Tuesday the first of March, Jacob's Bistro opened its doors for the first time.

It's tiny. It has six tables and a counter, and it seats twenty-six at a pinch. Its walls are warm yellow inside and rusty orange outside and its signage, already much commented on, was specially designed by the artist Conor Fennelly, who's related to the owners.

There's one of his paintings, an early work, hanging on the wall. If anyone asks they say it's a print. You can't be too careful.

The bistro opens from noon to three and from six to midnight, and on weekdays it has a staff of just two. On Saturdays the son of the proprietors helps out, and on Sundays it remains closed.

Its menu is simple: four lunch options, six dinner. There's a loyalty scheme for returning customers, and every week includes a no-warning lucky day, during which all diners are entered into a draw to win their next meal. And best of all, it's got a working fireplace.

In just ten days it's become a hit – queues at lunchtime, full house each evening – and it's already been favourably reviewed in a national paper. Gordon was described as 'Michelin-star chef Gordon Fennelly'.

Today is Friday, not Sunday, but the bistro is closed. *A private party*, the notice in the local paper said, *to celebrate the wedding of Caroline Plunkett, fashion designer, and Matteo Piccolo of Italy.*

You don't want to be working on that day, Caroline said. *We'll go someplace else for dinner* – but Eleanor insisted. She wants to show off their new venture.

She wants the wedding guests to see the delightful place she and Gordon have created.

As Cathy would say, *It's all good*.

She's still going to Cathy, still turning up every Monday morning at eleven. After about half a dozen Mondays she began to feel that she might finally be running out of tears. The pain hasn't completely gone away, but she's learning to live better with the broken stuff.

And once she turned a corner there, she found that she and Gordon started doing better too. It didn't happen overnight: she had to win him back. They had to talk, and they had to listen. A lot of talk, and a lot of listening had to happen.

But since just after Christmas she doesn't sleep in the spare room any more.

And Jacob. She and Jacob might take a little longer, but she thinks things are moving in the right direction there too. They're talking more, he's sharing more. And if they keep going the way they're going, there's every reason to hope they'll find a place where they can be comfortable together, a place like he and his father have.

Billy has helped. Billy was Eleanor's idea, and he was a good one. He came from the animal shelter, and he's a mix of about six breeds, by the look of him. Stub of a tail, foxy ears, stumpy little legs, trunk hard and round and hairy. He chews everything in sight – every table and chair leg in the house is destroyed – and still leaves the occasional puddle on the kitchen floor after eight weeks of telling him not to. He gives Clarence a wide berth and sleeps on Jacob's bed and digs up Eleanor's flower bulbs every chance he gets. And Eleanor and Jacob, between them, walk the little stumpy legs off him.

And Eleanor has a new man. His name is George and he's twenty-eight and his body is magnificent, and he's a personal trainer. *Stick with me*, he told her, *and you'll get back into shape*. And so far, so good.

While their guests sit by the fire and wait to be fed, she and Gordon bustle about the bistro's little kitchen. Eleanor plates up the asparagus and mushroom starters while Gordon attends to the lamb that's been cooking slowly for the past several hours with garlic, lemon and bay leaves. They toss salads and warm plates and decant wine, and steal occasional kisses.

And as Eleanor Plunkett Fennelly whips cream into soft peaks for the poached-pear dessert, she feels again the mild but definite wave of nausea that first made its presence felt two mornings ago, just after she realised she was ten days late.

And she doesn't dare to hope.

Acknowledgements

NUMBER THIRTEEN: LUCKY FOR SOME! MY sincere thanks to my tireless editor Ciara Doorley and all at Hachette Books Ireland, to my agent Sallyanne Sweeney at Mulcahy Associates, to Hazel Orme for copy-editing and Aonghus Meaney for proofreading.

Big thanks to knitwear designer Caroline Mitchell for her generous help with my research, to Christine Taylor of Choccywoccydoodah for her information – and delicious inspiration! – to Hilary Mullane for her invaluable tips along the way, and to Tess McCormack and De Ward for their input in the early stages.

Thanks to my family for their continued encouragement: Mam and Dad, who live down the road from me, my sister Treasa in Dublin, my brothers Tomás in Clare, Colm in the Philippines, Ciaran in California and Aonghus in Limerick. Thanks also to Barry and Aoife at Gallagher's Seafood Restaurant for lending their support with this new arrival.

Thanks to the wonderful booksellers of Limerick

and beyond, in particular to Collette, Caterina, Frances and all at O'Mahony's Booksellers; Nora and all at Easons; Evelyn and all at Easons in the Parkway SC; Vickie O'Sullivan at NCW Bookshop in Newcastlewest; Niamh in Lahinch Bookshop and Gerry of Bandon Books.

Thanks to Julie and all at Limerick's main library for their staunch support.

Thanks to my Facebook and Twitter friends, far too many to mention, who are always there with messages of friendly encouragement, and who share and retweet whenever I threaten – er, ask them nicely to pass on book news.

Thanks to Fred and Ginger, my feline housemates, who provide company and endless entertainment as I tap at the laptop.

A special thank you to Tessa Greally, whose chance remark inspired the theme for this book.

Thanks above all to you, dear reader. Where would I be without you?

Roisin xx

www.roisinmeaney.com
Twitter: @roisinmeaney
Facebook: www.facebook.com/roisin.meaney

The Reunion

ROISIN MEANEY

BONUS

MATERIAL

Roisin Meaney on
REUNIONS

REUNIONS? I RUN FROM THEM LIKE A SMALL mucky boy from a bubble bath. If I had a euro for every reunion invitation I've turned down since I left school about nine hundred years ago, I could give up writing in the morning. It's not that I have anything against reunions per se: on the contrary, I love the idea of them. Meeting up with people from the past and finding out how life has treated them, what paths they've taken, what ups and downs they've come through – imagine the different stories they'd recount, imagine the book fodder I'd get. It's just that in my case, an evening spent with people I used to know would be an exercise in acute mortification from start to finish.

My problem is my memory – or rather, my utter lack of memory. A goldfish would put me to shame when it comes to remembering stuff. I can't recall people I met the previous day, let alone someone I shared a classroom with thirty years ago. At any reunion I'd spend the evening apologising to people whose names had long dribbled through my sievelike brain. I'd have to speak as little as possible (never easy) for fear of exposing the bottomless depths of my amnesia, and pay constant attention to their remarks, so I could jump in with *I was just going to ask you about your brother* right after they mention that the self-same brother (whose existence, needless to say, would have been completely obliterated) had recently married.

To make matters worse, my best friend forgets absolutely nothing, and nobody. She and I were in college together; since then she's attended several reunions, and tells me all about them afterwards. *Oh come on, she'll say, you must remember so-and-so from Kerry with the red curly hair, she always wore black, and those big floppy hats, remember their house burnt down the first day of our final year exams, and her brother swam for Ireland in the Olympics, and her uncle was arrested for money laundering.* And eventually she'd get tired of my blank face and give up on me, and leave me feeling even more resolved never, ever to darken a reunion's door.

For years I got away with it. I resisted every attempt to haul me back into a group of strangers, or as good as, for a few excruciating hours. In the meantime my mother attended her fifty-year Teacher Training College reunion – she remembered *every single one* of her forty-odd classmates – and came home exuberant, having caught up with all their news (miraculously, only two or three from the group had passed on).

And then it happened. In the academic year 2014–

2015 the school I'd resigned from in 2008 to become a fulltime writer was celebrating its twenty-fifth year in existence, and as part of its anniversary events it was hosting a night for all past students, parents and teachers – and so my invitation was duly delivered, and I was thrown into a quandary.

As I was still living in the area, I was still meeting people from the school on a regular basis, either by accident or by design. On the one hand, it meant that turning down the invitation would be awkward. On the other hand, it meant that I'd have a few people at least to chat to without embarrassment; maybe I could even persuade some discreet ally to whisper names as others approached, and spare my blushes somewhat. So I decided to accept, and see what happened.

On the day in question, I suffered a crisis of confidence. I'd make a fool of myself; I'd insult people wholesale by not remembering them. What's more, I'd doubly insult them by not remembering their children, whom I'd taught. I wouldn't go, I'd invent a last minute family emergency. I paced the floor in my finery. I couldn't invent a family emergency: imagine if one happened the following day. I'd spend the rest of my life blaming my cowardly self for it. I'd have to go, and suffer the mortification.

So I went – and guess what? It was fine. I remembered a respectable number of people, and was graciously forgiven by the ones I forgot. I caught up with families who'd been through my hands, and was touched by the number of teenagers who approached me to tell me they'd enjoyed having me as their teacher, and who didn't mind a bit when I confessed to not recognising them. The funny thing was, as soon as they told me their names, their four and five year old faces popped immediately into my head: go figure.

Towards the end of the night, one of the mothers (Tessa, in the acknowledgements) remarked that a reunion might make a good theme for a book – and as soon as she said it, I thought *of course it would*. A ready-made structure, beginning with the year in question, and ending with the reunion year. The plot happening in the middle, a natural unfolding of life events. I was still writing my previous book, but as soon as it finished I began *The Reunion* (even the title fell into place), and this is what came out.

I do hope you have enjoyed it.

Roisin Meaney
ONE SUMMER

Nell Mulcahy grew up on the island – playing in the shallows and fishing with her father in his old red boat in the harbour. So when the stone cottage by the edge of the sea comes up for sale, the decision to move back from Dublin is easy. And where better to hold her upcoming wedding to Tim than on the island, surrounded by family and friends?

But when Nell decides to rent out her cottage for the summer to help finance the wedding, she sets in motion an unexpected series of events.

As deeply buried feelings rise to the surface, Nell's carefully laid plans for her wedding start to go awry and she is forced to make some tough decisions.

One thing's for sure, it's a summer on the island that nobody will ever forget.

Also available as an ebook

Revisit the island of Roone in

AFTER THE WEDDING

and

I'LL BE HOME FOR CHRISTMAS

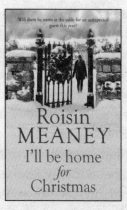

Also available as ebooks

Roisin Meaney
TWO FRIDAYS IN APRIL

It's Una Darling's seventeenth birthday, but nobody feels much like celebrating. It's been exactly a year since the tragic death of her father Finn, and the people he left behind have been doing their best to get on with things. But it hasn't been easy.

Daphne is tired of sadness, of mourning the long life she and her husband were meant to share, but doesn't quite know how to get past it. And she can't seem to get through to her stepdaughter – they barely speak any more, so Daphne knows nothing of the unexpected solace Una has found, or of the risk she's about to take.

When Una fails to appear for birthday tea with her family, Daphne suddenly realises how large the distance between them has grown. Will she be given the chance to make things right?

Also available as an ebook

Roisin Meaney
THE THINGS WE DO FOR LOVE

One crisp September evening art teacher Audrey Matthews sits alone in room six at Carrickbawn Senior College, wondering if anyone is going to sign up for her Life Drawing for Beginners class.

By eight o'clock six people have arrived. Six strangers who will spend two hours together every week until Halloween, learning the fine art of life drawing.

Nobody could have predicted on that cold autumn day the profound effect the class would have on its students and their lives.

Least of all Audrey, the biggest beginner of all, who is to discover that once you keep an open mind, life – and love – can throw up more than a few surprises . . .

Also available as an ebook